MW00653212

David Bickford is a Britis̲ State and Legal Director to the British Intelligence Agencies, MI5 & MI6.

David spent his working life diving into the cold murky seas of terrorism, espionage and organised crime.

At the forefront of the battle against international terrorism he was among the first to predict its onslaught.

David is recognised, both in the Agencies where he was awarded Companion of the Order of the Bath for his work and in the business, he now runs, for his ground-breaking solutions to defeat the terrorists and international organised criminals who threaten us.

David married his wife, Cary, in 1965 with whom they have three sons. David's life is filled with his family (his nine grandchildren keep him very occupied) as does his love of music, ballet, the opera, art and travel.

When he is not writing, David sees other areas of the law which need changing for the benefit of the public.

For instance, why can't the chatter between terrorists and organised criminals in their phone conversations be used as evidence to convict them? Surprising, isn't it, that these criminals can go free because this evidence is prohibited?

Why are there still agonising hurdles that women have to go through to get justice in the UK when they have been raped?

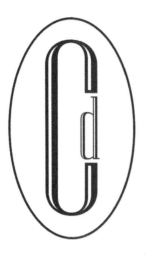

www.coinkydink.co.uk

KATYA

DAVID BICKFORD

Copyright © 2023 Coinkydink First published in Great Britain in July 2023 by Coinkydink Limited.

This edition published in March 2023 by Coinkydink (Publishing) Limited
2 Bermondsey Exchange
179-181 Bermondsey Street
London SE1 3UW

Copyright © David Bickford 2023
All rights reserved. No part of this publication may be reproduced, stored or transmitted in any form by any means, electronic, mechanical, photocopying or otherwise, without the prior written permission of the publisher.

The author asserts his moral right to be identified as the author of this work.

This is a work of fiction. Names, places, events and incidents are either products of the author's imagination or used fictitiously. Any resemblance to actual persons, living or dead, or actual events is purely coincidental.

Paperback ISBN 978-1-3999-4840-1
Ebook ISBN 9781739399306

Typeset in Adobe Garamond Pro by Coinkydink & Lorna Reid

Printed and bound in Denmark by Nørhaven

Coinkydink's policy is to use papers that are natural, renewable and recyclable products made from wood grown in sustainable forests. The logging and manufacturing processes are expected to conform to the environmental regulations of the country of origin.

Coinkydink (Publishing) Limited
A part of the Pretzel Film Group
www.coinkydink.co.uk

For my brilliant wife, co-conspirator and writer, Cary.

ONE

The InterContinental Hotel in Gibraltar was not designed to create a meltdown. The architects had positioned it on a cliff overlooking the spectacular seascape of the Bay of Gibraltar. All the rooms glowed with soft colours and lighting and they induced a state of tranquility in everyone who stayed there. Everyone, that is, apart from Katya Petrovna. She was impatiently pacing her room, clutching her mobile to her ear, listening to John Hammond the Director General of the G8 Intelligence Agency being unhelpful. He was insisting on sending her on an operation for which, as his Chief of Operations, she knew she was underprepared. The target was hidden and dangerous.

Trying once more to make him see sense, she deployed sarcasm as her weapon of choice. 'Yes, John, I understand you've planned this op but I haven't. Look, we're chasing this man Ronald Cartwright for half a billion dollars, so tell me, why can't G8 simply fork out the cost of a drone to suss out if he actually *is* in this place in Morocco? Why some elaborate deception op when he probably isn't there at all?'

She listened to his reply, restlessly shifting her mobile from one hand to the other as she gazed out of the huge window at the sun rising over the sea. She'd just arrived from Tunis where she'd spent three weeks with her team trying to track down Cartwright and the cash he'd stolen. There was no sign of him which wasn't surprising as the man who'd been Gadaffi's moneylaunderer would surely know his way around North Africa – that is if he was still alive which, in her mind was questionable. Now John was shunting her off again, this time to some new hotel development in Sidi Ifni. Why? Because a rumour suggested Cartwright was financing it and might be there, inspecting his investment. 'This is yet another rumour, John, just the same as the one that sent me to Tunis. And that's not all - over the last six months some word on the street or other has sent me chasing off to Hong Kong, Singapore, Abu Dhabi and now Tunis without a single sighting of him. What's different about this Sidi Ifni tipoff.'

She shook her head, impatient as John argued some more – found another persuasive reason not to go. 'You agreed my team would have R and R here after that wild goose chase in Tunis. They deserve it.' She thought about that as John sent another blast down the WiFi. She'd so far been given no idea of what to expect when she got to Morocco. She was in the dark as to whether Cartwright would be protected by minders. Half a billion dollars would pay for a lot of heavies.

She interrupted him. 'How do I know Cartwright won't have protection when we get to Morocco? He ran with terrorists when he was alongside Gadaffi - you know that, and I've got to prioritise the safety of my team.'

Her mouth hardened as he, in turn, interrupted her. Waiting for her at the airport was a chartered helicopter he had arranged for her to fly to Morocco. He had also assembled her team and told her they would be waiting in the chopper. John had clearly made up his mind, and there was no budging him – if he said she had to go into this operation blind, she would simply have to go.

'God, you remind me of my father – bullying, arrogant – '

His retort incensed her even more.

'You might think there's a difference between a KGB colonel and the G8 DG but I – 'she got no further. John had cut the call.

8

Quickly, she took out her flight bag and threw in a change of clothing - khaki loose pants, loose button-down shirt, jacket, cap, sun cream. Clothes for Sidi Ifni and the desert heat.

On her way through the foyer she asked the concierge to make sure her room was kept for her. She felt she might be back.

Making her way to the hotel car park she climbed into the hired Mercedes and drove down Harbourview road towards the airport. Inwardly seething at John's high-handed management, she was glad she'd got in that jibe about the KGB. Not that there was really any comparison between John and her brutal father but as John's Operational Chief she wasn't about to let him think he could always walk over her.

Usually, the traffic threading down the steep roads to the air terminal was light. Not this time, though. She was stuck in a queue of stationary cars and trucks, the drivers variously hooting their horns or leaning out to shout curses.

She switched on the radio and used the time to think about Cartwright. He had started his working life as an accountant in London, soon finding he had a talent for shifting dirty money through the shady world of tax havens. Some years ago, word had reached G8 that he'd been picked up by Gadaffi's regime in Libya to work for the corrupt dictator. His job had been to hide Gadaffi's mountains of illegal oil revenues. Cartwright had hidden this revenue for him through crooked financiers in offshore centres. The job had lasted until Gadaffi was slaughtered by a mob of angry Libyans. Cartwright didn't hang around for the same fate. He'd left Libya in a hurry, rumoured to have with him Gadaffi's personal fortune - half a billion dollars in cash which he'd loaded into shoeboxes and put in a convoy of eight Toyota Landcruisers. The convoy had then disappeared into the desert. The new Libyan Government unsurprisingly wanted their cash back and had asked G8 to trace the money and recover it. So far, the cash hadn't turned up and no trace of it had been found in any of the international tax havens. Was it still in the shoe boxes or had Cartwright actually succeeded in laundering it into accounts across the world?

The world of Libyan politics was like an ill-lit mine shaft, shadowy and dangerous. So far, she thought sardonically, she hadn't even seen either Cartwright's shadow or any danger. But John was convinced he was out there somewhere and if he'd survived Gadaffi's regime, he was, without doubt, dangerous.

These thoughts were suddenly cut short as the tall lorry she was following abruptly turned down a side road. She saw a sign immediately in front of her pointing to the airport. Instantly, she swung the Mercedes to the right directly in front of a truck loaded with vegetables. She ignored the driver's loud horn blast, skimmed past its front fender and accelerated into the sharp turn and into the airport's short-term car park. Unruffled, she slid to a halt in one of the parking bays.

Katya dumped the car there and, with no time to display a ticket, grabbed her flight bag from the back seat, glanced at her watch and started to run towards the towering glass facade of the main terminal. Almost immediately she stopped. A person running drew attention, and drawing attention was simply bad practice for any intelligence agent. She forced herself to walk, falling into her customary long, swinging stride as she quickly threaded her way through the parked cars and made her way towards the terminal's main entrance.

Without stopping she edged past a family of tourists struggling with outsize suitcases and, wielding her flight bag like a shield, she rammed her way through a group of students into the terminal. She shivered suddenly as the cold air from the freezing air-conditioning cut through her. Ignoring the commercial passengers queueing in front of the public check-in desks, she strode purposefully to the special check-in area for air charter helicopter crews and passengers. She went up to the Immigration desk and thrust her passport across the tall counter towards the officer sitting on a high chair behind it.

'Quickly, please, I'm in a hurry,' she announced.

Without looking up, the officer put out his hand and took her passport. He adjusted his round, steel-rimmed spectacles, and then very deliberately and painstakingly leafed backwards and forwards through the visas stamped in it before going back to the first page. Katya watched him slowly moving his thin lips as he read every line. She fumed. How long did it take to read the words written there? Katya Petrovna, born Moscow, passport issued Moscow, Russia, the date… Just her luck to meet with a bored, by-the-book bureaucrat when she was in a hurry. She narrowed her eyes, noticing the grubby collar on his uniform and the hazy smell of alcohol on his breath. Angrily she tapped her fingers on the counter to try to get his attention. He deliberately ignored her, shuffling his right hand sideways along his desk until it found an 'I Love Gibraltar' mug. His fingers curled around the handle. She realized he wasn't simply doing his job, he was being awkward and difficult on purpose—for some reason. But what? Her passport was in order, nothing was suspicious. Suddenly she remembered the words of Andrei Savin her training officer at the Russian Federal Security Service in St Petersburg - "Never, never push an official if you're in a hurry"

Resentment burned inside her. She leaned over the desk pushing her face close to his. 'You see that chopper?' She pointed to the Augusta AW 101 helicopter sitting on the apron outside, its rotor blades slapping the air, ready for the urgent departure John had ordered. 'The take-off slot is in exactly four minutes and I'm the pilot.'

He looked up, seeing her for the first time, taking in the deep violet-blue eyes, and the long waves of auburn hair, and he immediately regretted not looking up sooner. A suggestive smile flickered across his face but it came too late. She had already snatched back her passport, and moved to the automatic glass door that led out onto the helicopter apron. In seconds, she was gone.

She sprinted across the helipad towards the chopper. A furnace of searing heat rose from the concrete, mingling with the heady kerosene fumes from the Augusta's exhaust. She was now close enough to the chopper's open pilot's door for the backwash from the five spinning blades to whip her hair across her eyes, stinging them. She blinked and, brushing the strands out of her eyes, saw her co-pilot, Cato, frantically beckoning to her, mouthing 'two minutes' and holding up two fingers.

Typical of his humour to laugh at her discomfort, she thought. She hefted her bag through the doorway and laughingly mouthed at him, 'Back at you.' Then pulled herself up into the cockpit and climbed into the pilot's seat.

She turned to him and shouted, 'Thanks for warming her up.'

Cato, a tall, well-built West Indian simply nodded his head, a short braid of black hair falling over his aviator sunglasses.

Turning sideways, Katya pulled at the open door and slammed it shut. Immediately, the noise of the blades was diminished.

She studied the instrument panel: navigation compass, digital map, altimeter, auxiliary tank fuel gauge. She looked at Cato. 'All preflight checks done? Navigation fed in?'

His sunglasses glinted as he nodded again and handed her a headset.

She put it over her hair, adjusted the microphone and glanced over her shoulder at the two agents sitting in silence in the seats behind her. Oleg, a tall, blonde Ukrainian with whom she'd done more missions than she could remember, and Yas, a tiny, raven-haired Iranian, known for being taciturn but fast on her feet. She knew them both intimately. They were both in their 30s, and, like Cato, dressed for this op as tourists, in tee shirts, chinos, trainers. They had no tattoos, no designer sunglasses, no rings, no jewellery—nothing that might make them memorable or mark them out in a crowd to identify them. John had chosen them well.

She saw them both give her an expectant look - their eyes reflecting alertness and restless energy, qualities which marked out the true intelligence officer. They were waiting for her to deliver the mission briefing, but she hadn't time and wasn't ready yet. She would have to make them wait in patience - the most difficult skill for any agent to learn.

A voice in the control tower came through her headset demanding her departure.

She ignored it and took an extra ten seconds to care for her team. 'Good to see you,' she said to them. 'Sorry you're straight on to the next op without any rest. Way it is, I'm afraid. Seat belts all on?' She paused. 'Good, next stop Morocco.'

She murmured into the microphone, glancing up at the control tower as if she could see the air traffic controller listening to her, and then, with a skilled, gentle movement, she opened the throttle, pulled up the collective and lifted the eleven tons of machinery off the pad in a slow, climbing arc.

TWO

Flying at three hundred feet, Katya looked down at the intense blue waters of Gibraltar Bay. The only disturbance to the sea's stillness in the heat of the morning was the wake of a yacht, white and long like a smudge of white paint. She looked up and saw the stark outline of the North African coast ahead of them. Beyond it, lost to view in the hazy distance, would lie the yellow dusted Sahara Desert and, further away still, the green jungles of Central Africa. She'd been that deep into the continent on previous ops but this time her journey would end 325 kilometres south of Marrakesh at the small town of Sidi Ifni on the Moroccan coast, where the western edge of the Sahara Desert met the Atlantic Ocean.

Checking the navigation screen, she pressed the left rudder bar and tweaked the cyclical. The chopper banked steeply, flinging Cato and the team against the doors and armrests.

Katya laughed, 'Well, that should have woken you all up.'

Cato cursed. He was used to her playing this sort of practical joke, yet he was caught out every time. He opened his mouth to make his usual protest but she'd already turned to look at the team.

'Time for our briefing. I spoke to the DG immediately before take-off and, frankly, he made it clear G8 don't have a lot of intelligence for this op. Oleg and Yas, you were in Tunis with me so are fully briefed on Cartwright but you weren't Cato so I'll recap the main points for you. Our target is Ronald Cartwright. He's a British accountant who specialises in money laundering. He got first class degrees in finance and languages from Oxford Uni and Harvard—which means he's clever - but he's also a crook. For a number of years, he cleaned criminal money using international tax havens, then Gadaffi hired him to launder profits made from oil and dodgy oil sanctions. Cartwright was really smart and he was never caught. Then, in 2011, Gadaffi was assassinated and this is where things get a bit hazy. Word in Libya is that Cartwright snatched Gadaffi's personal cash fortune of half a billion dollars— and disappeared with it.'

'I've always thought the story was very vague – even more so now we've been chasing nothing more than a shadow half way around the world.' The tart comment from Yas, who always liked to triple check every detail of an op.

Katya valued her probing mind and, during their past ops together, they had developed a friendship based on mutual trust. She knew Yas was right about the vagueness of the intelligence and didn't try to dodge the question. 'The simple answer is, the information about the theft of Gadaffi's personal fortune has come from Libya's new government. They want their money back and they are using G8 to find Cartwright.'

'Not surprising really.' This from the tough, no- nonsense Oleg. It was the sort of down to earth comment he would make, thought Katya. He'd been recruited a couple of years ago by G8 from the Ukrainian army – a fearless man with strong determination and a bone-crushing handshake.

Katya thought Oleg's words echoed John's insistence on continuing the pursuit of Cartwright. Libya was young, foraging in a welter of political turmoil to find an identity. Erasing the horror of Gadaffi's memory was part of that and recouping the half billion he and then Cartwright stole from the Libyan people would go a long way to help. No doubt, G8 would gain politically if they found the cash but, for Katya, more importantly, she would crush a dirty thief who'd connived to steal money that should have helped the poor. She'd seen enough of that in her teenage years in a Russia that was emerging from the waste of the Soviet Union.

She heard Catos' voice. 'I know I'm new to this op, but why us? Why do we have to go and find Cartwright to get at the money? With all the financial tracking systems G8's got, it must be easy to trace that amount of money to a bank account.'

Katya kept her answer brief. 'In theory, yes. But even with all the computer power at G8's disposal, we haven't been able to find a single cent. Since the computers are of no use to us on this op we have to use the fall back tactics of physically tracking where and how the cash has been handled.'

She took his silence as a nod to go ahead with the briefing. 'G8 has recently heard a whisper that Cartwright might be involved in building a huge resort hotel and complex near Sidi Ifni on Morocco's Atlantic coast. It could be the Gadaffi money. So, our job is to find out if Cartwrigh*t is* still alive, and if he is, to try and persuade him, by every means at our disposal, to divulge where this money has been secreted.'

Oleg frowned. 'If this Cartwright was helping Gadaffi, he'd surely have had protection . . . And maybe that protection has stuck around to protect Cartwright, even after Gadaffi was offed.'

Katya nodded. 'Yes, that's absolutely true. We have to accept that that part of the op is completely blind. What's also certain is that those who served under Gadaffi will be violent and probably well-armed - not the types to sit down for a reasonable discussion about missing money.'

Yas spoke for all of them, 'You said our planning was sketchy— but we're not really going in against terrorists, based on just a rumour or two, are we?'

Katya knew there was no easy answer to the question but they all knew that no G8 agent should ever expect an easy ride. 'You're right, Yas.' She paused for a moment to emphasise that she was well aware of the threat to her team. 'Our flight time to Sidi Ifni is now one hour thirty-two minutes. I'll brief you in half an hour - if anyone wants some sleep . . .' She let the words hang as they settled back into their seats.

She glanced around the sky to check for other air traffic, and then made a small adjustment to the controls, sending the craft on a south-westerly course. They were flying parallel to the African coast now and, in contrast to Temara the waves below them now broke in white foam against tall sandstone cliffs. These reflected a deep gold in the bright sunshine which contrasted with the black jagged rocks jutting out into the water. The golds and blacks created an unusual mixture of light and dark. Unexpectedly, the sight reminded her of an FSB commander's remark when she'd joked about the imminent danger from the terrorist she'd just shot. "You're a true Russian," he'd said. "Light and dark."

She put the thought aside and meticulously checked the fuel gauge, temperature and compass, checked the airspace around her. It was clear of air traffic. Ahead she could see the sandstone walled town of Essaouira, still some distance off. Satisfied, she engaged the autopilot and settled back into her seat. Time to focus on what she had to do when they arrived at Sidi Ifni.

John had told her his plan was based on the assumption Cartwright was alive and financing the property development there. So, John had decided the best place for Katya to meet him would be on site.

She turned her mind back to John's outline of the op. He'd described the problem of how to arrange a meeting with Cartwright. She couldn't invite him to one, she didn't know where he was. So, she'd have to lure him in. A bribe? Hardly, if he was sitting on half a billion dollars. Then a threat? Possible. What did financiers fear most, apart from death? Obviously losing their money. So, she could threaten him with losing his investment. But how?

Someone nudged her shoulder, it was Yas. 'Tea?' She handed her a mug, answering the question in Katya's raised eyebrows. 'Yes. I've put in a teaspoon of jam, although how you can drink it I don't know.' She laughed. 'Disgusting.'

Katya smiled. 'My mother put jam in her tea.'

'That's the first time you've mentioned her.'

Katya shrugged dismissively.

Yas looked at her, sympathy in her eyes. 'Difficult?'

Silence.

Yas turned, handed a coffee to Cato and went back to her seat. Katya could be fiery if pressed.

The town of Sidi Ifni came into view. Katya was surprised by the beauty, even from the air, of its many art deco buildings, painted in blue and white – stripes, squares, curves of colour – all of them preserved as a monument to Spanish history.

It was the ugliness of the tall steel towers of the desalination plant in the distance that put to rest her doubts about John's operational plan.

He'd told her the locals in Sidi Ifni must hate the huge new hotel development Cartwright was involved in - tearing up the landscape, bringing in loud tourists, ignorant of the ways of the local inhabitants . . . How they would welcome someone, anyone, stopping it from destroying their way of life and a landscape much of which had remained unspoiled over thousands of years. The desalination plant would be used to fill swimming pools, not irrigate the desert for crops. There surely must be opposition to Cartwright's plans. How would that work? Protestors? They would be dealt with quite easily by the local police. Militant protestors?

John was right. They'd go in as ecowarriors. Threatening to damage the machinery and buildings. That would bring

Cartwright running. She had almost laughed at this suggestion. But now, having seen the contrast between the gentle town and the brutish desalination plant, she felt the stir of excitement.

John had arranged for a contact in Arizona to set up a shell nonprofit company called 'Our Desert' to support her ecowarrior cover. She nodded in appreciation. He hadn't had much time but he'd been thorough. His plan was workable. She turned on her microphone and began briefing the team.

They flew over the town of Sidi Ifni, along the coast towards its small airport. Below her lay an expanse of bleak, dark brown scrub dotted with low, sand-coloured buildings. A short runway, blocked with construction vehicles, ran parallel to a cliff that overlooked an uninviting, flat, grey sea.

She piloted the chopper straight in, aiming for the large white painted H. The landing pad was near a single-story building marked Terminal. As she touched down, the Augusta lurched sideways then slammed onto the tarmac.

Cato hung on frantically to the door handle, silently swearing. He knew Katya could scuba-dive, play a great game of tennis and sail a boat in a storm, but land a helicopter? Bloody hell, she nearly killed them all every time she brought one of these things in. He'd been on ops with her before and trusted her completely. He knew she always looked after her teams. He'd follow her anywhere, do anything for her, but this didn't prevent him from caustically commenting on her rotten landings.

As usual, she dismissed him with an amused laugh, saying, 'Choppy side wind.'

He stayed behind with her to complete the post-flight checks while Yas and Oleg climbed out and made their way up a stone pathway edged with tall date palms, to the Sidi Ifni terminal.

The post-flight checks completed, Katya asked Cato to stay behind and sort out all the equipment, and to bring it as quickly as he could to the rear of the car rental collection point. She wasn't worried about a customs inspection. A little corruption in the form of a cash bribe would sort that out.

There was no-one about. Katya went through the terminal and made her way to the car rental. There was no queue and she was quickly able to pick up the receipt and key for the Landcruiser John had booked for her. As she made her way towards it and bleeped the car door open, she heard someone running up behind her, frantically calling out her name. She turned. The seriously overweight man looked hot, red in the face and out of breath. He gasped that he was the rental manager and that unfortunately the vehicle was no longer for hire. There had been a mix up as it had been rented to another customer who was waiting for it and Katya would have to take something else.

He reeled as this woman with the piercing eyes palmed him a hundred dollars and told him, in fast, fluent, furious Arabic that she expected her contract to be honoured, and that she'd be taking the Landcruiser immediately. Trying to argue, he shook his head and wrung his hands. Horrified he saw five people arrive, seemingly from nowhere. He started blustering, sweat pouring down his face as they climbed into the car and slammed the doors shut. Ignoring him completely, Katya jumped into the driver's seat and started the engine. Mesmerised by her, the rental agent watched in disbelief as she drove off and wondered how he would explain what had happened to the customer back in his office, who had already bribed him.

As they drove away Katya turned to look at the two G8 agents joining them. 'Good to see you, Alexei and Irina.' She turned her attention back to the road, saying. 'You know Yas, Oleg, Cato.' She didn't wait for a reply. She looked at them in the rear-view mirror and said, 'You brought the weapons?'

THREE

Katya drove out of the airport and headed south on a narrow, metalled road leading to the development. Trucks were lurching towards her, hogging the carriageway as they went flying past in clouds of dust. Brightly coloured buses almost drove her onto the sand strip which edged the highway. The spectacular scenery of the burnt sienna Anti Atlas Mountains dotted with green scrub bush lay to her left, half hidden in the mid-afternoon heat haze. She hardly had time to look at it or anything else other than the road ahead. She caught herself swearing softly in Russian as she jolted off the tarmac to overtake a cart that was swaying wildly due to the huge mound of boxes it was carrying - the driver, totally oblivious to her, or anyone else's presence.

Cato glanced at her, admiringly. 'Whew! You can teach me some of that cussing,' he said. 'English doesn't hold a candle to Russian.'

'Don't you let your training officer hear you say that,' Katya laughed. 'While you're swearing – '

'The enemy's killing you – yes, I know.'

How much Cato reminded Katya of herself. He'd run at fourteen from his violent father and his single, alcoholic mother in Glasgow to a squat in London.

He was eighteen and on remand in Her Majesty's Prison Thameside for illegal computer hacking when Katya was told about him by a friendly police contact. 'He's bright. Could be useful,' he'd said. She went to visit him. The street scene he described of his violent teenage days in Glasgow was familiar to her from the cut-throat Moscow street scene she'd been caught up in during her own teens. She'd recognized a strength in him similar to her own, learnt from surviving a broken home and had persuaded G8 to take him on. Now trained, Cato was a self-assured qualified pilot and in charge of the team's Satcoms.

The local traffic started to clear and Katya looked in the rearview mirror. Alexei and Yas were talking to each other, Oleg and Irina were asleep, catching up while they could. She had personally recruited each one of them into G8, selecting complex individuals with backgrounds like her own, to whom struggle didn't come as a surprise at the first tough training session or, later, when they were out in the field.

Oleg loved to horrify listeners by ramping up stories of the ritual spiral of mutilation on the Ukraine Russia border and Irina would go one better with tales of the calculated barbarity of Hamas in Beirut. Each had survived the horrors by a combination of wit and courage and, in each of them, a violent streak could explode without warning. She relied on them totally which was some comfort, as what she was about to ask them to do would require all their understanding and commitment.

Cato touched her arm and pointed to an upcoming turning. She slowed the Landcruiser and swung off the metalled road onto an ungraded, narrow dirt track. They were now well south of Sidi Ifni. There were no landmarks, only burnt scrub and sparse brush spread out on either side of the trail. An air of desolation pervaded the area. It seemed a strange place for Cartwright to choose for a tourist hotel complex— if indeed that was what he was doing, she thought. On the other hand, the place was a postcard picture of the desert in this area. She stopped the vehicle and put on the park brake. Switched her mind to the explanation of the job she was asking them to do.

'OK listen up everyone. Don't forget we are now ecowarriors – Our Desert - the plan is to threaten to damage any machinery and the buildings so as to get Cartwright's attention if he is actually involved. The object of that is to persuade him to pay us off – so we can get his bank details. OK?'

'And if he isn't here, like Hong Kong and Tunis?' Yas, realistic as ever.

'We leave, like we did with them. OK? I want you all to be as menacing as you can, but no-one uses their weapon unless absolutely necessary.'

'That's difficult because we would have to leave the guns in here if we don't want them to be seen.' Oleg, preparing for a fight.

'Yes - when I see the layout of the development and can see how things are going I'll give you further instructions.'

There was a silence as they digested all this.

'Our slogan's "Our Desert". Chant it and chant it together, OK? Sounds strange because it's their desert, but DG set it up in Arizona so we have to go with it. Katya waited a second or two. 'Are you all on board with that?'

There were nods of agreement.

She thrust the gear lever into drive and guided the Landcruiser over a series of deep ruts along the track. The progress was painfully slow and it became obvious that whoever was constructing the site had absolutely no interest in keeping the roadway in good order. After about twenty minutes they crested a ridge. Katya saw ahead of them, spectacularly carved out of the scrub and sitting on a cliff overlooking a seemingly endless and very blue Atlantic Ocean, the distinct signs of a property development in the early stages of construction. There was a grid of roughly graded sand roads running alongside half- built sandstone buildings. As they got nearer, she could see that these foundations formed a clear layout: a central hotel building flanked by numerous cabins, the standard design for resort developments. At the eastern edge she saw a number of bulldozers and graders had been parked near a solitary, neglected portacabin. In front of it were a red- painted fuel storage tank and a green water tank, standing side by side. To the right of these, an area had been concreted over and, already, there was a large circle painted on it, with an H in the middle. A landing pad for helicopters.

Katya felt a sharp rush of adrenaline. Would they actually find Cartwright this time? She looked around. The prime location and the sheer size of the site made it obvious that this was an enormously expensive project— the sort of tourist resort that Cartwright would be able to invest in if he was alive and had half a billion in cash stashed away.

To the left of the track a sign declared in several languages that trespassers would be prosecuted. Without stopping, she turned the wheel sharply to her left, driving past the sign and on towards the portacabin. The whole place was deserted. There were no signs of activity anywhere.

As soon as they came within twenty yards of the portacabin, she saw its rickety door opening. Two Arabs stepped out, their white djellabas stained with dust and oil marks. Poking out from underneath the long garments, their feet, she noticed, were bare. She put them down as local watchmen and they were, no doubt, having to live in the cabin. She swung the Landcruiser towards them and drew up a few feet away in a cloud of choking dust.

Led by Katya, the G8 team all slid open the side doors, jumped out into the searing heat and started chanting loudly, 'Our Desert! Our Desert!'

The Arab watchmen both pointed at them, excitedly waving their hands trying to make themselves heard above the chanting. The noise attracted no-one else so Katya decided it was time for dialogue.

Knowing women didn't count for much in South Morocco, Katya had thought of handing over to Oleg to do the talking but, having seen the fuel tank, she'd made other plans for him.

'We're here to occupy this site on behalf of Our Desert', Katya called out, in English.

The team were chanting in unison now, their arms waving up and down in time with the words.

The Arabs started screaming in Arabic, their faces contorted in consternation as they saw the menacing figures stamping their way towards them.

'Do you speak English?' Katya shouted over them.

The Arabs fell silent, stared at her, then at each other. They started shouting again. 'Englis? Englis? No. No.'

'Francais? Katya held out her hands, palm upwards, 'Francais?'

The Arabs stared silently at her again. They moved towards her, gesticulating to her to leave, to get out.

Katya, shrugged, turned to the dark, sloe- eyed Yas.

'Speak to them in Arabic. I know I can speak it but if they think I can't, so much the better, I might catch some loose talk.'

Yas nodded and started to bellow in Arabic. The Arabs switched their attention to her and both of them started to speak at once. She furiously shook her fist at them which stopped their yelling. They looked at each other uncertainly, not sure what to do. After a moment, the tallest one, who seemed to be in charge, poured out a torrent of Arabic, punctuated by fast gestures.

She turned to Katya. 'He says this is private property. We must get off the site. It's Friday, Holy Day. The workers are not here and we should not be here either.'

Yas didn't need to translate, but Katya gave her credit for cleverly making it look to the Arabs as though she did. She said harshly in English, 'Tell them we are the Our Desert Ecological Warriors. We have come to occupy this development. It should not be here. The Western Sahara is sacred and should not be developed for tourists.'

'"Ecological" is not a word in Arabic,' Yas said, her eyes bright with laughter.

'Stop being smart.' Katya grated. 'You want a picnic, go home.' Always the same with Yas, she thought. A great agent but treated life as fun, although the husband she'd killed in Beirut for cheating on her might not have thought so.

Katya watched her walk purposefully towards the men to argue with them, gesticulation for gesticulation.

Finally, the Arab in charge threw his hands in the air and ran towards the portacabin followed by the other watchman.

Katya joined Yas. 'I didn't hear all that. What's happening?'

'They're fine,' Yas said, 'nice people. They're just worried, frightened by us.' She gave Katya a hard stare. 'You, in particular. They said bad things about you.' She raised her dark eyebrows, amused. 'I agreed about you. They're only watchmen not guards. No one expected any trouble here on such a remote site, so they don't know what to do.'

'Good.' Katya gestured to the team members to finish chanting.

They stopped as one and congregated around the Landcruiser, quietly talking among themselves. Katya and Yas followed the Arabs into the Portacabin.

It was sweltering in there, forty degrees, at least. The air, which smelt of a mixture of mint, couscous, acrid charcoal and sweat, steamed into their nostrils. Two bunk beds took up the far wall. A rusted stove stood against another wall, blackened from heat and smoke, and there was a large kettle on it with steam drifting out of the spout. An open cupboard next to the stove was littered with cans, bottles and plastic containers. A small, galvanised water tank stood, lopsided, on a couple of breezeblocks; a battered desk and two chairs completed the furnishings. A satcom on the desk was linked by a cable to the satellite dish by the window, its newness in complete contrast to the conditions the Arabs had to live in.

The taller watchman was shouting urgently into a mic connected to the satcom, demanding help. Katya rapidly thought through her alternatives. Take the mic and ask for Cartwright or wait - see if anyone responded. She waited.

After a stream of Arabic punctuated by frequent pleas for help the watchman threw the mic onto the desk. Turned to Yas. 'Someone will come.'

FOUR

Katya was thinking hard and fast as she left the cabin and made her way to the team who were standing by the Landcruiser. West North Africa was largely ungoverned. It was highly dangerous and no one under threat would be stupid enough to attend a blind meeting without backup. She looked at the helicopter landing pad. Whoever came would almost certainly bring their backup with them in a chopper.

Standing in front of her team, she briefed them quickly and fluently. She ordered Alexei and Irina to hide among the bulldozers and machinery by the Portacabin overlooking the helipad. Cato was to hide at the entrance to the development to forewarn her in case of an attack by road. She told Oleg to position himself facing the Portacabin and fuel tank.

'If it comes to it I won't avoid a firefight,' she told them.

Cato's eyebrows lifted in scepticism.

Her reply was curt. 'If it is Cartwright who comes, he's got to be convinced that if he's going to save his development he's got to pay us off. So we have to be prepared for a fight. I want you all to arm yourselves with grenades as well as spare ammo. If he brings a large team of minders with him we may not have enough fire power to outlast them for very long. So, I want Oleg opposite the fuel tank in case I need to torch it.'

Oleg climbed into the Landcruiser and started handing out the Bullpups - Russian Special Forces A-91 assault weapons favoured by G8 because they were foolproof, plus they also operated as grenade launchers. Useful for Oleg and the fuel tank.

'One other thing, Oleg— and it's important. I will be with Yas in the Portacabin. There's a bunk bed next to the south wall and we'll be sitting on it when whoever it is arrives. We'll remain there whatever happens. If we get into trouble or we need to convince him we have further back-up, I'll fire a shot. I want you immediately to rapid fire ten rounds through the wall six feet north of us.'

'Ten rounds rapid leaves a very small margin for error.'

'You're a marksman, you can handle it. If that stops the trouble or convinces him we are serious I'll fire another shot. If I don't fire, spray everything northwards of our position.'

She watched them take up their positions. She knew they were trained to think of only the roles they now had to play, using the down time to build up their strength and reserves, keeping only a part of their minds alert, ready to anticipate problems, to sense danger.

Katya returned to join Yas in the portacabin and, wordless, sat next to her on the bunk bed at the southern end. As sometimes happened in the moments before meeting a dangerous target, she thought of her father – he was the reason she was here. His severity was legend in the KGB and he'd been determined to forge her in his own image – even installing Helga, an ex drill sergeant, in the apartment to school her. How she hated that woman, who forced her to spend hours isolated in her room or days struggling through icy winter marches. She hardly saw her father except when he took her to the Black Sea in stormy weather to sail…

She'd allowed her thoughts to roam. She looked around the hut. It was no place for any human being to live in. Squalid, except for the satcom – and a new looking shelf covered in documents. She hadn't noticed it before. Paperwork meant the possibility of useful intelligence. Immediately she got up and went to it. The top of the pile contained blueprints. She searched for the name of the architects. There was none. Underneath were a dozen or so delivery dockets for building materials. She studied each one for the address of the supplier or logistics company. Nothing. The papers were devoid of any useful intelligence. The only thing of any use was a design of the development. A stunning series of white painted red tiled cabins on either side of a sand coloured hotel fronting a large swimming pool, the whole set in a lush green golf course. Unexpectedly the luxury of the development flashed an image of her mother, Galina – a principal dancer with the Bolshoi Ballet in Moscow. Occasionally she'd been allowed to watch her from the wings - elegant and beautiful against the rich scenery of her stage. A woman who had transported her for brief moments into a world of colour and beauty, sophistication and wealth. It was a door Katya would have loved to have opened herself, but she had never been given the opportunity to find the key - her father had made sure of that.

Yas touched her shoulder and pointed to her watch. 1600.

Katya glanced at the Arabs. They were listless now, like the fly buzzing lazily around the food cupboard. She wiped the sweat from her eyes and picked up a bag of maize from a nearby counter-top. Watched by the perplexed Arabs, she poured a line of it across the cabin floor from wall to wall. When she'd finished she dumped the bag on the floor and moved to join Jana again.

The Arabs looked at each other and shrugged.

Yas looked a question.

No-one said anything. A fly settled on a half-eaten date.

They waited.

FIVE

The Arabs heard the helicopter first, lifting their heads, straining to make out the direction the sound was coming from, desperate to make sure it was *their* people who were arriving.

The chopper arrived in a storm of dust, the sand swirling in all directions under the rotor blades.

Katya looked out from the Portacabin window. She felt her pulse rate increase and she tightened her grip on the Bullpup as she watched the helicopter's door slowly open. She caught her breath as she saw the first figure emerge. She had no trouble recognising the heavy set, jowly faced man wearing gold rimmed sunglasses. Abdul Ahmet. He was at the top of G8's list of wanted terrorists. Ahmet had protected Gadaffi, fought for him through the Libyan revolution, shooting, slicing, burning and torturing his way until his boss was eventually slaughtered – then he had shifted his fascination for violence to the world of terrorism where the killing continued under the guise of politics.

Katya mentally shifted up a gear, preparing herself for the switch in operational temperature, from tepid to boiling. Ahmet was frightening, cruel – poisonous.

She watched as he adjusted his lightweight charcoal suit jacket and looked around, hesitating. Probably looking for her, she thought. Walking away from the helicopter, leaving the rotor blades slowly rotating, he seemed to make up his mind about something. Presumably, she guessed, he was now satisfied the Our Desert ecowarriors weren't an imminent threat. He signalled to a figure sitting out of sight, in the co-pilot's seat.

Moments later a second man climbed out. He was Caucasian, sun tanned, elegantly suited, with a handkerchief flopping from his top pocket. Her pulse pounded. Cartwright. Greyer, leaner than his photograph in G8 records but, without doubt, this was Gadaffi's moneylaunderer.

The two men walked towards the portacabin, their eyes restlessly searching the half-built breezeblock cabins and hotel. Katya watched them, waiting for their backup to emerge from the chopper. None did. She wondered why.

As they neared the portacabin, she gestured to Yas who nodded to the two watchmen. Released, they rushed out, babbling in Arabic.

Ahmet brushed past them and barged into the cabin, closely followed by Cartwright.

The terrorist stopped in his tracks when he saw no one at the desk where the satcom was. He looked around the cabin, his eyes searching, then they narrowed to slits as he noticed Katya and Yas sitting on the bunk. His mouth tightened as he started towards them.

'No further than that line.' Katya pointed to the line of maize on the floor. Ahmet looked down and saw the ragged strip at his feet. He laughed scornfully. 'Are you joking? That's not going to stop me.'

He started towards her.

Katya felt behind her, drew out her Bullpup and put it on her lap. Ahmet stopped dead so suddenly that Cartwright staggered into him, swearing.

Ahmet quickly recovered, put his hand on Cartwright's shoulder and tried a charm offensive. 'I apologise.'

Katya ignored him, kept her eyes on Cartwright. Silent, arrogantly forcing him to speak first.

Cartwright studied her, momentarily pushed off course by the cold eyes challenging him over the Bullpup. He mentally shook himself. 'I thought you were a protest group.'

Katya kept her eyes fixed on him, wanting to keep the initiative, maintaining an expression of sheer arrogance. 'We're Our Desert - Ecowarriors - here to stop your development - '

Cartwright showed no emotion - pointed to the Bullpup. 'Western protest groups don't carry arms.'

Katya gave him full marks for his coolness, but then this man had survived the madman Gadaffi and had a globally feared terrorist as an ally. She raised the muzzle of her gun an inch. 'We're waging war. The desert belongs to the Arabs. – we'll demolish this place - return it to the desert unless you abandon it.'

Cartwright pointed to Ahmet. 'He's an Arab. So, you'd better talk to him.'

Yas stood up suddenly. '*You're* not . . .' she sneered. 'What are *you* doing here?'

Cartwright hadn't manipulated his way around North Africa just to be fazed by a couple of feminist trouble-makers, however striking the auburn haired one might be. He faced Yas, self-important. 'I was once in charge of this development. But it has been taken over and is now wholly owned by a consortium of Arabs, represented by my colleague here.' He gripped Ahmet's shoulder. 'There are no longer any western corporate ties.'

Katya looked at him contemptuously. 'So, as she says, why are you here if this is an all Arab development?'

Cartwright ignored her. Ahmet deliberately looked at his Apple watch with its graphite band, moving his wrist to show it off for effect. He then adjusted his designer shades for emphasis and looked dismissively at Yas. His eyes crawled over her body. 'I really haven't time for this.' His eyes flicked away and he scanned the cabin. 'Besides, you've got it all wrong. Our development will help our people. Many will be employed here, turning the desert into fertile land, and then the resort will bring in investment, creating many jobs. It is good for the local economy. So, please, just pack up and get lost.'

Katya knew she was fast losing control of the dialogue. Ahmet was running rings around her. She searched her mind for a reply.

Yas laughed. 'That's a joke, whoever you are. You're here to make cash for yourselves. Look at your watchmen. Look at the conditions of this cabin.' She swept her hand in an arc. 'Would you live here?'

Ahmet looked around mystified.

Cartwright broke in, conciliatory now. 'Yes, of course, I absolutely agree. We forgot the men in the field and we must do something about that. But you still don't have any grounds to protest about our being here.' He looked at his watch and then briefly out of the window.

Katya caught the gesture and knew it explained why Ahmet had had no back-up in the chopper. Against all the odds the mercenaries would be coming in by road. Rapidly she reviewed the options: wait here and have a firefight or bluff it out. In a fire fight her team could be outnumbered. There was little alternative. It all rested on Oleg.

She gave Cartwright a glacial stare. 'They're not coming.'

Cartwright tensed, uneasy, 'What do you mean, they're not coming? Who's not coming?'

Katya stood up, confident, brushing a patch of sand from her clothes. 'Your team. Your hired guns. We've got the road covered. When they come,' she moved the muzzle of the Bullpup suggestively, 'we will clear them out.'

Ahmet looked insolently at Cartwright. 'You told me these people were just a bunch of protestors. Nothing to worry about.'

Katya thrust the barrel of the Bullpup towards Cartwright. 'Contact them. Tell your men to turn around and go back. Otherwise, I assure you my people *will* take them out.'

Cartwright simply laughed. '*Your* people? Since when have ecowarriors had military back-up. You're joking.'

'You underestimate the seriousness of our cause and the size of our operation.' She lifted the gun's muzzle. 'And we'll take you two out first.'

Ahmet stared at her, summing her up. 'You're not the sort to kill in cold blood.'

Katya shrugged, fired a shot into the roof. Immediately Oleg fired a burst through the portacabin wall between Katya and Ahmet. The .50 calibre rounds smashed through the wood, splinters flying, leaving a gaping, smoking hole.

Cartwright dived to the floor. 'Shit! What the hell...'

Ahmet stood stock still. He wasn't a man who knew fear. But he had met women like her – terrorists. There was nothing these women wouldn't do to achieve their aims. Torture, random killing, came naturally to them. They had no safety net. This woman had just shown that. The bullets had burst through the wall not two feet from her – and, without doubt, she'd planned it that way. To feel fear in her presence would probably be wise. The moment his back up appeared she'd shoot him and Cartwright without hesitation.

Quickly, he climbed over Cartwright's prostrate body and hurried back to the satcom on the desk. Punched in a number. 'Return to Sidi. Immediately.' He threw the mic back on the desk, turned to face Katya. 'OK, so what do you want?'

Katya fired another single shot into the air and said coolly. 'I want... him,' she indicated Cartwright, 'to halt this development.'

She had nearly called him "Cartwright" but checked herself, realizing neither man had identified the other.

'Are you crazy? No. I mean what do you *really* want?'

Katya felt a surge of satisfaction, this was the first indication that he understood. That he realised there was a deal to be done. She feigned ignorance, looking down at Cartwright, lying prone on the floor, for an answer.

'He means money.' Yas explained to her.

'Money?' Katya acted the archetypal environmentalist. 'What do I want with money?'

Cartwright climbed to his feet, brushing a white carpet of maize off his suit. 'Why the hell do you want to halt this development? It's only just begun, just some trenches and a few walls in the scrub. There's no publicity in shutting this down.'

'Don't you believe it. I'll torch all your machinery and this cabin and take out that chopper. The whole thing will be videoed, posted on line. It'll go viral. That'll be publicity for our cause all right.'

'You and who else?'

'If you care to take a walk, I'll show you…'

'She's got back-up here, don't waste your breath.' Ahmet looked straight at her, sneering, 'You planned this very well. But you're not just aiming to knock all this down, are you?'

Katya stayed silent, watching Cartwright watching her.

Suddenly, Cartwright turned and walked to the door, ignoring Katya as she shifted her weapon to cover him.

She warned him, 'Don't try anything stupid.'

He ignored her again, stood in the entrance, wordlessly studying the helicopter, the machinery and then the scattered groundworks.

She waited. Silent.

His next words were barely audible. 'How far would you go to get publicity?'

Katya shook her head 'What?'

Cartwright raised his voice. 'I said, how far would you go to get publicity?'

'All the way. I'll blow this whole place apart.'

Ahmet interpreted Cartwright's thought. 'He's looking for the number you want.'

Yas nudged Katya. 'I told you he meant money, Katya. Now he means a lot of money.'

Ahmet was keen to explain. 'Your friend is right. I'm sure there is a figure we can settle on.'

Cartwright gestured impatiently to Ahmet. 'Don't even suggest it. I'm not paying a cent.'

Ahmet shrugged. "Well, it's your money. But I would think about it. We're here and our backup is nowhere.'

Katya stored the information that Cartwright was paying to build this place.

Cartwright read her thoughts. 'It *is* the money, isn't it? Oh, you've shown us you are very well organized and it would be easy for you to smash everything up.' Flattery was a ruse that Cartwright employed well. 'But it's the money you're after.'

Katya didn't want to sound too eager. Operationally she wanted the money with Cartwright's bank details attached but her cover demanded she play the ecowarrior role. She led him on a bit further, sounded hesitant. 'I'm not sure - I've got a bird in the hand here.'

'How much?' Yas, always practical.

'Not so fast', Katya interjected, 'we don't need money.'

'Before you reject our offer outright – '

'Come on it's good business.' Yas nudged Katya's knee. 'We can use it for our next protest.'

'How do we know we can trust him?' Katya murmured.

Cartwright put a hand up, slowly putting the other hand in his pocket. Katya tightened her grip on the Bullpup as he drew out his wallet. He held it up between his fingers.

'I think a hundred thousand would help towards your eco bank balance? That's a very sound basis for trust, I think.'

Silence.

'I thought so.' Cartwright put his wallet back in his pocket.

'You mean you haven't got a hundred thousand on you?' Katya asked innocently.

'No. I'm not stupid. You take the cash and still torch the place. If we have a deal, I'll let you know where to collect it.'

'No cash,' Katya said swiftly. 'I'll only take a Banker's draft - safer to travel with.'

Cartwright shrugged. 'Fine by me.'

'Not so fine,' Yas intervened. 'How do we know they'll pay up?'

'Well, who's going to stop you coming back here one night? I don't want a fight, I want to finish building. I'll be in contact, believe me. You can trust me. Now, can I give you a lift into town?'

'No, thanks. I don't fancy a free fall into the Atlantic.' Katya pointed to the helicopter. 'Goodbye.'

She watched them go, the helicopter gathering a storm of sand again as it rose and disappeared out of sight. Before the dust had settled she had come to the conclusion that Cartwright would already be giving instructions to suss out Our Desert. And Ahmet would be planning to make sure she'd never get her hands on that money.

SIX

Katya and her team left Cartwright's development to return to G8 Headquarters London, transferring flights in Gibraltar. She knew she must immediately report to John Hammond. The situation had changed dramatically now they had to factor Abdul Ahmet entering into the equation. With him in the picture, the lives of her team were now certainly at risk.

At Heathrow, she slipped through the secure police channel and took an unmarked Jaguar iPace from the G8 car pool. A fast drive and fifty minutes later, she was on the outskirts of Basingstoke on the M3. She eventually turned the car off the motorway and headed towards the town's ring road, driving past a line of anonymous houses until she came to an industrial estate filled with logistics warehouses. She eased the car along the side-roads darkened by the immense steel and carbon fibre buildings flanking them until she pulled up outside a warehouse that was painted a dull gun metal grey.

She always felt a tinge of excitement when she saw this structure, ugly and non-descript though it was. It was well-disguised and hidden amongst the other warehouses and yet it housed the headquarters of the powerful G8 International Intelligence Agency. The organization had been set up by Britain, the USA, Russia and the other five G8 countries to investigate and eliminate groups of terrorists and organised criminals who were dangerous enough to threaten democracy in these territories. It was through the Agency that nations co-operated, identifying targets and planning the complex intelligence operations which their agents often risked their lives to carry out.

She was proud to have been appointed G8 Chief of Operations only a year ago. She'd been told her outstanding astuteness, determination and courage had made her the youngest appointee ever. Whilst that was flattering, it was not the source of her pride working for G8. The real satisfaction lay in the fact that she and her international colleagues worked so easily together. As a team, they showed the world how national boundaries became irrelevant when sharing of intelligence was carried out with harmony and absolute trust. Of course, the Russians had pushed hard for her to be given the job as they knew the political kudos it would bring. But they found that the British, American and other G8 directors were equally pleased to have Katya's dynamism and leadership guiding the most difficult and dangerous part of their work.

Katya parked the car, locked it and walked into the building. Two discreetly armed security guards met her. She exchanged light banter with them as they checked her password and accompanied her down long empty corridors. The bare walls on either side were steel. There were no pipes, no cables—nothing into which anyone could insert spyware, nothing that could be sabotaged. It was a soulless, colourless place.

The guards led her through the directors' security screen and left her at a paternoster lift which she walked onto. She stepped off at the third floor where she crossed an oppressive, windowless hallway stretching away to left and right, before opening an unpainted steel door that led into a large rectangular conference room.

John Hammond, G8's Director General was there and turned towards her in one easy, relaxed movement, his grey eyes watchful. He was thirty-eight with sandy coloured hair and, as always, he was wearing a chunky cardigan over a plain open necked shirt. He wasn't particularly handsome or tall but there was an aura, a magnetism, about him which drew people in.

'Good to see you back, Katya - You have the Cartwright report?'

She saw him take in her white Prada silk blouse and black designer jeans. He raised his eyebrows. 'Had time for a change, I see.' He paused. 'We've been waiting.' A reprimand.

'Thanks. I picked this outfit up at Heathrow on my way through. Of course, if I'd known you wanted me still in desert kit I wouldn't have bothered,' she replied tartly.

There was a softening of his smile as their eyes met for a brief moment before he turned and walked towards a long metal conference table. There were computer consoles arranged along it and a large plasma screen in front of it.

'Everything alright?' John looked back at her over his shoulder.

Did his voice sound concerned? She smiled slightly at the thought. His razor- sharp mind probed the intricacies of chaos theory and mathematical equations not the sentiments of people.

As she sat down she pushed these thoughts from her mind and instead waved a hand at the two faces visible in the plasma screen in front of her.

'Lev, Walt, good to see you both.'

The greying, heavyset man on the left of the screen was coughing his usual cloud of tobacco smoke. Lev Leviatski, Chief of G8 Russia. At 54 he was the oldest G8 Director by some years. The average age of the directors was thirty-eight which reflected the burn-out rate in what was one of the world's toughest jobs. Taking on and successfully countering violent, cunning and sadistic terrorists and organized criminals soaked up an agent's stamina like a sponge in water. But Lev thrived on it, exhibiting the doggedness, typical of all Russians, which survived any horror provided one foot was put in front of the other for as long as it took.

Lev had heard her reply to John. 'Quite right, Katya, give John what he deserves. What is it you say… that English expression… "give him pepper"?' He spoke in a voice long grated by his continual use of his favourite Abdullah No 7 cigarettes. 'But you don't look tanned, I thought the desert would tan you, make you even more desirable.'

As Katya sat down she laughed, unfazed. Lev was ex-KGB, immune to feminism and would never change. 'Outrageous, as always Lev.'

Sitting on the right of the screen next to Lev was Walt Sable who shook his shaven head in despair at Lev. 'Need some help Katya?'

The wiry African American, Chief of G8 United States, had a didactic edge to his tone. Always precise in his manner, he'd grown up on the east coast of the States - majored in politics and law at Yale university and had worked as a political analyst on the Hill in Washington before moving to the FBI and finally picked up by G8. He always wore a suit and tie and, in a slightly old fashioned, correct way he never joined in the office banter that acted as a safety valve in the extreme pressure of their work. He found it disconcerting and he disapproved. But he liked and admired Katya. In idle moments, he thought he might be in love with her. That long glossy auburn hair, those stunning eyes, the straight nose— so typical of a Russian profile— leading to a full mouth and determined chin. She was lithe, quicksilver, beautiful, impetuous and exuberant, but underneath he sensed a sort of restless unfulfillment in her which he knew he couldn't satisfy. Besides, they worked together, so any relationship was out of the question.

'No need for assistance, Walt. For me, Lev is long past his sell- by date.'

They all laughed. She looked at John, who nodded for her to start her report.

She began. 'The information we received about Sidi Ifni proved correct. I met with the target Cartwright —'

'Was he attractive?' Lev peered provocatively out of the cigarette smoke.

Katya took no notice. 'Before I go any further you need to know that Abdul Ahmet accompanied him – '

Walt fairly snarled, '*What*? The bastard who gassed three hundred innocent Americans travelling on the Chicago El train?'

'Yes.' Katya saw that Lev looked shocked. 'The same man who killed those travellers on the Moscow Metro–'

'It was definitely him?' Lev, preparing for retaliation.

'Definitely. I don't mistake identifications.' She stopped as she heard a knock on the door.

One of the staff came in carrying a tray of coffee, tea and doughnuts. There was a pause as he put the tray down on the console and left.

'How come we don't get given those.' Lev sounded disgruntled as he saw the plate of cakes.

Katya smiled, 'They're nothing like our Pyshki doughnuts.'

'Ah, - those St Petersburg ones! Light and crisp.'

John looked unamused at the flippant interruption. But it gave Walt time to swallow his anger. John nodded at Katya to continue.

Taking a mug of black tea from the tray and, thinking she must remind them to bring jam next time, Katya continued the briefing. She quickly ran through the events at Sidi Ifni. 'I can confirm Cartwright is alive and involved in a hotel development near Sidi Ifni. It's clear from the layout of the foundations that it's of considerable size. Morocco's a cash society he can use it to pay for the build. That supports the intel that he took off with Gadaffi's money.' After describing how they'd found the development and how she had lured Cartwright there, she then moved on to his reaction. 'Cartwright seems convinced Our Desert is legit – '

Walt tapped one finger on his desk 'Good. So, we can trace him easily enough now you've met him.'

Katya shook her head. 'Not so fast, Walt. I said he seemed convinced, but he gave me nothing, no name, no details of the development owners, there's not even a sign there as to who it belongs to.'

'But there must have been something, Katya,' Walt said. 'Drawings, delivery receipts, that sort of thing?'

'Well, Katya's achieved two objectives,' Lev said. 'We've confirmed Cartwright is definitely alive and probably it was he who got away with the Gadaffi money.'

John looked thoughtful. 'The objective was to get Cartwright to offer you a bribe to stop you wrecking this Sidi Ifni project - get into his bank account that way. There doesn't seem to be any progress on that front.'

Katya absently fingered the gold necklace around her neck - something she did when she was unsure or had something controversial to say. She caught John's disapproving look. He was always warning her not to wear the necklace – telling her that the fingering of it was a tell— something people would eventually pick up on, something which would forewarn people of a thought or impending action. Lev also noticed the tell. He'd noticed it before, knew he should perhaps tell her, warn her but he kept it to himself, one never knew when that sort of information might be useful.

He looked at her. 'Something else, Katya?'

'Yes. I did a deal with Cartwright. I agreed he'd contact me to pay me a hundred- thousand dollars to leave his development alone.'

'And you really think he's going to do it? Why didn't you insist on being paid there and then?' Walt, critical.

'He told me he didn't have the money and, anyway, cash is no good. It's his bank details we want.'

'He'll now go back into hiding.' John, realistic.

She stubbornly fingered her necklace again, defying John and her training officers. She had her own private reason for wearing it and nothing and nobody, not even John, was going to stop her. 'I don't agree. He was shaken by my organization of the operation at Sidi Ifni. He's convinced I'm in it for the money and I'll turn the screw if I don't get it – and Ahmet won't forget being worsted. He'll hunt me down just to win back his self- respect. I have no doubt Walt's agents in Arizona will hear from Cartwright.'

'I hope you're right,' Walt said, grudgingly.

Lev stubbed out his cigarette and lit another. 'I agree with Katya that this is what we need to do.' He thought for a moment. 'I say we should continue with Katya's attempt to extort his bank details from him in return for leaving the Sidi Ifni development alone. We should wait for Cartwright's contact.'

John made up his mind. 'I agree.'

The big screen went blank as John switched off the connection.

SEVEN

As Katya prepared to leave the conference room, John held her back.

'Don't go yet, I want you to meet the new British Government Treasury Minister, Hugo Dempsey. He's just arrived and has asked for a briefing on G8's activities and you can help me.'

Katya grimaced. 'He probably wants to reduce the British government's input to our budget.'

John raised his eyebrows, 'Precisely. That's why I want you to brief him.'

Katya wondered why he wanted her to do the briefing. John was the DG, the one to handle politics. On the other hand, she was the Operations Chief, the expert at getting information. She laughed. 'So you want me to sweat him a bit?'

He strode off down the corridor, saying over his shoulder, 'Yes. If you can get him rattled, he might hedge off any budget cuts – when you've set up your briefing meet me outside the Tac Room.'

Katya watched him go, rapidly turning over in her mind how she might rattle a minister. She decided that shock tactics were probably the best approach. She mentally ran through her current operations searching for one that would shock the most hardened of politicians, men like Dempsey. It didn't take long. The most violent G8 target at that moment was Rosa Rulenski, a notorious Polish trafficker.

She made various arrangements with the ops personnel, went up in one of the lifts and arrived at the entrance to the TAC room just in time to see John greet Hugo Dempsey. The minister was heavyset with a beetle brow that somehow didn't match his expensively tailored suit – probably bought in Saville Row along with the shirt and tie. Taking this in at a glance she wondered what money he made outside his not so well-paid government post.

He was delivering a crisp greeting to John, 'Where are all your people? I've only seen two security guards since I arrived.'

John nodded. 'One of the reasons the G8 countries set up this Agency was to cut out over-manning. There used to be seven UK agencies alone dealing with terrorism and organised crime. Think of the duplication, triplication even, across a further seven countries. We cut out all that and established this central team of experts here.'

He broke off as he saw Katya. 'Join us, Katya, I want you to meet the new Treasury Minister, Mr Hugo Dempsey.'

She walked coolly towards him, held out her hand. 'Good to meet you, Minister.'

His wandering eyes slid over her. He was surprised to see so striking a woman in this of all places - violet eyes dispassionately returning his gaze. He took her hand and squeezed it slightly, 'Very good to meet -' He pulled himself up short. It wouldn't do to seem overly interested in her. He turned to look around.

Katya laughed inwardly. He'd be easy to manipulate. She stole a glance at John and saw the smile behind his grey eyes.

'Now if you follow me,' Katya said to Dempsey as she put her finger on a small glass plate alongside a steel door. A green light glowed. 'DNA security analysis. Please put your finger on the glass, Minister '

Dempsey said, sharply. 'You have my DNA profile?'

'This is what I want to show you,' she replied, ignoring the question.

The door clicked open to reveal the vast size of the warehouse.

'This is our Tactical Operations Room, the Tac Room,' she explained. It's where we assess intelligence and plan operations.'

'I've never seen anything like it.' Dempsey blurted out as he looked around.

The space was shrouded in an eerie darkness. There were no windows and there was no artificial light except for that emanating from eight large plasma screens that were mounted on one of the longer walls. On each screen, flashing up in many colours, were names of people, organisations, companies, banks, finance houses, dollar, yen, sterling - all linked together by solid or dotted coloured lines. Opposite them and built into one side of the building were four tiers of balconies going from the floor to the roof nearly forty feet above. The information and images on the screens were visible to over two hundred agents sitting at their individual workstations on each of the balconies.

Dempsey studied the flickering screens where the information displayed changed every few seconds as it was updated by the agents who were busy collecting, analyzing and collating it. He knew that, apart from a handful of people at the highest levels of the G8 countries, no outsiders had seen the Tac Room. He immediately felt a satisfying surge of adrenalin. This was power. Knowledge of this sort put him above his peers.

Katya read his thoughts. 'Yes, the Tac Room's classified Top Secret Ultra.'

Dempsey deliberately ignored her. Tall and beautiful as she was he didn't want her to feel important. 'What's that?' He said abruptly, turning to John and pointing to a chain of open fronted lifts that continuously wound up and down between the four floors, giving direct access to all the balconies.

'Paternosters.'

'I thought the EU had made them illegal?' Dempsey queried. 'They said with people jumping on and off them they were too dangerous to use.'

'Just one of many things that are illegal here, Minister.' John murmured, deadpan. 'They provide quicker access than closed lifts to all the floors in the building.' He dismissed the subject. 'You'll want to know about the plasma screens. Each of them reflects the most up to date computer analysis of information received on every one of our targeted organised crime or terrorist groups. The eight screens allow the agents to cross reference information – see if anything relates to their own investigation.'

Katya and John both stayed silent, allowing Dempsey to take in the breathtaking scope of the building and Top Secret Ultra.

After a moment, John turned to her.

'Katya's our Operations Director. To demonstrate how we work, she will take you through an operation.'

Katya moved easily to an operational console, knowing the thin material of her blouse accentuated the lines of her body. She quickly looked at Dempsey, catching him watching her, seeing his face redden.

She knew he was boiling inside, knowing he'd been set up to see and admire her. Crude, but still effective and he, the minister, had fallen for it. The expression on his face told her he would remember her making a fool of him. She watched as Dempsey turned to John, consciously ignoring her again. 'Tell me about G8 and your *unit*.' He emphasised the word 'unit'. Katya knew he had used it deliberately. It was less important than 'task force' and a damn sight less important than 'government'. He obviously hoped to put John back in his box, make him realise it was he, Dempsey, who was important.

John made him wait, studied him for a moment, then looked at Katya. 'You answer the Minister.'

Katya didn't hesitate. 'Organised crime is out of control and it's international. Thanks to advances in technology, it now crosses borders with impunity, corrupts bankers, lawyers, journalists, judges and, even, governments. These days it includes terrorism, illegal drug and people trafficking, fraud, kidnapping, extortion, movement of aliens, pedophilia, pornography, prostitution-'

She let the words hang for a moment before continuing.

'It has now become a trillion-dollar business. There is no longer a single cartel, there is no global Mafia. Instead we need to monitor a lot of gangs, the Triads in China, the Camorra in Italy and the terrorist groups such as Isis of course. There are also hundreds of criminals to keep track of. Like Rula Rulenski who I'm going to tell you about.' She paused. 'Before I do, you should know that the people involved in organized crime trade their commodities for cash, because it's easy to hide and very difficult to trace. Even with G8's resources at our disposal, we find cash used in illegal transactions almost impossible to find. The criminals employ lawyers, bankers, financial advisors and accountants to hide cash for them in places like private banks and investment trusts. In this way, the money can then be laundered prior to being made available again to the criminals via legitimate businesses, like import export, insurance,' she paused before looking at him and adding, 'and hedge funds. It's worth well over a trillion dollars a year.'

'Mine didn't.'

The abruptness of his defense took her by surprise. 'You're what didn't?'

'My hedge fund in Gibraltar before I joined the Government.'

Katya didn't probe, that would warn him of her interest. She could find out about his hedge fund from other sources. She moved away from the desk. 'Have you heard enough Minister? Would you like a break for some coffee or a further look round or would you like me to go on with the Rosa Rulenski operation?'

Dempsey assumed what he hoped she would see as a typically dismissive ministerial pose. 'I would like you to continue - over a trillion dollars a year! No wonder it's out of control.'

'One reason why G8 was set up.' She said, matter of factly. 'And this is how we do it.'

She turned towards the screen in front of the console, leant forward and speaking into the microphone, said clearly, "Rosa Rulenski". Immediately the name surrounded by a myriad of connecting red lines flashed up on the screen.

Katya started explaining. 'Rulenski controls prostitution rackets in Warsaw and Berlin. A combination of fear and pimps. Her prostitutes are forced to push seventy, eighty drug deals a month.' Katya motioned to Dempsey to stand nearer.

He leaned over her shoulder, suddenly noticing her scent, subtle, but at that distance very apparent. He recognized it as Picasso. Expensive, like her designer clothes - way over her salary band- he felt a hint of jealousy as he wondered who had paid for them.

She was talking again. 'Rulenski wants to expand. A month ago, one of our informants reported that she'd met up with a South African woman named Anele Dichter. They were negotiating the import of one hundred and fifty girls from the Transvaal area of South Africa for the French market. We planted a bug in Dichter's house. A week later we picked up a conversation between her and Rulenski.' Katya pressed a key on her keypad saying, 'This is part of what we heard.'

"Get them to Pietersburg and I'll take them on through Botswana, north through Libya and out of Benghazi to Narbonne on the French coast.'

'That'll take days. They'll be dead by then.'

'At their price, we can afford a ten percent wastage.'

'I told you these girls were cheap.'

The voices ceased.

Katya felt Dempsey's hand on her shoulder.

'So you managed to stop them, you saved those girls lives.' His fingers squeezed lightly. 'That's very impressive.'

Without flinching she allowed his hand to stay there, 'I didn't. In fact, ten Percent wastage was right. Fourteen of them died on the journey.'

'Fourteen?' he repeated. 'You let them die?'

'How could we save them without alerting Rulenski and Dichter?

She felt him stiffen and pull away his hand, but she didn't move, allowing him time to take in the horror of it.

'But you got Rulenski, Dichter, you prosecuted them?'

'No. Our algorithm suggested that we had sufficient evidence to prosecute Dichter. The problem was choosing a jurisdiction in which to do that. The UK doesn't accept telephone intercept as evidence, so the Dichter stuff wouldn't stand up in a UK court. The Germans had difficulties in securely providing the informant's evidence. So, the upshot was that the computer advised against prosecution. Do you want to see the detail?'

'No, thanks. I want to see what happened next.'

'Well we discovered that Dichter had made a major blunder. She'd used the Orianenberg Bank in the Netherlands Antilles for all her transactions over the past two years, so we were able to trace every one of them. Even a deposit of a quarter of a million made by Rulenski—presumably upfront payment for more women.' She spoke another command into the microphone and the screen lit up in a blaze of greens, blues and oranges. 'You can see the extent of Dichter's operations just by looking at the organisations and companies she used to launder the cash from her rackets. For instance, she used Franz Joseph estate agents in Austria, KMB accountants in Poland.' She hesitated, emphasising the next sentence. 'The Gonzales Brothers lawyers in Gibraltar–'

'How did you get all that information?' Dempsey shot out the question.

She shifted slightly in her chair, realising that when he'd run his hedge fund in Gibraltar he must have come across the Gonzales lawyers - they were leading lawyers there - yet he hadn't mentioned it.

'All the information that each G8 Task Force collects is automatically fed into all the other G8 computers, for instance those in New York, Moscow and Tokyo. That includes everything received from our informants and all digital intelligence, including satellite and drone surveillance.'

'The computers must have a massive capacity. I mean can you trace *anything*? Secret bank accounts, that sort of thing.'

There was an urgency about his questioning.

Katya exchanged a fleeting glance with John. Both of them were puzzled by the sudden sense of alarm in Dempsey's voice.

'Cash deals can be difficult but otherwise, yes, we can trace almost any financial transaction once it's in the financial system.' She paused, firmed up her response. 'To just about anywhere.' She noticed a slight bead of sweat just below his nose. 'Provided the algorithms have identified it as a target.'

'Target?' Dempsey flung the word out.

John stepped in. 'The algorithm works out which organised crime and terrorist group we should target, based on threat level.'

Katya looked directly at Dempsey. 'Or which individuals to target.'

His eyes avoided hers, switched to the screen, 'So, what did the computer decide about Dichter?'

Again, Katya thought Dempsey's question came at her fast, like a bullet, as if an automatic reaction to cover something he wanted well hidden. John's faint lifting of an eyebrow told her he thought so too.

Her answer stunned him. 'I didn't feed Dichter's information into the algorithm.'

'Bloody hell.' Dempsey obviously didn't care what they thought of him. 'You mean those women get away with it?'

'I didn't say that, Minister.' Katya replied quietly.

'Well, what have you done?'

She looked at John.

He stayed silent, giving her control, emphasising to Dempsey that if his number two could jerk a minister around then he, Hammond, could willingly do the same to a government.

'We siphoned Dichter's money out of her account to G8, so she's broke from that op.' Katya turned to the screen again. 'Rulenski had a quarter million dollars in Dichter's account and it's gone. The only explanation she'll believe is that Dichter double crossed her and stole it.' She pressed a key, switching off the screen. 'I guarantee Dichter will be dead within three months. Rulenski will see to that,'

Dempsey looked shaken as he stared at the now blank screen. 'That's what you do? Let them wipe each other out?'

'Sometimes. It's a positive outcome, given the vagaries of Human Rights legislation.' She looked at him. 'And, unless our budget's increased substantially, it's the most cost-effective way for the time being.'

Katya straightened up, keeping her eyes on Dempsey who was standing stock still, silent, staring into space. It was obvious he was unprepared for any of this. But she was taken aback by his extreme reaction. Of course, she had played him, made him uncertain, shocked him, forced him to be aware of her, teased him with her scent, but that shouldn't have produced this tense agitation in him.

Dempsey looked at John and jerked out his hand. 'Thank you for an interesting afternoon.' He smiled rigidly, once more playing the part of the supportive minister. 'We've got a fight on our hands with people like Dichter and Rulenski around.'

John shook Dempsey's damp, sweating hand. Then he pushed Katya's point about their budget allocation, saying slowly, 'Dichter will be dead, but Rosa Rulenski will still be in business.'

Dempsey slowly nodded, turned to Katya, and grasped her hand, fervently, 'You have been excellent. No, inspiring.'

As she watched a security guard usher Dempsey away, Katya looked at John. 'And if you believe that, you'll believe anything. What was eating him about our tracing capability, do you think? Something dodgy about his hedge fund?'

John pursed his lips, 'I'm not sure. It was definitely personal. Look into him and let me know if anything turns up - you did a good job, got him thoroughly disconcerted. Always keep ministers on the edge, is my advice. Control them or they'll control you.'

'It was easy.'

She saw again the smile behind John's eyes as he said, 'The extra spray of Picasso was useful.'

As they moved out into the hall John's mobile rang. He answered it, looked at Katya. 'It's Walt.'

'Yes.' He listened. 'Yes, Walt. I have that. Thanks.' He switched off.

'You were right. A typed note has been pushed through the door of the Arizona office of Our Desert.' He paused.

'And?' Katya said impatiently.

'You've been instructed to fly to Gibraltar where you'll be met and given further instructions. Walt's emailing the details.'

Katya eagerly started down the passage.

'Take care,' John muttered. Realising he might have been too personal, he added, 'It may be a ruse to lead you to Ahmet.'

But she'd gone.

EIGHT

The flashing red neon sign over steep stone steps announced the name of the club as El Fuego. This was certainly the name Katya had been given earlier by the man at the information desk in Gibraltar airport. She had followed the instructions Walt had relayed from Arizona, taking a long meandering walk in the hot morning sunshine to make sure she wasn't being followed. She stood outside a minute to mentally prepare herself to meet either Cartwright or Ahmet – or both.

Breathing deeply, she pushed aside the heavy curtain at the bottom of the steps and immediately started coughing in the heavy cloud of smoke rising from the spliffs and bowls of kiev and hashish in the hands of most of the people she could see. Quickly she scanned them. Cartwright wasn't there, nor was Ahmet. She knew then they had chosen a spot in the back of the room to cut off her escape when she met them. She took her time adjusting to the gloom and, choosing a table next to a wall and near the door, walked towards it.

She was intercepted by a waitress wearing a low-cut blouse and multicoloured skirt in the Spanish style. 'Mr Wilson will see you at his table.' Without waiting for a reply, she turned and walked towards the back of the room.

Katya stayed where she was. After a few paces, the waitress realized Katya wasn't following her. She turned and beckoned.

'Tell Mr Wilson I'm sitting here.' Katya said and took a seat at the table she'd chosen. She sat down with her back to the wall, facing the room.

The waitress was confused, not sure what to do. Katya ignored her and stared at the curtain. Her heartbeat had risen - sitting next to the curtain wasn't such a good idea. She could be surprised by an attack through it or hustled out through it by an assault from someone in the room. She was about to move when she felt a presence next to her.

'Not coming into the back room? You are careful, aren't you?'

Katya recognized Cartwright's voice. 'Very. I've no intention of taking that risk.'

He shrugged, sat down. 'I'm Ronald Johnson, by the way.'

She faced him, taking in his laid back coloured print shirt and Bermuda shorts. 'You should get to know yourself. The waitress told me Mr Wilson would see me.'

He sat in a chair opposite her. 'Wilson, Johnson. What's in a name?

'Plenty, as it will be on the banker's order you're giving me.'

'What are you drinking?'

Katya wondered why he instantly changed the subject. 'Yorsh, please.'

'It's a dump but they should be able to mix beer and vodka here.' Cartwright arrogantly showed off his international travel, revealing that it had included Russia where Yorsh was a national drink.

Katya wondered whether he'd had dealings with the same Russian *Mafiya* gangs which had roamed the Moscow streets of her early teens, he was certainly old enough. She remembered her own dealings with them. These had brought no profit, just hard lessons in survival. She felt a twinge of unease, what was it about this job that these memories kept coming back?

Dimly she heard Cartwright saying, 'Are you Russian? I wondered about that accent.'

Katya assumed her cover. 'Your guess is right, I'm second generation. My mother emigrated to the States.'

'No father, I bet. Explains you.' He nodded at the waitress. 'Beer and vodka mixed a third, two thirds, and a large Glenfyddich malt, just ice.'

'You know Russia then?'

'Worked with a few oligarchs, developing property.'

'In Russia or elsewhere?'

'Why? You want to demolish them as well?'

'It's why I asked. You–'

'Don't give me that crap. You're not interested in all this Our Desert nonsense. You're Russian – well, as good as - you have no interest in anything eco. You're just interested in money.'

'You're wrong–'

'An immigrant mother, no father– come on, you want to get out of that hole. The guts you've got – you're heading only one way - self-indulgence, luxury.'

She suddenly felt confused, her cover sliding into her real life. It was as if this man had seen into a part of her she had never recognized. With an effort, she shied away. 'What about the hundred thousand you're paying me for leaving Sidi Ifni alone?'

He studied her face intently. She was worried for a moment he was going to pursue his personal analysis of her. He had shaken her up.

Cartwright sat back in his chair suddenly.

Out of the corner of her eye, Katya saw the curtains part. A heavyset man, Spanish, long black straggly hair, torn jeans, slid through them into the room. As she turned to look at him she saw him give an imperceptible nod to Cartwright. It *was* a trap. Without thinking she jumped to her feet. The quicker she got out the better. There may be others outside but if she could surprise them by the speed of her actions she had a better chance than waiting. She shoved the table into the man, sending him sprawling into the curtain. She pulled it away from the door, took the steps two at a time. A man at the top spun around to face her – crumpled, choking, as she slammed her foot into his groin. She felt thick arms close around her from behind – her feet swept from the ground. She struggled but it was useless, she knew Ahmet would be waiting for her.

Her feet were placed on the ground again and she was bundled down the steps. The man she'd attacked was standing by Cartwright, rubbing his shoulder where she had charged into him.

Cartwright was grinning. 'Just seeing how you'd cope without your goons.'

Katya looked around for Ahmet. He wasn't there. She turned to Cartwright. 'You bastard.'

'I needed to see how tough you were,' Cartwright said. He watched her. 'I had a reason. What if I asked you to destroy another development of mine?'

She was genuinely non-plussed. 'What?'

Her question hung in the air for a moment.

Cartwright spelled it out, patiently. 'Supposing there was another development. Right in the middle of the desert. One that was more advanced. With the buildings more established on site. The whole thing backed by American investors.'

Katya was grateful to be able to get back into her cover. She stalled. 'You want this other development demolished? Why? You'd never get American investors again.'

'It's very simple. I built it in the wrong place.'

'The wrong place?' Katya was incredulous.

Cartwright gestured impatiently. 'It's in El Bayedh, in the

middle of the Sahara. We're building it for an investment company in Gibraltar. We badly underestimated the full building cost. Transporting materials across the desert, that sort of thing...' He tailed off, then delivered the punch line. 'So it would be the perfect way out for us if it was destroyed by you and your eco-warriors – saviours of the desert.'

'I see. You want the insurance?'

'Yes. But *you* get the publicity.' Cartwright smirked. 'It's a matter of trust between us. You've shown us you are well organised. You've just shown you can be violent – you'd demolish the place if it suited you. You'd find it easy with your talents.' Flattery was a ruse that Cartwright employed well.

Katya was conscious that she was going to have to press Cartwright further if she was to get at the Gadaffi cash. She needed Cartwright's bank details, not publicity. She played him a bit further, sounded hesitant. 'Why would I do that? I've got a bird in the hand with your payoff for Sidi Ifni.'

Cartwright was getting impatient. 'I'm not paying you for Sidi. I want this done and you can do it. A hundred thousand would help towards your bank balance. In return for your torching the development in El Bayedh for us. That's a very sound basis for trust, I think.

'Two hundred thousand.' The words were out of Katya's mouth before she realized what was behind doubling the price.

Cartwright stood up. 'Stay in Gibraltar. I'll be in touch,'

NINE

The chambers of the Gonzales Brothers, Attorneys- at- Law, Gibraltar, were housed in a traditional building with hewn stone walls and arched windows overlooking the sea. The brothers had inherited the large house and ornamental grounds from their late father, a respected barrister, and, because it gave an air of dependability and longevity, they'd clung onto it, refusing all offers from the developers who ravaged the ancient buildings around it and erected high-tech buildings typical of those favoured by the hedge fund and on-line gambling industries. Cartwright had always considered the house and grounds to be a shocking waste of space which could have been more usefully and profitably filled by a twenty-first century commercial centre – with a lift instead of the long flight of steep steps he was struggling up to reach the front door.

He blinked as he walked from the afternoon sunlight into the cool reception hall. Diego and Santo Gonzalez were there waiting for him, talking to each other. They were dressed identically in dark, expensive, well-cut suits and handmade shirts with gold cufflinks, an attire that they wore to convey respectability and wealth. Cartwright felt a tinge of satisfaction. They hadn't given him this much attention when he had first come to them years ago, just after he'd had to leave London in a hurry thanks to some ill-advised selling of time-shares on the Spanish Gold Coast. As a nobody he'd been at the bottom of the lawyers' pile, and he'd had to hang around for hours before they would see him.

Diego Gonzalez noticed the arrogance on the thin, narrow face, of the sharply dressed man walking towards him. 'Hello, Cartwright. Come this way.'

Cartwright followed them into their antique pine-floored office, admiring, as always, the light oak panelled walls which were punctuated by tall windows through which one could see the bay of Gibraltar and the white wake of boats on its dark blue water. Two overhead fans gave a colonial atmosphere to the room and, to the side of the long walnut boardroom table, he saw the glass display case with a model of the El Bayedh development inside it - a series of low, square, domed, model buildings, painted in pale yellows, pinks and blues, flanking a large mosaic tiled infinity swimming pool. Various labels marked out the areas designated for bedrooms, living spaces, restaurants and common areas. Above it, in gold lettering, was an impressive sign which read El Bayedh Desert Hotel Development.

'Beautiful, isn't it?' Diego beamed, 'It's a shame it's just a scam. We really should finish it one day.'

Cartwright shook his head. El Bayedh was indeed a scam through which a bunch of American investors had been lured by him, with the promise of a twenty per cent return, to invest in a hotel development in the middle of the Sahara Desert. Most of the investors were doctors, lawyers, professionals, all too busy undertaking expensive private cosmetic surgery and arranging large divorce settlements to bother about travelling into the desert to see what was going on with their money – until one day they would discover that Cartwright and the brothers and their money had all disappeared into the sand-dunes. 'It's cost too much already,' he said aloud. 'How much American investment have we got left, unspent?'

'A little over three hundred million dollars,' replied Santo, smugly.

'Have any of the investors visited El Bayedh yet?'

Diego scratched his beard. 'A dentist and his wife and a couple of film actors. But that was early days and there was enough development there to satisfy them.'

Cartwright gazed at the model buildings. 'Amazing. It's just like time-share selling. As long as you pitch the profit margin high enough, there's always some idiot who'll invest. Funny too that it's always the professionals who are the mugs.' He laughed. 'Beats me how their clients never figure out how stupid they are.'

Santo interrupted him, 'Even so, someone's going to wise up soon and I think it's time we got out and took the cash.'

'I'm glad you brought that up.' Cartwright looked around the room. 'We need a drink.'

Diego gestured to his brother. 'Gin and tonics, Santo.' There was no doubting it was Diego who ran the business.

'You ever heard of a protest group called Our Desert?' queried Cartwright.

'Who?' The brothers said together.

'Our Desert. They're an ecowarrior group, out to stop property development in the desert. They claim the desert belongs to the Arabs.' He paused for effect. 'They wanted to torch Sidi Ifni.'

Santo slopped tonic water onto the floor. 'What? Torch it? What the hell d'you mean?'

'What I say.' Cartwright looked at Santo as though he was half-witted.

'But it's not like the El Bayedh scam. The Sidi Ifni development is legit.' Diego put in, as though that meant something. 'I mean, Santo's and my personal money's in that one.'

Recovering from the shock, Diego pulled up a chair. 'Sit down. You had better explain.'

Cartwright ignored the summons, deliberately walked over to one of the windows and sat on the seat below it. He started telling them what had gone on with the Our Desert group at the Sidi Ifni development.

'They've agreed to demolish El Bayedh instead?' Diego shook his head in disbelief. 'I don't believe it. Why would they?'

'You'd better believe it,' Cartwright said harshly. 'And it could be very convenient for us. But first I need a hundred grand to pay them.'

Santo, totally mystified, looked at his brother for guidance, 'But we don't want El Bayedh demolished, I mean what for? It's a scam, we can just take the cash – we don't need it torched.' Then as an afterthought. 'And we certainly don't need to pay people to do it.'

Diego ignored him, leaning back in his seat shaking his head from side to side. 'It's brilliant.' He began laughing. 'Brilliant, brilliant,' he kept saying between gasps for breath. 'We blame these Our Desert people and we get our money out.' He wiped his eyes. 'When are they doing it?'

Santo stood with the tonic water bottle dripping in his hand, staring at him, bewildered.

Diego looked up at him, 'Don't you see, Santo? Cartwright has given us the answer - the perfect solution - the crown jewels of an idea.'

Santo looked at him blankly.

Diego almost patted him on the head. 'Santo, you just said we need to get out of this racket. You are right, some nosy investor is going to come along soon to El Bayedh expecting to find a luxury hotel complex and realise that his bucks have bought some skeleton concrete buildings and nothing else. If we simply get out with the investors' cash and leave those buildings behind, we'll have the FBI, Interpol– '

'And the Canadian Mounties – don't forget those four Canadian investors.' Cartwright added.

Diego nodded, 'Every law enforcement agency in North America and Europe will be hunting us forever. If the El Bayedh place is demolished by these Our Desert people, none of the investors will know their cash came into our pockets in some plush development scam. If it's blown up, it'll be in so many little pieces -'

'And the beauty of it is,' interrupted Cartwright, 'we become the outraged developers - after we have stashed the three hundred million in a Panama bank account, of course.'

Diego shrugged, took a gold toothpick out of his wallet, 'You know,' he said to Cartwright, 'the investment suckers will take months to sort out the mess with the Moroccans. It will give us time to liquidate and be long gone.'

He probed a back tooth.

'We don't want to wait,' said Cartwright. 'After Our Desert have done their stuff, the sooner we get the cash out to Panama the better. We don't need to take time to liquidate the company, it's a shell anyway.'

'Mmm, true.' Diego got up. 'Panama sounds good. It'll be well hidden there. Santo, where are those drinks?'

'Don't forget the hundred thousand for the Katya woman.' Cartwright added.

'Katya woman? Who's she?' queried Santo as he handed Cartwright a tall glass.

Cartwright raised it. 'She runs Our Desert. He drank deeply. 'I met her earlier today to set it up. I tell you, what a stunner.'

He heard a sound behind them.

'Thank you for the compliment.' Katya sidled into the room, holding up her iPhone, closing the door behind her. She looked around, gaining time to digest the enormity of Cartwright's fraud and the problem presented by her knowledge of it. The stakes were far higher now and Cartwright would expect her to react by demanding a higher price for wrecking El Bayedh. Also, these lawyers had only just been let in on Cartwright's scheme and that would mean haggling and delay. She saw Cartwright's upfront payment disappearing. But she had no alternative but to press on – everything depended on getting his account details. 'Nice place for us to meet.' She fixed her gaze on Cartwright. 'You did want me to meet your friends, didn't you?'

They gazed at her open mouthed. Cartwright was the first to recover, 'Katya. What the hell - where -?'

'You're careless, Johnson or Williams or whatever your name is. I followed you here. I assume from the nameplate on the front door, these gentlemen are Mr and Mr Gonzales, your brothers in fraud.'

Santo took a menacing step towards her, 'Get out.'

'No, I'm not doing that.' Katya calmly bent over the display case looking at the model. 'Very pretty. That bunch of uber-wealthy American citizens being scammed.' She raised her hand to stop Diego speaking. 'How much grief are they going to cause when they find out what you are doing?'

Diego glared at Cartwright. 'Is this the woman you were talking about? What the hell were you thinking.' He swung around facing Katya, 'I'm calling security.'

Katya pressed a key on her mobile, 'Go ahead, I recorded your interesting conversation about El Bayedh.' She moved her finger to hover over the phone, 'When I press this other key, it will be on social media within seconds.'

Diego promptly sat down.

'No? I thought not' said Katya. 'All those angry lawyers and doctors demanding their money back.'

Cartwright came out of his daze. 'Look, let's talk this over.' He raised the glass he was still holding. 'Drink?'

She waved her hand over the display case. 'No, let's talk about why you never told me this was a scam. You told me you wanted the insurance money. Now we're talking three hundred million dollars against what – twenty million?' She slapped her hand on the case. 'My price has just gone up.'

The creak of the overhead fans was the only sound to be heard. Katya let them whirr on for a second.

'There is no money,' said Diego, coming to life again. 'It's all tied up with the American investors.'

'Another lie you told me, Johnson. You told me you'd pay me a hundred thousand dollars up front to knock off this development.' She pointed at the model. 'Perhaps I'll go for the reward money instead. Apparently, the FBI are generous to informers where fraud is concerned.'

'Diego knows shit.' Cartwright cut in hurriedly. 'I mean, look at him, he's a lawyer, a black letter book man, he does what I tell him. Of course, you'll get the money.'

'Well, now I know you're getting three hundred million out of the El Bayedh fraud and the insurance money on top of the-' Katya shook her head as Cartwright started to protest. 'Of course, you'll claim the insurance, you're greedy, so I'll need that two hundred thousand.' Pushing Cartwright even further was a risk. She could hear her trainer complaining she never knew when to stop, but, she argued to herself, Cartwright mustn't be allowed to think her a pushover.

'You're Russian all right.' Cartwright looked her over. 'D'you want to come to my hotel and talk it over?'

Katya knew Cartwright was playing with her. She needed his commitment now. She must have his bank details. Time was slipping by. She eased herself away from the display case. 'The FBI it is then.' She turned towards the hallway.

'Wait.' The alarm in Cartwright's voice rang through the

room. 'Just wait until the job's finished and I can pay you off with a transfer - even if it's traced, I'll be long gone.'

Katya examined Diego's face for a minute. There was no mistaking the dogged look on it. There was no way he'd agree to a bank transfer upfront. She turned to face Cartwright.

'You don't think I'm capable of finding you if you don't pay up?'

He studied her. 'No, I do think you are capable of that.'

'So, I don't have to say any more. I'll let you know when I'm ready to do the job. And that transfer is now for two hundred thousand.'

She left them staring after her as she strode through the hallway, out of the front door and down the stone steps where she hailed a taxi.

Climbing into the back seat she told the driver to take her to the airport. Immediately she started to think about what she had learned from Cartwright and how she could turn it to her advantage. The first important point was Cartwright had let slip that the El Bayedh fraud cash would be sent to Panama, certainly to be laundered there. That information was important because if that was the preferred finance centre, the Gadaffi money was probably there as well. But how could the information be exploited to make sure of that? First, El Bayedh must be destroyed.

The cab turned a corner. Suddenly the sea came into view and, drawn to it as she always had been, she stared out of the taxi window at the flickering patterns on the waves under the hot midday sun. They were random, like the information she came across in her work—random, that is, until it had been sorted out to make a strategy or plan. As she watched the changing shapes dance on the water she worked out the planning of the operation to destroy the development at El Bayedh. Ahmet was the key. He was going to kill her, if only for humiliating him at Sidi Ifni. She had no idea when or how. If she was going to survive, she must find out. Fear shot through her as she realized the most certain way to find out was to meet him. But how? Ask him to help her demolish El Bayedh perhaps? She could then find out when and how he planned to help her. If she knew that, she could ambush him instead of him ambushing her. But if he did agree to meet her, there was no guarantee he wouldn't simply kill her and do the El Bayedh job himself.

Her view of the sea disappeared, cut off behind a dilapidated, domed building. Its exterior paintwork was scruffy and marked and it was probably awaiting the attentions of a property developer. But the building still seemed to be in use: two girls lounged there, leaning up against a wall looking provocative, smoking cigarettes. Most probably prostitutes Katya thought.

Instantly an image of Rosa Rulenski flashed into her mind. She caught her breath as an idea kindled—one that even she knew was brilliant. She almost laughed. Rosa and Cartwright! It was absurd to link their names. But was it really so laughable? Rosa was top of Katya's target list after Ahmet and Cartwright. Thinking laterally, the three of them made a neat triangle – joined together by violence, greed and cash. The idea started to take shape as the glimmerings of an operation designed to take out all three targets.

First, though, she must persuade John to agree.

TEN

Landing back in London Katya decided to skip briefing John and first spend some down time at her apartment.

She'd made good time from the airport and was now nosing her nondescript blue, G8 motorpool Ford down the traffic-jammed Thames Embankment. Evening mist was swirling up from the river, twisting and floating as it made its way around the buildings and down the busy streets. Commuters were hurrying along the pavements, intent on making their way to their buses and trains, heads bent low and coats wrapped round them as they tried to keep out the chill from the wind.

She turned the vehicle into Water Lane. No-one had followed her. She gave one last glance in her mirrors, saw it was all clear and turned the car into the garage attached to her ground floor apartment. Except it wasn't her apartment, it was the G8 safe house she was obliged to live in for a maximum of six months before she would be shunted to another safe house.

She resented the security, the gadgets, the fact that she had to keep moving because the G8 computers had worked out that she would only be safe for six months in any one place. Her job was not to question them, it was to complement them - to create the necessary strategy, tactics, political footwork and then convert the whole into a successful operation. Reluctantly, she accepted the algorithms' advice, even though she knew deep down that they couldn't possibly factor in the danger she faced every day. But, even if they could, fear or her own personal feelings could not enter into her work. So, she suppressed these emotions. If she allowed them to dominate her she would make a mistake. And any mistakes had to be made not by her but by her targets. This she achieved by manipulation, forcing targets into a corner - just as she had manipulated Dempsey and Cartwright.

She waited until the garage door automatically shut and climbed out of the car.

As she walked through the front door into the large sitting room she looked at the stark décor afforded by G8's meagre budget for safe house furnishings. White walls, grey upholstered sofas and the dreary utility brown coffee table. She wondered, not for the first time, how she put up with the G8 regulations for the housing of its senior agents. Nothing personal was permitted in the apartment, nothing that would in any way identify her, not a painting, no books. Everything was about security. Even the windows, which opened out onto a raised balcony just above the river's high-water mark, were secured with armour plated glass. She sighed, it was true the view of the Thames was breathtakingly beautiful but was that enough to soften the bleakness of this place?

Walking past a sideboard, her hand drifted across a framed photo. It might be forbidden to have any personal items but this one photo she refused to be parted from. It was of her mother dancing the lead role in the ballet Giselle at the Moscow Bolshoi Theatre. Her pose revealed her frail, dazzling beauty. Katya kept the photo not because she had loved her mostly absent mother – driven away by her father and too busy dancing or socializing to spend time with her - but because it represented a life far removed from the brutal one she was leading in G8. Colour, glamour and freedom were all evoked by the passionate way her mother had danced and lived. It was the sort of vibrancy she too craved. To be free to live the sophisticated life she wanted, not the ever-changing lives she was forced to lead as she moved from cover to cover to deceive her targets.

Was it the bleakness of this apartment and the nomadic lifestyle that brought on these thoughts or was it memories of the aching loneliness of growing up in Moscow in the nineties. Memories which never left her. Mentally, she shrugged off the many questions she sometimes dwelt on when alone. Living this way was what she knew, what her father had insisted on, what she'd been trained to do.

Turning from the photo she picked up her mobile, and, looking at her playlist, chose a track from the Ukrainian pianist Kapustin which she knew would relax her. She looked at her watch, it was getting late. One of her friends, Paul Foster, a late boyfriend, was giving a party on his boat. It was moored at Chelsea Wharf and he was leaving to pick her up in half an hour - she needed to hurry.

She turned up the music, kicked off her shoes, gave one last look at her mobile to check for messages and quickly walked into the shower room. Stripping off and standing under the warm water she felt it beat off her as she deliberately emptied her mind, soothed by the rippling cascade of piano music drifting in from the sitting room.

Twenty minutes later she was ready, dressed in tailored black trousers, one of her favourite white Prada tops, a wide silver belt with large silver buckle and a pair of new white and silver trainers. Her manicured nails were French polished. She'd swept her long auburn hair back into a silver clasp and lastly, as always, she'd put the simple gold chain around her neck. She looked at her reflection in the long mirror, twitched the belt and, satisfied, turned and gave herself a quick spray of Picasso.

Walking into the kitchen she poured out a shot glass of vodka and picked up a note on the counter left by Betsie, her housekeeper, who ran the apartment for her.

Betsie was fiercely protective and was the only person she allowed to boss her about. She squinted at the note, Betsie's handwriting was atrocious. *Don't forget furniture polish, luv,* it read. Katya's revenge on any male who called her "luv" would have been terrifying. She found it somehow endearing in Betsie who was now in her sixties. And had looked after Katya ever since her retirement from G8. She'd been a Registry Queen, as they were known in the registry department, where they filed all the information. She now ran Katya and the apartment with the same precision she'd applied to her job, fussing over her and continually telling her she should settle down and have a proper home, get married like Betsie and her late husband Bert. Katya smiled, John's name was mentioned frequently in these conversations - she wondered if Betsie had sensed something in her that she had refused to bring to the surface.

Had she allowed the tyranny of her parents to dominate her feelings? She shied away from the memory, then caught herself, wasn't that what Betsie meant? She was always hinting that it was time for her to face up to her past, to put it behind her, time to move on and settle for what she really wanted from life - freedom. It was the need for freedom that had driven her to the street life she'd led in Moscow when her parents had confined her to a life of homebound lonely drudgery.

Memories came flooding back of Helga – could she ever forget the name – coldly and dispassionately following to the letter the strict rules of military discipline and rigid regulations laid down by her father – the punishments she enjoyed giving her of starvation, of being locked up. She still felt herself shudder when she thought back to the cruelty of those early childhood years – the schools were relentless military institutions, talking forbidden, no friends allowed, regulation military haircuts, dull shapeless uniforms - the drab soulessness of the place, the endless unnecessary punishments from the harsh instructors. There had been no relief from the ugliness of it all. Until late one night she'd discovered an escape.

The picture was still vivid. Shivering in anticipation and fearful excitement, she'd waited for silence to descend on the house, except for Helga's snoring, before she'd climbed out of her bedroom window into the icy windswept mystery of Moscow. The excitement had built, the blackness of the sky seeming to wrap itself around her as she'd roamed the ill lit streets. They gave her a strange comfort – for the first time an escape from the friendless life she'd been forced to live.

There was the beer cellar, the first she'd seen, dimly lit in a dark side street - her heart in her mouth as she'd crept through the door, the amazing sounds which met her ears, discovered to be banned Western heavy metal music. Within the stained brick walls, people were drinking, loudly laughing, having a good time – it had seemed another world. One of the girls had pushed a cheap Yorsh into her hand. A kindly gesture she'd thought, only to discover that over the following nights other girls menaced her, bullied her to try drugs, prostitution. She'd resisted, knowing she had to find the nerve to become strong and street savvy if she wanted to survive and be part of the street scene. In the late nights on her way home she'd overcome the numbing fear when *Mafiya* members waited on corners to pounce if she didn't run - digging deep inside herself to uncover a rich vein of courage. Looking back, she'd found the excitement and danger of those nights on the streets and in the beer cellars exhilarating– she could still feel the overwhelming relief and freedom she'd felt.

She slowly finished her vodka, idly wondering what freedom would look like for her today. Maybe a ranch in America…a pipe dream but if she had the money…her thoughts drifted …she would have all the space and freedom she needed. She could breed horses which would give her excitement and adventure. Betsie was right about that.

The sound of Paul's riverboat horn brought her back to reality. She saw the vessel bump against the balcony railing. Swiftly gathering up her black velvet jacket, she gladly left the apartment, her thoughts and Betsie's promptings behind her.

ELEVEN

The evening had drifted into the early hours of the morning by the time Katya climbed off the boat and said goodbye to Paul and her friends. She slipped through the patio door, laughing, waving and promising to see them all again soon. The moment she shut the door behind her she heard the alarm go off on her computer.

Switching on the lights she walked quickly into the kitchen and touched a glass panel hidden under the countertop, wondering why G8 surveillance would want her at this hour of night. A cupboard door slid back to reveal a conference call screen showing John leaning on a desk, holding a mug in his hand.

He lifted it in salute. 'Have a good time in Gibraltar?'

'I'll brief you later, I've just come back from a party, it's the middle of the night or didn't you know?'

He gave no heed to the abruptness of her reply, saying, 'We have to talk plans.' As if he hadn't heard her.

'Can't it wait until the morning? People do sleep between one and six, John.'

He took a sip from his mug. 'Good coffee, this.'

Katya recognised his obstinate streak and, abandoning the thought of sleep, switched to being operational, became focussed on the plan she'd conceived in the taxi that took her to Gibraltar airport. 'I need to get hold of Rosa Rulenski- you know the Polish woman I briefed Dempsey about.'

John waved his hand in recognition. 'I know, the Rulenski

drugs and prostitution ring, but why Rosa all of a sudden?'

John watched Katya on his screen, staying silent while he waited for her plan to emerge. One of the things that attracted him to her, was her ability to think so laterally she surprised everyone.

'Cartwright's hotel development in El Bayedh is a complete scam, he's duped a whole bunch of North American investors into funding it but he's only pretending to build it, doing just enough work to make it look good. The moment we destroy it, Cartwright will disappear with their investment - all three hundred million dollars of it - and that money will probably not have been paid to him in cash. Why should it be? As far as the American investors are concerned it's a legitimate business enterprise.' She paused.

John let her continue.

She was used to his reserve, his lack of emotion and went on. 'Cartwright let slip that he'll send that three hundred million to a bank in Panama. That means we can trace it and the chances are it will give us a lead to the Gadaffi cash, too. I mean this is Panama, a tax haven and, given his background, he'll use one of his aliases – he's given me two already - or a numbered account in one of their private banks where it will be completely hidden.'

'So how does Rosa fit in? Why don't we simply find out which bank Cartwright's put this money in and take it?'

'I first of all thought that as well but then I remembered Rosa and the fact we've been after her for years with no success. So why not kill two birds with one stone?'

This time John did interrupt her. 'You're surely not going to involve Rosa in this scheme? She's not some pushover Katya, she's unscrupulous - kill without question— anyone who gets in her way.'

'We're talking about three hundred million dollars here, John. I think she could be tempted by an offer to split that with her. We can set up an operation where our undercover agent convinces her it could be stolen from Cartwright. I almost guarantee she'd be tempted. 'The cash would replenish what she lost in the Dichter op.'

'Yes, but what's Rosa's part in all this, I mean what would she expect to have to do for her share?'

'Our agent would tell Rosa that although they know about the cash they are unable to get into Cartwright's account in Panama to get hold of it. The agent would say that as Rosa knows all about moneylaundering in her business they would offer her a fifty-fifty split to help them get access.'

'What's to stop her taking all the money.'

'It doesn't matter, she'll know she can't take that amount of cash out of the Panama bank in one lump sum so she'll have to transfer it to one of her own accounts in a bank somewhere. We can then trace that and in turn the other assets she has stashed away. The end result will be that instead of just taking Cartwright's three hundred million we seize everything Rosa's got as well. Every Euro she's been paid from her prostitution rackets.'

'Aren't you forgetting the Gadaffi cash?' John questioned.

'Look, John, the computers still have no idea whether that's still sitting somewhere in those shoe boxes or whether Cartwright's laundered it. Our best bet is to follow the El Bayedh scam money in the hope it gives us a lead to the Gadaffi cash. As our computers can't do the job it has to be a boots-on-the-ground operation. We go to Panama and find Cartwright's account there. We wipe out both Rosa and Cartwright in one action.' She paused. 'Dempsey would be pleased, too, it saves the money we'd otherwise spend mounting two operations.' She saw the faint lift of his eyebrows and smiled. 'I knew you'd understand.'

'Oh, I understand alright, but how is this agent going to put the proposition to Rosa? Go up to her and say "Hi Rosa, I've got this great idea, I can lead you to three hundred million dollars—it's in Panama?"

'Don't be facetious, John, I've thought of that.' She paused before saying casually. 'I can be the agent.'

There was a moment's silence. She saw him frown and hurried on before he could object. 'Rosa's in Berlin, isn't she? And one of our stringers, Igor Paliakov, is there too. You know I can operate very well under cover there and I can use Paliakov as the cut out to introduce me to her.' She waited for a moment for this to sink in, then looked at him. 'I can do this John.'

He lifted his coffee mug and, deep in thought, drank some. He wasn't at all happy at his operations chief going on this operation, but it was complex and would need all her skill and judgment to bring it off. Resigned to the idea, he looked down and Katya saw him feed information into his computer. His eyes narrowed as he anticipated the response from the G8 computers working away to answer his search query.

Paliakov's photo flashed up on Katya's screen followed by a five-line cold officialese precis of a man's life.

Igor Paliakov.

Age 55.

Occupation: Property Consultant.

Stringer for G8 for nine years.

Present location: Berlin

The words dropped off her screen, leaving her with John's image.

'I know of him,' John was saying, 'Igor Paliakov – another one who thinks a go between can be an agent. Well I suppose we've got worse stringers.'

'Tell me about it,' muttered Katya. 'Do you know his story? Lev told me about him.'

She went on without waiting for his reply. 'It seems Paliakov made a comfortable living as a consultant sorting out land ownership after the two Germanys merged in 1989. He would still be doing it if he hadn't been persuaded by a vulnerable dark-haired Berliner called Rolfe to invest in an IT component production company. It was in Rostock up by the Baltic. One disastrous morning Paliakov woke up to find his Berliner had gone, vanished, together with a young, funky blonde, IT programmer. Paliakov's money disappeared with them. Lev heard about his story and thought, with his background, he could be useful investigating Russian *Mafiya* money laundering in the German property market'

'If Lev recruited him, he should be controllable,' John said. He thought for a moment. 'But what about his love life, it could be a risk if he's been that damaged?'

She shrugged. 'He's hardly looked at another man since his Berliner. But there is a downside, we know he still misses him and too much vodka really fans his rage that he was double-crossed.'

'And you propose working with him?'

'Well, you said at the beginning we've got worse stringers.' She bit her lip. 'I'll go and see him.'

She saw John lean forward to cut the connection.

'You know Ahmet's planning to kill me.' She announced baldly.

'Yes.' He waited.

'I'll need to meet Ahmet before I go to El Bayedh.'

'Why?'

'Well, I don't know how he's going to do it and that makes him very dangerous. If we're going to get Cartwright's account details I'm going to have to demolish El Bayedh. So I think it will be best if I see Ahmet and invite him to help me. I'm sure he'll agree because he'll think I won't be on my guard if we're co-operating. I can then plan how to get rid of him.'

'It's very complex, Katya. You really think you can successfully complete each part of the op., including the Rosa part?'

'Of course.'

She waited patiently, watching John silently thinking through the plan.

'It's outrageous.' He gave a half laugh. 'Only you would have dreamt this up. I'll leave you to do the planning. Just let me know where you intend to meet Ahmet and when – I'll arrange satellite surveillance. Just be on your guard.'

'Can I get some sleep now?'

Violet blue eyes met smiling grey ones.

'Of course.'

The screen went blank before she could thank him for his concern over the danger she would be in. She would have liked to have done that just to show him that she knew he cared. On the other hand, she wondered how he would have reacted to her gratitude. His inner feelings were a mystery. She looked at the screen for a moment. With Cartwright, Ahmet and now Rosa as targets would she be alive long enough to find out?

She tapped the glass panel and watched the screen disappear.

TWELVE

Katya had arranged to meet Paliakov at Berlin Brandenberg airport. She hadn't told him why she was coming. Rosa Rulenski's reputation would certainly be known to Paliakov and, if she'd told him upfront what the job involved, it was unlikely he would have turned up.

She waited in the crowded terminal. He was late and she stretched her fingers in annoyance at the thought that he had hedged off from meeting her anyway. She looked around to see if she could spot him and for the first time took in the modernist beauty of the arrivals hall. Its soaring glass walls and tensioned steel cables rose to a glass roof that seemed to float above her. The stark elegance of it appealed to the sophisticated side of her. Only the Germans, she thought, had the panache to turn what should be a mundane operational building into a structure to marvel at.

She made her way to the front entrance and stood waiting on the pavement, impatient and unamused at being kept waiting.

When Paliakov eventually arrived, he was driving a black Mercedes, indistinguishable among countless other black Mercedes parked outside the Terminal. She climbed in the front passenger seat, thinking he looked very Russian with his round face and puffy lips. He wore a baggy non-descript brown suit and one of the popular Russian knitted caps above square black plastic rimmed glasses.

She wasted no time in preliminaries. 'I want to meet Rosa

Rulenski,' she said, as he started the engine. 'You won't be involved, I just want an introduction.'

He blustered as she knew he would, 'That's not easy, I - '

'Of course, it isn't.' Katya cut in. 'I wouldn't be paying you to do it if it was.'

Paliakov changed lanes, moving the car into the exit road, 'How much?'

'Igor, can I call you Igor?' she said, smoothly.

He nodded.

She moved her hand forward and slammed the gear lever into neutral. He instantly reacted by braking hard. Vehicles behind screeched to a halt, car horns blared.

Katya took no notice. Instead, she grabbed Paliakov's jaw and forced it towards her. 'I have dealt with stringers like you all around the world. You're all shits and you're all on the make.' She yelled the words into his face. 'You're broke and I'm your last hope so don't ask me "how much?" like I'm a backstreet pickup. In fact don't ask me anything. I'm here to tell you, is that clear?'

Terrified by the brutality of the outburst, he could only stare at her. She shoved him away, 'Now do I get out of this car and let you rot or do you do as I tell you?'

Paliakov rubbed his face, he was almost crying. Without a word, he shifted the gear and let the Mercedes roll forward.

'Let's start again,' she said, conversationally. 'I want an introduction to Rosa Rulenski.'

He was silent, still touching his smarting jaw. Katya let him stew.

After a moment, he mumbled, 'It can't be direct.'

'Better,' replied Katya. 'So who is the go to?'

'It could be Mikhail Augsberg,' he said eventually. 'He's her enforcer.'

'That's dangerous. Why not a woman?' Katya queried.

He fell silent again. 'Of course, not a woman.' Katya answered her own question.

Paliakov bumped into Mikhail Augsberg two nights later outside Rudi's Restaurant. It stood opposite the majestic statue of Friedrich Schiller in the cobbled square of Gendarmenmarkt in the Friedrichstadt district of Berlin. It wasn't difficult for him to emerge from the shadows cast by the ghostly glow from the gently floodlit twin churches. And so create the collision that was to alter his life.

Katya didn't witness the charade. She was already inside the restaurant, seated at a corner table waiting to see if Paliakov made the contact and thinking it strange and rather surprising that Rosa's enforcer, Mikhail, regularly dined at Rudi's. She looked around the expensive and exclusive haunt of Berlin's sophisticated concert goers, most of whom had regular tables in the same way they had regular seats at the nearby Konzert Haus. Crisp white cloths covered the well-spaced tables and the exotic arrangements of flowers and flickering white candles made for a stylish setting. Seated at them were the beautifully dressed elite of Berlin. The colour, the clothes, the jewellery the women wore evoked a sudden and startlingly clear memory of the audiences she'd seen as a child at the Bolshoi Theatre. The soft lighting glowing from the sconces which shone down from the walls and up onto the framed photographs of famous musicians made the picture even more real.

A waiter dressed in black and wearing white gloves silently approached her. She didn't notice him and jumped as he tried to get her attention. Automatically, she ordered a Yorsh and watched him walk away to join other waiters who were making their way around the restaurant. Some carried notebooks for orders, others drinks on large silver trays piled high with food on oval platers all decorated with exotic flowers. The ordinary movements settled her down and, as she waited for Paliakov to arrive, she listened to the sound of music drifting down the room. Two violinists and a cellist were grouped on a raised dais at the far end of the restaurant playing soft classics.

She saw Paliakov and Mikhail come in. It seemed from Mikhail's enthusiasm that he had immediately been attracted to Paliakov. And watching Paliakov's response to Mikhail's blonde hair and wiry body she saw the feeling was obviously mutual.

They had only just met, but, satisfied the relationship would work, she regretfully didn't stay to eat but finished her Yorsh and, careful to avoid Mikhail seeing her, left. As she travelled back to her hotel she smiled at the thought of the restaurant's exorbitant bill dismaying G8's austere accountants.

She allowed Paliakov and Mikhail to develop an affair over a few enjoyable nights. Then she told Paliakov to begin murmuring hints to Mikhail about three hundred million dollars sitting in a lawyer's office in a tax haven somewhere.

Four days later he contacted her to say Mikhail wanted to talk about the money. He'd suggested they meet that afternoon for a drink at the Jagdschloss by the Grunewaldsee, a forest lake in the Charlottenburg district. Katya told Paliakov to agree. She didn't tell him that she intended to break into this meeting. That would make him look out for her and appear nervous. So, she arrived well before him and waited, hidden by some trees which overhung the water.

THIRTEEN

Paliakov had always enjoyed the walk around the Grunewaldsee. It was wilder than the other Berlin lakes and, in the hot summer days, his Berliner's body had compared favourably to the other users of the small nudist beach there. After a swim, they would go to the open-air café near the Jagdschloss, and drink Weisswein under the shadow of the tall pines. Remembering this as he walked along the familiar beaten earth path which skirted the lake, Paliakov stabbed the stick he was carrying into a grass patch by his feet, fighting back his anger, the humiliation, the loss.

Suddenly his left knee gave way as a large Weimar hound hurtled past, brushing him as it ran, tail erect like a periscope. It headed towards a pair of duck in the reeds which edged a marshy area of the lake.

'Lotto, Lotto.'

He turned at the shout and recognised Rosa Rulenski striding towards him. She was slapping a dog lead on her thigh and yelling at Lotto, who by now was thrashing around in the water. Paliakov immediately forgot his lover in a rush of nervous energy - mentally gearing himself into his cover story.

'Why didn't you stop him.' Rosa shouted at him, her German resounding off the bank of rocks behind her.

'Your bloody dog nearly had me over.' He shouted back in fluent German.

'This lake is for dogs.' Her German thickened as she came up to him and thrust the lead in his face. 'But they mustn't chase the birds. You should have stopped him.'

'If you'd bloody well trained him, he wouldn't have half killed me.' By now Paliakov's fury had nothing to do with his cover. 'And stop waving that lead in my face.'

Ignoring him she moved forward, saying quietly, 'While we finish the walk, you can tell me how to train a Weimar. And you can tell me about three hundred million dollars.'

He stared at her in simulated amazement. 'I - I don't understand what you mean.'

She turned around, her wide mouth creased. She was younger looking than her thirty-six years, with short, cropped, dark hair creeping out from under her fox fur hat. She wore a long fox fur coat, too, and kid leather boots with the tops rolled outwards. She tucked his arm closely under hers and started walking after Lotto who had, by now, abandoned his prey.

'You understand perfectly.' Her eyes ran over him.

Paliakov pulled away, looked across the lake, avoiding her eyes, simulating fear. 'I don't know anything about it.'

'I mean what you know about the money some lawyers somewhere have scammed and are going to hide in some offshore bank.'

The tone in her voice chilled him, forced him to look back at her. The stare she gave him was depthless. There was nothing sham about the fear it struck into him. He struggled to keep his voice steady but it sounded high pitched as he heard himself saying. 'What are you talking about?'

She pointed the dog lead at two men in tracksuits doing exercises on a lichen marked wooden bridge. It stretched over a small stream which wound away from the stillness of the lake to flow downhill out of sight. 'We can talk here or at my apartment.

If we have to go to my apartment it may be a little uncomfortable for you, that's all.'

He raised his head in relief. She had given him the opening he needed to be co-operative. 'Apartment?' He swallowed as he struggled to keep up the pretence of not knowing who she was. 'You're not police, then?'

'Police?' She burst out laughing. 'With a dog like that? You must be joking.'

Paliakov dropped his shoulders and smiled sheepishly. 'I thought you were police - the Russians - come to pick me up. You never know these days, there are more Russian police in Berlin now than before the Wall came down.'

She took his arm again with the same intimacy. 'Now tell me about your scheme. I may be able to help.'

She walked him across the bridge past the two men. They took no notice of her or Paliakov. One of them flexed his shoulders and took off at a high stepping run in front of them, picking his way over the pebble strewn surface. The other man waited and then followed them, practising boxing moves. Paliakov wondered what to do to keep up the pretence that he had no idea what Rosa wanted. She would be suspicious if he let on that he wasn't surprised by her accosting him. She must believe that he was only here to meet Mikhail.

He stopped suddenly, prodding a leaf with his stick while studying her face. 'Who are you? I know by your accent you're Russian. Where are you from?' Typecasting a Pole as Russian was deliberately provocative.

'Russian? I am a Pole – Warsaw.' She almost spat the words, slapping the lead against her thigh again.

'I am Russian,' he murmured.

'Yes. And I'm wasting my time.' She shouted to Lotto who came bounding up. She bent and attached the lead to his collar.

Palikakov stifled a gasp as he saw Katya coming up behind Rosa.

'A Weimar, isn't he?' Katya bent beside her to stroke the dog, speaking in Russian. Where she had appeared from Paliakov had no idea. 'It's a brilliant scheme,' she continued, looking at Rosa. 'It's guaranteed to succeed. But if we're wasting your time -' She shrugged her shoulders. 'I'm sorry.' She walked away along the stony path towards the Jagdschloss restaurant.

'Who the hell are you?' shouted Rosa after her. 'Wait!' Her Russian like her German was overlaid with a Polish accent.

Katya continued walking, quickly, her shoulders hunched - past the muddy junction with Umgehungs Chaussee, past the tall pine trees and along the rutted track to the restaurant. The white stuccoed building, interlaced with black beams, lay fronting the edge of the lake. Varied greens of pines and yellows of oak and beech trees formed its backcloth, which almost covered the moss-covered roof. There were quite a few people sitting at the well-spaced tables. They were casually dressed and, as yet, unaware of the drama unfolding before them. She stopped by an unoccupied table and waited.

Rosa arrived alongside Paliakov, breathing heavily, and walked straight up to her. 'I told you to wait. People don't ignore me...' She left the threat unfinished.

'Gluwein?' asked Katya, signalling to a waitress. She sat down on one of the wooden benches fronting a pine slatted trestle table.

Rosa promptly sat down beside her and nodded to the two men in tracksuits who immediately went to the next table.

'Let's talk about brilliant schemes,' Rosa said. 'Now who are you?' She gestured again to the track suited men. 'You know who they are? They do things for me. You don't talk to me and they will do things to you.' The words were spoken as a matter of fact.

There was no doubting in Katya's mind that Rosa meant

exactly what she said, but she knew that, if she caved in now, Rosa would have the upper hand.

She looked the men over. 'I wouldn't place too much confidence in them.'

'OK, so I don't want a scene, I ask you politely.'

Katya didn't reply immediately. She kept Rosa waiting, silently emphasising that she was in control. Then she said baldly, 'You take money off men by supplying them with prostitutes and drugs. I take money off men by finding where they hide it.'

Rosa lifted her chin, bridling at the bluntness of this opening. 'I'm not *prostytutka*.' She spat out the Polish word. 'Never. I took over my father's business. You - you may be, but not me.' Her anger mangled her German.

Katya moved on, seizing the opportunity to put herself and Rosa on an equal footing. 'Then we have a lot in common. My father was a conman. 'I think we have both done better than our fathers.'

'Your father didn't amount to much, then. You haven't shown me anything successful about you,' Rula retorted, rudely.

'Then listen and learn.' Katya quickly told Rosa a vague story about two lawyers who ran a property development company which figured an investment scam worth three hundred million dollars which they were going to transfer to a tax haven.

Katya stopped there as a waitress came up and took three tall glasses of steaming gluwein off a tray and handed them around.

Rosa turned on Katya, harsh. 'You haven't said anything. I mean where are these lawyers, who are they, where do the investments come from? And who are you? You're telling me nothing. Your friend here,' she pointed to Paliakov, 'promised Mikhail that he could get hold of the money easily.'

Katya shrugged, unconcerned. 'Well, if he hadn't, Mikhail

wouldn't have been interested, would he? It's you I want, not Mikhail.'

Rosa stood up, brushing her hands down the fur of her coat, smoothing the richness of it. 'I don't chase phantoms. And I don't like being made a fool of.' She signalled to her track-suited minders. 'As they will show you.'

The men got to their feet, slowly, in no hurry to inflict whatever pain they had in mind for Katya and Paliakov. Their living lay in shortening others' lives, whether by the ultimate effects of violence or simply by annihilation. Katya hadn't calculated that Rosa would have such a short fuse. She'd thought that she could play her along, create some sort of bond with her, lure her into the fantasy of seizing three hundred million dollars. Watching the hands of the minders flexing in movements they had practised countless times before as they approached their victims, she realised too late that she had underestimated this woman. She looked around her. The waitress had returned to the restaurant and, somehow, the place was suddenly deserted. She understood in that instant what she'd heard of Berliners. Years of living in fear had bred in them a sixth sense for smelling trouble.

'I'm alongside one of the lawyers,' she said.

'How?' Rosa rapped out the words.

Katya forced herself to speak slowly, to appear unconcerned by Rosa's bullying, 'That's for me to know.'

'Why do you want me?' Rosa turned away from Katya at that point and instead punched Paliakov's arm hard. 'You've already got this little worm to feed,' she taunted.Katya held her hands around the hot glass of gluwein, breathed in the aromatic fumes, 'Why do you think I went to the trouble of finding you?' Katya looked into the glass, keeping her eyes off Rosa, hiding her fear, knowing at any moment Rosa could turn on them, set her minders onto them. She said slowly, 'I am in a position to get this lawyer's personal account details. Paliakov tells me you are the person who can hack into the account and take the cash.'

'So why don't you get Paliakov to do the job?' Rosa addressed Katya as though he wasn't there.

Katya didn't hesitate. She looked at Paliakov derisively. 'Well, just look at him, would you use him to hack into a bank account?'

Paliakov winced as the words seared through him. One day, he thought, if he lived through this day, Katya would pay for humiliating him.

Rosa nodded slowly, sat down and sipped her wine. For a moment, she looked out over the lake which was mirrored in deep black, then suddenly said, 'You will regret it if you are not telling me the truth.'

Katya knew Rosa still wasn't ready to commit herself. She felt this haggling wasn't going anywhere and she had to break the deadlock. Either Rosa would bite or she'd set her minders on them. There was no middle course.

Abruptly she picked up her glass, slammed it down on the table, the gluwein spilling over. 'Very well, if I can't make you interested, goodbye.'

Rosa thrust out her hand, grabbed Paliakov's wrist, pinning him to his seat. 'You were right. We do have a lot in common. I think you're bluffing but I can't think why you should. You took a lot of trouble finding me – why, if you didn't have a good reason?' Still holding Paliakov's wrist she jerked him up from the bench, standing as she did so. He groaned as his arm bent sideways. She held it tighter, swung around to Katya. 'OK. You can have Mikhail. He does all my IT work and he'll tell you what to do. But from now on he will be part of your life, he will stay with you and not leave your side. In return, you will make sure that three hundred million dollars is transferred into my account.' She twisted Paliakov's wrist, hard, forcing him to sit down.

Katya started to ask a question. 'How - '

Rosa paid no attention – dictating the play. 'But make no mistake, if you don't pay that money to me, Mikhail will kill you both.' The words ripped out like machine pistol bullets.

Paliakov sat immobile, his face chalk white, trying not to let his hands shake.

Katya leant forward and put a hand on his shoulder. 'No need for that.' Her quiet tone contrasted with Rosa's stridency as she turned to the woman. 'And we're not paying all that money into your account. If it's a deal, we split fifty-fifty.'

Rosa's eyes flitted briefly towards her minders. 'You realise I could make you give me the name of the lawyer and his bank?'

Katya's violet eyes darkened. 'The money's ready to be transferred. Only I have that information and it will cost you a lot of time and trouble to get it out of me - and it may just be incorrect if you do.' She took a breath. 'You might *think* this is your gig, but it's mine and I'll organise it—until Mikhail takes over to hack into the account. Understood?'

'You think you're clever, don't you - you have no idea.' Rosa left the threat unspoken and instead started to stroke Lotto, looking thoughtful.

Katya didn't interrupt her. She had set up Rosa to decide for herself between her greed and her natural caution and she could do nothing more to influence that decision. But she did feel a little sorry for Paliakov because, if Rosa made the wrong choice, life would end badly for both of them.

The silence seemed endless, but it was broken suddenly by the shouts and laughter of two children running into the scene. They'd caught sight of Lotto and had started to run over to him.

Rosa's snarl, 'Stay away, he bites!' stopped them in their tracks and, as she glared at them, they ran away.

The interruption seemed to help her make up her mind. She

turned to Katya. 'OK, I agree. Fifty-fifty and Mikhail will help you.'

Katya remained reluctant. Rosa wouldn't expect an easy victory. 'I think we can deal, although you might be prepared to tell Mikhail to take the whole lot.'

Rosa was unmoved, 'You'll have Mikhail as a hostage to ensure I keep to the deal and, more than that, you will have my account number so what's to prevent you dipping into it?'

Katya shrugged, 'So it's a two-way trust that we have now? Take it or leave it?'

Rosa looked out again across the lake as if it would define for her what the word trust meant. She shrugged. 'Perhaps not trust exactly but, as you said, we do have a lot in common. I'll take the deal.'

Katya paused for effect before saying, 'OK. You be ready for Mikhail to get into the lawyer's account when I ask for it.'

Rosa stood up, pushed back her fur hat, shook the dog lead and watched Lotto wag his tail. Her eyes swept over the white faced Paliakov as she let go of his wrist.

'Cheer up,' she sneered. 'Mikhail likes you.'

FOURTEEN

The lobby bar of the London Holborn hotel was brightly lit, noisy and packed with media and TV production negotiators haggling over script credits and percentages. The informality and casual dress of the place and its buzzing activity were well suited to the occasional G8 rendezvous as the agents could blend easily into the background.

Katya was in London getting ready for her journey to meet with Ahmet and was the first to arrive for her meeting with John. He sometimes suggested meeting here; he liked to see what was going on and who was currently there.

She didn't buy a drink at the bar, the long queue seemed to go on forever, with people jostling and shouting orders at the hard-pressed bartenders. Instead she moved to a free table at the back of the room and hoped John would get one for her. She always thought this part of an in-house covert meet was tedious. The waiting, the pretence. She much preferred the challenge of meeting the opposition, the adrenalin of manipulating them.

'Bored?' John dropped into the seat opposite her, slinging his laptop and mobile onto the table.

Katya looked up. 'Of course, I'm always waiting for you.' She looked at his empty hands. 'Well, you could have got me a Yorsh', she said tartly.

He ignored the question. 'Tell me about Rosa, did she bite?'

She pushed her iPad away from her and leant her elbows on

the table. 'Yes. Rosa's on board.' She told him about the meeting at the Jagdschloss restaurant.

'That was dangerous to meet her without back up.' he said, when she had finished. 'Anything could have happened, Rosa's no Saint Theresa.'

Her hand went automatically to the gold chain around her neck. 'I'm glad you care,' she murmured.

'Alright,' she interrupted hastily. 'What's far more dangerous is my upcoming meeting with Ahmet. Time to find out what he's planning for me.' Her eyes smiled as she looked at him. 'A last drink before I go?'

He laughed and stood up. 'Okay, you've earned a Yorsh.'

FIFTEEN

Walt and Lev sat next to John at the console in the G8 Conference Room. Nothing John could say had deterred them from joining him to observe for themselves Katya's meet with Ahmet, the man who had destroyed so many lives in their cities. They burned with resentment at having failed to find and put him down and, now, if Katya succeeded in persuading him to join her at El Bayedh, there was a chance of doing just that.

The meet was so important that John had arranged for the satellite surveillance, known as G8SUR, to stream pictures of it to the large plasma screen on the wall in front of the consoles where they now sat. The satellite imagery and high frequency processes were state of the art and had recently been developed by the military for battlefield conditions. Not only did the technology penetrate buildings to give a clear picture of their interiors but it also captured sound. Like most new software, the system was complex to handle, prohibitively expensive and not wholly reliable.

Bearing this in mind, John had assigned the operation of the system to a specialist Information Technology team led by Guy Leaming. He was a Cambridge honours graduate and a scientist, a man of thirty-two, angular and prematurely bald. His parents had come to Britain with the early Ugandan Asian immigrants and he had all their wit and stoicism. He fed this into his team with remarkable results.

John was now watching Guy as he finished installing the

portable satellite tracking station in the conference room. It was a difficult job but essential to minimize the delay between any instructions issued by John and Guy's carrying them out. He and members of his team occupied the remaining space in the room. Quietly they busied themselves with calculating the geographical co-ordinates of Katya's meeting place and programming the algorithms which controlled the visuals and sound. John didn't interrupt them as he believed in delegation and, more important, that once delegated, he should leave the job alone unless there was an emergency.

He switched his thoughts to Katya's meeting with Ahmet which was to take place in Al Ain. The ancient oasis town lay in the desert some 170 kilometres west of Abu Dhabi. The meeting place was the Afwan Hotel. It was rumoured that Ahmet owned it through the nomineeship of Hassan Qarishi, a Dubai banker well known to the tax havens of the world. The remoteness of the place and the control Ahmet had over the venue left Katya totally exposed. The idea of having a G8 backup team stationed in Al Ain to perform a rescue mission was rejected. They'd be spotted in minutes. Whatever Ahmet wished to say or do would be watched by G8SUR and those in the Conference Room, but they would be powerless to intervene. Katya was on her own - like a bomb disposal engineer facing a ticking explosive.

Whenever she was in immediate danger, as in this meeting with Ahmet, John found himself tense. It wasn't that he was unsure of her. She never put a foot wrong and was the most coldly efficient operational agent he'd ever come across - a woman who'd survived her father's harsh Russian military upbringing and the life of a street kid in Moscow. Forceful, passionate and intelligent, she'd come out top of her recruitment interview. Intangibles like courage and duplicity had been tested, and her outstanding leadership and resourcefulness had led John to promote her to

Operations Chief. But he sensed there was a deep, hidden vulnerability to her. Something he had failed to find a reason for. When he saw her reports of successful operations he questioned whether this judgment of her had any foundation other than an insubstantial gut feeling. Whatever it was, as he watched Guy's preparations, he couldn't help feeling that perhaps he had been too hasty in approving her meet with Ahmet. The more he thought of it the more preposterous it was that she could actually find out from the man himself how he proposed to kill her. He had spoken to Lev about it, asked him if he thought the operation was too dangerous. But Lev was Russian, too, with all the Russians' contempt for danger, and he had no hesitation in supporting her. 'Throwing herself to the wolves – that's her job,' was his pithy reply.

'We're on.' Guy drew John's attention to the screen. Lev and Walt leant forward in their seats as if they could get a better view of what the screen pictured.

The G8SUR stream was already imaging in real time. The plasma screen showed Katya driving a Subaru WRX along the heat-hazed highway from Abu Dhabi to Al Ain. The desert stretched away in lumpy sand hills on both sides of the metalled dual carriageway. On either side of the road, lines of date palms stretched into the distance shading the central reservation. John could see no logical reason for their presence. In fact, they presented a continuous hazard to the high-speed traffic. On the other hand, as a show of the country's oil power they were spectacular. He watched, as a camel caravan came into sight. A string of a dozen heavily laden animals and their drivers were plodding along the side of the road. A biblical vision, incongruous in the setting, yet a forcible symbol in the new world that the old still held fast. A reminder to John of the soft face of the middle east which belied the savagery of the desert—and the savagery of Ahmet.

These thoughts made John tense even more as the screen picked up Katya's Subaru travelling very fast. Hardly slowing, it sped through the dust-cloud spewed out by the cement factory at Zakher. With the khaki- coloured Hagit hills on its left, the car streamed across the Wadi al Ain bridge, past the Al Jahili Fort, with its clay plastered circular battlement turrets, and slid to a halt as it drew up in front of the Afwan Hotel. The building looked almost a twin of the Fort and gave John more reason to believe it was Ahmet's headquarters.

There was a minute's wait as the G8SUR team reprogrammed the surveillance to reveal the inside of the hotel. The next image to appear was a large, palm-fringed central atrium. Boutique shops were ranged around it, painted in the rich greens, yellows, reds and whites of the Muslim world. Black lettering on signs over the windows showed them to favour the sales of fashion clothes, perfume, rich jewels and pure silver. In the centre of the atrium was a circular pond with a fountain spraying onto the water making it shimmer like the heat haze blazing off a desert dune. The effect was to send an image of such coolness that it seemed to John to penetrate through the plasma screen in front of him. To one side of it lay a suite of white leather sofas surrounding a large inlaid ebony coffee table. John watched as the G8SUR picture zoomed in on three figures seated on two of the sofas. Immediately words scrolled onto the screen identifying them as Abdul Ahmet, Jamal Tafir, Ahmet's number two, and Hassan Qarishi, Ahmet's banker. They wore white Thobes wrapped around their bodies and chequered Ghutras which covered their heads. Three other figures, clad in black shirts and trousers, came into view. They were carrying Kalashnikovs and were obviously bodyguards. They fanned out across the lobby and checked the front entrance.

John studied Ahmet, recalling the man's background. The G8 computers hadn't been able to determine the exact motives behind his terrorism. Hard information about Ahmet's early life had been difficult to come by, beyond the fact that he had been born and raised in the extreme bleakness of the Empty Quarter desert. Although he had fought savagely on Gadaffi's side during the Libyan revolution, Ahmet, unlike Cartwright, hadn't shown himself to be a close associate of Gadaffi's nor did he seem, like Gadaffi, to be a devout Muslim or to be wedded to any jihadist group. The G8 computers had concluded that Ahmet was a throwback to the distant era of desert tribal warfare and simply liked killing people. This made him treacherous and unpredictable.

The image changed abruptly to show Katya, wearing a white cotton midi dress with a tan belt and shoes, carrying a tan tote bag. She was unhurriedly walking across the white marble floor to greet Ahmet. The bodyguards followed her. After looking her up and down, the world's most wanted terrorist wordlessly gestured to the sofa opposite his. She looked at it, glanced at the fountain spray spattering it and, without a word, sat down on the sofa next to him. Tafir and Qureshi stiffened, then turned towards Ahmet, probably John thought, waiting for his reaction to her deliberate snub. The three body guards spread out on either side of him, holding their assault rifles across their muscular chests.

'Why does she always provoke trouble?' Walt muttered.

'Telling him he's not in charge.' Lev commented.

'With three Kalashnikovs pointing at her?'

Lev was silent.

There was silence from the screen too. Not a word was spoken as two waiters, dressed in pressed white shirts and black trousers, came up with a tray of tea and sweetmeats and handed them around. There was a sudden hiatus, the servants stood stock still, their faces puzzled and their eyes fixed on Ahmet.

John leant forward, on edge to hear the Arab's words picked up by the G8SUR scanners.

'What's this?' Ahmet demanded angrily.

Katya raised her hand to placate him. 'I asked them for jam.'

'Jam?' What for, there is no bread?'

'For my tea, I take jam in my tea.'

'Only Russians do that. You never told me you were Russian, what is this? Is this about Moscow? Are you here – '

'Moscow? What do you mean? You know I come from Arizona. My mother was Russian, so I take jam with my tea, like her. Anyway, what's Moscow got to do with it. I'm here to talk about -'

Ahmet ignored her, nodded at Jamil Tafir, his number two. Tafir gestured to the guards who closed in on Katya.

Ahmet spoke again. 'I will listen to what you have to say and then make up my mind as to who you really are.'

Katya started talking about the desert and camels and hawks.

After a few minutes of listening to Katya's inconsequential ramblings, Lev yawned. 'Hell. Why doesn't she get to the point?'

Walt smiled, used to the Arab custom of introducing business only after a long discussion of personal interests. Lev, usually so calm, had an intolerance of the Middle East.

Ahmet interrupted Katya. 'Tell me about Our Desert, why you are involved.'

Calmly, as if presenting her CV to a human resources manager, Katya gave him her cover story. She told him her background and how she'd been drawn to ecology and campaigning. She had been a student at Case Western University in the United States. She'd stayed on after becoming involved with Ivan Fadeyev, a Russian researcher with Grant Chemicals, who had been disgusted with the way the western mining and oil corporations ripped off the desert people. She had travelled to the Atacama Desert in Chile, where the copper mining companies stripped the land.

She spun the story, now starting to get animated. 'They take the copper and leave mounds of spoil which create acid mists. The desert people, the Atacameno, suffer burns to their skin, their eyes itch horribly, they get lung disease. Nothing effective was done to help them' She bent forward, getting into the story she was spinning. 'So, I took action myself. Someone had to help these people -'

Ahmet cut in. 'What about this Ivan Fadeyev?'

'He didn't seem to have the push to do anything positive himself other than to talk, so I set up Our Desert.'

'If he only talks, what does he achieve?'

'He talks, I achieve - to return the deserts to their owners. The desert needs preserving by all possible means - I don't care how.'

'You are very passionate.'

'About the desert? Yes.'

Ahmet shifted suddenly from the idly curious to the suspicious. 'You are also very persuasive and disciplined. Your attack on the development at Sidi Ifni was well coordinated. This development— the El Bayedh development— that you wish to destroy. Why haven't you done so already? I don't understand why you are here, why you want to talk to me?'

John watched as she remained silent. Ahmet had nailed the operational problem that Katya's plan posed for her. There was no reason for delay. There was no reason for her to meet him or talk to him.

Ahmet gestured, as if willing her to offer an explanation. She didn't respond. The silence went on.

Walt slammed his hand on the console. 'It's too tense. She's pushing too hard.'

'No.' The single word came from John. He started to explain but Lev interrupted.

'Look at Ahmet's face - the anger there at her lack of respect.

She holds the key to him getting a fortune in cash for him and Cartwright and she's not playing. He'll have to back down.'

'That's Russian thinking Lev. He's a desert animal, he'll kill her rather than back down. I – '

They saw Ahmet slowly nod his head as if he'd decided to come to his own conclusion. 'I understand. You need help.'

'Yes.' Just the simple affirmative from Katya.

'Explosives.'

'Yes.' Katya replied. 'And more.'

'More? You want more?'

'Yes. You can guess.'

In the Tac Room, on the giant screen, John, Walt and Lev saw Ahmet abruptly stand up. The bodyguards immediately closed in to protect him. He beckoned Abu Qareshi and Tafir Jamil to join him. The three men walked away from Katya and went into one of the shops. The guards ranged themselves outside.

Ahmet could be seen talking swiftly to Qarishi and Tafir but no sound came from the shop.

Lev looked up sharply. 'Something wrong with the surveillance, John?'

Walt quickly cut in. 'Has Ahmet activated counter-surveillance?'

Guy was bent over the controls. His head came up suddenly. 'Listen.' A loud thumping sound blared out of the screen mic.

Lev frowned, 'What's that?'

Guy shook his head. 'It sounds like a broken refrigerator in the shop.'

Walt grimaced, 'That racket?'

They waited. John clamped his jaw, knowing there was nothing he could do. Katya was on her own. 'Guy, will the sound return when they come out? It's vital it does.' He realized that the question was unanswerable. 'No. Forget it. We'll wait.'

Suddenly, they saw Ahmet walk out of the shop. He carried a pistol. Strode up to Katya.

John gripped the console with both hands.

Ahmet pulled Katya to her feet.

The sound returned.

'You cheated us. You told my colleague you could destroy El Bayedh. You can't, can you?'

Katya opened her mouth.

'This man – 'Ahmet pointed to a man struggling between two bodyguards as he was dragged into the atrium – 'This man also told me he could do something, and yet he failed. Prove to me you are better than him, show me you can do the job.'

'That's impossible, how – '

Ahmet thrust the pistol into Katya's hand. 'Kill him.'

Katya looked dumbfounded. 'That's crazy - are you crazy…what's he done…?'

Ahmet shrugged. 'As I thought, you can't can you?' He stretched his hand towards the pistol. 'Give it me.'

Walt half stood, as if he could get through the screen and into the atrium with Katya, to somehow help her.

'Kill him!' Lev shouted at the screen. 'Kill him.'

As if she'd heard him Katya jerked up the pistol. Aimed briefly at the man. Pressed the trigger. The noise of a flat explosion ripped out of the screen.

Guy flinched, lost control of the picture. A series of dizzying images followed as he wrestled with the controls.

The blur suddenly settled into an image of Ahmet.

He nodded his head at Katya. Sat down on the sofa, gestured her to do the same. 'So, we will attack El Bayedh together.'

A rush of breath from Katya whistled through the screen mic.

Ahmet turned towards his guards. 'You can let him go now.'

The guards loosed the man they were holding. Whimpering, he bowed to Ahmet.

Ahmet waved him away. 'Next time you will be shot - and not with blanks.'

Then he faced Katya. Laughed. 'I wasn't wrong about you.'

Katya recovered, said calmly, 'You get El Bayedh destroyed. A bunch of American investors will be financially ruined. And you'll have the cash to do more damage. As for me, Our Desert gets the publicity it needs to drive our cause forward. But you have a problem.'

John felt a moment of pride as he watched her professionalism.

Ahmet glared at her.

She went on. 'Our Desert can get into El Bayedh with no problems. They will travel in Our Desert buses, a group of eco-tourists visiting the desert. You're too well known in this region as running these tourist developments. If you try to go in by yourself, you'll immediately be spotted. Word will get back to the American investors.'

There was no reply.

Katya continued. 'You can hide with us in the buses.'

Ahmet's face tightened. The harsh lines around his eyes creasing.

Katya leaned forward, looking straight into them. 'Your men can pretend to be part of our operation— protectors of the desert. Who is going to challenge them if they look like naive, banner-waving, unarmed eco-protestors?'

Ahmet studied her for a long moment. Then abruptly beckoned a waiter. 'Bring more coffee – tea for my guest –and jam.' He leaned towards Katya, conspiratorial. 'So, tell me where I will meet your transport.?'

Walt fell back in his chair. 'She's got him. She's hooked him.'

'Why so surprised,' murmured Lev. 'She told us she would.'

John looked up at Ahmet's smiling face on the screen in front of him. 'Yes. But you can bet he won't be travelling as an unarmed eco-protestor.'

SIXTEEN

Katya had half expected to be detained by Ahmet's friends in Abu Dhabi, but she had boarded the aircraft to London without a hitch. She had arrived just in time to race to her apartment to change for another party Paul was giving on his boat.

She was pleased that she had taken so little time dressing that she had finished when she heard the familiar sound of a klaxon. She looked out of the window to see the stern of Paul Foster's river cruiser bump against the balcony of the apartment - the vessel's twin engines uttering a low-pitched growl as they held it against the incoming tide. Pausing only to secure her gold chain round her neck, Katya walked through the French windows and out onto the large balcony. She locked the windows with an ordinary key and pressed her finger against the light switch to set the infra-red security locks.

The party on board was obviously well under way. She could hear loud voices, laughter and music billowing from the boat's saloon. As she crossed the balcony she could see the main deck festooned with multi coloured lights. They flickered on the water as their reflection caught the swift running river. Above the lights, a line of flags flew from a halyard, like waving hands.

'Hi, Katya, hurry up. We can't wait all night.' Paul Foster was shouting at her above the noise. In his thirties, tall and dark haired, he was a successful Lloyd's broker. At one time Katya had been drawn in by his impatient and restless nature but she'd ended the affair when he'd showed signs of wanting a more permanent relationship. She had no intention of settling down, but they'd remained friends.

His mobile face lit up as he helped Katya over the balcony rail onto the stern deck. The scene in the saloon was clearly visible from there and she saw some of the guests were already dancing, while others were helping themselves to drinks. The sudden wash from a passing river cruiser made the waiters stagger a little, precariously balancing their trays as they moved around the gently rocking boat. Paul put his hand around her waist to steady her and smiled before he reluctantly left her to go to the wheel house. Like so many before him he'd never quite got over her.

Paul pressed a glass of Yorsh into her hand, quickly went to the wheelhouse and powered the boat into a tight turn away from the balcony. Katya staggered backwards her drink splashing over the back of a dark-haired man. She apologised and tried to brush it off.

'A pleasure!' he said, turning around to look at her.

Katya found herself face to face with Hugo Dempsey. 'What are you doing here?'

'I'm glad to see you can be surprised by something,' he said, his eyes skimming over her, taking in the fabulous midi pale blue dress she was wearing with the cool black wedged shoes and smart Chanel handbag.

He swallowed a sudden urge to know if the bag had been bought in London or was a copy bought in an overseas market, maybe Hong Kong - could she be tempted by money? 'Paul said he knew you and he's a friend so I invited myself aboard when he said you'd be here.'

Katya studied the man in front of her. Yes, he knew what he wanted. It had been obvious when he came to the meeting at G8 and equally obvious from the way he was behaving now. If he wanted to cut their budget, as John had suggested, he would see her as a target to pump for information, to find ways of manipulating and manoeuvring G8 to achieve that goal. What better way than to try and set up an affair with her.

Playing for time she said coldly, 'A wasted journey, I'm afraid.'

'Don't say that.' His eyes lingered on her as he moved closer. 'I never have a minute to myself these days, it's all work. The job's a nightmare, I spend all my time flying backwards and forwards to Europe at the moment, to Paris one minute to tell the French their economy's shot, Berlin the next, to cosy up to the Germans – '

A smooth voice interrupted them. 'Berlin? What about Berlin?'

Katya turned to see Paul there.

'You've been to Berlin, Katya,' he said, effortlessly inserting himself into their conversation. 'Tell Hugo about that time you and I had that fabulous Turkish dinner…' The note in his voice warned her that he would tell the story and it would be a long one. She put a hand on his arm. 'Sorry Paul, I've just seen Geoffrey Bale. Must catch up, I haven't seen him for ages.'

Paul and Dempsey both turned as she walked away, watching her thread her way through the crowd, smiling at someone here, touching the arm of someone there. Paul sighed to himself, thinking how confident and beautiful she was. 'Forget it, Hugo. There's no future there,' he muttered with a tinge of longing.

Dempsey pursed his lips. 'I'm not after a future…just a few nights when I'm not sitting in the House.'

Paul flinched as he saw the lascivious look on Hugo's face as his eyes followed Katya's lithe body. He still found it hard to think of Katya with someone else especially if that someone was as loathsome as Hugo Dempsey. He'd met the minister through a friend some years ago when on a holiday in Gibraltar. Hugo had introduced him to a few well-heeled clients there. The expat community kept a tight rein on their wives and partners whenever Hugo was around. Paul had been amused by Dempsey's reputation back then but there was nothing to amuse him now, given that predatory look in the politician's eyes. He turned away and watched as a tug swept past with a line of barges in tow. He'd known from the start that Katya wouldn't commit to him, but he'd clung to the hope that she might. It still hurt that when she'd had enough of him, she'd made it so obviously final. He suddenly needed another drink. And then he reflected hazily that needing to find a drink was something that seemed to happen quite a lot these days.

Dempsey noticed Paul's discomfort. 'Oh, treading on tender toes, am I?' he scoffed. Paul ignored him, muttered that he'd just spotted a colleague he needed to speak to urgently and made his excuses. He walked away back to the helm, leaving Dempsey alone and still watching Katya who was now leaning on the guard rail talking to an older man in a pin-striped suit.

G8 had set up Katya's day-to-day cover as a successful business woman who owned and rented out warehouses across London. Useful for her and useful for them as the warehouses had plenty of well-ventilated space where they could store their electronic equipment, high-tech plasma screens, complex servers and computers. Some were used for this and others as legitimate businesses. She had been instructed on the world of warehouse leasing and had already developed a reputation as a shrewd, hard-headed landlord. It would have staggered her friends if they had known she worked for G8.

Geoffrey Bale, one of Katya's tenants, was middle-aged, married with the statutory wife and two children, a large dog and a large house on an estate in the suburbs. He ran a successful business in one of her warehouses, importing tinned fruit and selling it on to small high street chains. This evening he'd already drunk a fair amount and she could tell he was in an inquisitive mood.

'Tell me, Katya, I've been asking myself how you make any money out of those miserable warehouses of yours? The site costs must be huge, but the rents are very low.'

She caught a glimpse of movement out of the corner of her eye and saw that Dempsey was threading his way towards them. She made a quick decision. Geoffrey Bale could be a dead bore with his questions, but, equally, he could be penetrating in his analysis of people. Better to wrestle with Dempsey's overtures. If Dempsey joined them, she could play the minister along, let him think she was interested in him and at the same time covertly give him just enough info about G8 through talk of the warehouses— to satisfy his curiosity. She could even talk about her financing them in a way that led him to talk about his hedge fund. John had given her a job to do, she would just have to handle it.

Dempsey made his way deftly past the DJ and a cluster of dancing couples. He arrived at the guard rail to see her laughing. 'What's the joke?' He looked at Geoffrey, 'I'm Hugo Dempsey, by the way.'

'I know who you are, minister,' replied Geoffrey rather stiffly and his expression soured as he saw Dempsey's hand slide to Katya's waist. She'd never let him come near her however hard he'd tried.

Unseen, Katya dug her nails into his knuckles. 'Lions tremble at my claws,' she quoted between her teeth.

'And I at a gazelle's eyes,' he murmured, withdrawing his wounded hand and sucking at his bleeding knuckle bone.

She screwed up her nose. 'First time I've heard Sultan Selina's poetry used as a chat up line.'

'You gave me the opening.' Before she could stop him, he told Geoffrey Bale he needed to talk to Katya privately, and with one powerful arm steered her away from the businessman, through the partygoers to a quiet and deserted space at the stern of the boat. The wake from the river boat trailed behind it, leaving an ivory path of glistening water as it passed underneath the lights on Westminster Bridge. It was getting late. The river traffic had almost disappeared and the Thames was quieter now as the vessel moved beyond the bridge. All that could be heard was the hum of the engines and the drift of music coming from the dance floor.

Katya was about to comment on the welcome change in noise level when Dempsey suddenly said, 'Where have you been lately? I tried to find you after leaving G8 that day.'

Katya wondered what he'd think if she told him she'd just come back from a meeting with a terrorist who'd love nothing more than to have an important British government minister like Hugo in his sights. She didn't reply.

'OK.' Dempsey persisted. 'If it's a secret you can't tell, tell me one you can. Who is John Hammond, really? What sort of man is he? If I have to work with him I need to know.'

She wasn't expecting the question about G8 to be framed in this direct way. She knew Dempsey would have been briefed by his staff about John. 'You've read his CV and you've met him,' she replied, coldly, hoping he would leave it at that.

'That's an obtuse reply. I meant is he in a relationship with you?'

She had had hours of training in dealing with interrogation shock tactics so this crude approach posed no challenge to her. 'Are you offering to take over?'

He looked her up and down. 'Of course. And I can sugar the pill if you wish. I can give you anything you want - even John Hammond's job…'

She looked out over the water, it was calm now, the lights of the embankment shimmering quietly on the surface, hiding the inky blackness below. How tired she was of coping with these men with their sexist comments and insinuations. If she'd been in any other organisation she'd have had them publicly outed and fired, but her job was to play them all - the sleazy money-launderers, the oily politicians and diplomats, the unpredictable terrorists - for information or to compromise them. Men like Dempsey – entitled, corrupt, ruthless—were everywhere in her world. Did she have to come on to him to see if she could find out more about that possible illegal hedge fund in Gibraltar? To see if there was a link between that fund and Cartwright and the Gonzales Brothers? Suddenly she felt in need of a shower to wash all the ugliness away. But she knew these thoughts were weak. She was G8, the Operations Director. She had to continue the game, to lead this man on, to see what information he had to offer. About illegal money, women - anything that she and G8 might be able to use.

Her training took over. She switched tack, baiting him by ignoring his question.

'John's CV, if you haven't already studied it, looks like this. He took a first in computer science. He then joined Michael Harris, a backbench politician, who ran a tyre distribution firm out of Manchester. Harris took on John to sort out logistics. He reduced their losses and mis-directions by over eighty-five percent and Harris rewarded John by appointing him as a director on his board.'

'That wasn't in his CV.' Dempsey was pushing for deeper information, information he could use to his advantage.

'When Harris became Prime Minister, he wanted John to head up G8. The civil servants all complained. "Hammond knows nothing about policing," they said, "Hammond knows nothing about intelligence, Hammond knows nothing about anything." Harris told them straight.' She lowered her voice and adopted a

Manchester accent, the Russian intonation very pronounced. "'Ammond knows about computers and 'e knows about tracking, so ee's my man." And that was that. John got the post.'

Dempsey laughed. 'Harris was right. Hammond is good at tech.' He touched her hand which was lying on the guard rail, 'And what about you, Katya? What's not on your CV?'

What was not on her CV was freedom. What was not there was trust. Nor the many lessons harshly learned to overcome fear, to manipulate, to evade and, at all costs, to prevail. But she didn't tell Dempsey this. She studied his face for a moment, deliberately softening her eyes, leading him to think she might make some confession.

His face relaxed under her scrutiny, his fingers tightening possessively on hers.

Abruptly she changed subject., 'Tell me about Gibraltar.'

She felt him tense. She seized the advantage, went straight on. 'I have never been. I hear it's a great place to stay— very chic.' She smiled. 'Lots of money.'

She'd taken him by surprise but he recovered quickly. 'You like money, don't you?' He replied, looking at her. 'Expensive clothes, Picasso scent.' He nodded at her bag. 'Chanel - shall I show you how to make some serious money...?' He left the sentence hanging.

She laughed, pulled her hand away from his, 'No, you'll never tempt me with money, I have my own salary.'

He shook his head, 'Believe me, you don't earn enough to live in Gibraltar if that's where you'd like to be.'

She leant against the guard rail and looked again across the water which was now streaked with the reflections from the navigation lights of a passing barge. It pitched gently as it chugged slowly past, on its way up river.

Music drifted towards them, soft now, muted. A laughing couple went past arm in arm. A tired looking waiter came up and offered them drinks from the tray he was carrying. They waved him away. The sky had darkened to a purple, stars were slowly coming out. Katya briefly thought it would have been nice if John had been there.

She abruptly pushed the thought aside and came back to the present. Dempsey was waiting for her reply.

She looked enquiringly at him. 'So how do you make enough money to live there?'

He laughed, 'You know very well it's a tax haven. You deal in them and know more about them than most people. For a start, you know one doesn't lose fifty percent of one's profits to the tax man. And you know very well the regulations are easy to dodge, if you know how.'

'Do you? Know how, I mean?'

'Come on, Katya, what do you think? Gib's the online gaming mecca of the world, so running a hedge fund from there is perfect. I did it for years. Gambling is just another name for risk-taking and running a successful hedge fund is all about risk.' He returned her scrutiny. 'If you ran a hedge fund and had the money you'd do very well there - you know all about risk. '

She shrugged 'But I'm like you— I can't run a hedge fund and be a part of government at the same time.'

'What if you weren't? A part of G8.'

She pretended to speculate.

'You would, wouldn't you?' he said, eagerly. 'You'd go there like a shot if you had the right introductions.'

She made as if she was considering the offer. 'Really? And who's going to do that for me? Not you. You can't, not if you want to keep off Parliament's Register of Interests.'

'I could set you up to run it. I haven't shut down my

operation, just mothballed it. That would get around the rules.'
He leant into her. 'Come on. Do it. We could – '

She broke in. 'Here comes Paul.'

'Bugger Paul. He would, wouldn't he. Just as you've become interesting.' He pulled out his wallet, and thrust his personal card into her hand. 'Call me.'

SEVENTEEN

Katya had bigger fish to fry than milking Dempsey for information. Early in the morning after the party on Paul's boat she drove to G8HQ and was in the TAC Room by 7.30am. There she planned her ambush of Ahmet very carefully. She studied photographs and a model of the El Bayedh development and made sure her team did as well.

It was half-built in a valley overlooked by sand dunes on one side and a shale cliff on the other. The only way in and out was by way of a track which ran down the shale cliff to a flat stony area. Two large water and fuel tanks stood there next to a litter of JCBs, bulldozers and other construction machinery. Skeletal concrete frames of chalets spread along the valley for about half a mile to a half-built hotel.

Her plan assumed Ahmet would arrive in the Our Desert buses he had agreed to use. She would hide most of her team and use Pierre and Carla to lure him in to the hotel area and ambush him before he and his terrorists left the vehicles.

She sent Oleg and Alexei to Tangiers to hire a Landcruiser and to collect the explosives Cartwright was supplying from the buildings materials depot he owned there.

The next day under cover of darkness, Katya and the team arrived at the development aboard a Sikorsky CH53K logistics helicopter. They set about unloading materials, weapons, a ten-man tent and a VW camper with the Our Desert logo emblazoned across its roof and sides.

Two days later Katya lay prone and still in a dugout they'd

built into one of the tall sand dunes overlooking the shale cliffs on the other side of the valley. Katya had been careful not to move from the dugout in case Ahmet had sent watchers ahead of him. For the last twenty-four-hours she had sweated there under the blazing, unforgiving heat of the sun and at night she'd frozen under the icy blue sky. She itched all over and had to fight against the urge to scratch which would have been enough movement to send a shower of sand over her through the gaps in the planks covering the dugout. Looking out at the fragmented buildings sloppily constructed, with mortar squeezed out between the blocks, and rebars drooping down from concrete beams, Katya understood why Cartwright wanted them demolished. If any investors came to inspect it they would discover it was all a sham. Cartwright would be on a serious fraud charge within seconds.

The thought was swiftly ousted by one that was more positive. The team she'd brought with her to El Bayedh had proved themselves at Sidi Ifni. They would have no trouble finding their way around the buildings in the shifting patterns of the firefight needed to eliminate Ahmet. She knew their courage, knew they would hang in there, killing Ahmet's men until the job was done.

She'd posted Pierre and Carla to the hotel area. Yas, Maxim and Irek were to hide amongst the concrete skeletons of the cabins.

She'd positioned Irina and Petrov to a dug-out they'd built next to the top of the track running down the shale cliff. They were to warn her when Ahmet's buses were arriving.

When would Ahmet come? Back in G8HQ Guy and the G8SUR team were on the alert to pick up any movement by Ahmet.

She thought of Oleg and Alexei. G8SUR hadn't picked them up. They should have been here by now. Probably held up by the notoriously bad tracks. Delay was a byword in desert travel.

More loose grains of sand fell on her face but, even though

she was lost in thought, she didn't move. Instead she gritted her teeth and shut her eyes, willing away the urge to run her hands through her hair and shake out the dust. She knew she had to stay completely focussed, she couldn't take a chance and underestimate Ahmet's determination to wipe her out.

Suddenly, the satellite mobile strapped to her forearm trembled. Cautiously she reached out a finger; pressed the text message button. It was from Guy. G8SUR had now shown that Ahmet's terrorists were on the move. Twelve of them were congregated at Ohanet, thirty miles to the north, where the Our Desert buses were parked. That meant his best route to El Bayedh was down the track Irena was guarding.

Another message. Three Chinooks flown by known contacts of Ahmet were refuelling at Daraj in Libya. She read the message twice, gripped by the danger it held, her stomach cramping in alarm. Could Ahmet be planning to attack her directly from the air or would he drop the attackers to walk in by stealth, probably at night and in numbers? She shivered slightly as she forwarded the message to warn Yas and the others.

She looked out of the observation slit, shifting her eyes west to east, flickering north. Searching. Painstaking. The rays of the sun on the shale cliff opposite were casting deep shadows. She trained her K15 thermal imaging binoculars on a particularly deep shadow near the top of the cliff and saw a movement inching across the blackness. She waited. There it was again. She tensed as she saw the leaves of a piece of scrub flutter in the slight evening breeze. Then she exhaled. Slowly. There was no obvious human activity there, it was just the wind. Her left leg twitched involuntarily. She tensed the calf muscle, slowly closing her toes towards her shinbone. She did the same for her right leg trying to ease the stiffness caused by her cramped position. A fly buzzed around the small opening, attracted by the smell of sweat and heat in the dugout. She wrinkled her nose, she wouldn't mind some of her Picasso right now. Waiting was the hardest discipline in these ops. Her thoughts drifted out of nowhere to John.

He was the first man she had failed to influence or manipulate in any way at all. In a stinking hole in the desert, in the sweltering heat, she had time to speculate on a possible Achilles' heel. If she could find one. His laid back, laconic attitude allowed no room for vanity. He was always ready to share his thoughts, using his quick, acute mind. So, self-interest was ruled out as a weakness. He was dominant and powerful, unafraid of taking tough decisions. He was not an easy target at all. She pictured him now, his customary relaxed stance, with a slightly backward tilt of the head - both of which seemed to emphasise the way in which he distanced himself from people. The only exception was when he smiled, sincerely, and that would always give his eyes a certain warmth. Perhaps it was that rarely seen warmth that gave a clue to his weak spot.

The tremble of the mobile brought her back to reality and the stench of the dugout. It showed the time was 6 pm, time for Irina to take over the watch. She pressed the send key on the mobile and imagined Irina swearing as her mobile woke her up, and as she too wondered why she was in a stinking hole, and forced to remain in it for hours. Like Katya, she'd be wondering why she'd taken this job at all. Such questions were common to G8 agents before and during an op. None of them ever found any logical answers. Each person had their own personal journey to go through.

Katya felt the Hum Assault Weapon digging into her ribs and, slowly moved her hand towards it. The HAW was designed to home in on vibration, particularly apt for its missiles to home in on the diesel engines of the buses. But how effective were they against the giant bulk of a Chinook? Those helicopters could carry over fifty armed troops. And he had three of them. Suddenly she felt cold; she knew she had badly underestimated Ahmet.

EIGHTEEN

Fifteen miles North of Katya's position, in a small desert settlement near Djebel Amour, a small wiry Berber emerged from a bleached-wood barn. His features were chiselled by the lamplight from the shed which also silhouetted his white chalwar, tunic and turban. He was carrying a pile of slim ice packs.

The light flickered through the orange trees which surrounded the settlement, picking out the strange shapes of two camels lying hobbled in the yard in front of the barn.

Inside it, stacks of baskets were piled up along one of the mud walls. The oranges inside them reflecting a pale yellow in the gas light. Alongside another wall were stacks of long polystyrene boxes. At the far end was a freezer room.

Carefully the Berber put the ice packs on the ground beside two of the polystyrene boxes lying next to the camels. He began sliding the packs, one by one, into the slim aperture between the outer and inner walls of each box. When he had finished, he nodded to his young son. The boy stepped forward and smiled, his features identical to those of his father's. He lifted a Russian Lobaev rifle into each box. They then began to fill them with oranges tightly packing them to hide the rifles.

NINETEEN

Oleg sat in the driver's seat of the black Landcruiser as it wound its way through the night along the rough roads leading to El Bayedh. He stretched his shoulders back, arching his spine, and feeling the relief as the stiffness eased. He and Alexei had been driving for hours since leaving Cartwright's warehouse in Tangiers and all of it had been on bumpy roads that were really little more than tracks. They had driven up to Cartwright's warehouse at the docks, collected four crates marked 'roof tiles', and driven out. It had been as simple as that. They had opened the crates in the back of the Landcruiser and found the explosives inside them had been made in Pakistan and the fuses in China. A curious mix, they had thought, until it occurred to them that Cartwright probably had property developments in both countries.

Oleg was jerked out of his reverie as he felt the front near side tyre puncture. This was the fourth puncture they'd had since leaving Tangiers and he groaned in frustration. He slowed, not stopping, because there was no way of knowing what had caused the mishap. It was probably a nail or metal of some sort, but it could possibly be something else. A bullet, a dart, maybe stop strips. If so, that would mean they had been hit by an ambush. Very improbable, he thought, but he automatically switched off the headlights. Nudged Alexei. 'Wake up. Puncture.'

Alexei shook his head. Looked round. 'Where are we?'

'Never mind that. Get out the K15s.'

Alexei reached behind him and lifted the K15 thermal-imaging binoculars from the back seat. He trained them on the darkness beyond the windscreen and slowly moved them around the vehicle, from window to window, searching for any unusual heat source in the cold night or for some sign of movement. Each time a hot spot was encountered, he searched the road behind looking for any sign of a stop strip, or any unusual disturbance.

He lowered the K15s.

'Nothing.' Alexei murmured. 'Nothing out there.'

Oleg followed the standard instruction for exterior vehicle maintenance for a two-man team, and said, 'I'll mend it. You stay here. Don't wait if anything happens.' He reached under the seat and took out his body armour whilst Alexei fixed the K15 to the siting mount of his Bullpup assault rifle.

Alexei sited the Bullpup, peering through the K15 into the empty darkness again for a possible threat. Oleg put on the armour then picked up a compressed air sealant pump, connected it to the electric output on the floor by his feet and unlatched the door. The next move was critical. He had to slide the door back and dive out to the ground in one move holding on to the pump, while Alexei slid across the seat to cover him. Oleg saw Alexei give a nod for the all clear then put the gear shift into neutral, jammed on the brakes and threw the sliding door back.

The shot took Oleg in the top of his head, just as he dived to the ground. Alexei dropped prone on the seat thrusting the Bullpup in front of him searching for the heat of the gun muzzle where the shot had come from. He didn't feel the second shot as it went through his left eye. His last thought was that there was too much light.

The Berber stayed where he was and kept still for a few minutes. Not because he was worried that either of the men who'd been shot would react in any way. He'd shot too many men and women to worry that they hadn't been killed and he knew he'd taught his son too well to miss his target. The Berber had been trained by his father who'd taken him deep into the desert with an old carbine where he'd taught him to sniff the wind and search the heat haze and calculate anything that might deviate a bullet. His father had been careful. He never spoke of his prowess and told him never to speak of his own. The only people who knew about him were those who sought their services in secret. The word spread furtively in the souks and waterfronts of Morocco and had reached the ears of Ahmet who, through an intermediary, had negotiated a contract for this kill. G8SUR had never heard of or seen the Berber. He wasn't included on their database, nor was the Berber's son, eleven years old now with two kills to his credit. One of them Alexei.

The son lay inside the polystyrene box waiting for his father to come. He knew the ice between the layers of polystyrene reduced the outside temperature, fooling the thermal imaging K15, because his father had explained it to him. It was cold though, even through his thick clothing, but he had to wait until his father moved from his own hiding place. He continued to look through the night scope on his Lobaev, which poked through a hole cut into the box, and watched the Starcruiser, now a ghostly glow on the track five hundred yards in front of him, the noise of its engine idly throbbing into the night.

There was a knock on his box. He carefully pushed up the lid, heard the slosh of water as the melted ice ran down inside the raised lid.

The Berber helped his son get out. Ahmet had been right, he thought. The ice inside the layers of polystyrene had countered the heat-seeking device. It had been cold in there, but only for a couple of hours. They had known for some time that the Starcruiser was heading for El Bayedh, so the Berber and his son had had plenty of time to choose their ambush site. Still, it had been much easier than the Berber had thought it would be. Not the shooting, that was always easy, but finding the target. He had expected it to be difficult to spot in the dark, especially after the Landcruiser head lights had been switched off. But, he was in luck. It had been careless of the driver to leave the courtesy light on.

TWENTY

Katya's mobile woke her at 4am. It was Irina messaging that there were no suspicious movements during the night. Ahmet must be very sure of himself if he hadn't posted watchers before his planned attack, Katya thought. But he was used to success, as his attacks on Chicago and Moscow had shown, so he may have grown complaisant. She hoped he had, and decided to risk going down to the valley to check out how the team members were doing.

She checked the HAW and tucked her knees into her chest as she edged to the wooden hatch at the top of the dugout and gently pushed it open. She wriggled out, making sure to replace the sand on top of the hatch, and then crawled away brushing out her prints as she went down the dune towards the large tent.

Irina was there, leaning against the VW, when Katya arrived. Katya asked her to wait a moment whilst she went into the large tent which stood nearby to check on Carla and Pierre. They were there stuffing the team's sleeping bags with their backpacks. When Ahmet arrived, the first thing he'd see would be the VW with their red and yellow Our Desert logo. This should reassure him that Katya was there with her team but, next, he would have the Chinooks' thermal imagers trained on the ten-man tent, searching to find out if anyone was inside it. The sleeping bags were to be distributed around the interior of the tent as decoys to look like people either lying down or seated on the ground. If the ploy worked, Ahmet should be lulled into believing Katya's team were in the tent sheltering from either the heat of day or the cold of night.

Katya wrinkled her nose as she stood next to Irina who, after lying all night in her dugout, looked rough and smelled terrible. Irina looked at Katya coming towards her and thought her stained desert clothing and tangled hair were disgusting. They spontaneously smiled at each other, each of them knowing exactly what the other was thinking.

As she opened her mouth to speak to Irina, Katya felt an alert on her mobile. A message from John.

"The three Chinooks—Ahmet and his men— in the air, travelling in your direction, ETA two hours."

Katya felt her stomach contract - the immediacy of the impending firefight suddenly hitting her.

The short message went on.

"G8 SUR observed twelve terrorists in Ahmet's group travelling in Our Desert bus along track to El Bayedh. ETA approximately two hours."

Katya repeated the messages to Irina, then said, 'OK. We now know for certain that the bus is on its way and to get here it has to travel along the track you and Petrov are overlooking up there'. Katya pointed to Irina's dugout. 'I want you to take Petrov and set up an ambush from your dugout - take out that twelve and their bus as they go past you.'

Irina wasn't happy, 'Isn't that too near to the development? I mean the pilots in the choppers will see us as they come in.'

Katya thought Irina had made a good point. The choppers would almost certainly open fire as soon as the pilots saw Irina's ambush sprung. 'True, so you've got to let the bus get in close, you'll have to delay attacking it until the last minute.'

Irina thought a moment. 'Yes. OK, but Petrov and I will only have our Bullpups, we can use grenades of course but twelve people are a lot for us to handle - we might not get them and I need to make certain - can I use one of the HAWs?'

Katya didn't hesitate. 'Yes, you can take the spare and I'm sorry I can't give you any more backup. Oleg and Alexei aren't here yet. Don't forget to double check -' Katya stopped. It was an unnecessary order. Nannying. Lev had told her early on in her G8 days that it was a weakness. "Delegate, don't nanny," he'd said.

Irina smiled. 'Double check Ahmet's guys are dead? Don't worry, if that HAW doesn't get them, this whore will.'

Katya waved her away. Irina overconfident as usual. Petrov had always said it was her only weakness. Katya knew how lucky she was to have the two of them, they worked together as a great team and she could always rely on them. She looked at her watch. Oleg and Alexei were late, but it was no use worrying. They'd either be there in time for Ahmet or they wouldn't.

She watched as Irina collected Petrov and walked away, their heads close together. Both she and Lev turned a blind eye to their affair because they were too good to lose. More important they trusted each other implicitly. It was an unlikely match. Irina was impulsive, strident, childish and dark humoured while Petrov was sturdy, methodical and solemn, unlike most Georgians. Katya had heard that when they first joined the St Petersburg police there had been trouble between them. Petrov was contemptuous of the slim, black- eyed girl and complained about her compulsive attitude. Until on one of their ops she'd raced through a fire fight to save his life.

The sky would soon begin to lighten with the sunrise and Katya turned to the other members of the team who were gathering around the tent. 'Any tea?' She asked, suddenly feeling cold.

Maxim thrust a mug into her hand. It was strong, black and hot, but without the usual mint. Smiling he dropped a spoonful of jam into it. Katya touched his arm, only Maxim could be so thoughtful. He'd spent time in Egypt as a diplomatic protection officer, often staying for weeks in the desert and had told her of his wish to retire there. "At peace" he'd said. She could imagine him there, like the Pyramids, solid, dependable.

She sucked greedily at the tea, then felt guilty that she hadn't asked Irina and Petrov to have some before they'd left. She thought of sending someone after them, but didn't. They were now on their way and needed to concentrate on what they were doing. She put the mug of tea to her lips and drank the rest down.

Dawn spread yellow and gold streaks across the Eastern sky - no wonder people became desert lovers. Its beauty was breathtaking.

Another message came through on the mobile. She checked it. Guy's G8SUR update. Ahmet was an hour out. The bus was nearing the junction of the approach to El Bayedh.

She looked at her team. 'Time to go.' She watched as Maxim and Irek went to their ambush positions, a HAW and three missiles slung over their broad shoulders. They brushed away their tracks as they made their way to the cabin structures at either end of the development. Irek checked his brushwork every few steps, always painstaking, thorough. She thought how good they were, what good policemen they'd been. How they'd both blossomed once they had joined G8. They seemed to have taken on a new lease of life now they'd been given the tools to really fight international crime.

Turning, she made her way back up the sand dune to her sordid dugout, again making sure she brushed over the dints made by her feet. The fetid air hit her as she opened the hatch and inched her way backwards into the hole, as she continued to brush the sand. After fixing the hatch in place she crawled over to the HAW and checked the weapon and its three missiles again. With three

Chinooks as targets she was to take out the centre Chinook with her HAW. Ahmet should be in that one protected from missiles by the other two. Or so he would think. But nothing was certain and the armourers at G8HQ had warned that if the targets were close together the missiles might hit one target more than once as their guidance systems became confused. Mentally, she shrugged. There was nothing she could do about that except to reload the HAW as fast as she had been trained to do.

She looked out of the slit to survey the area in front of her with the K15, trying to locate Maxim and Irek but she couldn't see them, they were well hidden. There was still no sign of Oleg and Alexei. They must have been delayed in Tangiers at Cartwright's warehouse or perhaps with mechanical trouble, or more likely by the terrain which was so awful. She thought of sending them a message but rejected it. Nannying again.

The tea still tasted strong in her mouth with an edge of sweetness from the jam and she edged a tea leaf out of a gap in her teeth. Chewed on it, relishing the flavour and tried to find another one, searching her teeth with her tongue, disappointed when she didn't.

She carefully unwrapped a malt tablet and put it to her mouth, grimacing as she felt the gritty sand stuck to it. She edged the water bottle over and poured some into her mouth. The malt tablet became smooth as she slowly sucked it. There was nothing else to do but wait.

An image of Cartwright came into her mind. When he found out that he had been outwitted by a woman who'd taken his scam money and his Gadaffi cash he would be livid with rage. But his fury would be trivial when compared to Ahmet's at discovering Katya had double-crossed him. Ahmet was a terrorist, he killed people and undoubtedly would kill her. She shuddered as she imagined his bullets hitting her body.

She forced her mind away by inching the K15 forward and scanning the valley and the hills in front of her. Nothing there. No movement. No breeze to flutter the scrub grass. No birds. No animals. Just the beginnings of a heat shimmer as the sun rose in the sky.

Her mobile activated a message. A personal text from John - Ahmet's approach was imminent. The bus carrying the group of twelve terrorists had stopped behind a ridge just in front of Irina's position, obviously waiting for the choppers to arrive. It ended *"Good luck."*

She hardly noticed his good wishes - keyed S into the mobile and pressed the button three times. SSS for standby. She sent this code to all the members of her team.

A faint noise crept into the dugout. Katya tensed as she listened. It faded, then filtered louder through the observation slit. It was coming from her right. She peered out of the slit on the eastern side of the dugout. The sun hit her eyes almost blinding her. She'd forgotten to put on her sun visor. She reached for it, mentally kicking herself as she squeezed her eyelids together, trying to shut out the bright spots behind them. The sound got much louder— and now she could make out that it was the beat-beat of the Chinooks' twin rotors. They must be very close now. She raised the hatch a little, ignoring the sand spilling over her head and raised the HAW until it was level with the gap she'd made. Looking through the weapon's sights she saw, etched against the sun about a mile away, the three Chinooks advancing, one behind the other.

Katya pressed the F key on her mobile, sending the open fire message to Irek and Maxim - threw off the hatch cover and shifted the HAW to her shoulder balancing it. The middle Chinook loomed large in her sights coming straight for her. She flicked the safety catch off, centred the laser sight on the large front rotor engine, pressed the trigger, fired the missile and ducked down to squat on the ground inside the dugout, not looking to see if the target had been hit. That would waste time. She then tripped the switch for the second missile and, straightening her legs as hard as she could, burst through the roof of the dugout, her back smashing through the flimsy structure as she flung herself forward, half in and half out of the hole. Two massive explosions jarred her body. She focussed her eyes on the scarlet, yellow and black billowing smoke to her left - to see what had been hit - Chinooks or her team.

Suddenly, out of the smoke, a Chinook burst through. Coming straight for her, low and fast and massive, the huge blades cracking through the air. She struggled to get the laser sight locked onto it. The pounding noise from the twin engines and the blades downdraft battered her, beating her back into the dugout, the hatch edge cutting into her stomach. She pulled the trigger. Flung her head down. Pressed her face into the sand. Shaking in the pulverising noise. The explosion lifted her up, flinging her out of the dugout. She went rolling, sliding, down the hill. Screaming. Scrabbling. Trying to slow down. To turn. To stop. Anything to get out of the way of the debris flying around her.

Suddenly the noise stopped as if just switched off. The only sound now was the crackle of flames. She struggled onto her knees. Dazed. Fighting to regain control. She reached for the Bullpup hanging from the strap over her shoulder. Swung it around, in an arc, searching. To the east she could see three great fires raging. The Chinooks had crashed there. The front of the one nearest the tent was intact, its rear a mass of tangled metal and flames. Missiles must have hit the other two in the front rotor housing - one of them completely destroyed, the other a tangle of smoking wreckage where the cockpit had been. Flames licked its rear fuselage which seemed undamaged. No-one was moving. Her eyes swept round to the north where a plume of smoke was rising about half a mile away. That must be the bus— Irina and Petrov's target. She couldn't believe how successful their surprise attack had been, Ahmet's terrorists had been pulverised.

Suddenly a raw crackle of firing startled her. She flung herself to the ground and rolled around to see where it had come from. She was just in time to see two black-clad figures slowly crumple to the ground as they sprang from the front of the damaged Chinook by the tent. Another figure climbed out behind them, unhurt, and started to sprint towards the tent which stood, immaculate amongst the devastation, like a standard on an ancient battlefield. Katya pushed the Bullpup forward into the firing position, heard a crackle of Bullpup fire come from Carla or Pierre in front of the tent. Saw the running figure stagger, stoop and stumble forward. Another burst of fire - the figure crumpled and fell backwards, a weapon dropping beside it. As Katya hesitated, another figure, and a second, leapt out of the rear fuselage of the other chopper, firing at the tent as they went.

Katya pressed the trigger on her Bullpup which sent bullets spraying towards the indistinct figures. The second of them saw the new danger and started firing at her. She felt the wind as the rounds snapped past. She knew she was fully exposed as she crouched halfway down the dune. The screaming pain would be inevitable as the bullets found their mark. She pressed the trigger again, beating down the urge to get up and run. The blast of another explosion smashed over her in a boiling wave, stones spraying against her sun visor. Sand forcing its way into her mouth. Choking her. Suffocating her. Desperately she fired off another burst through the haze of heat and dirt. This time there was no returning fire. She squinted towards the Chinook the men had sprung from. The rear half wasn't there anymore. All that remained was smoke, flame and jagged pieces of metal. No bodies. She coughed, an involuntary spasm, and fought to keep from coughing again as she watched the remains of the Chinook burning fiercely. She cast her eyes away to spot any further danger as she slithered towards the debris. She coughed again. It sounded loud, only the whisper of the flames to compete with it. There was no one there, at least no living person.

She looked up the hill, towards Irina and Petrov's position where the missile had come from. She saw them wave and felt the mobile alert on her arm. She looked at the message. Irina was saying she liked cooked Chinook for breakfast. Relief made Katya laugh out loud. Irina could be as funny as she liked in future, so could Petrov. They'd saved her life by taking out the rear end of that last Chinook. She waved back as she watched them standing there.

Katya looked around still dazed. They'd made it. She wondered if they'd all made it, wondered if there were any casualties. She stood up and started down the last of the dune towards the tent, sliding in the sand, feeling drained. Her trainer's words once again came to her. "When you're recovering, so's the enemy". Wearily she stopped and reloaded her Bullpup. She looked up and saw Maxim and Irek still holding their HAWs whilst walking quickly towards the tent. She was pleased. They'd done well and it looked as if they'd hit two if not three of the Chinooks. In the heat of the battle she wasn't sure of that and still had no idea whether she had hit one at all. Carla and Pierre had left their posts and had gone over to join Yas, Bullpup in hand, standing over the bodies in front of the tent.

Katya joined them. They stood looking down. One of the bodies was twitching. Still alive. It was Ahmet. A strike of bullets had smashed his thighs. He lay there breathing stertorously, blood oozing into the sand. No one went to his aid.

'You bitch,' he whispered. His eyes flickered onto Katya's face. 'Who are you?' The words rasped out.

'G8, you bastard.' She watched as his eyes started to glaze over.

'It's not over yet, bitch.' His lips curled back in the effort to talk.

Katya watched as he died. She felt no emotion.

'Photograph his body. And the scene.' She ordered. 'We need it for the record.'

As she started back to the tent she heard the sound of an engine coming from the north and looking up she saw Oleg and Alexei's black Starcruiser. They were just in time and would probably feel sorry they'd missed the fight. Katya knew she wouldn't feel sorry if she missed any fight in the future. She had thought she was going to die out there on that sand dune. She never wanted to feel that terror again. Never again wanted that fight to retain her control. She gave a shuddering sigh.

The two shots rang out almost simultaneously. She jerked her head up and saw Irina and Petrov fall, like leaves in autumn, almost in slow motion. The shock buckled her knees. She gasped. Ahmet's words tore into her. "It's not over yet."

The Landcruiser was careering down the hill. A burst of fire came screaming from it across to her right. She reeled, realising her stupidity. Trusting G8SUR. Trusting the intelligence. She should have questioned. Asked why. Why was Oleg late? She should have found out, should have seen the difference between nannying and caring. She started to run. Fired a burst at it. Hit nothing. The Landcruiser crunched onto the stones at the bottom of the hill and faced her in a charge, like a bull elephant, whining, rocking and grating in a cloud of red dust. The faces of a man and a boy contorted as they fired wildly at Katya's body. She flung herself to the ground, desperately aimed the Bullpup at the gasoline tank raised on its breeze blocks to the West of her and kept her finger on the trigger. A huge gout of flame erupted as she hit it. The fire flared out. Bright as the sun. Eating everything in its path. Devouring the Starcruiser as it screamed alongside.

Katya shook all over as she struggled to her feet and looked up the hill to where Irina and Petrov lay. Black smoke drifted overhead. Like a funeral pyre.

TWENTY-ONE

Katya sat on the wide balcony of her suite in the Hotel Intercontinental in Gibraltar, looking across the sunlit bay towards North Africa and the sands of El Bayedh hidden far in the desert. It was three days since the battle with Ahmet and his terrorists and she was still exhausted—so much so that she was barely conscious of how lucky she was to have got away from that killing ground alive. Her eyes clouded over as she relived the terrifying sight of the Chinook tearing towards her. Had she shot it down, or had that been Maxim or Irek? The confusion of the fight had left everyone in her team uncertain as to who had hit Ahmet's choppers. She only understood that every HAW had been fired and their ammunition supply expended - twelve missiles. A concentrated firepower that had demolished the Chinooks before Ahmet and his terrorists had a chance to deploy.

She still had no idea what had happened to Oleg and Alexei during their journey from Cartwright's warehouse in Tangiers to El Bayedh. There had been very little left of the Starcruiser when the fires had eventually died down. The only clue had been the twisted remains of two weapons and two lumps of charcoal. The weapons weren't Bullpups and this meant Oleg and Alexei had been ambushed somewhere and their weapons stolen, but she knew nothing more.

She had left the torn and blackened remains of the Chinooks littered, among the broken concrete structures. She had no interest in covering up Ahmet's attack and every interest in taking his share of Cartwright's payment to demolish the place. The bodies of Ahmet and his fellow terrorists she'd left where they lay, after making sure they were all dead. The fact there were no survivors might raise eyebrows when the news of the raid filtered out through the desert grapevine, but the only witnesses were her team and they would be long gone.

Except for Irina and Petrov. She had buried them under the rocky outcrop, side by side as they had been in life, overlooking the desert. Their grave bore no marker. They would lie together forever, undisturbed by the scorching sun or freezing, starlit sky. Later, in the silence of the night, she'd returned— not to grieve, it was too early for that, but to take a GPS position for a time in years to come when their story could be told. For now, everyone would think that the two agents had vanished.

She had summoned Cartwright to see the devastation at El Bayedh for himself. He'd arrived in his helicopter within hours. When he saw the carnage spread around the valley he couldn't believe Katya and Our Desert had slaughtered a well-organized terrorist group like Ahmet's. Dryly she had asked him whether he thought Ahmet had license to wipe out Our Desert as well as El Bayedh. He'd fumbled a hip flask from his back pocket and taken three or four hasty pulls from it before coughing and wiping his mouth to bluster and blame her for dragging him into it. She'd asked him who would he rather have as an ally. The unpredictable, lethal Ahmet or herself. Which was an unfortunate remark since it fired Cartwright up.

He'd eyed her up and down and said, 'C'mon Katya. I'll fly you to Tangiers then on to Gib.' He'd swigged from the flask and smirked. 'Pay off time'

She'd known she had to go with him to Gibraltar because she needed his cheque or a bank transfer with his bank details. El Bayedh was a side show to the main operation which was to trace the Gadaffi money Cartwright had stolen. But she didn't want to appear too eager. She still needed to convince him she headed up Our Desert and that the return of the desert to the Arabs was her objective. Cartwright must believe his payment to her was for her actions in El Bayedh.

'I've got to get my group out safely.' She'd replied, adding the promise, 'I'll follow on after you.'

'You've done your job.' Cartwright had waved his flask at the scene of destruction around him. Then circumscribing it in an unsteady arc towards her team he had raised his voice as the desert heat inflamed the alcohol in him. 'They'll be alright.' He'd grabbed Katya and folded his arm around her waist. 'We can have some fun in Gibraltar. Better than the bloody desert, I can tell you.'

She'd pulled away from him, snatching at her shirt as he tried to hold on. 'Do you think we did this for fun?' She'd shouted, pointing at the smashed and blackened Chinooks. 'Don't you get it, the desert's our life. This is what Our Desert stands for, what my members believe in.'

He'd grinned, 'Alright, alright, the desert's beautiful, nothing like it. But I've got to go.' He'd stood there, swaying slightly, hands on hips. 'Now, are you coming, or don't you want your money? Only way to get it is to come with me.' Normally, she would have fought him off, but she was desperately tired, on the verge of screaming her contempt for him. She had nothing left but the instincts ground into her by her training, so she'd let them take over, allowing herself to be forced into the straightjacket of the operation— to find the Gadaffi millions and finish him and Rosa.

Slowly, she'd pretended to look around at her team so as to gain time, to control her emotions. Her eyes had taken in Yas, who'd kept shooting until she'd personally killed the last of Ahmet's terrorists; Carla and Pierre, who'd raced out of the tent on Ahmet's arrival firing their Bullpups without a thought of their safety until the Chinooks had been brought down and burst into flames; Maxim, who cared enough to remember she took jam in her tea and who, with Irek, had fired the HAWs which had taken down their targets. These were the survivors, and she could think of no words that could ever show the depth of her thanks to them.

'You're right.' She'd shrugged. 'There's nothing else to do here. I want a bank draft, nothing else, or I don't come.'

He'd nodded. 'Done.'

So, true to the operational plan, she'd gone with him. To find out more about him and about the Gonzalez brothers and to see for herself the account details on the banker's draft which could lead to the whereabouts of the Gadaffi millions.

Before she'd departed, as Cartwright had stumbled towards his chopper, she'd quietly gathered the team to tell them she was going with him and that they should drive to Casablanca in the VW camper and from there take a scheduled flight to Lisbon and then on to Miami for R and R, keeping their cover as tourists.

They'd recuperate at South Beach, staying in assorted hotels along the sea front, spending the money G8 gave them in cash to cleanse the dirt and terror of El Bayedh. Oleg and Alexei and Irina and Petrov would become a memory to them. Then the team would return to G8HQ in Basingstoke. To be sent on another op.

Her op. was to continue…she felt her exhaustion deepen.

TWENTY-TWO

After a couple of hours sleep, a long soak in the hot tub, a massage and a change into a blue cotton top and a pair of white linen trousers she'd bought in one of the Intercontinental hotel's boutique shops, Katya returned to the balcony. Wicker furniture was scattered over the marble tiled floor and she sat in one of the loungers overlooking the bay. The safety railing was glassed in, allowing her an uninterrupted view of the harbour and the open sea beyond. The breeze caught the halyard of a moored-up sailboat every now and again and it rattled against the mast. The noise was somehow relaxing and helped her feel ready to meet Cartwright. He'd phoned to tell her that he'd set up a meeting with the Gonzales brothers that night and that he planned to give her the banker's draft for 200,000 dollars that he'd promised.

Her job was now to carry on the G8 investigation to find the Gadaffi cash. Once she had Cartwright's bank draft she could start to trace the account details of his payment to her—she was hoping that some transaction or reference in the same bank account might lead to the Gadaffi millions he'd stolen. Next, she would bring in Igor Paliakov and Mikhail to hack Cartwright's account, and transmit the entire balance into Rosa Rulenski's account. Then G8 would siphon all the cash out of Rosa's account leaving her and Cartwright bankrupt.

Katya knew the operation was complex and she set her mind to concentrate on the details. She picked up her glass of iced tea, spooned in strawberry jam and slowly stirred it as she watched the water in the bay ruffled by the strengthening evening breeze. The operation was proceeding as she had planned – Ahmet killed and Cartwright successfully lured to give her a possible lead to the Gadaffi cash – and she felt she should be relaxed and soaking in the balmy warmth with only the intermittent hoot of a horn or boat klaxon to disturb her. Perhaps it was the thought of Cartwright coming on to her yet again that was disturbing her. She considered it, but had to admit that Cartwright was only a small part of it. There was something bigger niggling at her mind.

She let her thoughts dwell on Oleg and Irina, Alexei and Petrov. She'd been close to them, but they weren't dear friends, they were operational agents. So why did she feel their loss so keenly. She opened the door to her inner self a little. Her mistakes had led to their deaths, it was no use denying it. She might have prevented Oleg's death. A text to him would have kept him alert, more watchful. She hadn't sent it. As for Irina, Oleg was late and Katya should have warned her of the possibility that Ahmet had associates which G8 SUR had not identified. That Oleg could be in trouble. She had been negligent and they had died because of it.

She passed her hand across her forehead, her eyes resting on a chunky ketch which was nosing its way out into the Straits, catching the breeze as it tacked its way to the Atlantic. She slowly realised that it wasn't only the deaths that bothered her, nor the fact that she had caused them. It was deeper than that. Why had she opened herself up to making those mistakes?

She fingered her necklace as she fought against the answer hazily resolving itself - her job. Her job. Lying in a stinking dugout in the blazing desert waiting to be blown apart, making sure Ahmet and his terrorists would not live to talk, laying herself open to Cartwrights pawing. Without it none of these things would have happened to her. She shifted uneasily in the chair. That was stupid. She loved the work, the analysis, the chase, the excitement, the danger that went with every op. She hadn't expected to, because her father had pushed her into it. But she'd found it was the only gene she'd inherited from him. Otherwise he was an arrogant, cold, bully who'd overestimated his ability to stay alive. She wasn't that person. She had her mother's genes, sophistication, a love of the arts, a desire for happiness, even though happiness had eluded them both.

The ketch tacked again, beautifully handled as the sails swung in unison, heeling the craft over, pushing it through the choppy waves. Sailing that ketch needed analysis too, and it was exciting, the uncertainty of a sudden squall or a rope jamming in a wild gybe. And she knew these dangers - they'd been drilled into her by her father during those brief holidays on the treacherous waters of the Black Sea. They had been more like military training camps, out in all weathers, all rules and regulations. Any show of weakness pounced on. Until she became as one with the turbulent beauty of the sea – absorbed, tranquil, at peace.

When was the last time she'd been completely relaxed with no worries about the future, no worries about the results of mistakes? She couldn't remember. Certainly not since she joined G8. John had seen to that, using her on job after job, promoting her rapidly until she was his chief of operations. John, the name jarred.

The high-pitched buzz of the 'phone made her jump. She looked at her watch. It was too early for Cartwright. She walked back inside and picked up the 'phone. 'Yes.'

'Reception here. Mr Cartwright to see you ma'am.'

She cursed. Then hesitated. He had probably arrived early to see what he could get from her. Didn't he ever give up? As she was about to tell him to wait, the thought struck her that she was getting depressed. Battle fatigue. Better to spend the time fending off Cartwright, she decided than to sit in a welter of self-analysis.

'OK. Send him up and have a couple of beers, and a bottle of Russian vodka sent up at the same time.'

She walked into her bedroom, checked her outfit in the illuminated full length mirror standing on the elegant, lime-washed floor. Her long auburn hair was once again washed and gleaming, clear of all sand and dust. She decided to leave it loose and let it fall in natural waves down her back. Picking up her lipstick, she looked into the mirror to put some on, then smiled at the incongruity of it. Here she was about to fight the man off and she was prettying herself up for him, to lead him on, to get him to tell her about his finances.

There was a knock on the door and Katya walked to the hallway of the suite, firmly shutting the bedroom door behind her. She opened the door to admit Cartwright who came in followed by a white-suited waiter carrying a tray laden with a litre bottle of Laphraoig malt whiskey, a carafe of water, two glasses and a plate of canapés. And some jam!

'How are you?' Cartwright peered at her. 'Beautiful– '

'Cartwright – '

'Ron, I've told you before, it's Ron.'

'If I call you Ron, you'd be all over me like a rash. Now stand back and stay there. Why are you early?'

'Oh! Well. If you're going to be all virginal…' He strolled straight past her to the balcony. 'We'll talk out here. You never know in Gibraltar; the bloody walls have ears. All those sodding Spaniards, wanting to know what's going on.'

He sat down on a wicker chair next to a table, passed a hand over his greying crew cut. His face was deeply tanned and lined with creases around his brown eyes. He looked younger than he probably was, Katya thought, doubtless imagining himself irresistible. As she took the seat opposite him she saw that the ketch was now a speck on the horizon.

'The walls have ears?' she asked innocently.

'You can't trust the Spaniards.' He grunted. 'Always shouting that Gibraltar is a nest of drug runners and money launderers. They pay the waiters and staff in hotels a lot of money for information. They've only got to see a new boat in the marina to suspect a new drug runner. The bastards got the Gibraltar police to turn over my boat from bow to stern when I first parked it here.'

With good reason, Katya thought.

'You got a boat?' Cartwright threw out the question.

'Hardly the thing you'd have in Kingman, Arizona.' She laughed. 'That's where Our Desert operates from and it's where I'll stay.'

He leant forward and poured out about four fingers of Laphraoig into a tall glass, slowly sipped it, 'Bloody marvelous.' He took another sip. 'Is it?'

She looked at him, puzzled. 'Is it what?'

'Is it where you'll stay?'

He poured out another glass with four fingers of the light gold malt and handed it to her. 'No ice, ruins it.'

She fumbled the glass as she took it. Whiskey splashed on to the balcony tiles. Leaving about one finger of liquid in the bottom of the glass.

'You're clever, aren't you?' he said. 'I thought so in Sidi Ifni. Too bloody clever for that Our Desert outfit. You'll get out eventually.' He gently swirled the Laphraoig in his glass. 'Why don't you get out now? Come away with me . . .'

Katya sighed inwardly. He'd tried everything else to get a one-night-stand. Now he was proposing a longer-term relationship. He really was a dead bore. 'Not with you, I won't.'

'What if I had three hundred million dollars to give you?'

She burst out laughing. Feeling a shiver of excitement now that they were close to her goal. She was genuinely amused.

147

'I repeat, three hundred million dollars . . .'

'That's rich. Trying to get out of paying me the money you owe us, are you? I thought we were going to the Gonzales brothers so that I can get paid.'

'No.' He rushed on. 'That money was for Our Desert. This is for us. I can get it. But I need your help.'

'You've had too much of that Laphraoig. It's the sun you know. Makes it go to your head.'

He put his hand on the glass-topped table between them, his fingers clenched, the knuckles white under the tan. 'Listen to me. I know you think I'm after your body - well I am, I admit that - but there's more. You're bright, clever, you organise things well. That bastard Ahmet fooled me. I thought he'd help you at El Bayedh to destroy the place. But not you. you had his measure.' He took a pull at his drink. 'You're like me and I've done well, got an apartment downtown, a villa in Marbella and a tidy bank account here. Enough to see me right. To see you right, as well.' She tried to interrupt but he swept on, leaning across the table, energy pouring from him. 'Don't stop me, this is important. I want more than that three hundred million. Of course, I can get money, earn it, sweat for it, graft for it. But I don't want to take the time to do all that. Bloody time, always ticking away.' He was speaking rapidly now, his words tumbling over each other. 'I need time to slow down, to do my own thing, go out in the boat, for a month, two months if I want. Not have to come back to set up yet another con.' He stopped suddenly, as if the thought overwhelmed him. He took a long swallow from his glass, rolling the Laphraoig around his mouth, savouring it, lost in his dream.

It was odd, she thought, but she felt some kind of sympathy for Ron Cartwright, some sort of empathy. Working his way into Gadaffi's inner circle he'd seen a chance to get rich, and had seized it. And now the lure of freedom lay before him. She understood the strength of that lure.

He spoke again. 'You can help me. I know you can.'

'Help? In doing what?' she asked, impelled by her training to stay on track, cut to the chase.

Cartwright took a slug of whiskey. His eyes narrowed. 'You didn't have anyone else backing you when me and Ahmet flew to the Sidi Ifni development to sort you out, did you? I mean you were bluffing about those extra people you said were monitoring the arrival of our backup?' He almost snapped the question.

Katya remained silent.

'I knew you were bloody bluffing.' He continued, 'I checked. There were no Europeans at the heliport at that time only Arabs.'

'That doesn't mean anything,' she said.

'Why weren't there any desert Arabs with you at Sidi Ifni, then? The only Berbers there were my watchmen. If you were working with Arabs, they'd have been there.' He rushed on, banging his fist on the table, 'I'll tell you why you didn't hire any Arab back-up. Because you wouldn't have been able to trust them not to report on you to their governments, with the result that you'd have got kicked back to America, that's why.'

She pushed her hair out of her eyes as a sudden breeze stirred it. 'That's rubbish. Come on when are we going to get my cash?'

'No, it isn't rubbish. I worked it all out after I'd seen what you did to Ahmet and his lot. I reckoned you were a sophisticated organization at Sidi Ifni and that made me assume you had a whole team behind you. But I had no idea just how sophisticated until I saw that battlefield at El Bayedh. Shit, taking out those Chinooks – Ahmet – his lot...'

She said nothing. Waited to see where Cartwright was going with all this.

'You've hacked into our communications, haven't you?' He said abruptly. 'That's how you knew we were coming to Sidi Ifni. That's why you took out my backup so easily. As for Ahmet...' He let the words hang.

She needed to find out what Cartwright had in mind. Her objective was to get her hands on the bankers draft he'd promised her. But if there was a possibility of taking the El Bayedh scam money instead, she'd take it. She fixed her eyes on his as she leaned forward, picked up the bottle of Laphraoig and poured a large measure into his glass. 'You keep drinking this.' She smiled. 'It'll clear your head.'

He scooped up a canapé and chomped on it.

'Pity,' he mumbled, a crumb dropping from his mouth.

His reply was manipulative, designed to pique her interest. She sat back in her chair crossed her legs, waited for him to explain. He'd be more eager to tell all if she showed no reaction.

He lifted another canapé, then brushed his shirt as some mayonnaise dropped on it. 'Damn. Bloody things. Why do they always fall to bloody bits?' He put it into his mouth, followed it with some whiskey.

He sucked his fingers. 'So, are you interested in that three hundred million?'

'Not if you're part of the deal.' She laughed.

'What if I wasn't?' There was an urgency to his voice now. It was almost as if he was pleading for his future.

At the back of Katya's mind, she fleetingly wondered why Cartwright needed the three hundred million so badly if he already had the Gadaffi cash. 'Well, Our Desert would be interested in the money, of course. Particularly after what we've been through so far. But not if -'

He didn't let her finish. 'Don't give me that crap. I've watched you. Our Desert is just a prop. You get a kick out of it because it's an easy outlet for your talents. It's simply a protest group. And you're nothing more than a demolition expert. A destroyer -'

'Don't you dare say that.'

'You didn't like that, did you?' He leaned back in his chair, studying her, the glass of whisky still in his hand. 'But I'm right. I can spot the difference between people who destroy things and those who build things – not just property, but businesses, financial empires - I've been a builder all my life.'

'Like El Bayedh?'

'El Bayedh was different. A scam to bring in money. If I had the whole three hundred million and didn't have to split it with the Gonzales Brothers, I'd build again. I wouldn't be sweating away at some poxy tourist development in the middle of a bloody desert. I'd aim for a real development, something to be proud of. A landmark. And I'd go on developing. Erecting buildings that future generations would point to and say. "That's a Cartwright. Cartwright did that one.' And with that sort of money I wouldn't have to work for it. Just put together a team and spend my time on my boat. Enjoy it all. Really bloody enjoy it all.'

She shifted in her seat, uneasy, unable to reply.

His eyes focussed, found hers. 'And you? What about you? The desert-spoilers will still be there when you're dead. There'll be no thanks for your efforts. You can go on destroying all you like but developers like me will keep developing wherever they want. And you can't destroy us all. You'll either be in a prison in Morocco or in the bloody prison of your own destruction. Makes no bloody difference.' He leaned forward. 'All your talent, all your ability, down the sodding drain. You're better than that. You needn't destroy. You can build.'

Katya felt oddly moved. No one had spoken to her like that before—offering encouragement—, certainly not her parents, not her trainer, not Lev, not even John Hammond. That name again. She hadn't looked on herself as a builder. Only as a destroyer . . . She let his words seep into her.

He noticed the change. 'I got to you, eh.'

She mentally shook herself. He was clever - clever with words, a devious, cunning property developer through and through. He knew how to get what he wanted. That three hundred million was a red herring. She'd never see a cent of it. She must stick to her plan.

She stood up. 'Time to go and see the lawyers. Two hundred thousand dollars is all Our Desert wants.'

He looked up at her, speaking rapidly, 'That three hundred million will be in a Panama bank. You hacked into my communications so you could hack into that bank. Use whatever tech expertise you've got. We could get that money and be away before they knew it.'

'Fairyland, Cartwright.' She walked to the door and opened it.

In his Mercedes, all the way to the Gonzalez lawyers' office Cartwright cajoled, swore and flattered, trying to win her over. Refusing to listen to him, she fixed her mind on the road ahead as he drove past the heavy sandstone buildings looming over the narrow road.

'Look at that,' Cartwright pointed out a block fortress with old, blackened cannon at its gates. 'The Governor-Generals used to live there, all guts and glory defending the Empire. Are any of them remembered today? Now look at that,' he nodded to a gold, glass, and steel fronted, triangular building with a single silver mast on top, shaped like a bullet, 'that's the Matosa Bank. Beautiful, elegant, the ultimate in sophistication, won the award for best architecture at Geneva. The Matosa family paid a fortune for it. And their name is secure forever.'

She didn't reply, but her eyes remained fixed on the silver spire until the car turned a corner and stopped in front of the Gonzales Brothers' office.

TWENTY-THREE

Dusk was falling and the stone building glowed a faint gold in the soft street lighting. Cartwright and Katya climbed out of the car and walked up the worn sandstone steps which led to the dark- blue front door. The gleaming, over- large brass nameplate revealed the importance and long heritage of the firm of lawyers that it guarded.

Reaching the top of the steps Cartwright was surprised to find the door slightly ajar. He pushed it open, holding it for Katya. As they stepped into the hall, the door immediately slammed shut behind them.

Cartwright spun round. Facing them in a dark recess beside the door were Diego and Santo Gonzalez.

'Shit, you scared me,' panted Cartwright. 'I thought you were bloody muggers. What the hell is going on?'

Diego Gonzalez walked forward while Santo guarded the door, leaning with his back against it, his arms folded. Diego pointed at Katya, 'We saw her with you, through the window, what's she doing here? We told you to get rid of her.' He tumbled over the words in his alarm.

Cartwright pushed Katya behind him, 'I told you, getting rid of her now is stupid. We do that and we'll have the FBI crawling all over us.'

Diego grabbed Cartwright's collar. 'She's not FBI, she's-'

Cartwright wrenched free. 'Get your bloody hands off me.' He rolled his neck checking nothing was damaged, 'No, you bloody fool, but she's as good as. Running a thing like Our Desert means she'll be on their files, so if she suddenly goes off their radar they'll be searching for her. And that will lead them to us. So, shut up and get her a banker's draft.'

Santo moved towards him. 'She's not getting our cash, Cartwright, you go fuck yourself.'

Without warning, he swung a vicious punch into Cartwright's kidneys. Cartwright fought for breath as he arched backwards only to double up as Diego's fist slammed into his stomach.

Katya didn't wait. She shoulder-charged Santo, crunching him against the wall as she opened the front door, flung herself through it and ran down the steps, two at a time.

She heard footsteps and a yell coming from behind her as she scrabbled around the corner at the end of the street. She half-crouched against the wall, doubled her fists into balls ready to smash into any pursuer; she tensed as she heard the footsteps and shouts drawing nearer. To her relief she saw a cab turn into the empty street, its headlights shining onto the cobbled road surface. She moved away from the wall and raced down the centre of the road towards the lights, waving frantically, refusing to move out of the way as the cab kept coming towards her.

The driver slammed his hand on the horn, the shrill noise from it blaring out into the night. He was then forced to slam on his brake as Katya kept coming at him. He skidded the cab to a halt, leaning out of his side window to furiously shout and swear at her to get out of the way. Ignoring him, she ran to the side of the cab, swung the rear door open and fell in. Grabbing the handle, she pulled the door shut, gasping, 'Hotel Intercontinental.'

The cab driver swore at her again, rich local Spanish words she didn't understand as she sprawled on the back seat. Looking ahead he saw two men chasing down the street towards him. He turned back and looked at Katya, she was pretty and pretty girls were made to be chased. But she was in his cab and two men were one too many to fight. He pushed the gear stick forward into first gear, executed a speedy U-turn, grinning as he chewed on his cigarillo. 'Hotel Intercontinental. OK.' He accelerated, leaving the two men standing in the middle of the street waving their hands in the air, still shouting and gesticulating.

Katya leant back on the seat, rigid with shock. Everything Cartwright had told her had been a bluff to lull her. And she had been thinking so much about herself she had fallen for it - all his honeyed words about building a new life and being too bright to stay where she was. His other words rang in her ears— "getting rid of her now". He was simply waiting for the right moment to have her shot and her body dumped in some waste ground outside the city. What a fool she'd been, pondering on the mistakes she'd made at El Bayedh instead of taking Cartwright's measure. She'd made the elementary mistake of underestimating him, treating him like a cheap fraudster. She'd never really asked herself how Cartwright had survived as Gadaffi's money man for so long. Gadaffi was a paranoid psychotic, so how devious and manipulative must Cartwright have been to be able to keep him onside. Lev would eat her alive for such negligence and, as for John— she couldn't face thinking about his judgment, not now anyway.

She sat up in the cracked leather rear seat and looked out of the scratched cab window, trying to concentrate. Striving to piece together what had gone wrong or, more to the point, what was wrong with her. And, above all, how to get out of this mess. But she kept seeing the moonlit ultra-marine sea, those hazy puffy clouds drifting across the sky, the distant mystery of the horizon and the sight somehow crowded into her, blocking out the sound and horror of El Bayedh. Instead, and unaccountably, she thought of the little ketch somewhere out there on the ocean, cruising peacefully under the bright stars, leaving behind its phosphorescent wake. Deep, deep inside her that sight had touched a chord, the simple beauty of it all, the freedom, a memory of the Black Sea not relived for years.

Her mind was on this picture when, through the window, she saw the shining pinnacle of the Matosa Bank. Without warning Cartwright's description came back to her: beautiful, elegant, the ultimate in culture, he had said. Had he in his crude way caught her subconscious longing for beauty and elegance – and freedom. When was the last occasion she had savoured these things? With her mother? Yes. It had been the last time she had watched her dance with the Bolshoi Ballet. Her hands went to the slim gold chain around her neck. The memory flooding back to the night her mother had given it to her. It was the last time she'd ever seen her. Katya could almost touch the scene, the applause for her mother at the end of the performance and again from the diners as they had entered the ornate gilded candlelit café, Don Giovanni. It was Moscow's late-night destination for ballet aficionados and she had found the richness of their jewels and dresses and their sophisticated chatter mesmerizing. And tumbling out of the scene came her mother's last words to the daughter she hardly knew, as she'd given her the necklace. "Remember, be kinder than your father. " Suddenly the words held a new meaning. She was leaving her daughter her legacy – she was telling her that her future lay not in the darkness inhabited by the corrupt but in the colour of the arts, the moods of the sea and the excitement of creation.

There it was, stark and, at last, acknowledged - she was living the life she'd been forced into by her father. A world of manipulation, corruption and violence. There was no kindness to give or to take. She'd forgotten the meaning of the word. However much she despised the man, Cartwright had summed her up. She was condemned now to a life of destruction and, finally, whether by way of conflict or simple murder, her life was forfeit, with no marker to show she had existed.

Through the cab window she watched the moon come out from behind a cloud, painting the wave caps in the bay a sparkling silver. They were almost beckoning her to join them. Cartwright's words rang true. She didn't need to be a destroyer. She didn't have to continue to live the agony of operational mistakes or the fear of losing her friends. Her talents could be turned to building a new life of fulfilment, excitement and satisfaction— a life outside the confines of G8.

The blunt force of Cartwright's judgment had brought her to face who she really was beneath the hard shell she'd adopted. Having uncovered the truth, she knew there was no going back – her life was going to change. It would take courage but she also knew she had that in abundance. From now on she was going to look after herself. Lead the life she really wanted to live.

A floodgate of emotion opened – she didn't need to be condemned to the life her father had forced her into, she *could* experience the excitement in the life her mother had shown her.

She caught sight of the Marina, the tall masts of the yachts glinting in the harbor lights. All paid for by the sort of money Dempsey had said was needed to live the life in Gibraltar. The sort of money…the words shocked her back into the real world. A real world of an expense she was wholly unable to afford.

How stupid to be lulled by Cartwright – to be conned into believing that sort of life was possible for her. She idly watched a long white yacht pull out of the harbor.

A flood of energy suddenly burst through her as she thought but why not? Why not the life for her?

She stretched towards the driver.

'I've changed my mind. Take me to the airport.'

TWENTY-FOUR

Arriving at Gibraltar airport, Katya got out of the cab and said goodbye to the bemused cab driver. Passport in her hand, she walked into the check in hall where the departure board showed that a BA flight to London had been delayed for an hour. She started pacing up and down in frustration. The delay meant the plane would only just get in to London before the night flight curfew. Most of the other passengers had gone through to the departure lounge or were shopping at the duty-free shops, so her restless pacing found few obstacles.

Was it possible to just take the three hundred million and run. Was it right? She'd spent her life fighting criminals, was she seriously contemplating joining them? Could she live a new life with the stink of corruption hanging over her? Could she succeed, even, if she tried? All she knew was that the money was in a Panama bank. If she tried hacking around the Panama banks, the G8 computers would soon track her and, in no time, she would be serving a long prison sentence.

She saw a half empty café and decided tea would help her concentrate while she waited for the next flight to London. She walked over to it and sat down on a high stool in front of a bored barista who was leaning on the dirty countertop. She ordered a tea with jam on the side and watched him as, yawning, he put a mug under the spluttering hot water machine. Her mood wasn't improved as he dropped a teabag into the mug and slid it across to her, splashing the water. She was about to push it back at him when out of the corner of her eye she caught sight of a kerfuffle further up the departures hall. A man had come marching through the entrance doors and was pushing past some angry late arrivals. She was about to look away when, to her horror, she recognized Cartwright. She tensed. He was looking disheveled and holding his left arm to his side. He looked around, spotted her and marched up to the café, his eyes blazing.

'You left me,' he said accusingly.

She had to admire the man. Sarcastically, she said, 'Did you really think I would hang around? Don't be so stupid - you were going to have me killed. What else would I do? Wait for a bullet?'

He ignored her, gingerly feeling his swollen mouth. 'You got that all wrong, it was me they were going to kill, the bastards. It was lucky my people came in. But only just in time - the sods were almost too bloody late.'

'You expect me to believe that? You -'

He didn't wait for her to finish, but continued blustering as he tried to convince her. 'I wasn't really expecting trouble, but I had my people watching me all the same. Just as well as it turned out.'

'I can believe you there. Because the trouble was for me and you knew it.'

He stepped closer to her.

Katya jumped down from the stool and swung it in front of her, 'I warn you, keep away from me.'

The barista paid no attention, he was gazing into space completely disinterested. Some of the few passengers seated in the cafe looked at them, some got up to leave others were suddenly busy with not getting involved.

Cartwright winced as he stepped back, 'Oh for god's sake put that thing down.' He held his arm. 'If you must know, I'm going to Panama, to the bloody bank. I need to find out what those bloody brothers have done with my El Bayedh cash and I need your help.' He rubbed his hand on his trousers, trying to clean a patch of dirt. 'Coming?'

She glared at him, pretending she didn't understand, hoping he'd tell her more, maybe tell her his bank account numbers. 'What are you talking about? What's in Panama?'

'I told you in the hotel, only you wouldn't listen. The Gonzales brothers have transferred that three hundred million to the Republic Bank in Panama. Why do you think I asked you for your help to hack into their account there?'

'You must know their account details so why do you want my help – '

'Well, I don't know the bloody details and it's pretty obvious you can help me find them after the hacking job you did in Sidi Ifni. I can't do it by myself. Besides, I want you.'

She put the stool down and burst out laughing, 'Ever the optimist, Cartwright. I don't want you – and the brothers will follow you to Panama, even get there ahead of you. And I hope they do.'

He stared at her but his eyes didn't see her, they were focused on something far away in the distance. 'That's a bloody joke.' He stopped.

'Why? What's the joke?'

He flicked a bit of imaginary dust off his jacket. 'Let's just say they're indisposed.' He looked around. 'Shit, isn't there a drink to be had in this bloody hole? That,' he pointed to the mug, 'looks totally disgusting.' He turned, stomped off to look for a bar, saying confidently over his shoulder, 'Coming?'

Katya was tempted. He knew the money was in the Republic Bank and that would make it easier for her to find it. The problem was he was more likely to get rid of her than to share the money with her. So, she let him go. Anyway, it was no use finding the money if she couldn't hide it again. It would be hopeless trying to keep it in cash, she'd need it to finance her new life. The worst thing was, if she found Cartwright's money, she had no one she could trust to hide it for her. The whole idea was a mirage. She pushed the mug of tea away from her. How ironic, she thought, that her work in G8 had been so successful that she'd stymied her own plan to get out of it. She'd have to remain an agent, then. Continue her life, sweating on the edge of danger as she targeted the Ahmets and Rosa Rulenskis and manipulated the corrupt Cartwrights and Dempseys. Her heart sank.

Suddenly she felt a surge of excitement. Hugo Dempsey – of course, his mothballed hedge fund. His proposal on the boat that he could revive it – if she would front it for him . . . The sly, corrupt scheme he'd suggested, the crazy idea that he'd break the rules and keep the relationship secret while he remained a minister. She could use him, she thought now. Transfer the three hundred million into his hedge fund! Play him along to get him to keep quiet. John had asked her and no-one else to inquire into the man's affairs. G8 would never find out, she'd stall any enquiries from John. And Dempsey himself would be a pushover. It was perfect.

She reeled in her racing thoughts – why would Dempsey agree to such a plan? He was certainly just the sort of man to be tempted by more money, and she'd already exposed his veniality that evening on Paul's boat - his love of money, the good life, his pursuit of her. That greed, combined with his vanity, all added up to him being a perfect target for corruption. On the other hand, this was a member of government, someone who was on his way to the top – why should he be tempted? Was her idea crazy? Was she letting her judgment be swayed by the enormity of the sum of cash to be won? But could she manipulate him enough to persuade him to help her? Could he be bribed with half of the three hundred million? Was half enough? He obviously wanted her, so maybe if she pretended she was part of the deal . . . But would he gamble his career for her? It was a huge risk if he betrayed her to G8.

She had to face the fact that she needed someone running a corrupt unknown set up and Dempsey and his hedge fund were ideal. She silently weighed the advantages and risks of such a plan, considering the question of whether Dempsey would allow himself to be bribed.

She tried not to get ahead of herself in her excitement. As she couldn't hack into the account, she'd have to get to Panama and use the old tactic of finding someone in the Republic Bank to bribe to allow her access to it. And if she went to Panama without informing John she would be suspect the minute she landed there. That meant she had to convince him that she still had an operational interest in Cartwright and Panama.

John Hammond. The name haunted her. Did he have a romantic interest in her or was she simply the chief of operations he rated highly? She'd never given herself time to face that question, just letting it lie until something happened to force an answer. That something had happened now. The moment she started to trace Cartwright's money for her own purposes she was in danger. One false step and John would be onto her however much he trusted her. To minimise that risk, she had to be in a position to manipulate him. This was the moment she must find out if he had feelings for her. She realised it was a sudden move and might alert John, but she had no time if she was to beat Cartwright to Panama.

Abruptly making up her mind, Katya left the café and carefully made her way through the arrivals hall, threading a path through the late passengers and baggage now choking the exit. Looking around she couldn't see Cartwright, or a bar, anywhere. She hurried through the main terminal doors and out into the heat and the noise and traffic of Winston Churchill Avenue, the main Gibraltar- to- Spain highway. Traffic inched past as drivers dodged pedestrians, sounding their car horns and flashing their headlights in impatience at the slow pace they made through the milling crowd.

The heat from the cobbles rose to meet her, the smell of fuel oil and dust rising with it. She licked her dry lips, took out her mobile and speed-dialed John's number in London. Out here, in the street, no one would hear her conversation and, if she kept moving, no one would notice her either.

Almost immediately she heard John's voice. Was there a trace of anxiousness behind it?'

'Katya. So glad to hear you. How is it going?'

'It's going well. There's been good progress. Not least in my being able to tell you the Gonzales brothers are out of it. They attacked Cartwright.'

'How do you know?'

'I was there.'

There was pause. 'Go on.'

'There was a fight. I got out. I'm at the airport. Cartwright's just joined me. He told me the brothers are indisposed - his word.'

'That means they're dead, then. Is the operation still viable without them? I mean, can you get to the Gaddafi money'

'From what he said the money due to me and Our Desert for the raid on El Bayedh should be in Panama by now. He also said he's going there to see if anything's changed. My hunch is he will stash the Gadaffi cash there as well.'

'I see. Well there's little point in keeping you in Gibraltar, then.'

She didn't reply, waiting before bringing up the question of her possibly visiting Panama, to tail their man. It was vital he agreed to her going there. So the timing of that question was essential.

'How are you feeling?' John asked suddenly.

Katya was surprised. He'd never bothered to ask her before. She felt strangely touched. Did he care more deeply than he let on? She wished she could see his eyes— they would have told her. Were they smiling? She hoped they were. She suddenly felt exhausted, it would be so nice if she could confide in him, or, better still feel his arms around her . . . She pulled herself up short. Was she losing her nerve, becoming sentimental and needy?

'A little tired maybe.' she replied.

'That's an understatement, surely. After that business with Ahmet.'

She smiled at the euphemism – John was still showing concern for her. It was the opening she'd sought. 'Nothing that some sun and sea won't fix.'

'You can't stay in Gibraltar.'

'No, of course not.' There wouldn't be a better time to put the question. 'There's sun and sea in Panama – I could use the time to find out if the Gadaffi cash was there...'

'No. Paliakov's there with Mikhail. He can sort out Cartwright and the Gadaffi cash, if we find it's there. It won't...' John stopped. Paused for a moment before saying, 'On the other hand, I reckon you deserve a rest. A few days in Panama helping Paliakov would do you good - yes, it's a good idea. Paliakov could do with some help. Can you fly there direct from Gibraltar?'

'Easier from Madrid.' She bit her tongue. Had she appeared too eager?

'Then get going. I'll text you his hotel details.' John rang off.

She didn't allow herself any more than a moment to congratulate herself. She dialled international phone listings, ran through the numbers and finding the one she wanted punched them into the mobile. She was taking a risk that her call could be traced but she hadn't time to set up a decoy route to avoid that.

Anyway, it was unlikely that anyone would want to trace the call. Dozens a day were made to this number.

A cultured male voice answered, 'Good evening. Treasury Minister's office.'

'May I speak to Mr Dempsey's secretary, please,' Katya sounded confident.

'Just a moment.'

Katya looked at her watch. It was going to be tight to catch the BA flight to London. She needed to see Dempsey in person before setting off for Panama. She needed to find out where he would be. A phone call alone wouldn't settle this business.

'Hello. Mr Dempsey's secretary here. Can I help you?'

'Yes. I'm calling on behalf of the Eisenberg Foundation, confirming our appointment with Mr Dempsey tomorrow at 6 pm.' Katya kept her voice clipped, assured, as she posed as an efficient secretary.

She waited as the diary secretary hunted for the non-existent appointment.

'I'm sorry. I have no appointment listed for you, and I see the Minister's at the Royal Opera House tomorrow night.'

'Oh.' Katya paused, as if consulting her papers. 'Oh, I'm sorry I've made a mistake, it's next week -'

She switched off, before the man asked who she was. It was unlikely a busy diary secretary would remember the call by the time Dempsey got back from wherever he was and even if he did, Katya had left no name.

TWENTY-FIVE

She re-entered the terminal. There was still no sign of Cartwright. Relieved, she quickly bought a ticket to London and fast tracked her way to the departure gate.

The plane finally landed at eleven o'clock at night. Tired and dishevelled, Katya found a taxi. She couldn't go back to her apartment in Water Lane – G8 surveillance would pick her up immediately – so she directed the driver to take her straight to the Mandarin Oriental Hotel in Knightsbridge. As she climbed out of the taxi she looked down to avoid being identified by the security camera. She shivered. It was cold and damp. The doorman at the hotel saw her shiver as he ushered her up the stone steps of the ornate Victorian building and politely asked if she was cold. She shook her head and tried to erase the memory of the stone steps she'd raced down just a few hours ago. The desk clerk had a less sympathetic reaction, raising his eyebrows superciliously as he looked at her crumpled clothes and registered the absence of baggage. A large tip and the handing over of her Platinum Card very quickly changed his disapproval to acceptance. He swiftly checked her into an executive suite.

She went up in the lift and used the keycard to access the suite. She was so tired she didn't notice the silk clad walls or maplewood furnishings. She flung herself down on the bed and her last recollection was of the star-shaped ceiling light looming over her. It brought back a memory of the moon shaped lights in the Berlin and Gibraltar airports.

She woke the next morning and she knew for sure she was going to strike out on her own. To achieve that goal, it was essential she spoke to Dempsey right away to get him on side. Phoning him was no use, she had to meet him. His diary secretary had let slip he was scheduled to go to the opera that night—she could contrive to bump into him there. She had no clothes, no make-up and her hair was a mess. She had no alternative but to take a risk and go shopping. She smiled to herself. It was just what she needed. Finishing breakfast, she headed for Sloane Street and the designer shops and boutiques. It was good to switch off after the grim days in Morocco.

She was mindful of G8's watchful eye on her expense account. The last thing she wanted, at this stage, was to draw their attention to the fact she was in London. Her G8 credit card account wasn't due for payment for three weeks so she used it – if all went well she'd be long gone by the time it landed in the G8 accounts department.

She found some summer outfits to take to Panama and couldn't resist some very expensive Ferragamo designer sunglasses and a couple of rather attractive wispy evening dresses. They were too gorgeous to leave behind. She stopped off for a coffee and then made her away along Knightsbridge, where she bought a very smart black suitcase and was tempted into buying some very high-heeled Jimmy Choo court shoes and a new black Chanel handbag. Finally, she moved into Harrods where she explored the cosmetics hall, buying a new bottle of Picasso, makeup and sun cream.

Her last call was to Sean, her hairdresser in Beauchamp Place.

'My god.' Sean exclaimed in horror when he saw her. 'What have you done to your hair?' His eyes dropped to her hands. He took one of them in his and looked at it. 'Your hands,' he wailed. 'Look! They're like sandpaper— so rough!'

"Archeological dig in Wales,' she replied cryptically.

'With that tan?'

She strode towards an empty chair, 'You know Wales, Sean. It's all wind. Now, get Lucille for my hair and repair me. Quickly.' She laughed as Sean, still muttering about her nails, picked up some nail restorer.

When she got back to the hotel, she caught the desk clerk's eye as he saw the designer parcels, her beautifully styled hair and manicured hands. She was amused by the thoughtful look on his face. He was obviously exploring what category to put her in - wealthy trust fund babe. Arm candy for a wealthy business man - too self-assured for that - more likely he was thinking she was a very successful business woman – probably twinning her with someone who sold ridiculously priced designer handbags or expensive jewellery. Still amused she went through the foyer and into the elevator.

She opened the door to her suite, dumped the parcels on the bed, tried out the latest Tiffany perfume one of the shop assistants had given her, poured herself a vodka and finally flopped down in one of the armchairs by the window. She sat looking out over the busy street, watching the buses and taxi cabs as they dropped off and picked up sightseers, lovers, business people. Even from the height of her room Katya caught the mood of hustle and bustle from the street below – the energy which seemed to soar up to her. Hugging her knees to her chest she stared out of the window.

Her first call after an early lunch in Covent Garden, was on the porter at the Royal Opera House stage door. She knew from G8 agents that some porters were notorious for leaking backstage gossip. They knew plenty about the regular opera-goers, all of it usually scandalous. They also helped the management as they developed a sixth sense when looking out for potential charity donors.

This porter scrutinized her through screwed up eyes and told her, through the corner of his mouth, that his name was Fred. She'd adopted an American accent which, together with her quiet, elegant charm, led him to sense a potential donor. He'd answered all her questions about the opera house and the important people who went to the performances with enthusiastic waving of his hands. He had no idea that he'd confirmed exactly what she wanted to know. That Dempsey would be visiting the Opera that night as a Patron. He'd also told her that he would be in his box by himself as his wife was in New York on business. All Fred was left with when she'd gone was the impression of a wealthy American tourist who would hopefully be back that evening with a hefty donation and maybe a large tip for him.

Back at the hotel it was the desk clerk who solved her final dilemma. For another large tip, he secured for her, at the very shortest notice and at an exorbitant price a seat at the very front of the Amphitheatre.

By the time Katya had finished getting everything prepared, it was time to get changed. She went up to her suite, showered and put on two of the morning's purchases: a short, backless black dress and the Jimmy Choo shoes. Her long auburn hair was shining and had been skillfully arranged by Sean to fall in soft waves down her back. Carefully she heightened the colour of her face, sprinkling metallic face glitter over her forehead and cheeks. She picked up her new handbag and checked the contents before generously spraying on her Picasso.

She looked at herself in the long hotel mirror and saw a startling image of her mother, of things ephemeral looking back at her. Unaccountably, she felt a compelling impulse to be with John. She wanted him to see her like this. Wanting…. Abruptly she turned away. There was no future in idle speculation— her father had taught her that.

On seeing her this time, the desk clerk was over-awed and

waved away her tip as he shouted at the doorman to get her a cab.

Outside the hotel the cold air crept into her – she climbed into the cab knowing she should have spent money on a coat and not the sunglasses.

Every time she flew home to London from an overseas operation she revelled in its feisty, in- your- face, atmosphere. Even Hong Kong went at a slower pace. From the cab, she idly watched the crowds going into the Underground at Piccadilly Circus. Abruptly, the sight took her back to the time of Ahmet's terrorist assault on the El Train in Chicago. The horror of the people killed, maimed – the photos, the reports. She clenched her hand on the door rest of the cab. There would be no more operations against the Ahmets of this world. No longer her responsibility.

The elaborate glass latticed front and white Georgian columns of the Royal Opera House came into sight - the epitome of the life she now wished to have.

She got out of the cab and walked up the steps and through the main entrance, into the foyer. It was her first visit to the ROH and even though she was only there to see Dempsey she felt an excitement. Memories of her childhood and the Bolshoi Theatre came flooding back as she saw the opera goers milling around, buying programmes, ordering drinks for the intervals, looking at their tickets, slowly moving into the auditorium. She went up the red-carpeted Grand Staircase and was captivated by the beautiful tracery of the Floral Hall with its magnificent barreled roof. She wanted to study it, but forced herself to move on, showing her ticket inside the auditorium and finding her seat under the magnificent blue ceiling with its white painted clouds.

She took a moment to look down at the magnificent red and gold curtains drawn across the stage: at the soft lights in their sconces, with their red lampshades, which shone above the tiers of boxes. They cast a warm glow over the Londoners and visitors finding their seats in the stalls.

The orchestra pit was filling up with musicians. An air of expectancy seemed to fill the whole House. She sat down in her seat at the end of the front row and took out her ten by twenty-five Opticron monocular glass. It was small, cheap and effective. She scanned the boxes, Dempsey wasn't there. She settled back discreetly deploying the monocular at intervals as the auditorium filled. Suddenly, he came into view, sitting down by himself at the front of one of the boxes to the right of her. She watched him flick open his programme.

There was a sudden hush and then silence from the audience as the orchestra started to play the overture. As the music ended, the curtains very slowly drew back. The opera she was going to see tonight was Faust. She watched Dempsey become absorbed as Faust was tempted by Mephistopholes. She smiled to herself. Faust, highly successful yet dissatisfied with his life, makes a pact with the devil, exchanging his soul for unlimited knowledge and worldly pleasure. Perhaps Dempsey recognized a parallel.

She wished she could watch the whole performance but, with time slipping by, she left her seat, eased her way through the exit at the rear of the gods.

Reaching the door to Dempsey's box, she silently pushed it open and sat down behind him in the shadows. She leant forward and whispered. 'Hugo. It's Katya.'

He was taken completely by surprise, half turned around, his eyes wide.

She hurried on. 'Katya Petrovna. Remember? You want me to go to Gibraltar.'

Dempsey didn't reply straight away.

She watched his face, imagining the sudden chill hitting him as he tried desperately to work out why she was there. Had their computers come up with something? Corruption, insider trading, criminal dealing, bribes? All of which, no doubt, had had a major part in building his hedge fund.

He stalled. 'I remember, Katya . . . Who wouldn't? Are you offering to go?'

Katya felt his hesitation. She needed to reassure him she wasn't there for G8.

'Yes', she replied, baldly.

At that Dempsey turned completely around to look at her. Even in the shadows she was dazzling. The black dress, the heady scent, those piercing violet eyes. He felt hypnotized - couldn't drag his eyes away. He was aware, though, that people would start being curious as to what was going on, would begin to look at him. He got up quickly to join her in the privacy of the darkened area at the back of the box.

'Are you on the level?"

She stood up and gestured with her hand to stop him. 'I'll meet you. At your apartment, after the performance.'

Before he could reply she had turned and slipped out of the box, walking swiftly towards the Floral Hall where she ran silently down the stairs and out of the main door. She needed to get to his apartment on Park Lane right away— to be there waiting for him when he arrived.

She took his card out of her bag, checked the address and hailed a cab.

TWENTY-SIX

Later that evening Katya was leaning over Dempsey as they sat on a white leather sofa in his Hyde Park apartment. Her words were rapid, spraying over the minister with the speed of shotgun pellets.

'Summing up. The Gonzales Brothers are dead. Cartwright is going to Panama. And when he gets there, he'll blunder around, make waves and probably alert the bank, so I need to move fast. Hammond has ordered me there to help Paliakov hack into the lawyers' account. I'll be there tomorrow and I can get that three hundred million but I need your help. I can't do it alone.' She sat back, her reflection shifting in the scenic window behind her.

As Dempsey absorbed the words, he began to understand this subtly perfumed, stunning and clever woman. Over the last two hours she had maneuvered him into listening to her outrageous proposal. It was both complex and corrupt. She had read him from their first meeting in the G8 Headquarters and then on the boat - had seen through his façade, his venality, his need to live without boundaries. This was her opportunity and she was giving him his - after just two meetings. She'd argued, persuaded, cajoled, enticed . . . All to draw him in and get him to agree to her preposterous plan. He was obviously tempted, but he was still unsure. It had all been too fast. He needed to slow down. Was G8 trying to trap him? Was she genuine? If she was, her quid pro quo with him must be colossal.

'What do you want?' His words matched hers for bluntness.

'I need to be able to use your hedge fund in Gibraltar to transfer the money into. At least for a few hours. After that I can arrange for it to be transferred elsewhere so G8 won't be able to find it.' Her violet eyes looked even larger as she tempted him. 'Leaving half for you of course.'

Dempsey felt himself weaken - he wanted the money and he wanted her but knew he had to see where exactly she was coming from.

'That's the first time I've heard you say something stupid, Katya. John Hammond didn't exactly approve of my Gibraltar connection, did he – I saw that during your briefing. He's probably investigating it right now.'

'You're right. But what you don't know is he's put me in charge of investigating you... I'll tell him only what I want to tell him.'

He opened his mouth to say something, then suddenly burst out laughing, it couldn't be a sting— it was too crazy. He looked at her. His greed overwhelming him. 'It's perfect.'

She bent down and picked up her bag off the sofa, took out a new pay- as- you- go mobile. 'Use this burner when we need to talk.' She tossed it on the sofa.

He nodded, confident, stretched out his hand to her. 'You're not going now, surely?'

'I'm only here for your help in getting that money,' she replied, coldly. 'Equal shares, nothing else. No bonus.'

'Bitch,' he said to the closing front door. But not in anger. He could wait.

Katya took a taxi straight back to the Mandarin Oriental, flung her clothes into a travel bag and headed for Heathrow.

TWENTY-SEVEN

Paliakov and Mikhail had been getting to know each other in Panama. Paliakov had been surprised to find Rosa's enforcer, Mikhail much more cultured than he'd expected. And he was charmed. He'd even started to forget his Berlin lover.

They were both, for different reasons, used to keeping a low profile – Paliakov working covertly as a stringer, Mikhail as a criminal. For this job, they were staying in a stopover apartment in Santa Ana, a rundown area of Panama frequented by the country's criminal fraternity. Mikhail had chosen the area because one of his Polish friends had recommended it.

Paliakov had thought the city would be as grim as their living quarters but a short walk away from the villa he discovered Casco Viejo, an old colonial borough which had been rejuvenated into a tourist hotspot. Over the last few days, he and Mikhail had explored the cafes, art galleries and gay bars there, even getting caught up one night in a noisy, colourful jazz festival. The Panamanians had turned out to be vibrant, welcoming people and they both found it amusing to join in the friendly way they all greeted each other on the streets. The only thing Paliakov hated was the hot humid weather, with never a cloud in the sky. He kept having to wipe away the sweat that was dripping down his face.

They had travelled by bus to the financial district of Panama City where they had found L'Espranca, a small intimate café opposite the Republic Bank. They could sit there, half hidden from the busy road, and no one would bother them. Mikhail would stay in the café while Paliakov went into the bank discreetly sidling among the teeming lunchtime crowd to chat up the staff to find someone who might help him access the Gonzales brothers' account. He'd been able to drift up in the lift and had found Enith, the girl who looked after the Gonzales account on the first floor. He'd flattered her and taken her out a couple of times to very expensive restaurants and had spoiled her with extravagant presents. She was slightly timid with limpid, dark eyes and had been seduced by all the attention. The flowers that arrived from him on her desk in the mornings had made her the envy of all the other girls in the office. On their last date in a restaurant he had promised her a gold bracelet she'd seen in a jeweller's shop window. The price he told her she'd have to pay for it was a promise to let him come into her office and use her computer when no-one was about. By now she was ready to do anything for him. As he put the band around her wrist and fastened it, she told him that the following day would be perfect— the girl she shared an office with was going out for lunch.

The day dawned, bright and hot as it always did in Panama. Paliakov dressed in a clean white shirt, and blue trousers, cinched at the waist with a thin snakeskin belt; black lace- up shoes and large Hilfiger shades. He stood under the ineffective ceiling fan in the apartment waiting for Mikhail to finish dressing. He would probably have looked suaver if he hadn't been pouring sweat. He grimaced. How he hated this steamy heat.

Mikhail joined him and together they took a bus into the centre of Panama City. During the slow journey through the honking traffic, Mikhail handed Paliakov a slip of paper - Rosa's Bank account details. Paliakov didn't look at it but swiftly put it in his pocket and turned to gaze at the brightly dressed suburban dwellers jostling and hurrying along the narrow pavements.

The scene changed suddenly from colourfully decorated

shops and apartment buildings to the skyscrapers of the financial district. There they got off the bus and Paliakov left Mikhail drinking a Seco at the café opposite the bank. How anyone could drink that Seco, all sugar cane distilled alcohol and served with milk and ice, was beyond him. Give him a tequila sunrise anytime.

He crossed the road and walked purposefully into the bank, mingling with the crowd in the banking hall before taking the lift to the top floor. No one paid him any attention. To them he was either a member of staff or some girl's boyfriend. It wasn't unusual for the girls to use their office for a date during siesta time so as to avoid the prying eyes in restaurants. And if the dates were with married men, the possibility of a whisper getting back to a wife.

Enith met him as he came out of the lift, took him down the corridor to her office and held open the door, reminding him he only had about ten minutes. He quickly looked up and down the corridor before going in. The office was empty. He sat down in front of her computer and started to work. Very fast.

It took him exactly one minute twelve seconds to open the Gonzales brothers' file. He searched rapidly through it for a mention of Cartwright's name. Nothing. Puzzled, he searched again. Nothing. Certainly no reference to Gadaffi's half billion dollars. He couldn't believe it, so he searched it again, this time looking for a coded account number. He looked at his watch, he had only two minutes before Enith would be back.

Suddenly he saw what he was looking for – a column of numbers and letters. There were seven of them, each with a name alongside. Bank account codes. He rapidly scanned them - Petra Handelsbaum, Luigi Rossi, Juan Esposito, Ronald Cartwright – There it was. Cartwright's bank account code staring at him from the page. He started to open the account- tensed as he heard footsteps coming down the corridor. They stopped outside the door. He froze as he watched the handle turn.

It was Enith. She beckoned him frantically. He shook his head. Without waiting to look at Cartwright's account, he took Mikhail's paper from his pocket and rapidly followed the instructions written there. Paid the money in both the Cartwright and Gonzales accounts by wire transfer into Rosa Rulenski's BlueLine Investments Account in Ambergris Island. He clamped his teeth together as he heard other footsteps approaching. He had to wait for BlueLine to confirm receipt of the transfer.

Enith shut the door and quickly ran over to him, straddled his lap and clamped her lips against his, gripping his face as he automatically recoiled from her.

The door opened.

'Oh' a woman's voice exclaimed.

The door slammed shut.

Enith climbed off him. 'You didn't like?'

'Very much, thank you,' he said politely.

She moved towards him again. Paliakov hastily pointed to the computer screen. BlueLine Investment still hadn't acknowledged that the money had been received. It should only take a minute or so and then he could transfer all the money in Rosa's account to G8. Despite the air conditioning he felt the sweat spreading under his armpits.

More footsteps - whoever it was had stopped outside the door. Enith drew in a breath, stretched over and shut down the computer. She ran to the door, grasped the handle with a shaking hand and opened it. A uniformed messenger was standing there and handed her some papers. As she said 'Thank you,' she frantically beckoned Paliakov with her hand behind her back, urging him to go.

He was about to reboot the computer when a tall, thin faced severe looking woman with short, mannish hair pushed through the door and stood there, one foot holding it open. She stared wordlessly at Paliakov, looking witheringly at him, plainly waiting for him to leave the room. As he walked through the door, he gritted his teeth to smile warmly at her – she was making him leave without a receipt for the payment into Rosa's account. He had no idea what moneys he'd transferred. Worse, he hadn't had time to move the cash on from Rosa to G8.

Katya arrived on a commercial flight which had landed at Tocumen International Airport some time before and, following Paliakov's emailed instructions, she had made her way to meet him at L'Esperanca café. On arriving, she'd ordered a Yorsh and a Seco for Mikhail. Without preliminaries, she sat down and asked him where Paliakov was.

Katya's face went white as he told her his partner was already in the bank making the transfer to Rosa. It couldn't be true! She felt drained- the dream of freedom was gone with the cash now already on its way to G8.

At that very moment Paliakov came out of the bank, blinking in the sunshine, and sighing with relief as he saw Mikhail waiting for him in the café, looking very attractive in his brightly coloured Bermuda shorts, patterned shirt and wide- brimmed straw hat. He walked over to his partner and sat down next to him.

'It's done.'

He loathed Katya, nodded at her, pleased with himself for having sorted it all out without her help. 'You needn't have come. All the cash is now in BlueLine Investments in Ambergris Island'. He smiled. 'Rosa's account.'

Katya kept her temper, drank some of the Yorsh. She put the glass down, looking puzzled. 'You said it's in Ambergris— in Rosa's account?'

'Yes.' Rudely ignoring her, he kept his gaze on Mikhail. 'You were telling me about that new fish restaurant, Mikhail. Come on, let's go and celebrate.'

They stood up. Mikhail gathered up his things and began to walk out of the café, waving at a taxi coming down the road.

Katya grabbed Paliakov's sleeve, holding him back. 'You transferred it to G8 after that?'

'No, I got interrupted before I could finish.'

Katya couldn't believe it. 'Then the money's still in Rosa's account?'

'Well, I didn't get the receipt, but I'm sure it's there. I'll do the transfer to G8 later. You should have got here on time. It's too late to complain.'

'No, I'm not complaining. I'm just checking.'

'Good.' Paliakov turned on his heel and walked up the road to where Mikhail was waiting with a taxi.

Katya stood and watched them go. She took the burner out of her bag, tapped the speed dial code for Dempsey's number. There was no reply. Desperately she tried again. Still no response. Where the hell was he?

TWENTY- EIGHT

Hugo Dempsey was wholly unaware that Katya was trying to reach him. He'd received an urgent summons from John and was on his way, in the ministerial Jaguar, to meet him at G8 HQ. He'd hidden the burner Katya had given him in a closet at his apartment, terrified the surveillance equipment he'd seen in the G8 Tac Room would find it on him.

His driver, Eve Pimm, closed the door of the car, climbed into the driver's seat and started up the engine. He was pressed back into his seat as the Jaguar suddenly surged out of the House of Commons courtyard into Parliament Square. It was pouring with rain, the car splashing through grey puddles and the windscreen wipers whipping away the large raindrops. Water from the heavy tires splattered over the pedestrians hurrying down Whitehall as they dodged the pools of water and hung onto their umbrellas.

Dempsey looked at the back of Eve's head. She'd been his mistress for the past year. She hadn't said a word about their usual evening together at her flat a few days earlier. She never did, she just took the two hundred pounds he gave her, dressed, and drove him home. Eve, Dempsey had decided, was becoming a bore. She was too expensive— and sulky if she didn't get her own way. She'd have to go.

Right now, he needed to concentrate on Hammond, whose summons to G8 had been unusually peremptory. Dempsey's first instinct had been to refuse, but when Hammond had added that it was to be a strategy meeting, something that only Hugo could help with, he had quickly changed his mind. If he was the only one who could help, he would have the upper hand in any decisions. That would be a welcome change from the last time they'd met, when Hammond had had the temerity to talk down to him.

Over Eve's shoulder, he felt a smug satisfaction as he watched the digital speedometer on the dashboard climb to 120 mph as they approached the de- limit signs on the M3. Only he, the Prime Minister and the Home Secretary had the right to travel at unpoliced speed. He smiled to himself knowing it raised his profile, made people look up to him.

But all this was nothing compared to the money waiting for him and Katya in Panama. He looked out of the window and for a moment thought of it all, soon to be hidden by him in a remote tax haven. Safe while Katya guarded it from any G8 investigation. He anticipated the excitement of turning that money into a billion-dollar hedge fund within twelve months. Free to operate out of Gibraltar, unfettered by irksome regulation.

He switched his thoughts back to the meeting with Hammond. The rain was now easing as Eve drew up outside G8 headquarters.

He walked to the entrance of the building, showed his pass to the guard and was allowed in.

The security guard, standing on the other side of the door, carefully studied the visitors pass and Dempsey's features before allowing him to go further into the building. Satisfied, he said, 'Mr Hammond's expecting you. He's on the second floor, minister. When you get there, you'll find him in the conference room opposite the paternoster You know your way.'

Dempsey looked around. There was no subordinate there to escort him -

Hammond showing his disrespect, no doubt. He bit back a blistering comment and angrily marched down the passage towards the paternoster and climbed in. As it passed each balconied floor, the open lift allowed brief glimpses of agents intently bent over screens or huddled in hushed conference – the planning of a complex sting operation or violent drug bust. The scenes passed him by.

He was too intent on working out why Hammond wanted to see him so urgently.

Almost certainly not about the budget. The deliberate brush off by the security guard could be the preliminary to awkward questions about his hedge fund? Had Hammond heard about his meeting with Katya. He suddenly felt uneasy – had he misread her? Had she set him up?

The paternoster lurched. The jerk concentrated his mind. He mustn't panic. He must simply fall back on his usual line of defence - he would play the power game.

As soon as he arrived at the entrance to the conference room, he flung open the door, cutting short Hammond's greeting.

'I hope this meeting is necessary, Hammond. It's my day for parliamentary questions - I'm extremely busy and-'

'My Russian and American counterparts think it's very necessary, Minister.' Hammond pointed towards Lev and Walt, whose faces were visible on the giant plasma screen on the far wall. They appeared to be sizing him up as he strode across to one of the chairs in front of the conference console.

'Counterparts?' Dempsey exclaimed. He had thought the meeting was just going to be between Hammond and him. Nothing had been said about outsiders. He felt his temper rise further.

'It is so good of you to meet with us, Mr Dempsey.'

Dempsey detected a note of insolence in the unmistakably

Russian voice. "Mr Dempsey." This man had said, not "Minister". As if he was dealing with the man not the politician. The hedge fund, not the budget. Another enemy in addition to Hammond? His reprimand of Hammond for misleading him about the members of this meeting would have to wait, baiting him now would appear juvenile. He heard Hammond say to him, 'May I introduce you to Lev Leviatski, our Director of G8 for Russia. And also to Walt Sable our Director of G8 for the United States.'

Walt's face became animated. He gave a broad, white-toothed smile. 'Hi. Good to see you Mr Dempsey. Welcome aboard, if I may say so.' Walt nodded towards a young man with a crew cut who was sitting next to him. 'Meet Cy Langton, our Yale lawyer and Task Force Tactician for Panama.'

Dempsey didn't pay any attention to the serious looking young man with the dark- rimmed glasses peering out at him from the screen. He was fixated on the one word 'Panama'. He was stunned. Why Panama? What the hell was going on? Had they found out about Katya's scheme to steal the money there? But how was that possible? She'd told him the money had only just been paid into the Republic Bank. He struggled to appear calm as he stretched out his hands and held onto the back of the chair. He grappled for something to say. 'I didn't know G8 targets could be geographical.' He realized what a stupid thing that was to say. All G8's targets would have a geographical element.

Walt's reply confirmed this. 'You've come right to the point, Mr Dempsey.'

Lev blew out a cloud of cigarette smoke. 'I said to you, Walt, that Mr Dempsey would be shrewd.'

'Good to know you're right, Lev.' Walt turned to Cy. 'Cy, go ahead and tell Mr Dempsey why Panama's a geographical target for G8.'

Hammond stepped forward to the console, pulled out the

chair Dempsey was now clutching. 'You may want to sit down for this, Minister.' He sat down on an adjacent chair and Dempsey followed suit, slowly, putting his hands on the console's steel surface, fingers steepled, pressed together which stopped them trembling and emphasised the listening position.

Cy spoke precisely in a slightly clipped Boston accent. 'You probably know most of what I'm to say, but please accept it as background. Panama is a major destination for fraud funds – and sometimes it's mingled with drugs cash which comes in mostly from Mexico, Columbia, Bolivia and Peru. The cash is difficult to detect because of the sheer volume of money and because of the secrecy practiced by most of the tax havens it's routed through.'

Dempsey moistened his dry mouth, trying, at the same time, not to swallow. Swallowing indicated nervousness. The last thing he wanted any of them to notice. What did they know? What was coming? For the first time in his life he was really scared. He moved his gaze from Cy to Walt and then to Lev, using his years of business experience to overcome the nerves gnawing at his gut.

Cy went on. 'Recently we persuaded the Panama Government to introduce anti-fraud and anti-money- laundering legislation. This required all their banks to report all financial transactions in excess of ten thousand dollars. They would report to the Panama police and the Panama police would then report to us at G8.'

Dempsey forced a smile. 'That must have taken a lot of persuading.'

Cy dodged the question. 'Information has been coming out of Panama by the ton. It's overrun our Panama tactical computer, but we're sifting through it and the programmers have been able to distinguish patterns of money-laundering in a number of particular tax havens.'

Dempsey could almost hear Katya's voice when she had explained money laundering to him, about patterns - how they could hide the cash in his hedge fund. He felt his face reddening, not sure whether it was from fear or excitement, but knowing he couldn't afford to show any tension or emotion. 'Patterns?' Dempsey knew his voice sounded shaky but he needed to ask the question to create a delay while he decided how to tackle this, decided how to react.

Cy paused. 'I expect I'm telling you stuff, you already know,' He adjusted his glasses and then, looking down, he shuffled some papers on his desk.

Dempsey was having difficulty breathing. What was going on? Why was Cy delaying the point of all this? He knew that there couldn't be any 'pattern' to the routing of the money to Panama as the Gonzales brothers had sent it from Gibraltar direct to Panama. Or so Katya had told him. But was that correct? Were Walt and Lev just playing him, before he was confronted with his theft? Did they know of the plan he and Katya had come up with? Or was he being prepared by Cy for a deeper interrogation by the big guns, Lev and Walt? And what about Hammond? What did he know? He clenched his hands together, fighting his rising panic.

Lev spoke again. 'Mr Dempsey, my American friends here are trying to tell you that the tax havens they are talking about are British Overseas Territories - major money-laundering centres. And, to put it bluntly, the British Government has known this for years but has failed to stop it.'

'Well, that's sure told him, Lev.' Walt leaned forward, looking to Dempsey as if he was coming out of the screen to confront him. 'That's what Cy was trying to tell you, Mr Dempsey. But Lev's right. Cy's far too polite, it's all that lawyerly diplomacy he learnt at Yale. We've come to the end of our patience with the British Government's lack of oversight of the monetary system in these British Territories.'

Hammond turned to Dempsey and said softly, 'Walt and Lev are referring, as you know, Hugh, to the islands, mainly in the Caribbean, which belong to Britain.'

Up on the high screen, Walt was speaking again. 'Mr Dempsey, your predecessor gave me and Lev here promises he'd freeze the assets in these places but we've seen no attempt to freeze anything - and no attempt to kick out the scumbags who hide their criminally acquired cash there.'

Dempsey was staggered by the bluntness of the attack. That sort of thing happened in business meetings, not in political circles where understatement ruled. The Russians were clearly furious. The Americans too, come to that. As this thought penetrated his brain, his stomach churned with relief as he realized that he and Katya were not, after all, the target of the meeting - the Katya scheme was safe from investigation. Then, in a roller coaster reversal, he realized with horror that if he personally didn't very soon crack down on these British tax havens, then his Ministerial career would be over. The Russian and American ultimatum made that very clear.

The switch from one threat to the other was almost too big for him to handle. He groped for something to say. He decided to divide and rule. 'Walt, I think Lev can speak for himself.' He stressed the words so that Lev was made to appear more important than Walt. 'I'm new to this, Lev. How can I help you?'

Cy recognized the slight and looked at Walt, raising his eyebrows. Walt shook his head. Both gestures were almost imperceptible. Even so, Dempsey picked up on the unspoken message. So far so good. He'd cut out Walt and Cy for the moment. He leant back in his chair and fixed his best, campaign-trail smile on the Russian.

Walt took no notice of Dempsey's put down. He laid out his demand peremptorily. 'Lev and I agree the only way to stop this mayhem is to freeze all the assets in these places immediately as promised.'

Dempsey's head jerked towards him. Freezing the assets meant stopping all financial transactions to and from the islands. That would be disastrous because Gibraltar would be included - where his hedge fund was, ready to receive three hundred million dollars from Panama. Panama! The cash was safely in Panama and that country wasn't a British Offshore Territory. It had nothing to do with Britain. The relief made him feel almost light-headed. Katya's scheme was safe, the cash could stay there for the moment. He could handle Lev and Walt now.

'I agree.' He brought his fist down on the desk, showing force and determination. 'Every bank, every trust, every mutual fund, everything, in every one of those places . . . We'll freeze the lot until an audit's done to sift out the criminal money. It's essential.'

Dempsey stood up, nodded towards Lev and Walt and then, dismissively, at Hammond. 'I'll speak to the PM.'

TWENTY-NINE

Katya sat in the L'Esperanca café for some time after Paliakov and Mikhail had left. She was trying to gather her thoughts. She had dialed Dempsey's burner three times in the last five minutes to get the account number he'd set up for the hedge fund they were going to use. He wasn't answering. Added to this, she was getting over the fact that one minute she'd believed Paliakov had sent the cash from Rosa's account on to G8 and she'd lost it, and the next minute she'd found that it was still in Rosa's account and still within her grasp. She was used to turmoil in the jobs she did for G8, but this was different. It was personal and added to the strain she was feeling.

Her frustration mounted - what the hell was he doing? Where was he? Abruptly she decided to move away to somewhere more private.

She got up, paid her bill, then hurriedly pushed her way into the crowded street. Halfway along it, she saw an iron grille gateway into a park and headed towards it.

As she passed through the gate she took in the peaceful manicured lawns surrounded by hundreds of beautiful fig trees, bowed down with the weight of their fruit. An oasis of calm. A striking contrast to the forbidding skyscrapers of the financial centre - where the world's cash was greedily swallowed up in Panama's hollow holding companies and shell property corporations.

A few yards from the entrance there was a bench, shaded by

one of the fig trees. She headed for it and sat down. There were few people here. One or two couples trysting on distant seats and some children knocking around a football under the watchful eyes of a group of mothers – or more likely nannies employed by financiers. Every five minutes she hit the redial button to try Dempsey's burner number once again. She waited there for over an hour, finding the fig tree actually did little to shade her from the gruelling heat. It was relentless and soon she was sweating, thirsty, tired and disheartened.

At last Dempsey answered.

'Where have you been?' she opened, tersely.

'With the Prime Minister,' Dempsey said curtly. 'Are you calling because you've got good news?'

'Not yet. Paliakov had to leave the bank before he had the receipt from Rosa's bank confirming his transfer. I need that before I can move the money from there into your hedge fund.'

Dempsey sounded puzzled, 'Did you say Rosa's account?'

'Yes, Rosa Rulenski, I told you in London, her account in Ambergris– '

Dempsey shouted in sudden panic. 'Ambergris? Ambergris Island in the Caribbean? What the bloody hell is the money doing there?'

Katya held the phone away from her ear. 'Don't shout - yes Ambergris -'

'Bloody hell, we're freezing all assets there.'

'What are you talking about?' Katya stood up abruptly.

'It's British! No-one can touch any money there.' Dempsey sounded frantic. 'I've just issued the freeze order – it had already been drafted and passed it just hadn't been implemented- I thought our money was still in Panama.'

Katya stared with unseeing eyes at the financial buildings beyond the edge of the park, speechless at the absurdity of what he was saying.

'But that's ridiculous. What do you mean?'

It was Dempsey's turn to spell it out, 'We can't touch that bloody money.

I've just drafted an order prohibiting any assets at all from being transferred out of all the British Overseas Territories.'

Katya felt raw alarm seep into her. She gave a shuddering sigh before clutching at one, final, straw. 'When does the freezing order come into force? You drafted it— but has it been issued yet?'

She imagined Dempsey's eyes flicking to his wristwatch.

'I'll get back to you!' he shouted.

THIRTY

Dempsey checked his watch, 7.15 pm. He reached for his office mobile to call his Private Secretary - swore as he realized he'd left it in the car. He couldn't use the burner and he'd had the landline removed from his apartment in case any of his women friends tried to contact him there - he'd told his wife no-one used landlines these days. Eve and the car had already left. He'd have to find a cab and get to his office in the Commons.

Fighting down his panic, he raced to the door of his apartment, flung it open and barged down the passageway. Would he get to his office in time? He stabbed the button to call the lift and paced up and down, almost beside himself with impatience as he waited for it.

The doors opened as it arrived and he was about to dive into it when an elderly lady came out. She moved very slowly, bent and overladen with bags of shopping. A spare bag sat on the lift floor. The woman had left it behind. Dempsey side-stepped her, threw it out of the lift. He stabbed the ground floor button, praying no one would stop the lift on the way down.

He sighed with relief as it came to a halt on the ground floor. He raced across the hallway, ignoring the porter's phone – no-one at the office would believe he would use a public telephone. He had to get to his office.

Out in the street he saw a taxi. Its light was off. He ran on - people cursing as he collided with them. A taxi was stopping at the end of the road. He shouted at the driver to wait for him.

'Emergency,' he gasped as he reached it. 'House of Commons. Get on with it.'

The cab driver tugged at his baseball cap, ''Ang on a minit, aren't you our Treasury Minister?'

'Just bloody get me there.'

The driver shoved the accelerator down. 'Right y' are, mate. But,'—he got in the last word— 'if yer talk like that in the 'ouse, make sure the bleedin' cameras aren't on yer.'

The policeman at the gate of the House of Commons recognised Dempsey and, without waiting, waved the taxi through. Dempsey climbed out of the cab and thrust a twenty-pound note through the window, mouthing his thanks to the cabbie who pushed it away, 'On the 'ouse, Minister, yer need it more than me.' He threw his head back in raucous laughter.

Dempsey pocketed the note, shot across the tarmac, ran up the steps to a side door. He pushed past the security policeman. Taking the stairs two at a time, he reached the first floor, plunged down a passageway and into his office. He crossed to his desk and snatched up the phone.

'Private Secretary, please.' He waited. His heart pounding. The sweat pouring off him. A voice came on the other end of the line.

'Jeremy? Hugo Dempsey here. Sorry to trouble you.' He caught his breath, tried to sound normal. 'Just wanted to know if the Ambergris freeze order has gone out yet?'

There was a pause.

'Well, has it gone?' Dempsey couldn't hide the sharpness.

'Yes. Sorry, Minister. I was just checking, Yes. It went out fifteen minutes ago. It's effective as from then and the press release has been emailed to all news outlets.' The private secretary waited. 'Is that all, Minister?'

Dempsey slumped in his chair. 'Yes, that's all, Jeremy. Thank you.' He buried his face in his hands. One hundred and fifty million dollars had just vanished from his grasp.

The private secretary put his phone down, pulled a handkerchief out of his pocket and wiped his thin, rather angular face. Shit. That had been close. He was new to the job of working for this minister and it seemed already as though Dempsey was everything he'd been warned about and more. Demanding. Dictatorial. Lethal to be with if things weren't done properly.

'Joss,' he called out to his own secretary in the next office. They'd stayed on to finish some work and it was late, but when she appeared through the door she still looked as neat and unruffled as she had that morning.

'Joss! That damned freezing order . . . Get the bloody thing off now will you. And send those emails to the press.'

She looked at him. 'Was that Dempsey on the phone?'

He returned her glance. 'Yes. Bastard wanted to know if the orders had gone out yet.'

'Don't worry I'll send them right away. He'll never know we did the job a bit late.'

THIRTY-ONE

Katya arrived in London after an exhausting journey from Panama. She'd been brought back by an encrypted email from John.

The plane had been packed full of noisy holiday makers. The luggage was delayed getting onto the carousel and there had been a long queue getting through customs. While she'd been waiting, she had reread it, trying to interpret its meaning. It was terse. She was to come back to G8 HQ immediately. He had never summoned her in quite such a peremptory way before. Had she slipped up? Had she been recognised in London on her way to Panama? Had Paliakov sensed she'd made some mistake while she was with him in Berlin – or Panama? He was a weasel— was always sniffing for scandal. After leaving her at L'Esperanca café, he had disappeared off somewhere with Mikhail and she hadn't been able to contact him again before she left. Did that perhaps mean he'd evaded her and reported her to G8?

As she'd watched the luggage slowly circulating, her thoughts had continued to tumble. Had Dempsey decided to turn on her? He could have done so—she knew she couldn't trust him. He still hadn't contacted her to tell her whether he'd managed to stop the freeze order against Ambergris, but she hadn't dared to contact him to find out in case G8 intercepted the call. Had his wife heard about her evening visit to his apartment? Was that the trouble? Or had he simply been piqued when she rejected him?

All these questions were still racing through Katya's mind as she climbed into the G8 car John had sent to meet her at the airport and to drive her to Basingstoke.

As the car pulled up outside G8's headquarters, the questions were still unanswered. She left her suitcase in the car, went through security and walked reluctantly, to the main G8 conference room. She had never felt this confused. It was as though she was wading through fog—an experience she'd not had since those first days at St Petersburg University so long ago. Days she'd hoped she had put behind her, days when she had been determined to go her own way only to be jerked back by her father who, as always, had her on a tight leash. But the emotions she'd felt back then were rising in her again. The moment she'd decided to strike out for freedom she'd found herself at the end of an invisible leash once more. This time it seemed as though John was her captor.

She reached the conference room door and stood there for a moment, as unprepared for this meeting as she had been for those with her father. She was going in blind. She took a deep breath to calm her nerves.

Opening the door, she saw John was waiting for her, sitting at the steel console, looking grim. She forced a smile, 'Hello, John. You don't look pleased to see me.'

'What happened in Panama?' He shot out the question.

She stalled, waiting for some further clue as to what he wanted from her. But he said nothing more to fill the silence between them.

'I would have thought that was obvious,' she said, quietly.

'Don't play for time with me, Katya. I asked what happened and, since I already know, I expect a straight answer.' He flung the words at her.

In a split second, Katya decided to act defensively—to blame Paliakov, 'If you must know, I didn't *do* anything. Paliakov disobeyed my instructions. Instead of waiting for me to arrive, he had already transferred the money to Rosa's account.'

John's look was harsh, uncompromising. 'Why didn't you arrive before he made the transfer?'

She silently cursed herself. She was unprepared. She should have known he would follow up her answer with this very obvious question. She could either bluff it out with a story of delay in Madrid, or confess to him about her unauthorised visit to London.

'I didn't understand there was such urgency, John.' This sounded a little bald, so she quickly played the sympathy card. 'I was beat, so I decided on a quick transit in London to freshen up - recover from El Bayedh— before heading for Panama.' She almost added, "Any objections?" but decided against provocation. That could come later.

John studied her long and hard.

She'd seen that look before, when G8 agents had gone off net. He used it to shake the truth out of them. She decided to hold the look, stare for stare. She was Russian, after all. And Russians did not back down. Especially not one who'd been a street kid used to fighting her own corner.

The silence was broken by Lev's voice, coming from the large plasma screen. Katya hadn't even noticed that he was online and watching them. 'I told you, John,' his Russian accent stronger in his plea in mitigation, 'Katya is not at fault.'

John turned abruptly to face Lev, his lips drawn back in anger.

'Yes, yes—' Lev cut in before John could say anything more— 'she should have gone straight to Panama. But even you didn't know, when you first gave her your orders, exactly what Dempsey was up to.'

Katya froze. So it *was* Dempsey who'd brought this down on her head. Had he given her up? Had G8 traced him using his burner to talk to her? It had to be the burner. And her number was on the burner's chip.

Dimly, through the brain fog, she heard Walt speaking.

'We should have known that man would rush off and issue the freeze order before talking to us again. He's a maverick.'

Lev smoothly drew Katya into the discussion, 'What do you think, Katya?'

Katya was completely at sea now. She knew exactly what they were talking about—the freeze order - but she wasn't meant to know about it. It was Dempsey who had told her, not John. She feigned ignorance. 'I'm sorry, Lev, but I'm unsighted on this. What's this about Dempsey?'

John didn't wait for Lev's reply. 'If you'd been in Panama on time you would have held back Paliakov and made sure of the transfer from Rosa's account to G8 .'

Lev continued to pursue his role as peacemaker. 'Katya, what John is telling you is that he requested that Dempsey issue a Treasury order freezing all assets held in British territories. And,'—he went on even as John tried to interrupt— 'this is a problem for us because Cartwright's money, and most probably the Gadaffi cash as well, which Paliakov transferred out of Panama— is now sitting in Rosa Rulenski's account in Ambergris where thanks to Hugo Dempsey it is now frozen.'

Katya could hardly believe what she was hearing. Relief made her burst out laughing, 'Is *that* all.'

'Yes. That is all. Just as I've told John.' Lev glanced down from the screen at John, 'But not with quite so much levity as you.' He shrugged, the way Russians do when making an argument that they know to be hopeless, 'You must do something about your sense of levity, Katya. Anyway, however much John wants it to be so, the freezing of the funds we are after was not your fault. Dempsey told no-one here that he planned to impose the freeze so fast. It was a complete surprise. As far as we were concerned, he was simply going to talk to the prime minister about possibly freezing assets in British territories. None of us expected him to go off and do it on his own without informing us. Being Russian and, therefore, a little paranoid, I personally suspect Dempsey did it to spite John for giving him such a rough ride the other day. Dempsey showing who's boss.'

'This isn't getting us anywhere,' John grunted. 'Somehow we've got to get our hands on that money in Ambergris.'

Katya had only half- listened to this exchange as she was already rapidly re-assessing her chances of getting hold of the El Bayedh scam cash. Her first conclusion was that any thoughts she'd had about having a life with John were now pie in the sky after the way he'd just treated her. Trying to shift the blame onto her for Dempsey's stupidity meant John definitely didn't care for her. She realised she had been fanciful about that. With that decision made, the fog cleared suddenly. She saw a chance to get Dempsey involved again.

'I'm sorry, John, but I don't understand the problem. Surely, all we have to do is ask Dempsey to lift the freeze again, thereby allowing us access to Rosa's Ambergris account. Then we can transfer her money to us. I can handle that easily, if you agree.'

John spoke slowly, spelling out his reasoning as if he was talking to children. 'We have announced to the world, through the press, that Britain's overseas territories are awash with criminal cash. That for years we've turned a blind eye to this worst form of corruption. And therefore, today, we have frozen their assets.' He paused as if to lend emphasis to what he was about to say. 'What you and Lev are effectively suggesting is that the first thing we now do is to further admit that we spent years tracing half a billion of Gadaffi's illegal cash, only to transfer it, for some odd reason, to a known organised criminal's account and then accidentally freeze it there, very conveniently, for her own use! Now we want to issue a

waiver so that we can instead transfer those criminal assets to G8.'
He shook his head at the stupidity of their suggestion. 'How is that
going to look to the public? Do you also expect me to explain it to
the Prime Minister?

It's political suicide. Certainly, the Prime Minister would veto
the suggestion.'

Lev put forward the obvious solution. 'Then we keep the
assets in Rosa's account until the fuss dies down and the freeze is
lifted. After that we transfer them to us.'

John kept his voice low, speaking in deliberate tones. 'There
is a further serious side to this. The island of Ambergris is governed
by locally elected Ministers. One unforeseen outcome of our
freezing their assets is that they may decide to retaliate. They have
the right to go independent, to leave British jurisdiction.'

'That's not in their interests, surely?' Katya said, trying to
sound convincing. 'They're too small to survive if they go
independent.'

'Come on Katya, you of all people know the government on
Ambergris Island is wholly corrupt. They'll go independent at a
moment's notice if provoked, and without warning – simply to lift
the freeze. Besides which, they are in Rosa's pocket. One word
from her, matched by a large bribe, and they'll do everything they
can to help her scatter all her assets around the world. Can you
imagine Rosa's reaction if she finds she's got the Gadaffi cash in her
account as well as her other wealth? The political fallout from this
mistake can lose us G8. The UK government will close us down.'

Katya saw she had nothing to counter this; decided to change
her tactics to appear to be on side. She became suddenly businesslike, reverting fully to her role as G8's chief of operations. In that
guise, she had only one purpose: to mastermind a strategy to
mitigate this disaster. 'What do the Ministers have to do to achieve
independence? Can we stall them?'

John nodded. 'I asked a friend at the Foreign Office. And he says we can.'

Lev choked slightly as he started to mouth words of protest, his eyes wide in alarm.

'Don't worry, Lev, this friend of mine doesn't know anything about our problem, or anything about our losing the Gadaffi money. I put the question to him as a hypothesis.'

Lev relaxed. He squashed out his cigarette in an ashtray on his desk.

John went on. 'To gain the island's independence, the current party in power, the Ministers, first have to have an election and then, if they win, they hold an independence referendum.'

Katya moved swiftly on to the next question. 'When might the Ministers schedule an election'

'Good question. Actually, they are in the middle of a general election right now. Polling is in four weeks.' He paused. 'To answer your question simply, Katya, – the Ministers have to be stopped from winning so that their opponents take over—a government friendly to Britain.'

Katya suddenly saw her chance. She had to get to Ambergris. Once there she might create the opportunity to get her hands on the money. She became persuasive.

'Then I'll take a team to Ambergris and I'll stop the Ministers winning. Can't be difficult to subvert an election in a small place like that-'

John cut across her, 'Sorry to upset a good plan but the opposition party is barely viable there. The Ministers can afford to buy what votes they need so they will win the election, and they will certainly make sure independence will follow. I doubt they'll even wait for a referendum. So there's no point interfering.'

Katya felt she was being propelled by some unseen force. She was going to get that money, come hell or high water. It was due to her and, as John was no longer part of her plans, it would buy her freedom. She was going to go as far out on a limb as she could to get it.

'Who's leading the opposition?' she asked crisply.

'Someone called Peter Thomas. He's an islander, he's honest and, I understand from my contact, a thoroughly good and decent man.

Katya's felt her heart jump. Peter Thomas. A name from the past. She couldn't believe it. Could it be the same Peter Thomas that she knew? She turned to look at Lev. 'Did he go to St Petersburg university? There was a Peter Thomas there with me, but he was Jamaican, I think.'

'Yes. That was the name. Did you really know him?'

Katya felt light hearted, she knew John couldn't refuse her going to Ambergris if there was the slightest chance of G8 getting out of this mess. 'Yes. And very well.' She caught the look on Lev's face. 'No, not *that* well, Lev. He was a good friend, very bright, just the person to win this election.' She hurried on. 'Look, I'll take the team with me. They're in Miami on R and R at the moment. I'll speak to Yas. Helping me to rig the election so Peter wins will be right up their street.'

John's expression was one of pure disbelief. It was plain he dismissed the plan as haywire.

'John, what other plan do you have?' she asked.

He remained silent.

Lev murmured. 'She's right, John, what option do you have?"

Walt snorted. "If the UN even get so much as a whiff of news that you're rigging that election they'll be all over G8 like a rash. We'd never survive. Don't, John—I repeat *don't*— get caught with your hand in that cookie jar.'

Katya wasn't about to let the opportunity slip. 'Walt, G8's whole raison d'etre is to out- manoeuvre the corrupt. I know every trick there is, and I don't care how I use them.' She looked directly at John. 'Back me up, John. If G8 can't get away with rigging this election by covert means to get the corrupt ministers out of power, we're hardly worth our government funding, are we? And you'd never have appointed me operations director, right?' She smiled.

Silence.

Katya pushed on. 'Give me four weeks in Ambergris and I guarantee the Ministers will be voted out.'

John knew he had no alternative but to let her go. If the Ministers were re-elected and went independent, the outcome for G8 would be disastrous.

Lev read John's thoughts, added some pressure. 'You have to let her go, John. Agreed, Walt?'

Walt still had reservations 'What if Katya's interference in the election is discovered? '

John made up his mind. 'Yes, go Katya, but Walt's right. Things could go wrong. You can't be hung out to dry— so I must be there as well. I'll arrange to join you.'

THIRTY-TWO

The next day, with everything packed and ready, Katya left her apartment for Heathrow and headed for Ambergris Island. Betsie had waved her off saying she really should stop gallivanting around the world and settle down. She'd added that she'd packed extra suncream into Katya's bag, "to make sure you don't get burnt by that awful Caribbean sun". Katya smiled, dear Betsie, she never left London but always found ways of caring for her no matter where she found herself in the world.

The check-in desks at Heathrow weren't busy, so she got through quickly for a change. Her flight was immediately called and, to her surprise, she found she'd been upgraded to first class - maybe John had forgiven her.

Landing in Miami, she checked in with Yas. In short time Yas had arranged passage in one of the small ex-wartime LST ships that still plied the passage from Miami to the Caribbean islands. Their tonnage and draught made them popular for navigating the small and shallow harbours in the outlying islands and Yas had taken advantage of this to load on the seven team members and a large cargo. Building materials, white goods and tinned provisions made useful bribes to counter those of the Ministers in the election.

Katya left Yas to change fifty thousand dollars into small bills to hand out to voters who preferred cash. Also, to purchase half a dozen quarry dynamite sticks and a plunger detonator - to be ready for all eventualities. She then boarded the Effendi Air Shuttle at Miami Airport, bound for Ambergris.

The aircraft didn't fly above ten thousand feet and the view from Katya's window was spectacular as the Caribbean Sea below showed her its myriad colours. But none of this prepared Katya for her first glimpse of the island—a spectacular sight suddenly visible out of the window next to her as the aircraft banked over the sea on its approach to Ambergris Airport. She gazed in awe at huge columns of yellow and amber coral heads, white water lazily washing over them. This was Ambergris— thirty miles long and twenty miles wide, rising out of the Silver and Navidad shoals near Cuba, surrounded by a maze of thousands of coral heads rising hundreds of feet from the ocean floor. Calm and beautiful in good weather, the place became a trap in the storms that regularly pounded it.

The aircraft's port wing dipped suddenly and the Finance Centre came into view, now holding six hundred banks and thousands of trust companies, dozens of insurance and mutual fund corporations.

The Finance Centre had been founded years ago by an ex-special forces officer, Major Tony Fanshaw, who, on retiring from the British army had bought an old sponger boat and set off. He'd found excitement in navigating his way to Ambergris. And, finding he loved the fishing life style of the islanders, had stayed. He'd bought himself a huge, falling down old building overlooking the sea and over the years had transformed it into the now luxurious Effendi Club. He'd had a passion for tennis and had built tennis courts for which the club became famous. And, as the island had no taxes, he'd set up a bank for the islanders, and for the travellers who came to his club. From there the island had prospered and grown into a tax haven.

One of the banks, she was sure, would be jealously guarding

the Gadaffi money and the three hundred million El Bayedh cash she was chasing.

Her mind turned to the election she was here to rig. Ambergris had become a stark political battlefield, where criminally inclined politicians were pitted against those who wanted their island to become clean and god- fearing. Not so subtle bribes - handouts for house repairs, furniture, white goods, donations of cash to the churches for the needy, and promises to builders of planning permission or high land prices for a development brought willing voters for the unscrupulous Ministers. These politicians were backed by thugs and Yardies, too. Brute force was another persuasive measure they used. Shop keepers found their stores torched and accidents happened to homes if the owners misguidedly voted for change.

The thought excited her. If crooks could win votes using these methods, she could use them to rig the whole election.

THIRTY-THREE

The plane jerked as the aircraft landed, and Katya's eyes focused on the airport. A single, one thousand five hundred metre runway was laid out alongside a small whitewashed, red-tiled terminal building, its entrance covered by a tall archway of trailing pink bougainvillea. Half a dozen medium haul jets stood on the apron, flanked on either side by rows of private aircraft, executive jets, twin- engined Ambergris Air Taxi Aztecs and a couple of crop dusters.

The morning sun's warmth embraced her as she walked down the aircraft steps. With the gentle heat, almost imperceptibly, came little shimmers of a damp breeze, just stirring the leaves of the banana trees and coconut palms lining the terminal building. Carried to her on the breeze, stronger even than the lingering smell of aviation gas, drifted a tantalizing perfume. Oranges? Nutmeg? Mangoes? Frangipani? Katya couldn't quite place it. She just breathed it in, feeling her limbs relax.

'Effendi Club, ma'am?'

The local boy standing there was diminutive, and striking in appearance, wearing a red fez over his black hair, and a startlingly white djellaba that enveloped him. Katya hadn't expected the staff of the Effendi Club to be dressed in Moroccan clothes and was amused to see a pair of Nike trainers poking out beneath the skirts of the long robe.'

'Yes, how did you guess?'

The boy pointed to the new Head Gravity Pro tennis rackets

clutched in her left hand. 'Only place to play tennis here. My name's Lewis. I take you through immigration, customs. Your bag please. Rackets, too. You give me large tip, pretty lady.'

Lewis drove to the Effendi Club as if his life depended on it. Katya's Travelex bag bounced about in the huge empty open body space behind the cab. The truck shot through a gateway carved out of a six-foot high, coral stone wall that stretched away on both sides for a good half a mile.

'There she is. Effendi Club.' Lewis ignored the frantic waving of a golfer as the Chevrolet's tyres squashed his ball into the paving. 'Beautiful, isn't she?'

That wasn't the word that immediately sprang to Katya's mind as the minarets and arches of the Effendi Club came into view. Preposterous, bizarre— but not beautiful, unless one was fond of Arab architecture in a Caribbean setting.

'Pink gin at midday,' Lewis said as he climbed out of the truck. 'I take your bags.'

'I don't like pink gin,' Katya grimaced.

'Only pink gin midday. Club rule.'

She began to wonder whether it was such a good idea to use this club as cover. The feeling increased as the shadowy interior revealed itself. It matched the exterior's middle eastern theme. The floors were tiled with pale blue, green, yellow and brown mosaic tiles picturing ancient Turkish ruins. Intricate woven tapestries hung on the walls. Pale blue painted wood and metal fretwork windows allowed tiny streams of light to filter into the darkness. A whirring ceiling fan added to the atmosphere of forgotten empire.

A short man of enormous girth greeted her with a large smile, his fez bobbing up and down as he bent over Katya's hand.

'Ms Petrovna, a pleasure to welcome any friend from Russia. I'm Emanuel, the day manager. Your first game is at 4pm. I regret it is not earlier but I thought you might like to get accustomed to the heat first. I trust I did the right thing?'

'First game?' Katya hadn't checked in yet.

'Tennis, Ms Petrovna. Tennis. That is why you came, is it not?'

'But checking in . . . Shouldn't I check in first?'

'We never check in here, ma'am. This is a club. Not a hotel. Now, pinkers is at midday. You'll just have time to see your room and freshen up beforehand.'

'Pinkers!' Katya almost groaned. That old colonial expression for gin and angostura bitters just about summed up the place. It was as far removed from reality as the ludicrous fez this man was wearing and the fact that everyone insisted on calling her ma'am. She decided to exert some influence. 'Where's the bar?'

'The Elgin bar, ma'am, through there.' He pointed into the gloom where she could just discern a dark wooden doorway.

'Twelve o'clock it is then.' Emmanuel beamed at her.

Lewis tugged at her elbow. 'This way, Ma'am, I'll take you to your room, you really want to go there first.'

Katya gave up, followed him through a fretwork doorway along a gloomy, dark mosaic-tiled passageway where sandalwood chairs and tables, many inlaid with ivory, hugged the walls. Lewis opened a solid teak door to a bedroom at the far end. She was met with a blinding light coming from a series of fifteen-foot high arched windows arranged around the huge room. There was only one wall, the rest were elegant thin pillars holding the glass panes. Sunlight streamed onto a thin, richly woven pale blue and cream Turkish carpet covering the middle of the floor. Katya strode across it, only half seeing the elegant carved teak furniture as she was drawn immediately to those fantastic windows and to the spectacular view.

The room was on the edge of a bluff. Twenty feet below her

a coral cliff split the waves that came marching in, emerald green and curling white, the colours thrown into sharp focus against the blinding blue of the sky. She'd never seen such a spectacular view. After the gloom of the Club's main entrance hall, the surprise was sudden and dramatic.

Whilst Katya showered and changed into a short sleeveless cream linen dress and cream sandals she reviewed what she knew of Peter Thomas, the man she was to rely on to lead the opposition against the Ministers. She had met him in St Petersburg during the early days of Russia's overthrow of communism. He was studying for a Masters' Degree in Politics, looking to a future where Russia would need to use the services of a tax haven to hide assets in case the drive for democracy failed and communism took over once again. They were both members of the Bugurusian Flying Club and had enjoyed vying with each other to perform ever more dangerous stunts. They hadn't had a relationship - the word jarred as Katya visited it, hastily putting aside a bad memory of her disastrous love affair with one of the postgrad students - but they were friends for the year he was there. They'd lost touch as most graduates do and hadn't seen each other for years until Katya had emailed him to say she was visiting Ambergris for a holiday.

Peter Thomas was a local islander. His mother, Tina, had been one of five daughters of an Ambergris fisherman who had been Fanshaw's closest confidant. On his return to Ambergris after his studies in Russia, Peter had gradually built up a business empire, becoming first a canning factory owner, then a property developer, then a banker. In all these roles he demonstrated all the talent and charm of the Caribbean people. His reputation for straight dealing attracted blue chip clients from around the world. After Fanshaw's death, he spoke out against the corruption of the Ambergris government whenever he could. Two years ago, he had set up an opposition party and had been elected its leader. In retaliation, the Ministers vilified him and his party.

This was the man Katya was going to help to win an election. He seemed tough enough and skilled enough, but it remained to be seen whether he was prepared for the real dirt of the fight ahead.

Katya walked into the Elgin bar, reluctantly took her pink gin and approached a group of people standing at one end of the dark room.

She decided to plunge in. 'Good afternoon. Katya Petrovna, I've just arrived . . .' She looked around the group. 'Can you tell me, why is this called the Elgin Bar? I thought Elgin stole the marbles from the Greeks so that's not very consistent with the Turkish architecture, surely?' She gave one of her most charming smiles.

She felt a hand on her elbow and heard a laugh.

'Hi Katya! So, you're still wanting to know everything there is to know, eh?'

Recognizing the voice and the laugh, Katya turned quickly around and gave a big smile as she saw Peter standing there.

He held out his hand. 'It's great to see you again!' He looked admiringly at her, 'it's been ages, how are you? What have you been up to? Welcome to Ambergris I hope you're making a long stay - I'm going to enjoy showing you the island.'

'Still with so many words, Peter? Yes, and that would be great and yes, it's great to see you too.'

They both laughed as Katya took the outstretched hand. He hadn't changed much since their university days - medium height with dark brown studious eyes, short curly black hair and a dark complexion. His lightweight suit hung lightly over his broad-shouldered frame and his white shirt cuffs showed off his well-manicured hands. He wore his thirty-eight years well.

Speaking with a slight American accent he said, 'We have so

much to catch up on. You were asking why the bar is called Elgin. Fanshaw, the man who built this place, hated the Greeks, something to do with his time in Cyprus during the troubles so for him he'd found the perfect name.'

'He must have been an unusual man.'

'He was. I knew him well. You would have liked him.'

They sat at the bar and chatted about their university days. Katya avoided talking about the election, there were too many people who might be listening. After a couple of drinks, Katya swallowing the pink gin in quick gulps to hide the flavor, Peter suggested he took her to lunch. Not at the club, but somewhere else very special on the edge of the ocean where, he said, they served the best conch fritters in the Caribbean. They drifted out into the sunshine, two old friends who had just met up again. Katya was pleased, relieved. Peter Thomas was as charming as ever and with his calm manner and energy looked as if he would be a very good operator indeed. She took his arm.

THIRTY-FOUR

Katya met Peter the following day for a game of tennis. She'd changed into a white tennis dress and, carrying one of her Head rackets, she'd made her way down the sandy path outside the Club which led to the hard court.

She was too good for him and, at the end of the third set, she used her strong forehand to send a ball flying over the net to bounce next to the white tramline on his side. He lunged to his left to try and reach it. The ball spun off the edge of his racket.

He flung up his hands to signal defeat. 'Two sets to one, you win. Come on, I vote we have a drink. I'm exhausted, I haven't run around this much for years.'

They walked through the gate, made their way to a terrace at the front of the Club and sat down at one of the tables overlooking a spectacular view of the sea. It was cool there, the palm tree leaves gently swayed in the soft breeze throwing shadows like pianists' fingers on the white table cloths. A waiter appeared with a tall, ice misted jug of rum punch and some glasses which he put on the table.

Katya leant forward and filled two glasses with the punch saying, 'You don't have a wife?'

'No, I've stayed single, no time!' He laughed. 'How about you? Are you married or in a relationship?'

'No'

Peter looked thoughtful. 'That time with that bastard in St Petersburg still holding you back?'

Katya shrugged - looking out across the bay she could still feel the shock of that night in the restaurant – the noise of his chair scrapping back as he'd stood up; laughing as he'd told her the affair had all been a joke, a bet he'd had with his friends.

She pushed the thoughts aside and, smiling, handed one of the glasses of punch to Peter, raising hers in a toast. 'Let's drink to our first game of tennis since Russia and to you becoming Chief Minister.'

He looked understanding and then, realising she didn't want to talk about it, moved on saying. 'Lovely as it is to see you, Katya, I need to know more about what you want from me. Why all the secrecy?'

Katya drove straight to the point. 'G8 want you to win the election that's going on here Peter and then you'll be able to clean up the corruption - put an end to the moneylaundering. If you do that we will arrange for the freeze to be lifted and you can get on trading as a legitimate finance centre.'

'Just how am I going to do that, do you propose? The Government Ministers have already started buying voters and are scaring others into voting for them by using their bullyboy tactics.'

She challenged him. 'Does that mean I'm wasting my time here?'

He looked shocked. 'Yes – no – that's not fair, Katya. You're asking me to do the impossible.'

'Peter, the reason Britain imposed the freeze is that the Americans and Russians insisted on it. There's no argument - we're going to work together.'

He waited to hear what else she had to say.

She carried on. 'The less you know about what I'm going to do here, the better. You have a Party to lead and you need to get on with that. What I can tell you is that I have a G8 team of six people coming in from Miami to help me. Their job will be to canvas voters for you in the same way the Ministers canvas voters.'

A look of consternation crossed his face as he realized the implication of her words. He started to protest then stopped abruptly. 'There is a man by the gate who's just standing there and staring at you. Do you know him?'

Katya turned, amused to see who was interested in her. She wasn't surprised to see it was John leaning on the gate, because she had been expecting him. What took her breath away was the expression on his face. It changed the instant he saw her, but she knew a longing look when she saw one, and she was caught off balance by this first clear indication of the strength of his feelings for her. The last time he'd seen her he had been angry, suspicious as to why she hadn't followed his schedule for the Panama bank operation and she had resented him for it. Suddenly, that had changed - the look she'd seen in his grey eyes had made her aware that she was more strongly attracted to him than she had thought.

Abruptly, she became aware that she hadn't taken her eyes off him. She mentally shook herself, and sharply pulled herself together.

'John, good to see you.' She smiled a welcome as he came up to the table. 'When did you get in?'

'Just now. Have you met Lewis? He's extraordinary . . .'

She laughed, covering what she felt had been an embarrassing moment by saying hurriedly, 'That's not the only extraordinary thing about this place. And you haven't yet met Peter,' she paused, 'and no, I don't include him in the same category as Lewis.' She laughed.

Peter smiled, holding out his hand. 'Katya hasn't changed. Hello, I'm Peter Thomas, leader of the Corporate Party – well, of course you know that.' He laughed awkwardly. 'Welcome to Ambergris. Katya has told me a lot about you.'

Something in the slight possessiveness of his voice made John look at him sharply. 'A lot?'

The smile continued to hover around Peter's mouth. 'Well, a bit more, I think, than strictly necessary for our work.'

Katya frowned at him – she'd caught the tone of Peter's voice and knew his remark had been made mischievously to find out whether John was interested in her.

'But that's us Caribbean folk for you,' Peter added hastily. 'Shooting the breeze is our favourite pastime.'

'Must be a new pastime of Katya's,' John said tartly as he sat down in one of the chairs.

Katya quickly poured out a rum punch and handed it to him whilst making some comment about the sea and the Effendi club. Afterwards she couldn't remember what she'd said, she'd just wanted to put an end to an exchange that had revealed a warmth and a totally out of character hint of possessiveness in John. What was going on? Did John actually care about her? Was he jealous? She nearly laughed. John, her detached boss? It was absurd.

Brusquely she changed the subject. 'I've told Peter he must win this election and then he can clean up the place. And when that happens I've promised him we'll lift the freeze; the banks will be able to trade again and communications will be restored.' She avoided John's eye as she picked up the glass in front of her and nonchalantly sipped it through an orange and white striped straw.

John felt as if he'd stepped into a miasma. He couldn't understand why he had suddenly felt jealous when he had seen Katya with her head thrown back as she'd laughed with Peter. He looked around so as to give himself a moment to assemble his thoughts before saying, 'One thing at a time, Katya. But in theory she's right about the election, Peter.'

Peter shook his head. 'I've told Katya but she won't listen. The Ministers are already winning this election with their bribery and threats. They're even talking about making the island Independent, I've never heard that before.'

He saw Katya's eyes literally change colour from violet blue to dark green, as if they were heralding a storm at sea.

'Let them.' Her voice was challenging.

She ignored his dumbfounded reaction and leant forward to speak softly to John, letting her comments be heard by Peter over the noise of the waves below. 'I have told Peter about my G8 team coming in from Miami.'

Peter frowned, trying to recover. 'I haven't agreed to that, Katya.'

Katya leant her elbows on the table. 'I told you my team will go around the voters personally on your behalf and will distribute white goods to them, TV's, videos, that sort of thing - lobbying for your Corporate party.'

Peter ran his hand distractedly through his hair. 'I don't like it, I don't want my party linked with this sort of bribery, I just want my own people to do the electioneering.'

Katya left him no room to argue. 'Forget it Peter, your people are too soft; they wouldn't last five minutes before the Ministers' thugs frightened them off.' She used the straw to stir her rum punch. 'I need a list of all eligible voters. Especially the ones who are undecided - the floaters - the people who might be persuaded to vote for you. Those are the ones we need to target. And yes, we will be bribing them, but you can salve your conscience by knowing they'll keep the freebies.'

Peter was visibly shaken. He slowly sipped his drink to calm himself. 'They've had the same recipe for this punch since Fanshaw built the club,' he said inconsequentially as he tried to avoid any more argument for the moment.

No-one said anything.

Katya filled the silence. 'By the way, there's a load of timber and building materials coming in tomorrow as well. Four of my team are going to do repair jobs for the voters. Home repairs are always acceptable and you'll be happy as they don't look so much like a bribe. We can win a fair number of votes that way.' She had debated whether to phrase the next question delicately or whether to get straight to the point. She decided to be blunt while Peter was so off balance. She found his eyes with hers. 'Do you think bribes are going to be enough to win the necessary votes?'

Peter's face tightened. 'Violence you mean? No. I hate all that. We never had violence here until the Ministers brought in their Yardie thugs. I won't be a part of that.'

John looked at Katya. 'Plain enough for you, Katya?'

She jumped up. 'I'm going for a swim. Either of you coming?'

THIRTY-FIVE

The offices of the Ambergris Corporate Party were situated in an old clapperboard-clad building on the sea front near the harbour. It was a double storey house with an upper balcony supported by iron pillars fixed to the ground below. The wood was painted white; the pillars, shutters and double front door a bright yellow. In front of the building was a tarmac road which ran alongside the beach. The sturdy, historic structure represented the image of the party and their tradition of fair business practices.

It was the target of Katya's first operation to win the election.

Her team had arrived in Ambergris early that morning on the LST from Miami. She hadn't contacted them. They knew their orders and she'd left them to get on with their various jobs.

Irek was the first of the team to start the op. His job was to keep an eye on Wesley Jackson. Wesley was a prominent Yardie on the Chief Minister's payroll and, with his permanent scowl, heavy build and bright orange and green Rasta hat, he was well known as a man to be feared.

Late that evening, Irek watched Wesley stagger into his house after a long session in the local bar. Satisfied Wesley had settled in for the night, Irek joined Maxim on the edge of the road in front of the Corporate Party office.

Although there was no moon that night, the canopy of stars in the sky cast a ghostly glow which made the yellow paint of the office window shutters and front doors shimmer against the white walls. There was no one about except for Carla and Pierre who were pretending to be lovers on the beach below. They watched Maxim and Irek carefully plant a package next to the front doors and pay out wire as they walked along the deserted road towards the harbour. The next minute a violet explosion blew a gaping hole in the doors.

Carla and Pierre had gone straight to the police. Their story was simple. From the beach, they had seen this man plant a package in front of the building. He'd run away but it was easy to follow his bright orange and green Rasta hat to his house.

Next morning Wesley Jackson was arrested. The Chief of Police, who was responsible for this arrest, quailed when, shortly afterwards, the Chief Minister barged into his office yelling that Wesley was innocent. The Chief of Police bravely pointed out that he'd had no alternative but to arrest Wesley. Everyone knew Wesley's hat, no-one would believe he was innocent. But - the witnesses were tourists. They would go home at the end of their holiday. There would be no trial because the paperwork would get lost. The Chief Minister would have to be satisfied with that.

He wasn't, but neither did he want a riot just when he'd nicely got the election in his pocket. So, Wesley stayed in jail and the Chief Minister made a pious statement denying any involvement and blaming unruly elements.

THIRTY-SIX

The following day Katya and John met for breakfast on the terrace of the Effendi Club. They were interrupted by Lewis bringing them an urgent message from Peter telling them there had been a bombing the night before.

They drove immediately into town to meet Peter and to look at the damage. They left the car in a side street and joined the large crowd of onlookers standing in front of the blue and white police tape stretched across the front of the government building. The people there were strangely silent as if trying to take in the meaning of such a blatant attack on a political party - something that happened elsewhere in the world, not on Ambergris. Their shock was mirrored in Peter's eyes as he stared blankly at the blackened hole in the once bright yellow front doors.

Katya was the first to speak, seeking the most important information. 'Were any papers damaged, Peter? Taken?'

'No.' Peter was trembling with anger. 'We have that to be thankful for. It had to have been done by that little creep Wesley. He's one of the Ministers' Yardie thugs.' He wiped the sweat off his face with the back of his hand. 'It was those bloody Ministers, they're behind it.' He paused. 'Of course, they've denied any involvement.'

'Of course,' John repeated, his voice cold, calm, matter of fact. 'So, who else have they found to blame?'

'The Police Chief said they've arrested Wesley and that they're making an urgent investigation. Nobody believes it. The

Chief Minister will make sure Wesley will be cleared and I guarantee he'll be out of jail by next week.'

The three of them walked onto the blackened wooden deck in front of the building and stepped through the hole made by the explosion.

Peter inspected the damage, still horrified. 'How could they?'

Katya tested him. 'It's unforgiveable, Peter. You should retaliate.'

Peter shook his head. 'Violence, you mean? No. Absolutely not. I've told you I won't have any violence.'

'So, what are you going to do?' she asked.

'I've called a meeting tonight. Here. For everyone to see the damage and to see what these Ministers are capable of. It will be a peaceful candlelit vigil. We'll show them how a democratic political party should behave.' Peter's shoulders heaved as he fought to control himself. 'I'm sorry, Katya.' He made a little bow to John. 'I must go. My party officers want me.' He put out his hand.

Katya took it, her eyes grave. 'I'm so sorry, Peter. I'm just glad no one was hurt.'

She turned to join John who was already walking away. They pushed through the crowd, crossed the road and made their way down to the beach. The smell of burnt wood from the explosion following them. It slowly receded as a welcome, salty smell of fresh shellfish overcame it.

The fish market stood on the shore by the small harbour. It was made up of a jumble of metal stalls and coloured striped canopies. They were blindingly bright now the sun had burnt off the overnight dew. In the sky beyond them, small puffs of white clouds slowly circled the heat-haze that was shimmering on the horizon. There was a slight swell to the sea and, after climbing over the coral heads, the waves were dumping onto the beach.

Katya pointed the waves out to John. 'You know one of my

first operations was to bug a meeting of PKK terrorists by the Black Sea.' Katya laughed. 'All I got was the noise of the waves crashing on the sand.'

John smiled briefly. They walked on past the market and down onto the beach. John bent down, picked up a flat stone and sent it skimming across the waves. 'Well, you briefed the team well. They did a good job on Peter's Headquarters. Just the right amount of damage and just the sort of crude explosive device the Ministers' Yardies would use.'

'Thanks. I'll tell Maxim and Irek. I had to have a word with Pierre though.'

John looked at her - raised his eyebrows.

She gave a short laugh. 'Carla said he took his role on the beach as a tourist on a dirty weekend a bit too seriously.'

'That's not what we're here for,' he snapped, 'I hope you shredded him.'

'Not too much.' She gave him a sideways glance. 'They made good witnesses. And one never knows what might happen on an operation like this.'

'Well it's not going to happen to you.'

She looked away quickly, not sure what he meant by that. Awkwardly, she changed the subject. 'What a disappointment Peter is, refusing to take the fight to the Ministers.'

'He's got a problem. If he bombs their offices in return, they'll just retaliate and they have some very nasty help, so he'll lose that battle.' John tossed another pebble between his hands. 'The G8 computers deduced there's a hidden groundswell of hate for the Ministers— but it's yet to ignite into an uprising. It's our job to light the fuse to make that happen - and without Peter knowing.'

Katya wanted to change the subject – wanted to probe what John had said earlier, "well, it's not going to happen to you". She decided that trying to attract him in her usual style – as a provocative, sensuous, enigmatic Russian- wasn't working. She was sure there was a weakness in the glacial dam that he'd built around himself. There had been the failed affair with that girl in his past. If that girl had found a vulnerable spot, then she could too.

She kept her eyes on the foam from the surf rippling up the sand. 'It isn't easy being dispassionate, is it?'

'Dispassionate?'

She caught the pebble as it left his hand. 'Calculating, I mean . . . If I'm violent, it's in the heat of an operation. No time to think— I just react and thank god I'm alive at the end of it. But when I have to analyse, plan, manipulate, like I'm doing to Peter, it's so cold . . . hard to not care about the harm inflicted. I find it difficult to be human sometimes. Don't you?'

'I'm a mathematician. When I'm working, I'm a mathematician – and only a mathematician. Emotion gets in the way of the calculations, so I try to not go there.'

'But don't you need to relax? You can't relax without getting some kick out of life.'

'Getting kicks means not being in control. You ought to know that.'

She turned to him, the violet blue eyes alight with laughter. 'Well, you've seen my file. You know everything about me,' she paused, mischief lurking in her eyes, 'well, nearly.'

John didn't answer. She left the silence hanging until, abruptly, she pointed to one of the cafes on the shoreline. 'Come and have some clam chowder.'

She went to take his arm, but he shook her off.

'Why push me away?' she asked.

John looked past her, over her shoulder. 'We'll make a mistake if we mix our private lives and working lives.'

'I only suggested having clam chowder. How does that mix the two?'

He hedged, awkward. 'I didn't mean - I just meant it's a mistake.'

Katya drove on, seizing the initiative. 'Have you never made a mistake?'

'Not that I'm aware of.'

She tossed the pebble in her hand and threw it into the water. 'Everybody makes mistakes.'

He stopped walking. 'I'm a mathematician, calculating, remember?'

She looked directly at him, flicking the hair out of her eyes. 'I can't think of anyone I'd rather make a mistake with.'

His mouth hardened. 'We're not having this conversation.'

'Is that an order?'

'It's a fact.' He turned and angrily bent down to pick up another pebble. And then he abruptly changed subject. 'Cartwright's in Panama now, apparently, looking for his money. Paliakov kept watch on the Republic Bank after you left and spotted him going in. The bank clerk Paliakov recruited has reported to him that she told Cartwright his bank account had been closed for official reasons.'

Katya stiffened, she didn't want Paliakov anywhere near Cartwright. Trying not to sound too concerned she said, 'Why do we need Paliakov to tail Cartwright?'

'Because we don't know what money Paliakov managed to transfer into Rosa's account in Ambergris – or whether it included the Gadaffi money. As you know he was interrupted when he made the transfer from Panama to Ambergris before he could confirm what amount had been transferred. And we still don't know.' He looked at her. 'You were late getting to Panama, you remember?'

John went on. 'Dempsey's freezing order couldn't have come at a worse time. Any hint that we are trying to get into Rosa's account now could get back to Dempsey or worse the PM. And that'll be the end of G8. It's all down to the election. It's vital that Peter is elected.'

THIRTY-SEVEN

After Katya had parted from John, she met up with Yas down by the harbour. They mingled among the crowds in the busy fish market, unnoticed as they pretended to discuss the prices and variety of the wares on sale. Walking side by side, their heads bent together and occasionally jostled by an eager shopper, Katya briefly congratulated Yas and the team on the success of the op the previous night. Afterwards she briefed her on the next stage of the mission. Yas nodded her understanding of what she and the team had to do and drifted away to blend with the shoppers.

Katya spent the rest of the morning making sure everything was in place for their attendance at Peter's vigil at the Corporate Party HQ that evening.

She met John at the Club later that same day and they made their way out to the hired Volkswagen in the car park and drove out to Peter's HQ.

The roadway was soon cluttered with people on their way to the vigil. They all carried candles. Church candles. Large. Tall. Flickering and flaring in the faint evening breeze. The crowd was almost silent - only a low murmur of muted conversation could be heard as the throng of people wound their way to the meeting place. Katya noticed how well dressed the people were, even the children. She remarked on it to John.

'They're members of the Corporate Party.' He flashed back,

impatiently. 'Financiers, bankers, businessmen. Of course, they're well dressed.'

'No. You're wrong. It's the candles.' Katya replied.

'Candles?' he queried.

'They're church candles.' She turned to him. Put her hand on his arm. 'They are in their best suits and dresses because they feel as if they're going to church, to a burial service - they are mourning what feels like the end of their Party.'

Not for the first time John admired her reading of human nature. He wondered if his predominantly mathematical analysis of every situation was as productive. Katya had summed up the situation in two pithy, instant, sentences. She had summed him up in much the same way when they had talked on the beach that morning. He tensed slightly.

She took her hand away, aware of how wary he was.

'Well, I don't like the candles.' She gestured to them. 'The Ministers will see all this as a sign of weakness. These people are party members, they should carry placards, not candles. They should be shouting slogans. Instead, they really believe a peaceful demonstration will make an impact.' She frowned. 'Peter believes it as well. He's too honest to be a politician. The Ministers will eat him alive.'

They parked the car a little way from the office in a side road and got out. They walked back to the main road, joined the milling crowd and moved with it to take up a position on the sea wall, opposite the office.

Peter was already in the office, standing on the balcony with his fellow candidates, each of them carrying a candle. The murmur of the crowd stopped as Peter stepped forward carrying a microphone. He looked around. Raised the candle he held in his other hand.

'Thank you for coming. Thank you for showing concern that democracy -'

'Shut your face. Shut your fuckin' face.'

A man in a yellow Rasta hat had leapt onto a lamppost opposite the building. He scrambled up it, yelling. 'You fuckin' coconut pig.'

Another man dressed in a grey business suit clawed at the man's legs, shouting, 'Fuckin' Rasta shit. Fuckin' Ministers' man.'

He swore as the man on the lamppost fell on him.

The crowd reeled. Backed away from the flailing fists and feet. Knocked over a young girl. The girl's father lashed out. Shifting the crowd as he picked her up. People trampled on other people. Swearing. Throwing punches. Candles flying. Burning. Scorching. The chaos spread.

Peter shouted at them. Desperate. He stretched over the balcony. 'This isn't the way. This isn't -'

He got no further. A candle smashed into his chest. Hot wax sprayed over him. He reeled back. Clawing at his face. Staggered as a man burst through the door onto the balcony, screaming, 'Get the Ministers! Get the Ministers!'

The crowd started growling. An ugly, urgent sound. The fighting spread. More screaming as more candles burnt arms, legs, faces. The screams then drowned by the sound of sirens. Police. Climbing out of their wagons. Waving batons. Clubbing those nearest them.

The man on the balcony screamed louder. 'Get the bastards! Kill the fuckers.' His fists urging on the crowd.

The growl turned to a howl as the crowd became a mob. Hurling themselves on the police. Candles now weapons of hate. Burning, hitting. The police staggered back. Unable to cope. Started running. The mob screaming after them.

Katya broke away. Running blindly, away from the mob,

seeking shelter. She turned into a quiet alley, looked around for John, saw him just behind her.

She felt an irrational bubble of laughter well up inside her. 'I can't believe that went so well. Irek climbed that lamppost quicker than a cat.'

John shook his head. 'That fight under it looked so real.'

Katya got herself under control. 'There's no love lost between Irek and Pierre.'

'Who threw the candle at Peter?'

'That was Carla. She's got a good arm on her.'

John nodded at her. 'I'm impressed yet again. It was a good riot. Well organized. The Ministers will know they've got a fight on their hands now.'

Katya bent her head. Carefully peeled some candle wax off her arm. She looked towards the next operational step, taking care to be helpful and imaginative. 'Can I start sending the team out with the white goods? Once the voters hear about this riot, they'll think the Ministers might be vulnerable after all. A few gifts of fridges and televisions will soon have them thinking Peter is a shining knight.'

'Yes, good idea.' John replied. 'But tell our team not to be too obvious when they give the free goods away. Bribery is subtle, it's not as easy as starting a riot.'

Katya smiled. 'Hot blood, cold blood. I'll tell them.'

They came to the end of the alleyway. John looked out and started walking into the road. She followed him, picked her way through a rubble of candles, pieces of wood, stones and broken glass. It was eerily deserted, just the wind in the palm trees blowing debris through the square. The crowd had gone. Evaporated as fast as it had got out of control.

They found the Volkswagen where they had left it and drove

in silence back to the Effendi Club. They picked up their keys and walked down the dark passage to their rooms.

When they reached Katya's door, John walked on without a word.

'Aren't you going to say goodnight?'

'Goodnight.' He flung over his shoulder.

'You're not still going to be cold blooded? Not after all that excitement. Why won't you bloody relax?'

'Don't swear.'

'I know, I know . . . While an agent's using valuable seconds to swear, the enemy's killed them. I read the training manual.'

John turned and walked back to face her. 'If you're going to keep being indiscreet I'll send you home.'

'I'm sorry. It's just…' She reached out to touch his hand.

He pulled away. She looked at him, confused. 'Is it because I lost the team members at El Bayedh?'

A look of concern crept into his eyes. 'It's got nothing to do with them or your work - look we should both get some sleep - concentrate on the job.'

As she started to unlock her door, she said, 'One day you're going to find out that life runs on passion, not on mathematical analysis.' She opened the door and turned her head. 'When you do, you know where to find me.'

She shut the door behind her with a snap, leaving him standing there, bewildered. He raised his hand to knock, only to let it drop. He walked slowly to his room.

Her words had made him restless, uncertain. He knew he wouldn't sleep. He slung his clothes on a chair and pulled on a robe, poured out a brandy and took the glass with him out onto the balcony. The darkness of the horizon was broken only by the white horses of lazy waves and the intermittent flash of a firefly. He drank some brandy and leant on the railing.

He was going to have to face it, after all these years of shutting off emotional ties and walling up his feelings, Katya was dominating his thoughts. He had to admit to himself that he wanted her badly. Badly enough to take the risk of letting her through his defences.

THIRTY-EIGHT

Peter's house overlooked the sweep of a pineapple field which ran down a hill to the sea, half a mile away. On either side of the field the broad leaves of a banana plantation swept around and up the hill behind the house. The veranda was shaded, its coolness enhanced by the pale blue swimming pool just below it. Traditional Caribbean pale green wooden furniture was spread across the large area with bright coloured cushions on the loungers and chairs.

John and Katya sat on loungers talking with Peter. He was depressed, upset and disillusioned that his supporters had turned the rally into mob violence. 'How could my people have rioted like that? How could they? I've told them again and again, we don't meet violence with violence.'

He picked at the crease in his trousers. 'If we can't get that through our heads we're no better than the Ministers.'

Katya leaned forward, concern written across her face. 'No. You did win last night, Peter. Not in the way you wanted, maybe, but what you saw was your Party coming together, finding its resolve. When that candle hit you, suddenly your supporters had had enough. They're only human and they used the only way they had to get back at the Ministers for attacking their party - you.'

She got up, walked to the edge of the veranda and paused there. Framed against the flamboyant colours of oranges and reds behind her, she turned, allowing the effect of this to emphasise the words she uttered, 'It's the Chief Minister's corruption and greed that drove your people to riot last night. It's your people who represent what this island stands for, not the Ministers. Tell them that.'

John looked at her. Her face was animated, her fingers gripping the balustrade behind her, and she was tense, utterly absorbed in what she was saying. She was right, but he wouldn't have used those words, that passion. There was a depth to her, a compelling belief in her own personal values, that he'd failed to see before. So far, when they'd been together, he'd only seen the flirting, the casual frivolity, which seemed at odds with her formidable record in the field. But now that contradiction was explained. Beneath her seductive exterior was a fiery passion that went far beyond sensuality. It was the hidden guiding principle of all she did and all she thought. What she had said at the door of her bedroom last night suddenly became vividly real. . .

He dragged his thoughts from her, saying abruptly, 'Look, Peter, they rioted because they wanted to get back at the Ministers. Good. Now you'll get their vote. What more do you want?'

Peter jerked his head up. 'That's a terrible thing to say. People were hurt. Don't you care, John?' He stared at the G8 man, realization slowly dawning. 'You don't care, do you?' He gave a speaking look at Katya. 'Does he care about anyone?'

Katya moved away from the veranda rail. 'Don't look at me, I'm just here to do a job.' She added harshly, 'John's personal feelings are none of my business.'

Peter turned to John. 'You're a fool, John, if you believe that.'

John abruptly got to his feet. 'I've got work to do.' He turned to Katya. 'Has the lorry load of timber and stuff gone to the Coral Bay Ward?'

'Yes, it went down with Maxim earlier. I'll come with you.'

She stopped in front of Peter, 'Have you got that list of voters I asked you for - you know, the floaters, the ones we can buy?'

He nodded. 'Under lock and key in my office.'

She put a hand on his shoulder. 'Good.' She looked towards John then back at Peter, 'He does care, you know. He just has an odd way of showing it.'

She joined John and they walked down the coral lined stone path. The humidity from the low banana palms drenched them as they went towards the gate which opened onto the sand track where their truck was parked. She was deep in thought.

When Peter had blatantly asked John whether he was attracted to her, she had had no trouble telling him she wasn't interested in John's personal life. And, meaning every word of it, she'd heard the harshness in her own voice. Then she'd seen John's reaction to her words and instinctively knew she'd at last awakened some response in him. But it was too late and too ephemeral – not to be trusted. She had no intention of being seduced by him and then rejected. And she had no intention of abandoning her plan to get the money. But, she now realized, if John was attracted to her, he was malleable— and that could work to her advantage.

Carefully she set about her new strategy. She reached for the driver's door to the truck.

'As I just told Peter, you have an odd way of showing you care about me.'

Her inference jolted him. He had waited until the right moment to tell Katya how much he wanted her, but he'd been dismayed by the curt reply she'd given Peter when he'd asked if he cared for her. Now she'd given the opposite impression. It certainly wasn't the time to declare himself so he merely said, briefly, 'You're too sure of yourself. Get in.'

Satisfied, she didn't answer and climbed into the driver's seat.

'Can I drop you off in the town?' Her voice sounded flat, dull.

'Sure.' John, conflicted again, welcomed the opportunity to

be away from her. He needed time to recover from his bewildering changes of mind.

Katya pulled the truck up at a café alongside the beach, climbed out and stood for a moment looking at the vehicle as John, after sliding into the driving seat, drove away.

THIRTY-NINE

Katya waited in the café, watching the fishing boats lethargically being unloaded after a night at sea. Then she picked her way through the fish stalls and stacks of boxes of red mullet, grey grouper and green lobster tails to the headquarters of the Corporate Party. The doors had been renewed but the woodwork of the whole building was covered in splashes of candle wax and dirty smudges.

The ground floor was in turmoil. Election canvassers, secretaries, researchers, milled around trying to gain access to computers, calling instructions at the top of their voices. Katya pushed her way through the bustle and noise, a baseball cap hiding her auburn hair, sunglasses covering her eyes. She reached an open iron staircase, which led upstairs to where doors led off the small landing. She walked to a door to her left.

It led into Peter's office which took in the whole of the front of the building, with shuttered windows and wide French doors leading on to the balcony overlooking the sea. Two large ceiling fans creaked as the blades slowly circled over a large teak desk. There were leather chairs and a tall, glass fronted bookcase lined with leather bound volumes of old ledgers. It smelt of history.

Katya closed the office door behind her and slid a small wedge under it. She looked around. On the walls were paintings of ancient British sea battles. Swiftly she lifted each one, looked behind them, then replaced them. The desk was her next target. Each drawer opened quietly, revealing nothing, except spare writing pads, a bottle of ink, a muddle of pencils and pens. She meticulously returned all of them to their original position. There was no computer or laptop.

She studied the old leather-bound books standing upright and unopened for years - opened the glass doors, felt behind the only book that leaned sideways. Gently probed. There was a click. A shelf of books shifted downwards revealing a safe.

Quickly she opened her bag, took out a small digitalised scanner and settled it just below the safe lock tumblers. She watched the scanner, watched the numbers appear. Listened for sounds of movement on the landing outside. Pulled the safe door open. Dropped the scanner in her bag. Riffled through the papers in the safe. Not for long though. What she wanted was on top of the second file. Peter's list of floating voters - those to be bribed - the original, bearing his ink signature and date.

Suddenly, she heard the scuff of feet on the stairs. She hesitated, debating whether to go on or give up. She bit her lower lip, took out her iPhone. Photographed the list. Saving the images. Saving the names. Saving the signature and date Peter had written there. The steps sounded closer. A fine bead of sweat lined her upper lip. She closed the safe. Reset the combination. Controlled the urge to run. Pushed the shelves back. Closed the glass door. Bent and took away the door wedge. The actions mechanical, deliberate, perfectly drilled.

She heard a door open and close; then slipped out and down the stairs, un-noticed.

FORTY

The old fortress, built by Jem Tebbard a notorious 18th century pirate, housed the Ambergris International Telephone Exchange which linked the undersea telephone cable from England to Venezuela. The advent of satcoms had seen the last manager close the exchange and depart in 2005. Leaving the fortress bleak and empty, save for the antiquated equipment.

That is until the G8 computers assessed the equipment could still be used for international phone calls. It was a loophole in the freeze which had been closed by John.

Two nights after Katya had reached Ambergris, six Marines arrived by helicopter from the British Navy Guardship cruising off Bermuda. Only the sound of its blades chattering in the black night sky gave away its presence. It was invisible, even when it rose above the cliffs from its journey across the sea to skim over the rocky outcrop below the Telephone Exchange. It had barely touched down when containers began tumbling out of its side door followed by five Marines in battle fatigues carrying light arms. Silently they hefted the containers and fanned out.

Just before the helicopter took off, the commander jumped out. He was followed by a huge flat headed dog; as it landed, it let out a low growl.

'Shut up, Tank,' the commander hissed.

Nodding to the Marines, he led the way up the bouldered slopes to the Telephone Exchange. The crenellated outline of the old fortress which housed it was indistinguishable from the rocks in the inky blackness. It took less than a few seconds to open the door. They spread out inside. Their night vision goggles taking in the interior, the old switchboards, the wires, the old telephones and the old wooden stools left behind by the cash strapped company that had operated it.

'Bloody 'ell.' One of the squaddies muttered.

'Quite,' said the commander.

FORTY-ONE

That same night, two miles away from Tank's intermittent grunts as he chased out the rats littering the Telephone Exchange, Katya was hidden in a clump of casuarina trees on the Effendi Club golf course.

She was making a call on her mobile to Dempsey; the risk was high. G8 SUR was programmed to let through all G8 calls from agents as top priority but she knew they were logged and a direct call from Ambergris to Dempsey on her number would raise alarm bells. She had to redirect the call and disguise the number she was calling.

She connected her mobile to the laptop she'd bought in London. Not as cutting edge as the G8 ones but good enough for her needs.

The laptop processed the number through a series of cutouts until she heard a dial tone. Then Dempsey's voice.

'Hello.'

'You have a name to help me contact the Chief Minister?'

'I'll call you,' he muttered.

She moved away from the trees and made her way to the shore. Hugging the low cliff, she scrambled over the coral rocks to the clubhouse, picked her way up the bluff through the darkness to the Effendi Club, let herself in through her bedroom window. She smiled to herself.

She'd known John wouldn't be there.

FORTY-TWO

The morning room of the colonial-style Ambergris mansion was stuffed with antiques. Louis Seize furniture, gilded desks cheek by jowl with inlaid tables. The pictures covering the walls included two Pisarros, a Klimt, three da Vinci sketches and, incongruously, three Ionists. The Chief Minister was sitting in front of a cherry wood marquetry table wondering, for the hundredth time, how much his legal adviser was worth to own all this.

'Well?' he barked.

The man he had addressed was his statistician. He was a grandson of one of the Old Bay Street boys who had built Freeport in the Bahamas. The statistician coughed nervously, fingering his black tie.

'I'm afraid things are not looking so good.'

The Chief Minister's seat creaked as he shifted in it. 'Things aren't looking so good? I'll say. We can't get any money in or out of the island, all accounts are frozen. All Satcom communications cut. The Marines have taken over the landline Telephone Exchange. We've had a riot. The voters are changing their minds. The island's awash with new televisions, fridges and roof repairs. It's like a goddam Wal-Mart out there.' He stood up glaring. 'How fucking bad can things get?'

Linus Beecham, his legal adviser, moved towards the table from the shadows by the window where he'd been standing. 'The important thing is the election,' he said. 'We win and we can go independent. Get the marines out. Move our money again.'

The statistician turned to him. 'The margin is almost unworkable. If the voters keep leaving you at this rate you will have lost the election by tomorrow afternoon.'

The Chief Minister brought his hand crashing down on the table.

'It's goddam G8. Ever since the freeze, I bet they've been mucking in our pond. Their fingers are all over this mess.'

Linus Beecham put out a hand to steady the crystal decanters rocking on the table, holding on to the glasses as they rattled on their tray. 'G8 wouldn't dare touch the election. The UN would crucify them. It's the Corporate Party at the bottom of it.'

The Chief Minister snatched up one of the glasses and splashed in some gin from a decanter. 'Don't be a fool. The Corporate Party haven't got the money or the brains for this kind of disruption.' He tossed back the neat gin. 'And d'you think an unelected party can just put a call through to London and ask to have the marines take over our Telephone Exchange to stop our wire money transfers? No, it's G8 I tell you.'

Beecham took the glass. 'Then that's another reason why we've got to win the election.'

The statistician leaned forward tapping his finger on the table. 'Transfer our money to the Cook Islands. It'll be safe there.'

'Sure, why not, and we can follow it. Get the hell out of here.' The Chief Minister glared at him. 'How can we, you fucking idiot, with our communications knocked out?'

FORTY-THREE

The morning after Katya had called Dempsey, she climbed the steep basalt road to the Telephone Exchange. She wanted to see how she might be able to use the landline to transfer the three hundred million to a safe haven. The front door was closed. She pushed it open and stood with her back to it peering through the gloom of a dark passageway.

Tank stood there about six feet away. The dog was colossal. Black. His huge head lowered, rolls of fat gathering at his neck, long rangy front legs supported by paws the size of soup plates. Katya looked at him and swallowed. A signal for Tank's massive rear haunches to bunch up as he launched himself down the corridor. An earsplitting bark pounded through his flaring mouth. Katya stood stock still, preparing for the impact. It came with devastating force. Pinning her against the door, which slammed shut. The soup plates were on her shoulders now, the teeth an inch from her face. Suddenly a mammoth tongue leapt out. Slobbering over her ear.

She heard a posh English accent. 'You bloody idiot, Tank. Get off. Sorry about that. You're lucky. He must like you. He either licks you or tears your throat out. No knowing with Tank which it will be.' The commander came hurrying down the passage and held out his hand. 'Hello – You must be Katya. I'm Storky.' He grinned, answering Katya's unspoken question. 'Thus, christened after I delivered a baby in a bombed out building in Afghanistan.'

He looked at his artificial hand. 'Usually gives people a bit of a shock. Lost it just before I delivered the baby.'

Her eyes strayed to the Military Cross ribbon on his chest. Storky's eyes followed hers. 'No. That was for when I got Tank.'

Katya laughed. 'Having met him, I can understand why.'

'After this,' Storky raised his artificial hand, 'they transferred me to signals. Good of them really. I could still go on ops.'

Tank gave a low growl.

'Shut up, Tank. I was stooging around in Helmand when I met Tank. He came out of nowhere, kept hanging around my hide. Loped off when I gave him some chocolate, but he kept returning. Damn near got me sussed. I daren't move because I thought he'd kick up a fuss. Anyway, when the time came to withdraw I decided to take Tank with me. He'd kept me on my toes, obviously a bloody intelligent dog. I decided to train him. Devil of a job getting him back to camp, but I made it.' He paused to light a huge briar pipe. 'It took me just two days to find out Tank's as thick as four planks. Not an ounce of brain in him.'

Katya laughed. Pulled one of Tank's ears. 'Well, he fooled me.' She let go and Tank rambled back down the corridor, his tail thumping the walls on either side as he went. 'Thanks for seeing me. I want to use your secure equipment for a video conference with London.'

'Of course, come into the ops room.'

He turned and motioned Katya to follow him. What he had said about Tank was true. He was thick, but for ten years now the dog had one invaluable asset. Storky was always able to gauge the reaction of visitors to Tank's greeting. Most cringed in fear, losing his respect right away. Others gritted their teeth, fear of making a fool of themselves overcoming their terror. This woman remained ice cool, her face a mask of concentration as she analysed Tank's attack. She'd taken Tank's weight standing upright, knowing the door would help her take the impact, and she'd shown no surprise when she'd shaken his artificial hand. He knew he could work with her.

They reached the ops room. 'It's a bit of a shambles because the landline hasn't been used for so long, but it works.' He watched her as she took in the dusty switchboard and the old black telephones on a long desk below it. 'Not what you're used to in G8 I would think, still it's all we've got.' He nodded to one of the two Marines on duty. 'Fix up the video link, Beth. G8 in London.'

Beth nodded, humming quietly as she fiddled with the electronics she'd connected to a plasma screen on the desk. The screen lit up showing Lev and Walt.

Katya didn't hesitate. 'What's the score, Lev? Are we winning?'

Storky was startled at the abruptness of Katya's greeting. This man was surely her superior.

'As you can see, Katya . . .' Lev, unperturbed, pressed a button on his workstation. Across the screen in front of Katya there appeared data for each of the Ambergris Electoral Districts, the number of electors, the number committed to Peter, the number bribed with white goods and the number bribed with house repairs.

Lev took the ever-present cigarette from his mouth. 'For all practical purposes, you've done it. You are almost at the point of no return. Peter and his Corporate Party are on schedule to win.'

Walt cut in, 'Practical purposes are not practical results, though. Tell her how many more voters must be swayed to be certain and so we have a comfortable margin of error.'

Lev went on. 'The key is the Ambergris finance minister's aunt, Conchita Ybarra.'

'The Minister's aunt? Can you believe it?' Walt exclaimed.

'This Conchita Ybarra is well respected and her opinion goes a long way.' Lev stabbed his desk with his forefinger. 'She could gain us twenty votes. Buy her and you won't need to buy anyone else.'

Katya's mouth turned down. 'How are we going to turn this woman against her own nephew?'

Lev pressed another key on his workstation. The election statistics on Katya's screen were replaced by a bank statement. The balance showed fourteen million dollars. The statement was in the nephew's name.

Storky whistled.

She pressed the print key and watched the hard copy emerge. 'Thanks, Lev.' She nodded. 'Walt.'

The screen went blank.

Katya turned to Storky. 'Can we talk somewhere?'

He pointed down the corridor. 'Come into my office.'

Tank scrambled to his feet and let out a growl as his head hit the table. 'Do belt up, Tank'

Storky opened the door to a small chamber smelling of damp and must. It had been hewn out of the solid coral and it was pitch dark. He picked up a desk lamp and switched it on, casting a dim light onto the crevices in the walls, creating deep shadows there.

Katya went straight to the point. 'The problem I want to discuss is what happens if the Ministers win the election, declare Independence and decide to take over the landline to Venezuela.'

Storky cleared his throat. 'As I see it, once they can connect to Venezuela's banking system, they are into the international financial network.'

'In a nutshell,' Katya agreed. 'And once they've done that, the Ambergris banks can wire transfer all the money they like through the cable via Venezuela and into the world markets. It would take G8 months to track it all.'

Tank yawned loudly.

Storky ignored him. 'Well, if you want to stop them, it's no good demolishing this exchange. They can build another one in a week. At least, one good enough to handle financial transactions for big investors prepared to pay to get their money out.'

Storky fumbled in his desk drawer and took out a bottle of local rum and a couple of glasses. 'Sorry it's not vodka.' He poured out a couple of glasses. 'No room in our kit.'

She took a glass, thinking at least it looked like Yorsh. 'Could you blow up the cable offshore?'

Storky sipped his rum. His aquiline nose wrinkling slightly at the un-accustomed taste. He much preferred beer.

Tank broke the silence with a growl.

'It's no rations if you don't dry up Tank. Well, we've got scuba gear. That cable's only sixty metres down under the outer marker buoy.' He reached for a chart behind him, traced a depth contour line with a finger blackened by his pipe ash. 'See?'

'That's not deep water, the Ministers can get divers down and mend it easily. That's no use.' She leant back.

'No, they can't mend it,' he said, 'to do that requires specialist equipment, special wiring. They don't have the expertise here, it's all in the UK.'

There was a loud bark. 'Tank, you bloody mongrel. I take it if there's trouble you want me to blow the cable?'

Katya looked at Tank. 'Why bother?' Laughing, she pulled his ears. 'Just let him chew it.'

FORTY-FOUR

It was midday and Katya sat in the shade of Peter's garden, looking out across the plantation to the ink blue sea and the floating white clouds above it. She had been teaching Peter how to mix Yorsh. He was staggered at the amount of vodka she poured into the half pint of beer in her hand, and she'd laughed at him. 'You wouldn't have survived as a street kid in Moscow. This was all we could afford, cheap beer and cheaper Vodka. Street food, too. Palmeni, Chebureki, cheap but solid, like your conch fritters.'

He was fascinated. 'A street kid? You couldn't have been. You never told me when we were at Uni.'

'No.' She smiled, wryly. 'But, yes, I was one, from twelve to seventeen. They were my only friends, some mafiya types as well, but only for protection.'

'But your parents, why did they let you roam wild?'

'They were hardly ever there and if they were, my father wouldn't let me go out. He told me I must never make friends—people were dangerous, not to be trusted. He told me to remember he was KGB and that at all times he would know if I was obeying his rules. There was no way out, I had to stay at home - at least when he was there.' She shrugged as if it was the norm. 'You can imagine, the loneliness was stifling. There was no relief, not even at school. The rule there was the same: no talking, no playing - just work. When my parents were away, which was most of the time, I got out - after midnight when the housekeeper had gone to bed. And then it was easy. The apartment was on the ground floor and I could just climb out of my bedroom window.'

'Wasn't that dangerous in Moscow?'

'You remember Russia then, changing from communism to capitalism - the *mafiya*, the gangs in the streets, black-marketeers, men feeling up girls in nightclubs.' Her eyes lost their focus as she remembered. 'Yes, it was dangerous.' She paused in reflection. 'I only did it to be free – you know, escape the harshness and loneliness of home ... and yet... if I was honest there was a certain glamour in it. The music was so new, so way out - Pink Flamingo, Stop the Night.' Her eyes lit up. 'And the clothes – the knock offs from Prada, Gucci, the colours -' Almost guiltily she brought her gaze back to him, back to the present. 'But now I don't think about those days. Tell me about Conchita Ybarra -'

She broke off as John walked on to the veranda.

'I was just telling Peter about Conchita.'

John looked down into her glass. 'And about Yorsh, I see.' He picked up Peter's glass, sniffed it, "You drink that much Vodka and it'll kill you.' He looked across at Katya. Smiling grey eyes met challenging violet ones. He looked back at Peter. 'She's been drinking this stuff since she was born.'

'Yes,' smiled Peter. 'She told me.'

'Tell us about Conchita,' John said abruptly.

Peter was excited. 'If we can win over Conchita Ybarra we will definitely win that district. And if word gets out that her nephew has lost her vote, we will win other districts as well – I mean he's the finance minister. Voters are bound to ask why his aunts abandoned him.'

'But if we fail to win her over, she could do a lot of damage to you,' John said. 'What's so special about her?'

'She was a kind of midwife who became a guru. People

trusted her, sought her advice. She dotes on her nephew so people support him even though he's totally corrupt.'

'Yes, he's got a fortune stashed in his account here,' Katya said.

Peter looked at her. 'She doesn't understand her nephew's partying - running with the Yardies. She hopes he'll find his religion again which is why she still supports him.'

'Well, she won't when she hears about that cash he's sitting on,' said Katya tersely. 'But the question is, should we approach her?'

Peter paused. 'I know it's difficult, but I think she's worth approaching. You might persuade her to vote for us.'

She finished her Yorsh in one swallow, put down her glass. 'Well, if we're going to coerce her, there's no time like the present.' She turned to John. 'Let's go.'

FORTY-FIVE

Later that day, Katya climbed the path to Peter's house to tell him about her visit to Conchita. She was already regretting her decision to give him the good news personally. The rain was falling in stair rods, soaking her. The noise of it all was deafening as the droplets beat on the roof of the veranda and rattled through the banana leaves, the frangipani and the bougainvillea. The latter bowed deeply as the heavy drops exploded on it. They hung over her pouring a steady stream of water onto her jacket. She broke into a run only to stop to shake her foot after it splashed into a puddle. She was not happy, even less so when she saw John was already on the covered verandah, coffee cup in hand, watching her with an amused smile on his face.

'You should have worn that.' He pointed to the swimsuit in her hand.

She ignored him as she climbed the steps. 'Good afternoon, Peter, lovely day. I came prepared for a swim but not under your banana trees.'

Peter grinned. 'Welcome to one of our calmer days.'

'If this is calm, I'd hate to think what stormy is. It reminds me of the Black Sea.' She glanced at John. 'Squally.'

'Don't blame me, Katya, I told you to bring wet weather gear, it was you who packed swimwear.'

'Is that what I should be wearing?'

Peter laughed at John's embarrassment. 'You're not going to pass up that offer, are you?'

Katya ignored him. 'Conchita Ybarra is now on board. We need to talk about that.'

Peter put down the mango he'd begun peeling. 'I was telling John I don't really believe it, she's always voted for that bloody nephew of hers.'

'Conchita was bought the moment she found her nephew had stashed away fourteen million dollars. She'll help a further swing in votes to the Corporate Pary. And that ties up the election. What's important now is what you're going to do after you've won it.'

'That's easy.' Peter replied. 'I'll keep the freeze in place until every account in the island has been thoroughly investigated.'

The rain stopped abruptly as if evaporated by the sun emerging from the clouds.

He picked up a couple of lemons and squeezed them into a jug.

'How did you persuade her to vote for me?'

Katya looked hard at John. 'By him being brutal.'

John returned the look. 'You didn't have to soft soap her. We had her nephew's bank account details— that's all we needed.'

'She's an old lady.'

'She's an operational target.'

Katya mentally cursed herself. She didn't need this bickering. The last thing she needed was for John to carry out his threat to send her back to London and G8. She searched for something to say.

Peter stopped pouring rum onto the lemons in the jug and looked uncertainly for a moment from one to the other. The tension needed to be sorted out. They clearly needed to spend some time alone together.

Suddenly, he put the jug down. 'Do you mind if I leave you? I've got to get down to the office and brief the election committee.

You two stay here and use the pool. Ask the staff if you need anything. Enjoy your rum punches – or Yorsh if you want it.'

He waved away their protests and walked down the veranda to his car. Hooting the horn and waving goodbye, he left them alone.

Leaving John at the table Katya walked over to one of the loungers. She sat down, stretched out, not speaking to him. She felt he was so on edge with her that anything she said might alienate him. Time was getting short if she was to make any kind of arrangement with the Ministers to get that three hundred million— and perhaps the Gadaffi money— out of Ambergris. She couldn't afford to have John in a mood where he scrutinized her every action. She couldn't have him as a partner for life, she knew that, but she needed him on side and whether that meant putting their relationship back on an even keel as it had been or something more didn't matter. So, she said nothing but waited for the heady scent of the frangipani and hibiscus and the lazy silence of the afternoon sun to have a soothing effect on him.

Sometime later, John came over and sat in the nearest lounger to hers as if to make peace. Wordlessly, they looked out over the island as the sun slowly sank, throwing purple shadows across the pineapple fields.

'These colours remind me of the nights when I was allowed by my mother to watch her ballets, the scenery, costumes...' Katya stopped. Her hand went to her neck as she ran her fingers down the gold chain there. She looked towards John. 'What do you know about my mother?'

'Bolshoi ballet star. Slim, redhead, very beautiful.'

Katya knew he was mentally reading from her file.

'No. I don't mean that. I mean her makeup - her character.'

'Disappearing with that young dancer after your father's murder?' He pushed his coffee cup away. 'Too passionate for my taste.'

A vivid image of her mother flashed before Katya - elegant, perfumed, leaning across the restaurant table that last night she'd seen her, when she had fastened the gold chain around her daughter's neck.

Katya abruptly got up, she suddenly didn't want to talk about her past. 'I'm going for a swim,' she said.

When he heard her by the pool John deliberately didn't move, but he watched her body as it arched through a dive into the pale blue water. He shook himself and looked away to the faint shapes of the palm leaves as they shivered in the breeze. He tried to understand his own behaviour.

He'd never had difficulty in discouraging women who came onto him. A short, polite sentence or two, freezing them out, was sufficient. But for some reason he'd needed to go out of his way to upset this woman. His jibe about her passionate mother was irrational. He knew the mother's passion also simmered in the daughter. But instead of slapping down the daughter, he'd attacked the mother. Where was the logic in that?

Katya surfaced and tossed the water out of her hair, droplets sparkling in the pool lights. 'Are you coming in?'

'No.' His answer was short, tight.

Katya swam slowly towards him and rested her arms on the blue tiles edging the pool. 'What are you really frightened of, John? I'm not an operational target, yet you push me away all the time? Why?'

He didn't hesitate. His reply was blunt and uncompromising. 'My life is about dealing with chaos theory, making sense of the irrational, minimising risk. There's no place for sentimentality. And there's no time for it either.' He didn't sound very convincing.

She looked up at him, the water trickling around her eyes and down to the corners of her full mouth. 'I heard different. What you did for Betsie when her husband died, what you've done for her boys . . .'

'Betsie talks too much.'

Her mouth widened to a smile, the pale blue water now reflected in the violet of her eyes.

'Maybe, but underneath the man who bullied Conchita this morning is the man who helped Betsie. They're not the same.'

He was silent.

'I know you've had women before, John.' She let the silence build. 'So what's different with me?'

Abruptly he walked over and, to her complete surprise, bent down and lifted her face between his fingers.

'Nothing's different. That's the whole point. What happens if I'm thinking about you and not the job? If you're killed? What do I say then?'

Katya drew herself up and put her lips next to his.

'You say that at least we didn't waste the time we had.'

He jerked back, 'I have no time, Katya. Not for this.'

Her eyes followed him as he got up and walked away. He didn't look back.

FORTY-SIX

In the small hours of that night Katya was 'woken by a call from Dempsey. He just said. 'Your contact is Linus Beecham, the Chief Minister's lawyer.' The line went dead.

After breakfast, Katya found Linus Beecham's name in the phone book and decided to take a cab to his address. She had chosen a dark brown, sleeveless linen dress. Her hair was tied back and hidden under a brown baseball cap. Her sunglasses kept out the early morning sun and hid her face. In her hand she carried a small brown leather briefcase.

She arrived at a huge, two-storey, colonnaded house. Painted grey and white it cast a shadow over the bright vegetation and immaculate lawns surrounding it. It was more than a house— it was a mansion, a statement of wealth. Katya asked the cabdriver to wait and walking up to the front door she pressed the gleaming brass doorbell.

A maid opened the door.

Katya smiled at her. 'Mr Beecham, please.'

'Who shall I say is calling, Ma'am?'

'Brenda Stirling. Newsweek magazine. I have an appointment.' Katya moved into the hallway.

The maid hesitated. Katya raised her chin, threatening a row.

'Sorry ma'am. Please go into the morning room.' The maid pointed to a door at the side of the hall. 'I'll fetch Mr Beecham directly.'

Katya took her time inspecting the room, taking in the priceless furniture and paintings. Linus Beecham reeked of money, and this was only his morning room. The man "who did the Ministers' legal work", as the cab driver had put it, obviously charged top rates and more. This was certainly the man she needed to be able to get to the Chief Minister.

She was ready when the door opened.

Beecham was short, his grizzled hair glossy black over a broad, flat face creased into a suspicious gaze. The eyes flicked over her. He put out a hand, the fat, spatulate fingers rejecting her. 'I don't forget appointments with Newsweek.' His nasal, North American accent quickened. 'So, who are you?'

'I have something for you— or at least, for your Chief Minister.' Katya reached into her bag and took out a copy she'd made of Peter's voters list.

He went to take it but she held back. 'The names on this list have been targeted by the Corporate Party. They are bribing them for their votes.'

Beecham looked at her in total disbelief. 'What are you saying? Who are you?'

She repeated her words.

He rasped out the next question; now the typical lawyer seeking evidence. 'If it's true how d'you know all this?'

'You don't need to know that. A few enquiries will show I'm right.'

He looked her up and down. 'What d'you want?'

'Access to the Chief Minister.'

'What for?'

'None of your business.'

Beecham's eyes crawled over her, his flat features immobile.

'Is that all the names?' He pointed at the paper she held.

'No. One of them. You get the rest after I've seen the Chief Minister.'

'One? What sort of idiot do I look like?' Beecham's mouth tightened.

'An idiot who wants to win this election. The name on this list holds the key to a district. Without it, your man loses.' She spoke slowly, keeping her eyes on his, watching them dilate slightly. He stood there a moment, his eyes trying to lock on hers through the dark sunglasses she was wearing.

'Let me see that,' he said abruptly.

'Is the Chief Minister here?'

'Tonight. Here. Eleven thirty.'

She'd be with John tonight, she thought. 'No. This afternoon, three o'clock.'

'The Chief Minister's busy then.'

She put the paper in her bag.

'No. Alright. This afternoon, three o'clock.' Beecham held out his hand.

She gave him the paper.

He looked up in shock. 'Conchita Ybarra. Bought?'

She looked at him, impassively.

'You're damn right we'll go down in that District.' He looked up. 'Is the rest of the list like this?'

'Do you want to know, or not?'

'I'll see you get your meeting.'

'I didn't doubt it,' she replied.

The cab was still waiting for Katya. She climbed in and looked out at the ocean as the driver raced along the coast towards the Effendi Club.

The meeting had gone well. She knew the Chief Minister would be there to meet her, Beecham would make sure of that. She now needed to make sure of Dempsey and also find out what was going on with Cartwright and Paliakov. The last time she'd seen Cartwright was at the airport in Gibraltar. He'd be wondering what had happened to her - why she hadn't tried to get her cut of the El Bayedh cash from him. And the last she'd heard of Paliakov, he'd been tailing Cartwright as he tried to find out what had happened to the accounts in the Republic Bank in Panama. If Cartwright was blabbing about her, Paliakov might get to hear about it. The result didn't bear thinking about.

FORTY-SEVEN

Katya had showered and changed and met John on the tennis court. She had caused him so much grief with her serve during their game that he'd given her the match and was marching off the court. That suited her well – denting his ego would keep his mind on her as a woman rather than as an operational agent.

She was about to chide him when Peter came barging up to them, his eyes wild.

'It's Conchita Ybarra,' Peter burst out. 'She's been killed.'

Katya was genuinely horrified. 'But she can't be dead. We were with her only yesterday afternoon.'

Peter spoke in a low urgent voice. 'She was found in her water tank in the garden this morning, floating face down. She was murdered.'

'Calm down, Peter,' John broke in. 'First, are you sure it's her?'

'Of course, I'm sure.'

Katya shook her head. 'It's one thing that she's dead, it's another that she's been murdered. She could easily have fallen in the tank. She was very unsteady on her feet.'

'She'd lived there almost all her life, there's no way she'd have fallen in.'

John turned to Katya. 'She was doing her washing, hanging it out on the washing line when we saw her, wasn't she? She may have decided to clean the tank at the same time.'

Peter leant forward. 'That's the point. She never cleaned her tank. A boy did it for her. She never went near it.' He hesitated, rubbed his fingers together. 'Did someone see you with her?'

Katya leant her racket against the fence. 'We were very careful to be alone when we saw her. There was no one else around.'

'Then she must have said something to someone.' Peter pressed his fingers against his temples.

Katya looked up sharply. 'I think you're jumping to conclusions. She was a very independent lady, she could easily have cleaned the tank herself.'

John's voice hardened, 'It would be a mistake to voice your suspicions, Peter. If your other voters think she was murdered they will be too frightened to vote for you.'

Peter took his hands away from his head, his weary, troubled eyes on John. 'Suppose it was murder, though, I can't go on, I can't be responsible for-' His voice tailed away.

Katya said sharply. 'Concentrate on what you're going to do without her.'

'Nothing.' Peter looked blank. 'We can't do anything, we'll lose the Finance Minister's district without her support.'

'What about the bribes? We've got loads of stuff left.' John was curt.

'Conchita could have swung it. Without her, bribes won't do any good.'

'Then concentrate even more on the other districts. You can win them, *are* winning them.' Katya urged. 'You can't give up now. You need to look confident. Go about saying you're going to win, that you must carry on. It's what Conchita would have wanted. It's now all about your presence, confidence.'

Peter straightened up. 'You're right, of course.' He rubbed his eyes, 'I just wish I didn't feel so responsible -'

Katya put her hand on his. 'I'm sorry about Conchita. I liked her very much.'

FORTY-EIGHT

At three o'clock that afternoon Katya was watching the Chief Minister enter the morning room of Linus Beecham's plantation mansion. Aged forty-two, tall, thin, he'd been in power four years now. His face was tinged with grey. Long lines creased his cheeks. His brown eyes were strangely dead for a man who wielded so much authority and they now rested dispassionately on her.

'You're the woman who gave Linus here Conchita's name?' He nodded towards Beecham, who was standing by the fireplace.

The man's eyes crawled over her and told her all she needed to know about him. Used to his own way, bullying if he didn't get it. She'd bully him first, put him off his well-trodden path.

'A man as stupid as you didn't deserve to get Conchita's name.'

He started forward, his large hands clenching into fists. 'You dare talk to me like that, you bitch.'

A picture of Ahmet seared through her mind - drenched in blood, gasping the same last dying words "you bitch". She leapt to her feet. 'Don't ever call me a bitch.' She started for the door. 'You want the list of voters swinging to the opposition? Forget it.'

The Chief Minister glared at her, struggled with himself, then shrugged his shoulders. 'OK, I didn't mean it. I apologise.'

'I did mean it,' Katya snapped. 'What sort of an idiot kills off his main asset.'

The Chief Minister hunched his shoulders.

Beecham interrupted again. 'What do you mean?'

'Conchita Ybarra, killing her.'

Beecham and the Minister exchanged glances.

'We didn't-' Beecham started.

Katya cut him short. 'Don't go there. You killed Conchita and to make things worse you killed her too soon.'

The Chief Minister stared at her. 'Who are you, woman? Coming here telling me what I do and don't do?'

She chopped off his challenge, 'You know it, too. If you'd given her a good fright, she'd have told the voters it was your Yardies gave her a beating and the voters would have been terrified not to vote for you. Then, with the list of voters I've got, the other Districts would have tumbled your way. Instead you've lost that opportunity.'

His eyes slid to one side.

She saw the tell. He was inwardly cursing himself. She added salt to the wound. 'You want the list of voters?' She held up her bag.

'Yes, I want the goddam list.'

Katya looked at Beecham; pointed to the Chief Minister. 'Is he going to be sensible? Can he be sensible?'

Beecham shifted uneasily, wondering where this terrifying woman had come from. 'Depends what you want.'

'You are one of the crudest people I've come across. All I want to know is can he do as I tell him?'

The Chief Minister exploded, making Beecham jump. 'I don't take orders from anyone, particularly some goddam woman so why don't you get out?"

Katya decided she'd needled him enough. Businesslike, she said. 'I've some money locked up here. I want to get it out.'

The Chief Minister laughed, but his eyes remained dead. 'So

do we all. Goddam British Government's got us frozen.'

'I have no doubt you're making plans to take over the Telephone Exchange.'

The Chief Minister's eyes crept up to hers.

She ignored him. 'And you then intend to wire your money out to Venezuela.'

'That's our business.' Beecham chimed in. 'And I don't see where this is getting us.'

'It gets us to the point that I know if you try and use the landline to Venezuela, the Marines are ready and able to cut the cable. So, forget any idea of trying to get your assets out by using it.'

'Shit.' The Chief Minister slumped in his chair.

Katya leaned over him. 'You didn't really believe you could take over the landline while the Marines are here, did you? That's as stupid as what you did to Conchita. Of course, they will cut it before you can use it.' Katya pointed her finger at him. 'On the other hand, if you use my list, win the election and go independent immediately, you can get your hands on the Telephone Exchange and hopscotch your money all over the world and hide it. You'll have just enough time to get out of Ambergris before-'

He snorted contempt. 'That doesn't make sense, why would I have to get out? I'd be Chief Minister for another term and the island would be independent.'

She shook her head. 'I can't believe this. I'll spell it out slowly. Conchita's death stinks. When you win the election, you were going to lose before you killed Conchita, the UN will come piling in to investigate her death. They'll almost certainly declare the election corrupt.'

'Sounds like total fantasy land to me.' Beecham looked at the Chief Minister.

The Minister kept his eyes on Katya. 'So how would taking over the Telephone Exchange help you?'

'I've told you. I've got money here I want to get out. This freeze is going to stay unless you win this election and go independent. The only way I'm going to get my money away from here is to make sure you win.'

'Go on.'

Immediately you go independent you'll open up the Telephone Exchange so as to get your money out before the UN come piling in. I want a one- minute slot there first.'

'In return for the list?' The Chief Minister didn't move.

'Without it, you'll lose the election. Guaranteed.' Katya kept her voice flat, unemotional. 'My way you get a hundred and sixteen voters bought and paid for. Another forty to be visited.'

Katya reached for her bag. The Chief Minister watched the movement, warily, relief showing in his eyes as she pulled out the list.

'Just like that?' He questioned.

'Yes, just like that. I want one minute of your time, not much to ask.'

He slowly nodded, watching her like a cobra.

She handed the list to Beecham. 'I don't expect you to fail to deliver. A one- minute slot, immediately upon your party winning and you taking over the Telephone Exchange.'

The Chief Minister's eyes widened, terrified, as they caught sight of the Beretta .32 she'd hidden behind the list and now pointed at his stomach.

She said matter of factly, 'You don't want another death just before the election, so call off your Yardies. And remember, if you do fail me I'll find you.' Her eyes lasered into each of them in turn. 'Wherever you are.'

FORTY-NINE

That evening Katya had a message from Storky. She was summoned to an urgent video call with Lev. The insistence of Lev's summons made Katya uneasy as there was no immediate reason for her to speak to him. Her mind raced as she analyzed the implications. Had someone in the Minister's camp talked about Conchita's murder? Had there been a witness at her house when it had happened? Had she herself left some clue behind when she'd opened Peter's safe and taken the list of voters? Had someone seen her at Linus Beecham's place? And why wasn't John summoned to the meeting with Lev?

She found Storky in the Telephone Exchange setting up the secure link with G8 in London. Tank lay on the floor, growling and waving his tail.

'He's happy,' said Storky. 'He must've caught a dozen rats in this hole. There are rooms here that haven't been opened in decades.'

Katya hardly heard him. She was closely watching the satellite link, trying to keep her nervousness under control, mentally acting out reasons for her past visits to the Chief Minister and Beecham. 'Are you sure this room is secure for a video call?' she said.

Storky laughed. 'We've got no plans of this place. I haven't got the means to make a proper recce. As far as I can see it's as secure as a sieve at sea.'

The satellite link screen sprang to life, revealing Lev's features.

There was no preamble. 'You'll want to see this, Katya. G8SUR surveillance video.'

Lev's peremptory launch into whatever evidence he had almost unnerved her. She simply nodded, not trusting herself to speak.

The screen suddenly filled with a violent image of Rosa Rulenski screaming in Polish at Mikhail. The translation scrolled at the bottom of the surveillance picture.

'You come here to tell me my money's frozen in Ambergris? I can't use it? Are you crazy?'

Katya was taken completely unawares. She frantically tried to assess what was going on. Dimly, she heard Lev's voice. 'We've managed to get G8SUR fixed on Rosa Rulenski's place in Krakow. It was all quiet until Mikhail joined her there. He made a flying visit, leaving Paliakov in Panama. I think the result speaks for itself, here's some more.'

The screen showed a terrified Mikhail pleading, spreading his hands. *'Rosa, be reasonable…'*

Katya watched the spittle fly from Rosa's mouth.

'Don't you fucking argue with me you useless piece of shit. Find Paliakov and get to Ambergris and don't come back without my money.'

'Rosa-'

His voice broke into a scream as she snatched up a glass vase and slashed it in fragments across his face. Clutching his cheek Mikhail staggered from the room blood pouring between his fingers.

'Good for her,' Lev laughed.

Katya found something to say. 'We'd better warn Paliakov that Mikhail's on his way.'

'Loaded for bear,' chuckled Lev.

Tank yawned loudly.

'Tank, you dumb idiot.' Storky shouted.

Lev looked up, startled. 'What was that?'

'Our guard dog.'

Katya didn't need to force a laugh. It came spontaneously, from sheer relief. 'He's the only thing defending the Marines from the Ministers, Lev.'

FIFTY

Rosa Rulenski had petrified Mikhail. He had thought she was going to kill him. He'd immediately emailed Paliakov at their hotel to say he was returning to Panama.

'Mikhail.' Paliakov stretched out his arms as he met him at the airport.

'At last.'

Mikhail took Paliakov in a strong hug. 'I've missed you.'

'What happened to your face, Mikhail. Such a terrible cut?' Paliakov stroked the fresh scar with his fingers.

'I got drunk,' laughed Mikhail, 'walked into a glass door.'

'Poor boy.' Paliakov spoke in Polish, leaving Mikhail to carry his suitcase as he headed towards the terminal's exit. 'Come on, I've got my car in the long-term lot, I couldn't find any space in the short. Bloody chaos, as usual.' He kept his arm across Mikhail's shoulders as they pushed and jostled their way across the heaving terminal and out to the courtesy bus stop.

Mikhail looked up at the burning sun as they climbed off the bus onto the hot car park pavement. 'Wonderful. Krakow was freezing as hell. I'd like to stay here forever.'

Paliakov gave Mikhail's shoulders a squeeze. 'First, we go to Ambergris. Get the money out. It might take a bit of time, though.'

Mikhail stopped walking. 'You don't really think Rosa will keep her bargain, do you?'

'My fifty percent? Of course she will. She couldn't have done it without me. And now she knows she doesn't need Katya – it's me she needs for future deals.'

Mikhail lifted his head, facing Paliakov square on.

'Rosa's orders to me were to kill you and Katya the moment the money was transferred to Ambergris.'

Paliakov's eyes widened. 'But you didn't. Was that because the money was frozen and she couldn't get it right away?'

Mikhail took Paliakov's arm. 'You know better than that.' He touched the scar on his face. 'It wasn't a glass door - she gave me this. Glassed me without warning.'

'Then-'

'Yes. If I don't get her money out of her account in Ambergris, I'm dead. You too. I can't get the money to her while this freeze is on. And I can't go back to Poland empty handed.'

'You mean? - '

'I'm getting out, leaving her – '

'But a hundred and fifty million -'

'Forget it. You never had it. It was just a dream.'

'And you?' Paliakov hesitated, 'And me?'

'We're going to Punta Mala. From there we can explore Panama, Columbia, the whole of South America. Forget Rosa. Forget everything. It's just you and me now.'

Paliakov bent his head to unlock the car, hiding his other hand as he brushed it quickly across his eyes, brushing away unexpected tears.

They climbed in. He started the engine, looked in the mirror, then stopped.

'Your seat belt, Mikhail.'

As Mikhail looked down, Paliakov leant into the side pocket of the door, found the icepick he'd put there and slid it into his hand.

He leaned back. Silently drove it into Mikhail's heart.

Mikhail's mouth opened to scream, but the breath left him before he could utter a sound. As the darkness clouded in, he could only think about the tears in Paliakov's eyes.

Paliakov got out, shut the car door and walked over to his own vehicle parked a few meters away. He got in and drove slowly and sadly out of the car park. He had loved Mikhail, but there was no safe future with him alive. Rosa would see to that. So Mikhail had to die.

He drove carefully through the City traffic to the Poritilla district and turned left into a small square. It was bordered by modern office buildings with some shops and a local café at street level. It wasn't lunchtime yet, so the square was deserted except for a handful of doves and some ubiquitous sparrows foraging underneath the iron and slatted wood seats there. Paliakov hardly noticed them as he found a parking slot and walked over to the café, slowly, so as to keep the appearance of nonchalance.

The bartender hardly noticed him either, just another tourist, dressed casually, certainly not employed in the City, so he merely nodded at him. Paliakov sat down at an outside table and ordered a local beer. Idly, he sipped it, thinking of Mikhail and the good times they'd had.

His thoughts were interrupted by a lean set man with a crew cut who noisily plumped himself down at another table, opened his newspaper and started reading it. Paliakov recognized him immediately. It was Cartwright, the man he'd been following since he'd arrived in Panama a few days previously.

Paliakov almost laughed as he visualized the scene to come. He launched himself out of his chair and strode over to Cartwright and grabbed his wrist. He leant down and whispered loudly, 'There's a dead man in your car at the airport.'

Shock surged through Cartwright, blabbering automatic words of denial. 'What the hell... Who are you?'

'Cartwright, isn't it?'

'Get lost.' Cartwright tried to pull his arm away. The relentless pressure strengthened.

'I haven't got a car at the airport.

'It's hired in your name.'

Cartwright tried to struggle to his feet but Paliakov bent his wrist back and forced him to sit.

'We don't want you running off with our money, do we?'

Cartwright winced in pain. 'Shit let go of my wrist, bastard. I don't know what you're talking about.'

Paliakov gripped harder. 'The Gadaffi money you stole – in the Republic Bank.'

'What Gadaffi money?' Cartwright stopped suddenly as the truth hit him. 'Shit, it's that bloody woman, isn't it? El Bayedh. You're Our Desert. That cow set me up - someone took my money.' He stared wildly at Paliakov. 'It was her. Wasn't it?' He started struggling again. 'She knew about the bank - but it's my bloody money.'

His words didn't immediately sink into Paliakov's brain. His mind was too focused on the pleasure of inflicting pain.

Cartwright ranted on. 'She was all sodding sugar in Gib, took me in. It was you she met in London, wasn't it?'

'London?' Paliakov involuntarily let go of Cartwright's arm.

Cartwright brought it to his chest, rubbing it with his other hand. 'Don't try and deny it.'

Paliakov couldn't believe what he was hearing. As far as he was concerned, the only women involved in the op were Katya and Rosa. And Cartwright hadn't met Rosa, didn't even know of her existence. He decided to deny everything, to force Cartwright to tell him some more. 'You're talking crap.'

The words were hardly out of his mouth before Cartwright

started shouting again, oblivious of the spectacle he was making. 'Shit! I know bloody well she bought a ticket for London. You can't deny you saw her.' He went into a paroxysm of coughing, trying to catch his breath.

Paliakov thought rapidly. That could explain why she was late meeting up in Panama. Who had Katya met in London, then? It wasn't Lev or G8, he knew that. She'd told them she was travelling direct to Panama from Madrid. Why was Cartwright so sure she was going for the money? Had she been tempted? Lev's star agent tempted by the lure of riches? The woman Lev constantly singled out, and measured favourably against the men, making them feel inadequate? Paliakov remembered how humiliated she'd always made him feel whenever G8 had used him. How she had slapped him down in Berlin. He suddenly felt certain she had been tempted by the money. Now he must make sure of his theory.

Cartwright mistook Paliakov's hesitation, wiped his mouth, 'Look can we make a deal?'

'Tell me first—how d'you know it was me she met in London?'

Cartwright looked at him. He didn't understand why he was telling this bastard all this, the sod must know it already. Who the hell was he? Where had he come from? But if he played along with this man, there might be a chance to salvage some of the money.

'I don't know. Why would you be here otherwise?' Cartwright rattled on, trying to please. 'When she and I met the Gonzalez brothers in Gibraltar they got scrappy. The bitch didn't help me, just lit out, left me to deal with the bastards. She left me flat, so I checked her air reservation to know where I could find her.'

Paliakov let go off his grip on Cartwright's arm. He had all he wanted to know. It fit. Katya hadn't travelled via Madrid. She'd stopped off in London. For no operational reason. There could only be one answer to that. He was sure. Well, not sure but he could think of no other answer. The money. Just too much to resist. He punched some numbers on his mobile.

Cartwright shakily stood up. 'You talking to her? Tell that bitch I don't -'

Paliakov spoke into his mobile, 'Police?'

'What the hell are you doing?' shouted Cartwright, not caring who could hear him.

'What I said I'd do.' Paliakov looked Cartwright over. 'Avis Car Rental here. We've found a body in one of our Blue Dodge Saloon's at the airport.'

'For god's sake.' Cartwright grabbed his arm, his face white.

'Yes, rented in the name of Ron Cartwright.' Paliakov shook him off.

Cartwright shoved his chair away, almost fell as he scrambled from the table to run down the street.

Paliakov watched him go, stretched to ease the tension in his shoulders and sat down. Of course, the Panama police wouldn't hold Cartwright for long. At least, not by Panamanian standards. Two or three months, then they'd find the forensics didn't match up.

It didn't matter though. Two or three months was more than Paliakov needed to investigate Katya, prove she was on the take and deliver her to Lev. He savagely remembered her contempt of him and vowed she'd pay for it. He could almost see her in the cells starting a twenty-year sentence and for once he'd get the recognition he deserved for putting her there. And that cow would know it.

He smiled at the young waiter who approached as he beckoned him. He paid the bill and hurriedly left the café. He knew exactly what he was going to do. He would fly to Ambergris, directly to the location of the money.

FIFTY-ONE

The election crisis came swiftly. Forced by Katya.

She had to know the current state of voting. The Ministers had to win. She needed them to win to be certain of getting her cash. She needed the cash to be able to eliminate John from her mind. She needed the three hundred million to be free.

Which was why she needed this meeting in the Telephone Exchange.

John, still awkward - the memory of her in the pool seared in his mind - sat beside her as she talked to Walt and Lev on the satellite link.

'We need the computer forecast on the election voting because, if there's been any change, we need to know where the weak links are.' She used the word "we" to emphasize this was John's request as much as hers. He must be seen to be fully involved if anything went wrong and she had to face an inquiry by G8.

The screen flickered as numerals flashed in an equation. They stopped at a series of numerical predictions.

Katya slowly read out the figures. District after District showed the Ministers in the lead. She had difficulty covering her sense of relief at this reversal of the earlier prediction of a landslide victory for Peter's Corporate Party. The Chief Minister had used the list she had given him to good effect. With the Ministers now firmly in power, Rosa's cash was within her grasp, free of any UK government freeze. Just a few more days to wait.

She controlled herself, edged her voice with a tinge of alarm. 'On these calculations, Peter's already lost the election.'

Lev shrugged, an "I told you so" gesture. 'Voters are human beings. They know the difference between a new television and a murdered old lady.'

Walt cut in. 'But it's only three days to voting.'

Lev's voice was icy. 'Then winter will have come early.' His eyebrows came together as he concentrated. 'What is your contingency plan, if the Ministers win again?'

John looked at Storky who was leaning casually against the wall.

Storky pushed himself away and leant down to speak. 'That's why I was serious about our lack of security here. We need to keep out communications here open. There will be at least a two-hour delay between the Chief Minister declaring independence and my team blowing the cable. With the team out doing that I'd only have four men left to defend this place. If the Ministers were determined enough, they could get their men to come charging in and take over the landline.'

John stepped in. 'And once that happened the Ministers would have time to wire their money out of here through Venezuela into the world markets.'

There was silence. It was Lev's voice that broke it, sounding like a lorry on loose gravel. 'There is some information which you should all know before you make any decisions.'

He was succinct as usual, 'I won't bother you with the details or the sources of the information. A finance company named Annaba Trust is one of the fronts for heroin trafficking out of Afghanistan, and its only real purpose is to distribute funds for terrorist activity against the West.' Lev scrunched his cigarette into an ash tray on his desk, lit another. 'Annaba Trust is registered in Ambergris and is solely owned by Linus Beecham, the Chief Minister's Legal Adviser.'

'Who?' Katya rapped out the question, steeling herself in order to look convincing.

'The Legal Adviser to the Chief Minister, Linus Beecham. Two months ago a number of spread payments were made to the trust by Ahmet.'

'Ahmet? My Ahmet?' Katya broke in.

Lev squinted at them through the haze of fresh cigarette smoke. "Yes, the payments were made a couple of weeks before you killed him.'

John explored what Lev had said. 'Ahmet was Gadaffi's minder. What you're saying is that Ahmet may have had Cartwright's ill-gotten Gadaffi cash all along. Spread it to Beecham when he thought it was safe. To fund his terrorism? So maybe Cartwright never had it?'

Lev nodded.

'Linus Beecham financed Ahmet's terrorist activity from here in Ambergris? Beecham laundered terrorist cash? Kept it on deposit?'

'Yes.'

John looked grave. 'The fact that Ahmet and his group have been eliminated in no way diminishes the guilt of the Chief Minister here. He had to have approved of Beecham's actions. He is just as culpable as Ahmet for those terrorist attacks – equally guilty of the murders of those innocent civilians.'

Lev struck a match. 'So, winter must come early for the Chief Minister, too, John.'

FIFTY-TWO

Early the next morning Katya and John leant against the perimeter fence of Ambergris Airport.

Katya lowered her Swarowski binoculars. 'I don't like this, John.'

The decision to assassinate the Chief Minister suited her plans, but if they were going to succeed, she must not appear too eager to be part of killing him.

'We don't have to like it'. He replied harshly. 'We just have to do it."

'But it puts us on a par with Ahmet.'

'Ahmet was a terrorist. The Chief Minister is a terrorist – well, as good as.'

Katya didn't argue, instead she looked down the length of the runway where the Chief Minister would die.

Strutting around the ponds on either side were hundreds of egrets, brilliant white waders which had lived and bred there for centuries. Peter had told her they were protected birds on the island.

John echoed her thoughts. 'There were seven individual bird strikes at this airport last year. Did you know that?'

She saw this remark as the opportunity to put forward the first part of her plan.

'I'm sure we could give Peter better support to win this election.'

John straightened up, drawing on the stubborn streak he held in reserve, 'We've got less than seventy-two hours before voting starts. The election's lost. The Ministers will get in again.' He faced her squarely, his words final. 'We've got to do it, there's no alternative.' He pointed towards the ponds. 'Those egrets are used to aviation noise, but they'd be startled by any unfamiliar sound, particularly a sudden sound.'

She followed his gaze and watched some of the egrets wading in one of the ponds, their heads darting into the water, feeding. She thought back, to when she'd seen the desolation in Lev's face as his words covertly suggested the solution to the wrong party being set to win the election. "Winter must come early for the Chief Minister."

Katya glanced sideways at John as he scanned the runway again. She felt herself tighten as she remembered that stubborn streak in him had led to his humiliating rejection of her. Now she would use it for her own ends.

She shifted topic, preparing the way. 'How can you be certain you'll knock out the Chief Minister's plane?'

'We'll get a sight of the daily flight plans. See what time he's taking off.'

Katya was silent for a moment.

'Is something wrong?' he asked.

'No. The plan's good.' She hesitated deliberately, leading him on.

John leaned towards her. For a moment, he was distracted by his closeness to her. He fought against it, said roughly, 'Go on.'

Katya bent down and pulled a piece of grass, fiddled with it between her fingers. This was going to be difficult. She had to go along with the plan to assassinate the Chief Minster yet she had to keep him alive. Preventing John from killing him was fraught with the risk of her exposure. She knew now that his feelings for her were conflicted. This would surely create tension in him which could spark other deep emotions - impatience, anger, suspicion. She would have to handle him very carefully.

'Well, I was thinking that the Chief Minister's schedules are haphazard. You remember Peter commenting on it . . . the flight plans might change at the last minute.'

'You think we might not get the correct take off time?'

'I think it might be better to be certain.'

John studied her. He saw her point. There was a risk, small but catastrophic if they got the wrong plane because the Chief Minister altered his schedule at the last minute.

She hesitated. 'If he was flying to an election debate, I suppose the risk would be reduced. He would try and be there on time…'

She let the sentence hang. Looked at him, gauging the right moment to withdraw. He opened his mouth to reply.

'Forget it,' she said quickly. 'I'm being too cautious. You've obviously thought carefully about this. I-'

'You mean arrange a meeting between him and Peter?'

She nodded. 'A public meeting. They couldn't refuse.'

'That would give us a definite fix on his time of departure?'

She nodded.

Abruptly, he turned and walked to their Volkswagen.

FIFTY-THREE

The rain steadily drummed on the roof of Peter's house, sliding off the palm leaves in steady rivulets, raising little spurts of water on the surface of the pool. She looked at John, sitting at the breakfast table opposite her, watching Peter.

Peter was being difficult. 'Why should I give the Chief Minister the credibility of a head- to- head debate?'

John reached for his glass, slowly drank the fresh orange juice, trying to curb his impatience with Peter's intransigence.

Katya shifted her gaze from him to the low dark clouds obscuring the sea in the distance, saying, 'Things change quickly in politics, Peter, like the storms here. One minute blue seas, the next a maelstrom. Everything was fine until someone in your Corporate Party leaked the list of voters you were targeting. You've got to accept that and realise that people are now terrified to vote for you because of that leak. You personally have to stand up to the Chief Minister. He had Conchita killed and it's up to you to tell the voters that. To tell them the truth, face to face with the man who did it.'

'I should never have trusted my committee.' Peter reached for the list in front of him. 'But I've known them all my life, they're the leaders in my Party, they needed to know who we were aiming at for votes.'

'A lesson to learn,' John said, brusquely, shifting his gaze away from the swimming pool, trying to erase the memory of Katya's arcing dive into the water, her long hair streaming out behind her.

There was a silence. Katya filled it by pouring tea and spooning cherry compote into her cup. She deliberately took a sip, sizing up Peter through her eye lashes. 'If you think you made a mistake, Peter, you must do all you can to put it right.' Peter jumped as she rattled the cup in its saucer. 'You've got to meet the Chief Minister in public and it's got to be televised. Let the people see you tear into him, accuse him, fight him. You owe it to Conchita.'

Peter slowly got to his feet and walked to the edge of the veranda. He looked out across the pineapple field. A haze misting up now as the sun dried out the rain and the steam began to rise from the rich vegetation. Katya joined him, leant against the balcony rail, following his gaze.

'I've said it before, Peter, and you have to believe it. This is what you stand for. An island that's united…that cares for the farmers and fishermen as well as the financiers. Not a place ruled by crooks and greed and corruption. Tell them that. They know you, they'll trust you.'

Peter didn't move, the sound of the cicadas suddenly becoming loud in the silence.

'Yes. I know.' Looking into the middle distance, he paused a long moment. 'You're right Katya. I have to do it.'

FIFTY-FOUR

The Chief Minister climbed into the Air Taxi Piper Aztec aircraft parked by one of the hangers at the Ambergris airport.

The pilot started the engines in a crack of exhaust smoke and, whilst carrying out his preflight checks, taxied the aircraft past the terminal. The Chief Minister gave his usual wave to the small crowd of people standing amongst the bougainvillea plants on the observation platform on the terminal roof. No one waved back. He didn't care, their votes weren't worth anything. He'd sewn up all the districts and the election was already won with two days to go. So he didn't mind going to this debate with the Opposition Leader. What a nobody Peter Thomas had turned out to be. Frightening as hell one minute, sucking in the voters, turning that bloody Conchita to vote for him. Then, as soon as pressure had been brought to bear on those two-timing bastards on that list, he'd caved in. No riots, no violence, nothing, just words. It showed he had no guts. You had to have guts to be Chief Minister, to govern, to get what you wanted.

He tightened his seatbelt, watched the pilot speak through his headphones to the tower and thought how satisfying it would be, after the election, to make Ambergris independent. A visit to the Telephone Exchange, half an hour on the landline, and he'd be away, out of Ambergris, his assets spread across the globe.

His view of the airfield was suddenly blocked as they went behind a large hangar on their way to the runway.

Lying in the tall plumed reeds at the far end of the airstrip, John watched the Piper Aztec roll behind the hangar. A few moments later, it appeared as a shimmering shadow in the heat haze at the start of the concrete ribbon. The whine of the twin engines rose in tone as the Aztec started on its journey down the runway. One or two egrets lazily flapped to one side or the other, no longer bothered by the noise.

The grasses either side of the runway flattened as the plane gathered speed, the prop wash gushing behind, the sun glinting off the cockpit window.

John saw the nose wheel lift, gracefully leading the rest of the plane into the air six hundred yards from the end of the runway, keeping low as the wheels retracted.

He pulled the trigger. The report of the short twelve bore was flat, like a plank dropped on concrete. The noise startled a hundred egrets out of the grass. They rocketed skyward, screeching wildly, their plumage scrabbling for lift as they clawed their way through the sky, looking for safety, bunching together, wheeling in a frenzied mass.

Seconds later they were spewing blood as they tore through the propellers, and smashed through the windscreen into the pilot's face. Cramming the air intakes. Pulling the plane down, port wing sparking, scraping the runway, cartwheeling the fuselage. A spume of dust, propellers cutting earth and coral. A swathe of grit. Sheets of spray, doors bursting open. Screams high above the noise of the tearing, rending metal.

FIFTY-FIVE

From the Terminal Katya watched the fire engines race across the tarmac to the site of the crash. She stayed where she was. It was too late to do anything useful about the inferno under the black eddying smoke at the edge of the airfield. She heard the screams of the people around her, registering their shock, and then saw the surge of movement as the crowd broke up. Some were running across the field towards the broken plane, others towards the Chief Minister as he climbed out of his Aztec. His eyes were fixed on the spot where Peter had died, where he would have died if his aircraft had taken off first.

He stumbled as his feet touched the ground, dazed, still unwilling to believe what had happened, hardly able to credit Katya with his life. Remembering how she'd stood by the window in his house urging him to trust her. Trust that she had persuaded Peter to arrange the debate so that both he and Peter would fly at the same time to a neutral meeting place in the north of the island. That Peter had arranged the flight plan so that the Chief Minister would fly first as befitted his political rank. Trust her that she had heard a whisper that someone had planned a bird strike to crash the first aircraft, that someone had arranged for the Chief Minister to be assassinated. That if his aircraft took off first, he would die.

Even as the Chief Minister had boarded his Aztec he didn't believe her. True, she'd given him Conchita and the other names to help him win the election but this was something altogether different. This was an assassination plot, hardly credible. It was only when the pilot announced they were ready to take off that he felt a surge of panic and told the pilot to wait behind the hanger while he sent a last-minute text. A few minutes later he heard Peter's Aztec maneuver onto the runway and lift off. Then the screaming egrets, the smashing impact of the crash, the roar of flames.

Safely on the tarmac, the Chief Minister leant against his plane's fuselage. A stream of cold sweat plunging down his back. His breath coming in short gasps. Darkness reaching into his brain.

He could be dead now. Smashed. Beyond recognition. Burned. Beyond dust. The anger started to smoulder. That bloody bitch had been right. The Opposition had tried to kill him, wipe him out. But it didn't make sense. That little shit, Peter Thomas, hadn't the guts to do this. Someone else had to have planned the sabotage.

He hardly heard the shouts of the people as they came up and crowded around him, jostling him towards the terminal. His Yardies violently ploughed through the milling mob, flanking him, guarding him as he strained to shut out the noise, trying to think. Who was it? The Americans? The Brits? Who? G8? Would they try again? How long before they did? That bitch had told him nothing. Just a whisper, she'd said. Who the hell was she? He felt cold again. He'd only been interested in the opposition's voters list. He hadn't believed her story about his proposed assassination. Until now.

A microphone was thrust at him. He pushed it away. 'Get the fuck out of my face.'

He saw the shock register on the faces around him. A sudden silence. He realized what he'd said. His anger out of control.

'I'm sorry. I'll make a statement in a minute. I'm too shaken at the moment.'

He turned to the Yardy nearest him. 'Get me to the VIP lounge. Clear it and I want Beecham there, nobody else.'

The VIP lounge was small. Empty except for the teenage waitress staring out of the window. She swung round, fear stabbing her, as the Chief Minister and his Yardy burst in.

'Get me a drink.' The Chief Minister nodded at her. 'Bourbon. Leave the bottle.'

He turned to the Yardy. 'I want the Aztec fuelled and ready to fly to Surinam, Paramaribo Airport, in three hours.'

He had held out his glass to the Yardy to pour out another slug of Bourbon when Linus Beecham burst in, panting, his hair plastered over his face.

'What the hell happened? I heard you were in a plane crash.'

'Forget it.' The Chief Minister swallowed the Bourbon. 'We're getting out of here. I'll tell you about it on the way.' He grabbed the bottle, stabbing his finger at the Yardy. 'You will take the Telephone Exchange. Right away. I don't care how many men you use, but do it quietly. Those damn British marines are around and I don't want a fight and I don't want them wrecking the Exchange while you're trying to get in. Use the tunnel. Surprise them. Once in, you'll hold all calls until I phone. Understand?'

The man nodded.

The Chief Minister splashed more Bourbon into his glass. 'You'll let the woman in. No one else. Just the woman. She can use the telephone. But she has no more than five minutes. Then get her out.'

The Yardy nodded again. He knew the woman. Had watched her go in and out of Beecham's house.

'What can I do?' Beecham took the bottle and drank from its neck.

'I want you to stay with me, then go to the Telephone Exchange as soon as those fucking marines have been taken out.

You'll take details of all my accounts and you'll transfer them by hopscotch to my accounts in the Cook Islands, as we arranged. Once you've done that you can wire out your own money. You'll have about two hours.'

Beecham's face was streaked with sweat. He wanted to ask questions but he'd never seen the Chief Minister like this. If he said they had to get out, then they had to get out. The questions could wait. His mind jumped to the twenty-three special accounts, and to his own account, which had to be cleared out and hopscotched to eleven accounts in the Cook Islands. Two hours would be enough and then he'd be on that plane. He began to feel a little better, thanking his foresight for having planned for just such an emergency. The accounts were set up all across the world. They just needed activating.

'Right. I'll need my laptop. Will you come to my house?'

The Chief Minister walked ahead of Beecham into the washroom. Sluiced his face with water, tasting the salt of his sweat. He looked in the mirror. The bitch deserved five minutes. Without her he'd not be watching his reflection. And he wasn't going to cross her. He wasn't going to watch over his shoulder for her for the rest of his life. She was deadly. He looked at Beecham.

'Take the woman with you to the Telephone Exchange. Let her wire out her money first. First, you understand.'

FIFTY-SIX

Katya stayed among the shadows in the crowded Arrivals Hall when the Chief Minister came out on the narrow balcony overlooking it. He was alone, gripping the wooden rail as his dead eyes slowly cowed the crowd below him into silence. They nervously shuffled, like cattle outside a slaughterhouse, searching for his Yardies. The word was out that the Opposition Leader had perished.

The Chief Minister's words came at them like sledgehammer blows. 'What you saw just now was no accident. The crash you witnessed was an assassination attempt on me. I have it on good authority the British government tried to kill me this afternoon.'

The hall erupted into chaos. The crowd surging towards the balcony. Shouts of anger mingled with yells of disbelief.

He held up his hands. Didn't wait for silence. 'As of now Ambergris is Independent. A state of emergency exists. I am flying to Britain to see the British Prime Minister and I'm charging him with murder.'

The last words were drowned out in the noise as the crowd broke into opposite camps. The fuse lit for scuffling then fighting as they came to terms with the meaning of it all. But the Chief Minister didn't wait to stop it.

Katya watched him leave. She tried to reach him but was blocked by the milling crowd. She turned and raced through an open door out onto the airport apron, skirted around the back of the building and was just in time to see the Chief Minister's

Mercedes accelerate down the access road. She knew instinctively that with him had gone her chance of siphoning Rosa's account. He was getting out. Without pausing she shoved her way towards the cab rank at the rear of the Terminal.

'Wait. Wait.' The shouts came from behind her. She ignored them, she wasn't waiting for anything, kept running towards the cabs.

'WAIT - it's me, Beecham.' He was yelling to be heard above the turmoil in the Terminal behind him.

Katya turned and saw Beecham, breathing heavily as he came running towards her.

'I was coming to see you.' He panted, bending double, gulping in air, pouring sweat in the heat. He caught his breath just enough to say. 'The Chief Minister sent me. I must take you to the Telephone Exchange.'

Katya almost laughed in his face. They had taken her seriously. She touched her handbag, felt the Beretta there.

His face registered the threat. 'There's no need for that. I'll take you back to my place first.' He staggered as a running woman barged into him.

Katya grabbed his arm to steady him. 'No way, we'll go straight there.'

'You're perfectly safe, the Chief Minister has given you five minutes to transfer your money out but we have to wait for-' He stopped, not sure whether this was information he should be telling her. She threw him a look that started him again. 'The Marines, they have to be cleared out of the Exchange - our men are there now - come on.'

He started to shove his way past two men arguing in front of him but Katya pulled him back. 'You'll need me if you're going to take the Exchange from the Marines.'

Beecham shook his head. 'Our people know a secret tunnel

into it which backs up to an old cupboard in the Main Exchange. The Marines will never expect them in the chaos. It'll all be over in a minute – and we can go as soon as I get the call the Exchange is in our hands. Quick, we can use my car.'

She let him go, she didn't need him. 'I'm still not going back to your place, it's too risky. I'll meet you at the Exchange.'

Beecham nodded. 'Okay. But you'll have no more than five minutes, don't forget.' He fought his way back into the crowd and vanished.

Katya stared after him, oblivious to the people shoving and barging past her. She had expected this to be a moment of triumph. Countering John and keeping the Chief Minister alive so successfully was a high point. Very few people ever got the better of John.

Her emotions were mixed and this surprised her. Operationally what she had just achieved differed in no way from her G8 work. Her objective had been to save the Chief Minister, take her money. She'd accepted there might be casualties in the crash, but Peter's death had shaken her. She had liked him, had grown close to him, even admired his naïve goodness, felt his despair. These emotions had somehow got tangled in her relationship with John, as if Peter in his simple way had drawn her to John, at the house, on the tennis court, at the swimming pool - so that Peter's dying had somehow strengthened the unspoken bond between her and John.

When she'd learned of his death, her first thought had been of John, of his shame and utter disbelief that he'd killed a friend instead of his target. And that stirred an emotion so deep in her she sensed danger, the danger of getting involved. She instinctively thrust It away. She must accept John was a lost cause, must focus on what she was doing, on what needed doing next.

So, she left the airport and made her way to the Telephone

Exchange. Carefully. Searching for surveillance, altering direction, on the watch for the Chief Minister's double cross, evading John and the G8 Team.

As she reached its outer wall she could see the door was hanging off its hinges. By it was a Yardy, the one who had watched her come and go from Beecham's house. He beckoned.

She pulled the strap of her bag around, her hand lightly resting on the Beretta and slowly crossed the street.

'Not necessary,' the Yardy called, pointing at the bag. 'The landline's set. You've got five minutes.'

She took out the Beretta. 'I'll trust this anyway.' She waved him aside.

In the hallway, four Marines were sprawled across the floor.

'Dead?' she asked.

The Yardy laughed. 'No, Ma'am. They weren't expecting us. We broke in through the tunnel. Used tear gas.'

She looked at them. 'But they're unconscious.'

His face didn't alter as he produced the small lead weighted sap.

'Don't want to kill 'em. Navy Guard ship come in and shoot us up.' He grinned. 'So, we used the old ways.' He kicked one of the bodies. 'They so modern these days, they forget the old ways.'

She heard a growl and caught sight of Tank lying over the inert body of Storky. 'What are you doing about that?'

He laughed. 'That? He just licked us all over. Tear gas didn't fuss him at all. A couple of chocolate bars and he was ours.' The face behind the dark glasses focussed on her. 'Five minutes.'

It only took one. She opened her laptop, the connections clicking through like clockwork. Three hundred million dollars and the money in Rosa's account, flowed out of BlueLine Investments through Caracas to Nicosia into the account of Richard W. Foster in Jahal Bank, Nicosia, Cyprus. She had chosen the name Richard

W. Foster because she knew no-one of that name and, because it was a special account, the money could sit undisturbed there until the time came for her to move it on. She felt a shiver of excitement.

FIFTY-SEVEN

Paliakov had arrived in Ambergris on a private charter six hours before the air crash. The passport he'd picked up in Panama said he was Juan Hernandez, accountant.

He had hired a small Skoda from the car rental desk at Ambergris Airport, slung his holdall in the back seat and had driven to the Sunny Paree Condominium complex north of Harvey Town. A thin Danish girl in a cotton mini dress showed Paliakov along a weed-strewn path to a peeling cabin, the orange paint stripped in great gashes by the onshore salted wind. A wooden slatted double bed, a sofa and a built-in cupboard served as the furniture. A slab of wood holding a sink and covering a fridge was called the kitchen. The bathroom didn't stand inspection.

The girl smiled the smile. 'Fifty dollars for extras.'

Paliakov shuddered. He closed her hand over a twenty-dollar bill. 'I'll let you know.' He forced a smile in return.

He had nothing to do for the rest of the day, at least not until past midnight when he planned to get into the BlueLine Investment offices and see if he could hack into Rosa Rulenski's account. Bored, he switched on the television which relayed local news only. The sofa was plastic and sagged so he lay on the bed and cursed the heat. There was no air conditioning. He idly watched a mosquito fly around the window before closing his eyes and catching some sleep.

It was three thirty in the afternoon when the first news of the air crash came through on the television.

Paliakov sat up, tense, analysing the information, turning each piece over. The Opposition Leader had been wiped out in the first fatal bird strike ever in Ambergris.

Still listening to the news, Paliakov went to the creaking fridge and took out a bottle of beer, opened it and sat back on the bed, thoughtfully drinking from the bottle, trying to ignore the awful warm taste. He tried to seek logic through the chaos. When things happened like this it was rarely coincidence. The egrets had damaged aircraft but never crashed a plane before.

The pictures of the crash scene suddenly disappeared. A reporter excitedly cut in, announcing the Chief Minister had accused the British government of trying to assassinate him. He had declared Independence and was flying immediately to the UK to see the British Prime Minister.

Paliakov drew in a sharp breath as he realised what had happened. He was right, the crash was no accident. He started to pace the room, thinking fast. It bore all the hallmarks of a G8 operation. In fact, it looked like a typical Katya operation. What Lev called "subtle and unattributable"- unattributable to G8. But then killing the Opposition Leader didn't make sense. G8 had arranged it so that he would be the election winner. So why kill him? Was it an accident? Hardly, it was a Katya operation, she didn't make mistakes like that.

His heart started pounding. Suddenly it struck him. Of course! Katya was after the money. She'd turned, just as he'd guessed in Panama. It all made sense. The only communication link on Ambergris was the landline to Venezuela. It all fitted. Katya needed access to the landline to get Rosa's money out. She needed the Chief Minister to get her to the landline. He could only do that by going independent. Killing the Opposition Leader sealed the deal.

Paliakov spent no further time on analysis, he knew he was so right. He'd got her. It was nearly five-thirty and he'd have to work fast.

It was six o'clock when he backed the Skoda into a parking place opposite the BlueLine Investment office. The light was still on so he sat back to wait. There was hardly anyone around. It was much cooler now and a breeze was getting up. He watched the street lamps swing in the wind, short gusts that sent them bobbing on the wires strung across the road, throwing odd shadows across the buildings. Out of the corner of his eye, he saw the light go out in the Blueline office. The front door opened and shut. A woman walked away, pulling at her khaki skirt as it was tugged by the wind, probably a security guard.

He waited a few minutes. Then, forcing himself not to hurry, strolled across the road. He was inside the BlueLine office within ninety seconds. Very slow by operational standards. But what little skill he had learnt was by way of lunchtime sessions with operational officers in the G8 practice room in Moscow.

Once inside, his expertise took over and he thought again how lax these offshore financial firms were, not spending the money to secure their computers. He was into Rosa's files in minutes. Searching for the El Bayedh three hundred million and the Gadaffi money. It wasn't there. He searched again. The same result.

He settled down. Went through every file in BlueLine. There was nothing there. His stomach churned. The money had flown, but how and where had Katya hidden it? He must think. He took his mind back to the TV broadcast. His acute memory analysed the pictures and the reporters' words. They had been full of images of the crash and the Chief Minister declaring independence and the fight at the Telephone Exchange. He shook his head. Of course. The Telephone Exchange – he'd been right, she would have used it to transfer Rosa's cash immediately after the plane crash - but to where?

He wasted no more time but immediately fed in a request to the computer to track all landline communications relating to BlueLine Investments for the last five hours. He didn't have to wait long. There it was. Routed via Caracas from BlueLine Investments to Jahal Bank, Nicosia, Cyprus at 4.48pm that day. She'd got the money out less than an hour after the crash, while he was sitting in that dump of a room working out what she was doing.

He felt heady. But he had more to do.

He opened the most recent BlueLine file and typed in the Jahal Bank Nicosia. There it was – the account she'd transferred the cash to - Account Richard W. Foster 77077631. Cartwright's three hundred million dollars plus change. He'd got her. He could get the money. Suck it out into a G8 account then tell Lev. His sweat dripped on to the keyboard. He wiped it away. Fed in some more data.

The response was instant. Jahal Bank was a mixed private Hawala bank. Paliakov suddenly went cold. He slumped back in his chair, exploring the Hawala system in his mind. The Asian underground money transfer, designed to avoid exchange controls and taxes, was so simple but effective- and secret. There were Hawala bankers all over the world.

Katya was really smart. That three hundred million was now cash in the Hawala end of the bank's system. Non-transferable except by a Hawala transaction. Paliakov was shattered. It was incredible. The money could only be taken by her. It was now completely hidden.

Paliakov wiped his face with his hand. He'd never get her. He couldn't go to Lev, he had no evidence that it was Katya who'd made the transfer. There'd be no recognition for him now, just the same dreary life as a G8 stringer.

He began to shut down the computer programs when abruptly a thought struck him. It was unlikely the Hawala banker at Jahal Bank knew Katya personally, he simply knew her as Richard W. Foster, the name in the account. Cartwright's money, the three hundred million, was available to anyone who showed up at Jahal Bank proving they were Richard W. Foster. He felt a flush surge through him. Three hundred million dollars. His heart started pounding.

He switched off the computer. Unsnapped the front door lock and walked over to his car. Staggering slightly as a heavy gust of wind swept down the street. He'd got her – and he might yet get some cash. But a thought suddenly struck him - where was the Gadaffi money?

FIFTY-EIGHT

Paliakov was losing his temper. In his job he had to be patient, but he wasn't used to leg work and he'd been combing Harvey Town in his car searching for Katya for what seemed like hours. He had to find her, had to stop her from getting to Cyprus and the Jahal Bank. Only she stood between him and that cash.

The tiny Skoda was buffeted from side to side as he drove along a narrow road to a place called the Effendi Club. He'd been told it was a special place for tennis players. And Katya was a tennis player. For the first time he felt a twinge of optimism.

He'd just parked the car outside what looked like a Club when a small figure ran out and opened his door.

The figure peered in. 'Small car for large driver,' it said.

Paliakov glared at the man dressed in Moroccan clothes.

'I'm Lewis. I get your baggage. Give me keys, please.'

Paliakov struggled out of the car. 'I'm not staying. I'm looking for someone.'

Lewis ran his eyes over him. A knowing look came into them. 'Me? They tell you down town? Two hundred fifty dollars. All right?'

Paliakov nearly hit him. 'No. I don't want you, you little prick,' he shouted.

Lewis stepped back. 'Sorry. Sorry. When you guys look for someone here, it's usually me.'

The words cut into Paliakov. Red hot, stabbing at the boiling resentment in him. 'Ms. Petrovna. I'm looking for Katya Petrovna.'

Lewis's eyes changed, became wary, seeking the advantage.

Paliakov saw it. He pulled out a hundred-dollar bill.

Lewis's hand closed on it. 'Yes. She here.' He paused. 'Well, not *here*,' he added.

'So where is she?'

Lewis shook his head. Paliakov measured him. Even he could take out this little shit but he knew it wouldn't do any good. Lewis would only talk for money. He pulled out a fifty. Lewis nipped it out of his fingers.

'Down by fisherman's wharf.'

'What the hell's she doing down there?' The words, let out on impulse, with another fifty- dollar tab on them, fuelled his rage still further.

'I reckon she's with the Hammond fella.' Lewis put his forefinger to the side of his nose as he watched Paliakov's face. 'I know you wouldn't be interested. But the Hammond fella is, I tell you, all over her like a rash.'

He turned away, disinterested now, bored of Paliakov. 'Anyhow that's where they is.'

He looked at the cash in his hand. 'You mind down there. Storm coming.'

But Paliakov was past caring. Hammond was involved. It was always the same. These fucking businessmen were always the same, show them some money and they were yours. Like those bastards in Berlin. Leaving him like that, taking his cash, taking his Berliner. Now Katya with Hammond. The same thing. Done a deal with the Chief Minister and lifted the money. Now they'd light out together. The hell with them. He'd find them. Destroy them. The money was going to be his.

The drive to the wharf was treacherous. It was dark, no streetlights, the wind coming in spurts, rocking the small car. The wharf gradually came into view, dimly lit by lights swinging wildly on wires stretched above canvas awnings which thrashed over the stalls. Fishermen were under them, struggling to take them down.

He looked for Katya through the windscreen, searching among the shifting shadows. The sky beyond was pitch black, a bubbling white line streaking across it. He stopped, struggled out of the car, bent his head against the wind. A plastic box skittered towards him, caught his shoe. He bent down to get rid of it.

'Sorry, man. It got away.'

Paliakov looked up. A white-haired woman was grinning down at him, pointing at the box, her hand clawed with arthritis. He smelt the stink of fish on her.

'Have you seen a tourist woman down here. Maybe with a man?' He shouted against the wind.

'You too late. She down there.' She pointed along the coral shoreline. 'Been there an hour now.' She doubled up in laughter.

Paliakov swung away. Left her standing there, cackling with laughter. He stumbled across the litter- strewn market place towards the shore in the direction the woman had pointed to. Kicking away plastic bags and debris as it blew across his feet and into his legs. He put his hand under his shirt, eased out an old Smith and Wesson. He'd picked it up at a pawnshop behind his hotel in Panama. Stripped it to get through the baggage search, relying on the lax security for private charter flights.

Battling against the wind, struggling to stay upright and cursing the weather, he scrambled down to the foreshore slipping and sliding onto the coral beach. The waves smashed into the shore, whipped up by the wind, rattling the loose stones as they were sucked back into the ocean. Paliakov felt a glimmer of fear.

Here on the edge of the water, he might not get away. Might be sucked into the back surge.

He tried to move more quickly but the loose coral made it difficult. Dimly he saw a wooden jetty poking into the sea, rusted metal piles diving below the broken water. A couple of fishing boats lay alongside sharply rising and falling with the force of the waves. The old kind of boats, forty feet long, high prow, a sweep to the stern, with a stumpy wheelhouse. They were deserted. Heaving and tumbling in the surf.

The wind changed suddenly, tore at his face. That was when he heard the faint sound of voices. The woman's voice, the Russian Rs unmistakable. Katya.

They seemed to be to his right. On the jetty. He eased his body forward. Feeling for loose stones; lumps of coral. His hands touched the wood of the jetty. They were walking towards him. Away from the coming storm. Their hands joined. Hammond's head close to hers. Paliakov felt the bile rise up in him. He could almost taste the hate surging through him. His chance had come to get even - to eliminate the only threat to his getting the money and to ruin Katya. He straightened up. Tightened his grip on the Smith and Wesson.

FIFTY-NINE

Katya was the first to react. She saw the figure coming towards them; saw the pistol glinting in a sudden flash of lightning. Immediately she thought of the Beretta lying useless in a drawer back in her room and decided to be cool. It was always safer to pay off muggers, they were unpredictable. She didn't have much money anyway so he could take it, probably wanted it for drugs. She nudged John.

Paliakov stood still, watched them. 'Don't recognise me, do you Katya?'

Her head whipped up. His Russian instantly identifiable.

'Paliakov!' She tried to adjust, to be operational, to find a way out. But the thought of the money kept getting in the way. Did he know? Had Lev sent him? For the first-time ever she knew panic.

It was John who saved her. He slowly walked towards him. 'Paliakov. What are you here for?' He nodded at the pistol, 'Had trouble in town?'

Paliakov stepped back, 'Don't you come near me, you bastard.'

John stopped in his tracks. 'Hand over that weapon, immediately. What are you doing here? Have you lost your reason?' His voice was cold, angry.

'Reason, you shit? I'll give you three hundred million good reasons.' Paliakov waved the Smith and Wesson at Katya. 'And that cow, too.'

John watched Paliakov's face, the black rimmed glasses

fogged with salt spray hiding his eyes, the mouth working as he spat out the words, highly charged, almost incoherent, about to blow at any moment. He stepped in front of Katya, protecting her. Whatever was on Paliakov's mind, it had something to do with her, some wild sort of grudge. John had seen this kind of thing before.

'Pull yourself together, Paliakov.' His voice was sharp, commanding. 'Give me that.' He held his hand out again.

Paliakov pulled the trigger. Splintering the wheelhouse of the nearest boat. A sliver slashed John's cheek as the bullet whined into the sea. Katya started forward. John held her back, shoved her behind him. 'No. It's you he wants. He's insane. Keep behind me.' John wiped his face with his hand, shaking the blood off his fingers.

The movement drove Paliakov's mind nearer the edge. John's closeness to her, his protectiveness…he was picking up Katya's contempt for him, too.

'She won't get the money. That bitch you're protecting. In Jahal Bank.' He started shouting as the wind whipped around his words. 'I know it's Hawala. But I can get to Cyprus. I can get it.' His voice rose hysterically.

A heavy gust swung one of the boats into the jetty. A fishing net came loose from its boom, dropping and unravelling across the planking. Katya shifted to avoid it. Stopped as Paliakov levelled the pistol at her.

'Onto the net, you cow.' Paliakov knew what he had to do now. 'You.' He motioned to John. 'Join her.' Paliakov jerked the gun towards it.

A heavy rain started to fall, driving into them. The wind suddenly increasing. A slash of lightning streaked through the clouds, its brightness flickering across Paliakov's face. John sensed what was coming. He knew Paliakov was totally over the edge. He tried one last time to bring him back to reality. 'Paliakov—' He got no further.

'Shut up. You're with her, you shit. Get on that net. Or she gets it.' He raised the pistol to Katya's head.

John lunged forward. Tripped over the tangled net. Fell sprawling at Paliakov's feet.

Paliakov kicked him. There was no response. 'Tie him into that net, you fucking cow.' Paliakov's voice was wild, screeching above the wind. His head to one side, he was half doubled over against the gale that swept down the beach. The salt spray from the water hitting his face.

Katya struggled with John's unconscious body as she dragged him further onto the net, tussling with the wet line, looping it over his hands.

'Tighter. Tie him in, I said.' Paliakov stepped nearer. Katya tied the knots as loosely as she dared. She eyed the gun, waiting for a break.

Paliakov stepped back. 'You get in too.'

She hesitated.

'Get in!' He yelled. 'Or do you want this?' He shoved the gun forward.

Katya climbed into the net. Paliakov grabbed a loose line hanging from a pulley on the boom, and jerked it. The net started closing. Katya launched her weight against it. Stumbled as her foot caught. Her hand thrust through the mesh. Trapped. Throwing her off her feet. Suspended. Swinging. Terrified.

Paliakov heaved on the line. Ignored her scream. The pulley jerked as the net closed. Finally tying the line off he made sure Katya and John were locked in. The boom swayed as the waves slammed the boat into the jetty.

The wind was howling louder, making Paliakov's voice inaudible as he shouted at them. Clambering on board, he tugged the wheelhouse door open. He paused then, gasping for breath as he tucked the pistol into his waistband. He looked out across the harbour at the mass of storm clouds coming in, at the sea boiling under them. The waves were rearing up over the coral heads, smashing into each other in a flail of white. He turned the ignition key. This was retribution. Making sure she never breathed again. Never fucked up people again. Never lived to find him.

He climbed out onto the jetty. Picked up a boathook and smashed it through the side window of the wheelhouse, using it to shove the throttle full forward. He stepped back. Almost in a trance. Watching the sea churn as. the revs hit full power. As the boat wrenched the mooring ropes, ripping the cleats out of the jetty planking. As the boat reared away from its mooring. Plunging into the waves. The boom frantically swinging. Rising, falling. The net slamming their bodies into the water. Then crashing them back into the wheelhouse.

SIXTY

Katya knew she was drowning. The net had dropped deep into the sea as a huge toppling wave lurched the boat over. The boom swinging with it. Her hand was still caught in the mesh. She couldn't move. Couldn't reach for the surface. Find air. Her lungs started to heave.

As the darkness closed in she felt the futility of it all. Her mind drifting to John. To his final attempt to protect her. The only good thing in the whole mess. She could feel his body against hers. It was a pity she couldn't tell him. Couldn't tell him that despite everything, despite her betrayal, despite her killing, despite her deceiving him, she was still able to love. To love him. For she knew now she did love him. Her mind started fading. Drifting away. But the thought was still with her when she blacked out.

The sharp pain in Katya's leg kicked her brain awake. Her body had smashed into the wheelhouse as the boat staggered crazily in a roll passing through the harbour entrance into the maelstrom of water around the coral heads. Coughing. Retching. Seawater flowing from her mouth. Her lungs seared with pain. Her eyes burning hot. A red mist floating in front of them. She gasped as the net struck a shark pole. Jarring her shoulder. The giant hook scraping her forearm as it snagged the mesh. Tearing through the net.

She gagged as a huge, breaking wave washed right over her. Forcing water into her lungs. Smashing her onto the deck as the mesh parted.

She lay there, pain searing through her back, hazily watching the net as it swung over with the boom. With some sort of bundle tied in it. There was a high-pitched noise in her ears. Rising above the wind and the drumming rain. She tried to fix her mind on it. Felt the throbbing under her body. Must be an engine. Her mind froze. She was on the boat. John. The bundle in the net. John. Desperate, she reached for the wheelhouse door. Wincing at the pain in her back. Hung on to the handle. Hauling herself up. A surge of fear as she saw the sea for the first time. A white, angry, seething, screaming mass of foam and black water. Rearing up - twenty, thirty feet. Thundering down in creaming surf - towards the boat. The prow smashing forward. Driven by the whining of the engines - on full power. Burying the nose of the boat in the oncoming wave. Tons of water pouring towards her.

She fell to her knees. Clinging to the handle. Her head bent to her chest. Waiting. Until the water surged past. Split by the wheelhouse. The boom swinging over. In its wild dance. Katya snatched at the net. Frantically dug for John. Tearing. Fighting. Pulling. Struggling. Crashing to the deck as John came free. Knocking the breath out of her.

Then sliding, slipping, shouting with agony, she dragged him to the wheelhouse. Snatching the door open. Tumbling him in. Heaving the door shut. Jumping forward to pull him back. Away from the wheel as it spun frantically; the spokes a blur.

She worked on him then. Blanking out her pain. Pumping his lungs. Forcing her breath into them. Not caring about the sea. The storm. The waves. As they pounded the small cabin. Without him nothing mattered. She could die with him if he died. She held him in her arms as she clung to him. Her breath coming in great gasps. Sweat pouring down her face. Mingling with the seawater dripping from her hair. Her mind a blank. Until she became aware of a different sound. A different rhythm to the boat. It was a low growling noise. Fading then booming. The boat no longer rising and plunging through the waves. But juddering as mountains of water slammed into it from different directions.

Katya clawed her way up the side of the cabin to stand unsteadily on her feet. Peered out of the windows. Water streaming down them.

She saw it then. Black and glistening in the lightning. Terrifying. A massive coral head. Ten feet out of the water. Streaked with foam as the surf threshed over it in a deep rumbling growl. A huge back rip piling up the waves. Sucking the boat towards it.

She felt the fear surge through her. Reached her hand to the wheel. Tried to catch it. Yelled as the spokes mashed her fingers. The wheel spinning furiously as an opposite wave caught the rudder. Tossing the boat on its other side. Sending her sprawling. The sound nearer now. Menacing. She began the same scramble again. Reaching for the wheel. Waited. Until the wheel spun to its stop. Then she grabbed it. With both hands. Threw her weight against it. The bow bit deep into the water. Lifting the stern. The engine screaming as the prop came out of the surf.

She felt a hand on her shoulder. John, now on his feet. Clinging to the radar mount. There was no time for him.

'The throttle lever,' she yelled at him. 'Pull it back.'

He looked blankly at her, not understanding.

'John,' she screamed, forcing her words to rise above the howl of the wind, 'Pull the throttle lever back.'

He shook his head, trying to clear his senses, trying to blank out the pain as he caught the throttle lever. Pulled it right back. The engine coughed.

She yelled with fright. 'Not too much. Forward. Not too far.' Katya fought the wheel. Turning it to the right. 'More. A bit more.'

The nose of the boat moved forward; at an angle. Up the side of a curling wave. The crest broke over the small cabin. The noise drowning Katya's orders. Suddenly the bow slid over. Tumbling the boat into the trough.

'Throttle back,' Katya yelled, 'I'm going to turn. Throttle half forward up the next wave. Pull it back when I say.'

Her body hunched over the wheel. As she used all her strength to move the spokes. To control them.

John shifted the throttle forward. Crawling the boat on a diagonal up the next wave. The coral head loomed directly in front. The swell dragging the boat onto it. John threw up an arm. To protect himself when they hit.

'Now.' Katya spun the wheel. The boat leaning over. The stern slipping around. The bow pointing down the wave. John desperately pulled the throttle back. Heard the engine cough. He felt ice fear reach down his spine. He shoved it forward. Then back.

The boat slammed into the trough.

'Full forward. Full forward,' Katya screamed. She felt the next wave surge the boat towards the coral head. The bow lifted as the prop bit. Driving the boat at the wave. Gradually losing speed as it crawled high up the slope. The coral head almost under the stern. Katya flung the wheel the other way. Sliding the boat sideways back down the wave. Into the trough. The crest towering over them. About to break. To throw them onto the coral. At the last minute, she swung the nose into the wave. The whole force of the surf tumbled on the boat. Pushing it down. Water pouring into the wheelhouse. She glimpsed the coral head as they swept past. Half submerged. Instinctively John pulled the throttle back. The boat literally shook. Water sluicing off as it rose to the surface. The coral head now disappearing behind them.

Katya stared at him. Dark rings around her exhausted eyes.

'It'll be OK now,' she gasped. 'We'll turn again. Keep on the throttle. Forward up the wave. Back down.'

Abruptly a silence descended. The wind stopped. The wave tops settled. Massive but without the streaming spume. Katya looked at John. The desperate weariness vanishing as she realised what was happening.

'The eye,' she yelled. 'The storm. It's the eye.'

'No need to shout.' He smiled.

She gave a shaky laugh, took his hand. Slammed the throttle forward. The boat surged towards the shore.

'I never did a seamanship course,' he said unsteadily. Light-headed. Relief flooding through him. No longer on the edge of death.

'I spent my teens on the Black Sea.' She coughed. 'You learn fast there or drown.' She leaned towards him. 'Thanks to you, I didn't.'

She kissed him.

Her feelings for him were clear now. As they had always been if only she'd let them surface. But she must keep the money and John must never know. She could find a way. Had to find a way. She took John's hand again to push the throttle forward.

She steadied the wheel as they surfed a wave. The harbour entrance was in front of them. The town lights now visible through the scant, misty rain which seemed to welcome them.

The wheelhouse door slammed open in a howl of wind. A sheet of rain blotted out the town lights. A flood of water foamed around their feet.

'It's back,' John yelled. 'The storm.'

'Hold on,' Katya shouted. 'Full power. We can make it straight through the harbour entrance.'

A wall of water, thirty feet high, towered seething over the stern.

Fear again tore through her as she loosened her grip on the wheel. The stern out of control. Gasping with effort, gritting her

313

teeth, she grabbed the spinning spokes. Cried out as they cracked into her fingers.

John put his shoulder to the door. Pain searing down his side and back. Slammed it shut. Turned and put his arms around Katya instinctively. Held onto the wheel spokes with her.

The stern lifted. The angle steepening until they stared, petrified, into the trough twenty feet below.

In an endless roar of white foam, the wave snatched the boat, hurled it, tearing, grinding, onto the coral beach.

SIXTY-ONE

They lay on the deck of the wrecked cabin listening to the keel of the boat grinding on the coral beach as the storm raged over them. Exhausted, sodden, clinging to each other. Too weak to move, or talk. Just feeling the warmth of each other. Drawing strength from one another.

She felt close to tears for the first time since she was a child. She just held her hand out to him.

He took it in his. 'Paliakov'll pay for this. Pay for what he's done to you.'

She swallowed. 'What was driving him? He must be mad.'

John squeezed her fingers. 'I thought he had a grudge at first. Getting at you. But it was the money. He tried to get rid of us. You heard what he said.'

She returned the pressure of his fingers. 'Something about a bank. Cyprus, wasn't it?'

He nodded, trying to concentrate as he felt pain stab down his back. 'Jahal Bank. Did he say it was Hawala?'

'Yes.' She arched her back, weariness surging through her body. As the adrenalin of terror receded. 'We've got to stop him from getting it - the money. We have to find it before he does.'

'You'll have to do that. I've got to clear up the mess I made here. Do something about the Ministers.' He passed his hand over his face. Told her it wasn't so much the killing of Peter that gnawed at him, that was excusable, an operational hazard. But it had left the corrupt Ministers in control and completely undermined the operation itself. That was what he had to put right. She would have to deal with Paliakov and the money.

Katya agreed with him. She needed him caught up sorting out the problem of the Ministers so that she could slip away, get to Cyprus and hide with the money. After Paliakov, after the storm, after John had helped save her life, her near drowning had made her face the truth of her relationship with him. And her deception of him had taken on a new meaning. She wanted the money and the freedom the new life would give her but she now wanted John as well. The two weren't compatible. Or were they? She shook her head, too tired to think. She would sort it out later.

'Come on,' she said wearily. 'You sort the Ministers out and I'll find out exactly what Paliakov did with the money.'

They slowly made their way back to the Effendi Club.

It was after three in the morning when they finally made it back to the Effendi Club. It was deserted except for the ubiquitous Lewis. He looked at them in astonishment. Taking in their soaking, torn clothes, wild hair and blood trickling from cuts.

'Hello.' He bowed; the tassel on his fez describing a little arc. 'Been love making?'

He was reminded of Paliakov as John glared at him.

'OK, OK, just joking.' He waited. Looked at Katya, decided it was safer not to mention the man who had been looking for her.

John pointed towards the bar. 'Get us a drink Lewis. Rum. And be quick about it.'

'Yorsh for me, Lewis,' Katya called after him.

Lewis hurried down the corridor to the Elgin Bar, took out bottles of Harvey's Special Rum, vodka, beer and three glasses. He ran back, panting, hurriedly poured out two large measures of rum and a pint of Yorsh, gave them their glasses and raised his own.

'Lovers and departed Ministers.' The rum disappeared down his throat.

'That's no way to talk of the dead, Lewis,' John spoke sharply.

'I said Ministers.' Lewis looked at his glass, poured out another rum. 'I meant Ministers. I'm drunk, I don't mind telling you,' he said. 'I'm glad drunk those rat bastards have flown - flown.' He poured the rum into his mouth.

'What do you mean, the Ministers have flown?' John grabbed his wrist.

Lewis pulled away and did a little jig.

'The Ministers flew off with their money. That's what I heard. Flapped away before the storm hit.' He took a pull from the bottle. 'Juan Ybarra knows.'

'Juan Ybarra. Conchita's nephew?' John queried.

'Yes he's stayed, he heard the Yardies killed his Ma - got a lot of help and searched them out.' He stopped, poured out some more rum. 'Huge fight, bodies everywhere, ended up at the Telephone Exchange.'

'Go on.' John took the bottle from him.

'That's 'bout all there is.'

'Who's in charge?'

'Chief Minister and his crowd lit out. Corporate Party's running things they say, what's left of it. I don't care. Long as those bastards have gone.'

Katya took John's arm. 'Thanks Lewis.'

Leaving their drinks untouched, Katya held John up as they limped down the dark passageway to her room.

SIXTY-TWO

Katya took John straight to her bathroom where they cast off their sodden clothes and wrapped themselves in the thick Effendi Club bath robes. Exhausted, they were both silent, just glad to be alive.

As she worked on his cuts and bruises she was thinking fast. As long as John thought Paliakov had taken the money she was safe from the discovery that it was she who had deposited it in the Hawala bank. Katya knew she had to nail Paliakov as the traitor but to do that convincingly she had to find out how much G8 in Basingstoke knew and there was only one person who might tell her – Lev. She must speak to him before John could get to him. She needed at least four or five minutes on the call because Lev would ask questions, he always did, and she would have to answer them persuasively.

She finished working on John's wounds. He was still shaky but was reviving fast and it would be only a matter of minutes before he recovered enough to want to speak to G8. The only thing she could think of to give her time was to persuade him to take a long shower to ease his pain. So, she turned the water on to hot and almost pushed him into it, telling him to stay there while she made them hot drinks in the suite's galley kitchen.

She quickly made her way to the sitting room with its spectacular windows which looked out on the jumbled waves now picked out in bright moonlight with the passing of the storm. She grabbed her phone off the coffee table, ran to the small kitchen punching the speed dial to Lev. It only rang once before she heard a familiar voice. Keeping her voice low and level, she replied. 'Lev, Katya here.'

'Katya?' A surprised pause. 'Where's John?'

She heard the alarm in Lev's voice, fumbled with the kettle, pouring water into it. 'He's OK, Lev. I'm phoning because we have a problem.'

'Peter Thomas, you mean?'

Katya gripped the phone. This was the dangerous part of their conversation. If she was to learn from Lev whether he knew any money had been transferred to the Hawala account in Cyprus, she had to let Lev know the Ministers had fled with their cash. But she mustn't let him suspect she knew how it had happened. 'No. That's been resolved. The Ministers have left the Island and the Corporate Party are in control. There's some rumour they took their money with them.'

'That explains the activity.'

She switched on the kettle, pretended not to understand. 'What activity?'

'Between four and six your time last evening there was a series of transfers from Caracas. We didn't pick them up until an hour ago but we traced them back to Ambergris. It seems a number of people used the Landline to Venezuela.'

Katya's mind raced. Lev had confirmed what she'd feared. G8 had already discovered the Ministers had taken their money with them. 'That's very bad news, Lev.' She paused slightly, asked the crucial question matter of factly. 'Have you traced the money on from there?'

Lev's voice became muffled as he spoke to someone in his office. 'We're doing it now. The computers are tracking. It looks like they used simple hopscotch, so we should get to it quite quickly-' He broke off as someone spoke to him, then repeated it to her. 'They tell me it'll take about three days to track all of it and get it back. Except one transfer— it went Hawala apparently.'

She spoke carefully, taking two mugs down from an overhead cupboard. 'It's why I'm calling you Lev and not John.' She listened to the silence down the connection, at the same time she listened for the noise of the shower, relieved as she heard the water still rattling against the glass panels.

'Hello? Are you still there Lev?'

'Yes. I'm here. What about John? He is alright, isn't he?"

'Yes, yes - well, no - I wanted to tell you myself. It affects us, the Russians in G8. It's Paliakov.'

'Paliakov? What about him? He's in Panama, R and R.'

'He came here, Lev.' She paused, trying to break the news gently.

'What are you telling me, Katya?' Lev's voice was harsh, demanding.

She spelled it out in a rush, getting over the hard ground as quickly as possible. 'He tried to kill us. He's gone over. Taken the money.'

'What?' Lev almost shouted the word then muttered something she couldn't catch.

Katya realised he suddenly sounded tired, incoherent. She tried again. 'Paliakov came here. Told us he'd siphoned the money out of Rosa's BlueLine Investment account and had sent it to Nicosia to the Jahal Bank. Hawala.' She hesitated a second as if working out a problem. 'I didn't understand what he was getting at when he said that because there was no way he could have sent out that money with the freeze still on here. Now you've told me about the landline it all makes sense. His is the transaction that the computers spotted as Hawala. He must have stolen the money in Rosa's account.'

There was a long pause. Katya let Lev think while she shook some coffee into a mug.

Then he asked the question she had prepared for. 'Why did he tell you where the money was?'

Again, she took a risk and took her time answering, pretending to think, to revisit the scene, even as she dropped a tea bag into the other mug.

'You should have seen him, Lev, he was completely out of control. He was going to kill us. I don't think he cared what he told us. Once he'd transferred the money out of Ambergris he had to get rid of us. Who else was in a position to get to Rosa's account? And we would have then found out that he had to be hand in hand with the Chief Minister to be able to access the landline at the Telegraph Exchange. And if he was working with him, was it another part of the deal to kill Peter? I wouldn't put it past him.' She pictured the scene before she spoke again, summoning her terror to make what she was saying totally believable. 'Lev, he was out of his mind. I think he had some sort of hatred of me. I think it had been boiling up for some time.'

She heard Lev blow smoke into the phone. In a long sigh.

'I know about Paliakov. He had a side, you know.' He hesitated. 'Katya, you were sometimes . . .' He paused. 'Perhaps I should have stopped you; but I know your need to blow off steam.'

Katya heard the shower stop. She had to bring Lev's focus back - Paliakov must not get to that money, at all costs he had to be stopped. Her voice quickened. 'You'll take it from here then, Lev. Paliakov's gone after the money but he can't do it remotely. He'll have to go to the Hawala banker and personally instruct him what to do with the money. So G8 will trace Paliakov - arrest him?'

There was another silence. She knew she had only a minute or so before John came into the sitting room, she also knew she couldn't hurry Lev. The kettle hadn't boiled yet. She forced herself to wait.

'You said things were resolved your end? In Ambergris?' Lev spoke haltingly.

'Yes. The crisis is over. If you can get the Ministers' assets back, we'll be all right on the G8 end. There need be no publicity that we nearly lost it all.'

'Then I want to ask a favour, Katya. I only ask because I trust you and you are a fellow Russian after all.'

She knew what was coming and knew she had succeeded. She would let Lev think she couldn't let him down, that if she did, the whole of G8 would suffer as well as the Russian part of G8. It was the reason she'd called Lev and not let John do it. 'You want me to go to Cyprus. Get the money back. Eliminate Paliakov.'

'If it was just me, I wouldn't ask you, Katya. But it is for us Russians. A scandal will hurt us and we're too young an organization and Russia has too many enemies.' Lev sounded sad. Hating to say the words.

She had no time left but she forced herself to go slowly - hurrying too fast would only arouse Lev's suspicions. 'I know Lev, I would ask the same of you. They would point the finger at us - I remember the KGB and the corruption, my father...'

'I'm sorry, Katya.'

'We'll always have bad ones like Paliakov, Lev. It's doing something about them that matters.'

She waited as she heard someone talking to Lev, her stomach knotting as she strained to hear the click of the bathroom door opening.

'The BlueLine transfer out of Rosa's account.' Lev's voice was stronger. 'The account number is 77077631. The name is Richard W. Foster.' He paused. 'Katya-'

Katya didn't let him finish. 'It's between you, me and John, Lev. No one else needs to know.'

'Thank you, Katya. I won't forget.'

She tossed the mobile on the coffee table just as John walked slowly in, his body wrapped in the bath robe. The only sign of the last five hours ordeal were the dark lines under his eyes.

He saw her cuts and bruises, her hair streaked with salt, her eyes red with fatigue and his face softened, 'Go and have your shower. I'll see you in the morning.'

She opened her mouth to tell him to stay. But that would open the way for his thoughts to stray to Paliakov and the money and how it got to Cyprus. So she let him go.

SIXTY-THREE

Cato landed the chartered Embraer Phenom 300 on the Ambergris airport runway with a thousand feet to spare. The aircraft's twin turbofans ruffled the reeds beside the ponds and the plumage of the egrets which strutted nearby. As he parked he saw Katya there signalling him not to shut down. He gave the thumbs up, set the engines to idle.

Katya ran forward, unlatched the door and climbed aboard.

'Cato. Good to see you. We need to take off for Miami right away.'

Cato's first thought was she never changed, she looked as beautiful as ever, always in a rush. His second thought was security. 'OK well shut the bloody door then.'

Katya laughed. 'No, hang on John's coming, he can shut it. What's the flight time?'

'Cruising, about an hour, a bit less if you're in a hurry - knowing you it'll be a lot less.'

She laughed again. 'Got any drinks on board?'

'In the rear. Coffee.'

Her mouth turned down. It was his turn to laugh. 'No, it's alright, there's tea as well.' He saw her eyebrows raise. 'Yes, and raspberry jam.' He felt the pressure of her hand on his shoulder as she turned and hurried towards the back of the cabin. She was in a remarkably good mood he thought.

As Katya strode down the aisle to the galley at the rear she heard John climb aboard and Cato speaking to the tower requesting permission to take off. The door slammed shut; the turbo fans started their soft whine; they lifted off.

John would want to talk about Paliakov and that was fraught with danger. She wasn't really worried about losing the cash Paliakov was after. She'd given Dempsey clear instructions what to do with it when she'd been with him in London. She was pretty sure he'd carried out those instructions, otherwise he wouldn't get his share of the three hundred million. Unless he decided to run with the whole lot himself.

She recoiled from that thought. Could she bear to lose the money having got so close to it and to her freedom? Without the money, there was no chance of being free, her loneliness would have no end. Unless… unless there was a chance of a life with John. What about John? She loved him, wanted him and was sure he loved her, wanted her. The problem was how much did he want her? Was it enough to commit to a lifetime together? Would he leave G8 for her? His motive for working in G8 was different to hers. She'd been given no option by her father's tyranny but to work in intelligence. In John's case, he was dedicated to the work. It was a question that nagged at her because in it lay the key to her freedom.

She dropped two teaspoons of jam into her tea, picked up the two mugs, and walked back down the aisle to the seats. Putting the mugs on the table, she sat down opposite John. He lay back, head on one side, asleep.

She didn't wake him, content with the intimacy of him near her, and silently took a magazine from the rack by her seat and began leafing through it. It had the usual glossy pictures of multimillion dollar residences. All beyond the resources of any G8 officer or most other people for that matter. Idly she turned a page to see yet another five-bedroom apartment overlooking Central Park in New York. What a waste of time looking at property she

Katya

didn't want and would never be able to buy she thought and looked up to see if John was awake. He was dead to the world. A page fell open advertising a three-thousand-acre spread in Montana, an eight-bedroom ranch house, bunkhouses for staff, stables and corralling for horse breeding. She caught her breath, read the details again. Three thousand acres nestled a valley in the white- capped Rocky Mountains, pictured with a huge lake, green pasture. That was freedom – half of that three hundred million would swallow up three thousand acres and a lifetime of living there - she felt a frisson of excitement.

Suddenly Cato stood at her elbow, holding out a sheet of paper looking puzzled. 'This just came through from Maxim in Ambergris, it's for you.' He nodded at John. 'Well, it's addressed to John, but you'd better read it as it's marked urgent.'

She took the note and scanned it as Cato stood over her. It was simple and to the point.

'URGENT

To: DG G8

Time: O652 Zulu

Body recovered from Ambergris Harbour 0640 hrs. ID Igor Paliakov confirmed. Cause of death drowning. Instructions please.

Maxim.'

Katya stiffened, her hand reaching for her necklace. She couldn't believe it. Paliakov dead. Paliakov really dead. She felt lightheaded, the money was hers. The ranch was hers. And if she asked the right question in the right way John would be hers too.

Dimly she heard Cato speaking. 'Wasn't he a Berlin stringer? What was he doing in Ambergris?'

'Good question, Cato. Tell Maxim that if he or any member of the team are asked about Paliakov they are to deny all knowledge of him and leave his death in the hands of the

Ambergris Government. There must be no link to Paliakov or G8. Make that very clear, OK?'

Cato wanted to know more but Katya was obviously shocked at the news and anyway it was never a good move to question her orders unless there was a very good reason. He nodded and turned towards the cockpit.

Katya nudged John's arm. He awoke suddenly, saw her and sleepily smiled. 'Sorry, I must have dozed off.'

'Paliakov's dead.'

He sat up, fully awake now, incredulity spread across his face. 'Dead, how?'

She pushed the note across the table. 'Drowned, the bastard must have been sucked into the sea after he left us.'

He read the note. 'I'm not sorry about that.' He immediately went operational. 'We need to reply to Maxim.'

'I've already done that. Told him to tell the team to deny all knowledge and leave it to the Ambergris Government to deal with. There's nothing to link Paliakov to G8. Nothing to link G8 to Ambergris at all.'

'Good.' He noticed the emotion in her eyes. 'He was irrational. It had nothing to do with you, he hated you for some reason. And he had to kill us if he was going to get away with the money. Always remember that.'

Katya felt a weight fall off her - he had no idea. 'Thanks John.'

She broke in as he was about to say more, the timing could not be better for what she had to say. She took in a breath, 'John, I'm thinking of leaving G8.'

She saw him flinch. Was that a signal that he was only interested in her as his Chief of Operations?'

He took his time before replying slowly. 'I'm not sure I could cope with that - G8 could cope with that… '

It was time to persuade him. She gave him the magazine and pointed to the page advertising the ranch. 'I've just seen this, it made up my mind, I don't know why - I just saw it - it's something I've always dreamed of - if I don't leave G8 now…' She stopped there, letting the picture of her future hang, afraid to add words that might reduce its meaning.

She watched him take in the photos of the place, read the description.

He looked up. 'By yourself?' He queried.

The question took her by surprise, she'd expected him to ask how she could afford it. Did the words mean his uppermost thought was he might want to be with her? There was a pause as violet-blue eyes looked steadily into grey ones. 'If I had someone to come with me, I'd take them.'

'Would it have to be this place?'

It was a start, something she could build on. 'Not necessarily, as long as it's somewhere where we can have space, time; maybe breed wild horses…'

'Would I have to leave G8 as well?'

The question came at her like a thunderbolt. It was what she wanted but also what she dreaded. He would come, but would he really commit. She had to make sure. 'You mean live with me somewhere else, do something else?'

The grey eyes hadn't left hers. 'Nothing fazes you, does it? You're not at all surprised I want to be with you.'

She laughed. 'But do you, John?' She put the question direct. 'Want to commit, I mean?'

'Well, I couldn't afford to be with you on this ranch.' He pushed the magazine over to her. 'Not if I left G8.'

She felt the conversation was like a Tac Room operational meeting and, laughing, said so. He laughed with her, but his gesture told her that he was hesitant, uncertain of abandoning his career.

Tactically she felt it was now or never. She had to explain how she had the money to buy the ranch and live there. The explanation would be a lie so it had to be convincing.

She knew that what she was about to say could throw suspicion on her. On the other hand, the risk was balanced in her favour - Paliakov was dead, John was full of sympathy for her for the way Paliakov had tried to kill her, and G8 had an assassination in Ambergris to hide.

She started quietly. 'My file doesn't reveal this and even Lev doesn't know.' She saw his expression change. Committed, she slowly went on, 'It's about my father.' She shook her head as she saw he was about to interrupt. 'No, let me finish… It was the old KGB…you know how they secretly hid huge sums of cash…protecting themselves …' He nodded. Her voice grew stronger as she started to build the lie about her father. 'My father did…hide money…' She made an excuse for him. 'It was the old communist regime, you know, anyone in the intelligence world knew how to make money and hide it.'

John stopped her. 'You don't have to tell me this, Katya. What your father did or didn't do isn't visited on you, it was a different world.'

'No John you need to hear this.' She paused, gathering her thoughts. 'He knew the Chechens were treacherous and he'd been warned not to get in too deep. The last time I saw him he told me this and told me where he'd hidden a fortune in cash for his future. I don't know why he told me, I only knew him as controlling and cruel - but then perhaps, after all, he trusted me - he'd trusted me when we sailed together in the Black Sea…' She broke off. 'I've never touched it. I was in the FSB by then and said nothing because they'd have sacked me, I mean they were clearing out the old Soviet intelligence stables- and he wasn't popular-

'I never knew.'

It wasn't the three words by themselves that told her John believed her, it was the way he said them, his sympathy for the life her father had forced on her rather than any concern about his corruption which he accepted without question.

'So - you . . . you can buy your ranch.'

Katya felt relief flood through her. The last obstacle to her future with him had been removed. He believed her. The spectre of G8 hanging over their heads, her head, had been lifted. 'John. I want to leave all thoughts of Russia, of G8. Leave it all behind. I'd do that with you.'

His next words were flat, a question to himself. 'I'm not sure I could leave G8 straight away, I'd need to think about it.'

Her euphoria gave way to dismay— she had to persuade him. 'Not even for me?' For the first time, she spoke the so far unspoken. 'I know you love me John.'

His face softened. 'I know that too. Look, give me a year to tidy up and pass on the reins to a successor and I'll join you. Fair?'

'Promise?'

He looked up as Cato bent over the table. 'Landing in Miami in ten minutes.'

SIXTY-FOUR

It was just after dawn when Katya and John landed at Heathrow. It was drizzling rain, the pavements already shiny, puddles forming in the grey paving slabs made greyer by the low cloud.

The queue for cabs tailed back for yards, and they waited, too tired to talk. Finally, they came to the front of the queue and Katya told the driver to take them to her apartment. John didn't argue, he was pleased to be able to get somewhere just to sleep.

Betsie opened the apartment door just as Katya was putting in her card.

'Katya!' She exclaimed, scandalised by this breach of security. 'Well, I never did. You look all in, dearie, get yourself inside this minute.'

'Hello, Betsie. I've got John with me. He's going to be staying.'

Before Betsie could say "John?", she was scandalised again as he kissed her cheek, saying. 'Hello Betsie.'

'Get away with you, John.' She screwed up her apron and laughed. 'Never mind him, dearie, we're just good friends.'

Katya, tired as she was, threw her head back and laughed too. Her auburn hair flying across her shoulders, the violet-blue eyes sparkling. Betsie caught their expression as they rested on John. She felt her eyes watering, she'd been on at Katya for so long to find someone to settle down with.

She turned away to hide her emotion. 'I suppose you'll be

wanting a cup of tea.' She sniffed as she went towards the kitchen. 'Mind, no kissing behind my back.'

Katya and John burst out laughing as they moved towards each other.

'Don't forget the jam, Betsie— 'John stopped as he heard his mobile ring. He answered it, listened and raised his eyes at Katya as he said. 'Hello, Prime Minister.'

After a minute or so he put the mobile back in his pocket, saying thoughtfully, 'The PM wants to see me at the House of Commons right away. Dempsey's making trouble apparently. Something about Peter's death in Ambergris.'

Her mouth tightened. 'I always knew Dempsey was a nuisance - he never liked you from the start.'

'I know and I might need some support.'

'I'll come with you, I was there in Ambergris and Dempsey wasn't, so what can he say?' She hoped her words sounded confident and to emphasise them she leaned forward and kissed him. 'Seeing him off will be nothing to what we've been through.'

'I loved you through all that,' he said, suddenly.

She kissed him again. 'As I told you, you have a funny way of showing it.'

He laughed. 'That's your redeeming feature.'

She pulled back. 'What is?'

'Your sense of humour.'

'Oh, that.' She laughed with him and turned towards the kitchen to say goodbye to Betsie. Her brain raced as she tried to work out what Dempsey could possibly want. Why was he drawing attention to himself in this way when he'd just banked a fortune?

She took her car out of the garage and drove them rapidly to the House of Commons, effortlessly threading through the traffic despite her mind being wholly occupied by Dempsey. What worried her was that Dempsey's raw ambition might have led him to believe he could hide the money and at the same time trample over G8 to further his career. The next step on that career ladder was the Chancellor of the Exchequer, and his greed for the job was blatant. It now seemed he was about to take credit for successfully freezing the assets of the British Territories and blame John for bungling the Ambergris operation. Katya knew only too well how ambition could lead to disaster. She'd led enough targets down that path.

It was in her favour that John still had no idea that she and Dempsey had met in London and had now successfully banked the El Bayedh cash. As she drove, she concentrated his mind on his own relationship with Dempsey and not hers. She made him re-cap his run-ins with him, first when he introduced him to G8 and later when he allowed Lev and Walt to bully him into freezing the British Territory's assets. It wasn't surprising, she told John, that Dempsey would use any excuse to retaliate and probably get him sacked so he could appoint his own puppet Director General of G8.

Dempsey was getting to his feet to address the House when they arrived. They had a glimpse of the Chamber as a Clerk led them to the PM's office, the faces of the Members expectant as they anticipated what was rumoured to be a major Parliamentary speech. Even at ten o'clock in the morning, when most Members were at home or already in the Bar, they had all come to hear him.

The hum of speculation stopped abruptly as Dempsey began his speech.

'Mr Speaker, Honourable Members, the fight against organised crime and terrorist money-laundering has reached a new plateau. A point at which we need to review the balance of power between the G8 Agency fighting it and the governments funding the fight.'

'You were right,' muttered John to Katya as they moved on.

The Clerk ushered them into the PM's office. The PM looked up from his desk, searching behind them.

Instead of the usual greeting he said urgently, 'Where's Lev?'

Katya couldn't hide her surprise. 'Lev? Are you expecting him, Prime Minister?'

'Yes, it's urgent and I told him to meet me here.'

'What about?' queried John.

'He told me what you and Katya have told me. He said we've achieved exactly what we set out to do and got rid of those bloody Ministers. Now Dempsey's got it into his head that we should expose the death of the Leader of the Opposition. Something he's picked up about the Chief Minister and an assassination plot. Dempsey refuses to speak to you, John, so I need Lev here. If Dempsey won't see you, he can listen to Lev who can put an end to this damaging speculation.' He narrowed his eyes at John. 'There's nothing in this assassination nonsense, I presume, John - G8 played no part in the Leader of the Opposition's death?'

Katya spoke first. 'Dempsey'll have a hard time proving the word of an ex Chief Minister who's just skipped Ambergris having raided its Treasury and taken the cash with him. I was there. Of course it's not true.'

A sudden roar of cheering echoed from the chamber. They turned and looked at the screen on the wall opposite the PM's desk.

'Looks like Dempsey's giving it to them.' The PM looked down at his desk, absently riffled the papers there – on edge. 'He's good at that,' he muttered. 'We must find Lev before Dempsey goes too far.'

The cheers broke off. A silence descended. Then muffled exclamations followed by a buzz of chatter.

'What the hell is going on?' The PM looked at the screen again. 'What the hell's that?'

Katya turned her head, saw a message on the screen.

From BlueLine Investments Ambergris to Jahal Bank Nicosia Pay three hundred million dollars to Richard W. Foster Account Number 77077631

She drew in a breath. Clenched her hands. Swallowed to stop the sickness rising in her throat. What was Dempsey up to? Her eyes remained fixed on the screen. Dimly she heard John speaking. 'That's a transfer from Ambergris - it can only be from the Chief Minister.'

The PM looked shocked. 'BlueLine? What's that? Where is this coming from?' He looked around as if he expected the Chief Minister to be there. 'My god the press will have a field day. It's got to be stopped.'

Katya was paralysed, speechless as John was the first to move.

He picked up a phone on the PM's desk, dialed a number and spoke into it. 'Where's the television screen controlled from?' He listened. 'OK.' He slammed the phone down, pushed Katya towards the door. 'We'll sort this out,' he called to the PM over his shoulder.

As they ran down the deserted corridor Katya heard Dempsey struggling to make himself heard above the hubbub in the packed Chamber. She was still completely shattered by the message on the screen, sweat bursting out of her every pore. Her senses sharpened as she passed the open door into the Chamber and saw the MPs all standing up, waving their Order Papers, shouting, 'Shame. Shame.' All she could think of was how could Dempsey be such a fool as to risk everything by attacking John.

She felt John push her ahead of him into the Control Room.

As the door opened Lev quickly looked up from the control panel in front of him. 'You've come. Good. You know why I'm here?'

John didn't hide the surprise in his voice. 'Lev. What-' He

stopped, became urgent. 'You've got to stop this, Lev. Paliakov's dead. The cash is safe, he can't get it and Dempsey can't hurt G8, it's all over-'

'No, John, listen to me -'

'No, you listen to me, Lev. Once the details are out no-one will believe the Chief Minister or Dempsey— they will both be finished. You can't create a scandal with the British Government, Lev, the PM won't stand for it.'

'The British Government?' Lev drew savagely on his cigarette. 'Do you think that's what all this is about, John? This is about people, not mathematics. You think it was only Paliakov? It was Dempsey.'

'Dempsey?' John almost shouted his surprise. 'He's making it up to get rid of me in order to put in his own man to head up G8.'

Katya's hand went instinctively to her gold necklace, her face white, swallowing to control herself.

Lev pressed a key on the control panel, half aware he had noticed her tell. The screen flashed up another message.

"To Basu. Jahal Bank. Split the package at your discretion to Tarsus Development London. Account Number 8040070."

Katya's stomach contracted. She thought she was going to faint. Dempsey had followed her instructions to the letter. It would take moments to find out her three hundred million was in a Hawala not a hundred yards from here. A blind urge crashed through her to save herself, to confess before it was too late, to tell it all, blame Paliakov - the name sprang to her lips, 'Paliakov…'

Lev looked straight at her. 'You think that was Paliakov? Watch. The call to Jahal Bank came from this number.'

"0793774798017" The number blazed out on the screen.

Lev went on remorselessly. 'That's Dempsey's mobile number. The computers tracked it. G8SUR has located the mobile itself. It's in his jacket pocket as he speaks.'

'Dempsey? It's not true.' Katya hardly heard her own words.

'I can't prove it. But I can get close.' Lev pressed another key. Words scanned across the screen.

"Yes. Hello."

"You have a name to help me contact the Chief Minister."

"I'll call you."

Lev went on. 'That call came from Ambergris. Routed through Houston, Guatamala, Mexico City, Caracas and Paris. The voices were electronically distorted, but it was routed to Dempsey's mobile.'

Katya's heart pounded, her fingers wrapped around her necklace, there was a chance things would go right, Lev had Dempsey firmly in his sights.

John was still in denial, 'That doesn't mean a thing. It might have been Dempsey's mobile but that doesn't prove he was using it.'

Lev's face didn't move. He vaguely thought Katya seemed overly nervous, she was fairly clutching that chain of hers. He dismissed it, went on. 'Then believe this.' He pressed a key. 'This occurred at four twenty-five this afternoon.' The message flashed across the screen.

"To Lee Chin Investment Trust Singapore From Tarsus Development London. Transfer three hundred million dollars to Hugo Dempsey Account Number 446619732"

A red mist swept over Katya's eyes. She felt a great band clamp across her chest as the immensity of what Dempsey had done to her took hold. All gone, stolen - her life - her freedom – her future with John. The years she had been tyrannized, the years she had sweated terror in G8, the funeral pyre in El Bayedh, the promise of a future with John. The pent-up dam burst in a blaze of uncontrolled fury.

'The bastard!' She screamed. 'The son of a bitch. He's taken the money. My money. My share!'

She dived through the door, down the corridor, shoving people aside, shouting Dempsey's name.

John stood stock-still, unable to move. The colour drained from his face as he stared at Lev for an explanation. Any explanation. Lev stared back, knowing deep down he should have guessed that tell of Katya's was more than just worrying about G8's reputation. Silently thinking to himself, my god, what has she done...

"She's got a gun. She's got a gun." They heard the shouts as they echoed up the corridor.

John's heart was in his mouth as he tore his eyes away from Lev's to fling himself through the door and race down the corridor to stop her. Pushing away shouting, questioning faces.

Katya heard his shouts. She raced around a corner towards the noise of the Chamber, kicking aside a policeman striding to meet her. She slammed open the Chamber door - saw Dempsey standing by the dispatch box, open mouthed in fright.

'You bastard.' She yelled. 'You took the money. It's not yours. It's ours. It's mine.' She jumped up onto the front bench waving her Beretta.

Ministers flung themselves to the floor as they saw the gun. The members froze as they watched her scramble along the bench towards Dempsey - blocking two security guards who were trying desperately to get through them. Dempsey was struggling to shove past the other Ministers, yelling at them to move, kicking at them to get away.

Above the noise Katya screamed at him again. 'You double crossing bastard!'

Dempsey turned then. He saw John forcing a path through the stunned MPs to try and reach her. 'Stop her, Hammond.' He was frantic. 'Stop her.' He saw a space under the seat and dived into it, shuddering with fear, knowing she'd kill him.

John saw Dempsey duck down. He shouted at Katya. The words drowned in the screaming surging mob.

Katya charged her way across the bench, forcing a path through, pushing and shoving people out of the way. She jumped down in front of Dempsey, bent over him, raised her arm and levelled the Beretta.

About to pull the trigger, she caught sight of his mobile lying on the floor. She couldn't believe what she was seeing. It was the burner. Lev was right, Dempsey had brought his burner with him – the key to unlock three hundred million dollars. She grabbed it. Ignoring John's shouts over the screams all around her, she kicked Dempsey aside - flung herself towards the gap behind the Speaker's Chair. Dodging the hands trying to grab her and waving her gun she forced her way out of the chaos into the unguarded side passage beyond; ducking unseen into a doorway as two security men rushed past her on their way to the Chamber.

She heard heavy footsteps coming towards her. She only had minutes to get out of the building. The next door along the passage would lead to the secret passages and corridors that only G8 used to get in and out of the House. She reached it in seconds, quickly opened the door, made sure the passage was empty and desperately raced down a flight of stairs and into a tunnel, blindly following its twists and turns. So far no one was following her, but she could hear the muffled shouts and the clatter of heavy footsteps above her and knew John and the security guards would catch up with her at any moment. Gasping for breath she made it to the outer door which led into the street. Cautiously she opened it - no-one there. She slipped through it and saw a group of tourists. Dodging the traffic, she raced across the road to join them, her sanity returning. Suddenly, close by, she heard John's voice and the shouts of the security guards, followed by two gun shots. Her whole body shuddered.

EPILOGUE

The ketch tacked again, beautifully handled as the red sails swung in unison, heeling the craft over, gently pushing it through the choppy waves ripping from the Bay of Biscay through the Gibraltar Straights.

Katya touched the helm slightly, giving her a better view of the Hotel Intercontinental, marvelling that it was only six weeks since she had sat on the balcony there, drinking Yorsh and enviously watching the ketch that changed her life. It was incredible that her luck had held as she'd kept running, successfully breaking out of London to cross France, then Spain and on to Almeria where she'd bought her own ketch.

She wondered idly what had become of Cartwright and smiled. He was a survivor. He'd be running some scam somewhere fleecing another lot of naïve professionals, eager to lose their money in his latest get rich scheme.

She certainly wouldn't be an investor. Although, with the El Bayedh three hundred million at her disposal and locked far away from G8's prying eyes, the loss of a few million might be worth the amusement.

Nothing to amuse her about Dempsey, though. Her face hardened. She'd spared him only because he'd taken his burner to the House, leaving her to find his bank details. It had taken seconds to hopscotch the three hundred million into her own completely hidden accounts.

Slowly her thoughts turned to John. She knew she had loved

him. But to have given herself up in the hope he would have forgiven her would have meant years of prison, confinement, disgrace. It would have come at too great a cost. Her freedom. She knew she'd done the right thing though. The Gadaffi cash had been in Beecham's private account in Ambergris, nothing to do with Cartwright. She'd blocked Beecham from transferring it and had left it for John and G8, so completing her last op for him.

His love for her, her life with him, the ranch, the wild horses - would he actually have given up G8 and gone with her? These were questions with no answer.

She stretched her arms and looked up at the cloudless blue sky, suddenly feeling the freedom she felt when she was flying.

It was time to move on.

Excitement started to build in her as she turned to the horizon, looking forward, past the jib, towards the Atlantic.

End

A NOTE FROM THE AUTHOR

Although I worked in the Intelligence and Security Agencies, the characters and plot in Katya are entirely a work of my and Cary's imagination. That is not to say that I would not like to write about those who work in intelligence. But nothing I could say would adequately do justice to their bravery, dedication and sacrifices they make to protect democracy and keep us safe.

I really hope you enjoyed this book and thank you for supporting me on my journey from the Intelligence community to the world of writing.

KATYA THRILLERS COMING SOON

The Informer

A Cold Winter

DAVID BICKFORD

The Informer

Katya Petrovna is a risk-taker. It's what led her to leave her job at the Russian Federal Security Service and join the new G8 Intelligence Agency. But her reputation as headstrong and independent precedes her, and G8 wonders if she's ready for their dangerous missions.

When a Russian woman is caught at London Heathrow airport with a suitcase full of cash, John Hammond, G8's Director General, assigns Katya her first operation: infiltrate a Russian mafia-run casino on the Black Sea.

Katya goes undercover as the daughter of a wealthy ex-KGB officer looking for a good time. But as she delves deeper into the casino's operations, she finds herself out of her depth. The mafia's reach extends all the way to a Chinese Tong Casino in Macau, where they're running a brutal trafficking operation. And with each step, Katya's mistakes put her in even more danger.

She tries to recruit Kirill, a casino floor manager who she knew as a street kid in Moscow, as an informant. But as the stakes get higher and the risks greater, she can't be sure if he's on her side or working for the mafia. Katya's descent into the dark world of the high-stakes casino trade is a nightmare of cruelty, torture, and death, but she can't stop now.

The girls in the trafficking trade need her to do what she does best: take a gamble.

DAVID BICKFORD
A Cold Winter

Lev Leviatski, Soviet Political Adviser in Cold War Berlin is on the brink of treason. The young, enlightened Russian patriot is appalled by the news that Soviet troops are secretly massing on the Afghan border. He sees the pending invasion as a hole which will swallow the Soviet Union and destroy the Russia he loves and for which his parents died in the battle for Leningrad.

He tries to tell the Soviet command to pull back from the brink but the KGB, which he hates, silence him. So, secretly, he plans to create a major crisis in Berlin to alert the world to what is happening. The risks are enormous both for Lev and the wife and son he adores. And the risks increase as every move he makes is countered by the American Political Adviser, Mike Peterson, - a man who's determined that the Soviet Union must be smashed in the mountains of Afghanistan, so he can rescue the East German girl he loves.

As Lev plots and counterplots, he descends into a savage battle for supremacy over Peterson, ruthlessly shattering the lives of innocent Berliners to gain any advantage. A fight which flashes into such intensity, he forgets that, in the dangerous labyrinth of the underworld of the East West undeclared war, the KGB is silently waiting.

Will Lev be able to expose the truth and prevent an impending invasion? Or will he meet his downfall at the hands of his fiercest rivals? Find out in this electrifying tale of espionage, power, loyalty and love.

ACKNOWLEDGEMENTS

My heartfelt thanks for all the hard work, dedication, and support the whole team has provided throughout the journey of bringing this book to market. It has been an incredible experience to work with such a talented and committed team, and I am deeply grateful for your contributions.

My publishers Pj and JD at Coinkydink are outstanding, and all my thanks go to them for making this such an exciting journey.

Sue Poulsen, editor extraordinaire and to her son, Jack, for those final touches.

Larissa Murray's narration is sensational. Her tone, voices and energy throughout the story are simply magnificent. larissamurray.com

Photographer: Adam Whitehead - @adamwhiteheadphotography

Stylist: Natasha Royt - @natasharoyt

Jacket Designer: James Macey - blacksheep-uk.com

Interior Jacket: Lorna Reid

Web Design & Hosting: Ryan Hawkes - pretzelfilms.com

www.davidbickfordcb.com

Made in the USA
Coppell, TX
02 October 2023

22316911R00193